FAGIN'S BOY

Christina E. Pilz

Blue Rain Press
Longmont, Colorado

Christina E. Pilz
Blue Rain Press
Longmont, Colorado
www.christinaepilz.com

Publisher's Note: This is a work of fiction. Names, characters, places, and
incidents are a product of the author's imagination. Locales and public
names are sometimes used for atmospheric purposes. Any resemblance to
actual people, living or dead, or to businesses, companies, events, institu-
tions, or locales is completely coincidental.

Cover Design and Editing by Jennifer Quinlan; Historical Editorial
Logo by D. L. Pilz
Author Photograph by Bryan Sanburg
Book Layout ©2013 BookDesignTemplates.com

The Library of Congress has cataloged the paperback edition as follows:

Fagin's Boy/Christina E. Pilz – 1st ed.
ISBN 978-09-89727303

This book is dedicated to...

Fredrick L. Pilz (Dear Old Dad)
who introduced me to the spirit of Christmas Present,
oh, so long ago.

My sisters, Caren and Diane,
whose love is boundless and uncountable.

And to all those orphans out there.
You know who you are.

"*Where have you been, this long, long while? Ah! The same sweet face, but not so pale; the same soft eye, but not so sad.*"

—*Oliver Twist* by Charles Dickens

Table of Contents

Fagin's Boy

CHAPTER 1

Oliver Twist: The Further Particulars Of A Parish Boy's Progress

Oliver stood in front of the looking glass that rested, tipped back in its oval frame with curlicue ends, on top of the chest of drawers. He slowly took off the somber black top hat he was wearing, and with his fingertips, placed it on the chest of drawers. The looking glass told him what he already knew: that his face was white with cold, his hair crushed by the hat's brim and sticking out from his ears, and his eyes looked as flat as the pieces of silver that had been pressed upon Uncle Brownlow's dead and forever-closed eyes. Oliver could not see, now or ever, the angelic beauty that so many had told him he possessed. But what did that matter when everything in his world was no longer as it had been.

The small room around him was clean and warm and snug under the eaves, the baseboards and wooden floor shining with the particular brilliance of many scrubbings and hand-

2 ᴏ Christina E. Pilz

rubbed wood oil. The floor was covered with several patterned pieces of carpet. Bright wallpaper along the inside walls
brimmed with small country flowers. To one side of the window, on the single white wall, hung two small watercolors
that Aunt Rose had done for him depicting the small cottage
in Chertsey; on the other side was a colored print of a map of
England.

It was a nice room, tucked way up at the top of the house,
full of cloudless echoes of privacy, with only the maid and the
cook to trouble him at the other end of the narrow passageway. But it did not belong to him; none of it was his. Not the
prints on the wall nor the ornaments on the bookshelf nor the
white scalloped drapes, not even the wash basin with the
pitcher and the tiny, almost unnoticeable crack along the handle. None of it was his. Not anymore.

Nothing was Oliver's except for his clothes, his books, and
the miniature portrait of his mother, which was a painted
copy of the large one that used to hang in the parlor. The
original had been lost in one of the moves to or from the
country which had been made in recent years as Uncle
Brownlow's illness had retreated or advanced. The doctors,
one of whom had been Mr. Grimwig's personal own, had
called it consumption, but neither the good summers in the
country nor all the plasters and blisters in the world had kept
Uncle Brownlow from being taken home to God.

Oliver had not minded being tucked away at the top of Uncle Brownlow's townhouse. It allowed him to be away from
Mr. Grimwig, who had often said, regardless of who was listening, that Oliver was a bad seed, born to be bad, and likely
to hang. Uncle Brownlow had often chided Mr. Grimwig
about this, but he would chide him no more.

Oliver was yet too numb to cry; his body felt stiff against the onslaught of sorrow that battered against his breastbone. With a hard swallow, smoothing the placket on the fine black wool of his suitcoat, Oliver regarded the bookshelf under the window and concentrated on the row of books there. He looked at his botany book, which was mostly about flowers that could be planted in churchyards. Then at the grey-bound collection of Dr. Johnson's poems. Then at the green geography book he'd studied from cover to cover so many times the edges were frayed. And then at the much loved *Cobwebs to Catch Flies*, which he'd practically memorized by now and sometimes still took down just to muse through the pages and pretend that everything was all that it was. It was the first book Uncle Brownlow had ever given him.

With one last glance at his own tired expression, he turned away from the looking glass, away from the stark, stiff outline his mourning clothes made against the clean white walls. Away from the image that reflected more of the kind, sweet young man that people thought him to be rather than any of the anger he carried inside. Once or twice, he might be able to imagine it flickered there in his eyes, but mostly, the people he knew saw what they wanted to see. Young Oliver Twist, diligent in his studies, kind to all, extremely good and wanting for nothing.

Looking down at himself, he touched his collar, slowly, feeling the last tingle of the dampness from the flakes of snow that had vanished in the relative warmth of the room, sensing the tug of threads beneath his fingers. He wanted to loosen his cravat, but he needed to remain respectably dressed. He also needed to go downstairs in a moment to join the somewhat solemn assembly that were now drinking cups of tea and partaking in whatever plates of cake Mr. Grimwig's housekeeper could press upon them to accept. And he wondered, when he got down to the parlor, whether Mr. Grimwig would throw him out now or later.

He knew that thought was some untended result from his own dark musings and might never happen. Uncle Brownlow had asked Mr. Grimwig to look after Oliver, and look after him he would, till the trumpets came for him. Mr. Grimwig was a gentleman, and as such, he would keep his word. Of course, there was no telling in which way he would keep it, whether it would be with kindness or with hard looks and scoldings and thumps of his cane.

Probably the latter; Oliver had read once about how chameleons could change their color. Mr. Grimwig was no chameleon and would not, very likely, ever change. At least that made him predictable, which was something to be thankful for, as was the fact that Mr. Grimwig had not cast Oliver out into the freezing winter streets. It was well within his right to do so, especially since, in Mr. Grimwig's mind, Oliver had never been a trustworthy boy, never worthy of Uncle Brownlow and his kindness.

Oliver thought about washing his face and hands in the basin at the washstand, but that would just delay what must come, and he wanted to have it over with. For he was a gentleman, and he knew how to behave at a funeral reception. He'd attended enough of them, starting at the age of nine at Mr. Sowerberry's undertaker's shop.

"Oliver!"

The voice came from the bottom of the stairs; he'd heard it often enough. Mr. Grimwig, unable to mount the stairs most days, preferred instead to stand at the bottom and shout and pound his cane. Uncle Brownlow had found him and his pounding cane amusing, but then, they'd always been the best of friends.

"Oliver Twist!"

He needed to go down. If he'd been a braver lad, he could walk down the steep staircase with his head high and look everyone in the face and take their kind words with the aplomb of the heroes in his favorite books, not letting any of it affect him.

It wasn't an aspiration completely doomed to failure even if, as was very likely, Mr. Grimwig would meet him at the bottom step with a pinch to the back of Oliver's arm. The pinching had replaced the head-thunking that Uncle Brownlow had finally objected to some years back. Either action, however, would be accompanied with a hissed warning about workhouse boys and how easily they tended to go astray.

Mr. Grimwig had never forgiven Oliver, even after these five years, for what he ostensibly felt was the outright theft of the new suit of clothes, the stack of expensive books, and the five-pound note, none of which had ever been returned to Uncle Brownlow. Mr. Grimwig had held Oliver completely at fault for this theft, even after the event of his abduction back into Fagin's gang had been exposed as being completely out of the boy's control. The theft only proved, in Mr. Grimwig's mind, that one couldn't take in a workhouse orphan without experiencing, at the very least, a heartache. Especially not after the boy had been in the company of a gang of pickpockets.

"Oliver *Twist!*"

Oliver did not want to give Mr. Grimwig a chance to up-braid him, in front of guests, no less. Though Mr. Grimwig might enjoy it, Oliver most certainly would not, so he opened the door and hurried down the stairs.

The carpet runner muffled his steps as he descended, stumbling down the risers in his haste. He paused a moment at the top of the last flight of stairs, rubbing along the inside of his left arm, over the scar from the bullet that Giles had shot him with. Even though the scar didn't ache now as it some-times did, it was a touchstone upon which he could place his fingers and take a deep breath and manage whatever Mr. Grimwig might have to say to him.

The parlor, the small library, and the shining landing on the first floor were stifling, the air pressed and close compared to the rooms above. From the many grates, Oliver could feel the warmth of the coal fires mixed with the press of people. Everyone was dressed in solemn black and brown, standing together, talking in low voices in a way that told him they would soon be talking loudly.

The funeral of Mrs. Bedwin, the former housekeeper and his old nurse, had been like this. She had caught a chill two springs ago and left this world in her favorite grey silk dress, white pelerine, and black bonnet—her Sunday best. And after the mourners had come back from the graveyard, well, their exhaustion had put them at their ease, and the feeling that they were all joined together in something commonly shared had relaxed their guard. As it had been thus, it was now.

Oliver could hear sounds of immoderate chatter and see the ease of movement and gesture among the guests. Funerals did that; once the burial and church service was over, people tended to tire and were less inclined, it seemed, to stand on ceremony. And that was just the way of the world.

CHAPTER 2

Treats Of A Funeral Reception, Whereupon Oliver's Future Is Determined

"**O**liver, come here at once."

Oliver stopped on the bottom step, and, ignoring his unhappy reflection in the looking glass that hung on the wall next to the front door, scanned the gathering to see where the call from Mr. Grimwig had come from.

Mr. Grimwig was waiting, taking the spot nearest the fire in the parlor. Of course, he was always the one nearest the fire. He gestured, a scowl already in place as if Oliver had spoken back to him in a disrespectful manner, or, perhaps even more damning, had refused to approach altogether.

Oliver hurried over to him; it was best not to make matters worse. That Oliver had complied as soon as he was able didn't matter. Mr. Grimwig was cross with him from the moment he got up in the morning to the second his cap-covered head hit the pillow.

He nodded at Mr. Grimwig and the two men who stood at his elbow. The two men had cake plates in hand, cups of tea balanced on the edges of the plates. They were dressed in black out of respect for Uncle Brownlow as well as Mr. Grimwig, and one of them had a parson's collar. Mr. Grimwig, as accounted by Uncle Brownlow, knew a great many people in London, though he was not inclined to share any of his activities or business with Oliver. But it was good that the men were standing there, presenting too much of an audience for Mr. Grimwig to do more than scold.

"I blame it on too much time alone with his books, gentlemen," said Mr. Grimwig. "It puts too many thoughts in that foolish head."

Mr. Grimwig often talked about him this way, in the abstract about a boy who might or might not have been Oliver, as if Oliver wasn't even there. But in spite of the sudden anger that boiled behind his eyes at the explicitly untrue remark, a funeral reception was neither the time nor the place to say what he really thought, so he didn't say anything.

"But never mind. Did you know, gentlemen, that the number of workhouse boys turned criminal is shockingly high? Why, I have the numbers right here in my head, if you'd care to hear them."

The two men shook their heads as if astonished by this fact. But Oliver noticed that the head shaking seemed shallow at best, and that the men weren't scowling at him. In fact, they seemed to be eyeing him kindly, as they might eye someone who has lost a beloved guardian.

"I'm sure," said the parson, "that the numbers can be turned either this way or that, and that even an orphan can rise to do good works. What about Dick Whittington and his cat?"

"He wasn't an orphan," said the other man.

"We are all orphans eventually," said the parson, and both of Grimwig's acquaintances nodded sagely, as if this were the cleverest thing they'd heard in a good long while. And, if Oliver wasn't mistaken, they also looked a tad relieved when Grimwig nodded also.

"There's many a man who has made his mark in the world," said Mr. Grimwig. He then spoiled any kindness that might have been lurking in his words by saying, "But I've yet to see anything remotely approaching that potential to apply it in young Twist here."

Oliver felt his jaw tighten even as he opened his mouth to protest, but it wouldn't matter.

Mr. Grimwig had never liked Oliver, of course, but then he'd always made that quite plain. Now that Uncle Brownlow was solidly buried in the frozen ground, his distaste for Oliver and all that he was would be clearly shown, and probably daily if not hourly.

Mr. Grimwig tapped his cane twice to bring everyone in their party to attention.

"This is Oliver Twist, of whom you've heard me speak," said Mr. Grimwig. Then he added with a snap, "And he's not my nephew or anything close to a relative."

Oliver sighed. It was only a little after noon and already he was assured of getting a huge dose of Grimwig's dislike of him.

"This is Parson Greaves." Mr. Grimwig nodded at the parson.

"We've met, young Oliver," said Parson Greaves, holding out his hand for Oliver to shake. "Though it's been some time ago."

The parson had a young face, and as Oliver shook his hand, he realized this was the incredible reading parson that Uncle Brownlow had often talked about with a little smile playing on his lips, and that Oliver had met during their last visit to Chertsey. The incredible reading parson could read as fast as a blood horse could run and knew at least ten languages, and when in his cups, could sing filthy ditties in Old English as easily as a nun might say her prayers.

"Pleased to meet you again," said Oliver, his throat feeling thick over the words.

"And this is Mr. Beauchamp, of the Pear Tree Court Bookshop."

Mr. Beauchamp, somberly dressed in dull black wool and a mismatched brown waistcoat, was slightly bald and round but pleasant for all that. As he nodded at Oliver and held out his hand, Oliver realized where he knew him from. This was *the* Mr. Beauchamp, from the very bookshop that Uncle Brownlow had been perusing when Oliver had watched the Artful Dodger and Charley Bates steal his silk handkerchief.

At that moment, with that memory pounding in his head, Oliver found that he couldn't manage a proper greeting, let alone a simple hello. He felt a rush of heat across his face as he realized he'd not recognized Mr. Beauchamp, even though he knew him fairly well from the bookshop. But then, the circumstances now were different; Mr. Beauchamp was completely out of place when not surrounded by dark shelves of used books.

"Gentlemen, may I introduce Oliver Twist, my friend's ward."

"It's a sad day, Oliver," said Parson Greaves.

"Thank you," said Oliver. He kept his voice steady and watched as Parson Greaves and Mr. Beauchamp looked at him, which people tended to do for a little while upon meeting him. He'd experienced those stares and assessing expressions for years now, ever since he'd been sold to Mr. Sowerberry when he was nine.

He'd sometimes imagined they must see a greasy spot on his lapel, or perhaps a stray hair or a speck of smut on his cheek. But that had never been the reason. It was Mr. Grimwig who'd finally explained it to him, in his way, some years ago, and several times since then, as he and Uncle Brownlow waited for Oliver to adjust his cap in the slender looking glass that hung in the front hall.

"That boy is as prideful as a peacock!" Mr. Grimwig had said, exploding. "As in love with his own reflection as any Narcissus!" But before Oliver could gather his anger fast enough to deny it, Uncle Brownlow had ushered them both to the steps where they could hear church bells ringing and see the beautiful spring day that beckoned them.

Since then, Oliver had been attuned to such comments, and the looks that went with them. Or, as now, the looks that spoke without a word. It could be that he was wrong; the two gentleman might be thinking something else altogether. Or perhaps not. His only hope was that even if they saw him and admired his face they would not think him vain.

"My dear friend Brownlow was not his real uncle, of course," said Mr. Grimwig. "The boy has relations in the country, a poor curate and his wife near Chertsey, and, from the tell of it, some additional kin near Lyme. But none that could take him in, or that would want to, I'll be bound."

Grimwig was talking to the gentlemen, who all listened with polite interest on their faces as if Oliver wasn't standing right there being so maligned. Oliver felt a flash of rage beneath his breastbone and a great, swamping desire to state, quite clearly, that Uncle Brownlow *had* been his real uncle, in every way that mattered.

But instead of protesting, Oliver turned his face away, feeling the heat there, to look at the paintings on the wall. The red velvet atop the mantel. The little stag made of Chinese porcelain. The wreath of dried flowers and hair that Uncle Brownlow had kept near him everywhere he went. Oliver had liked to imagine that the hair had belonged to his mother, but he'd never asked, and now that Uncle Brownlow was gone, he'd never know. Certainly Mr. Grimwig wouldn't know, or even if he did, would never stoop to share that information with Oliver.

"Will you remain at home?" asked Mr. Beauchamp. He had the rough, hearty voice of a bookseller, the typed that easily urged passersby to step into his shop. "Or will you find a position at a university?"

Parson Greaves laughed. "Of course, Beauchamp, you would urge more education on the boy. Can't you see he's destined for the church?" The parson winked at Oliver in a friendly way because, of course, even the most angelic looks could not gain one entrance into the seminary, and Oliver was a poor religious scholar at best.

"Well, Oliver," said Mr. Beauchamp. "Do you have any dreams? But of course you do, all young men have dreams."

"Oliver dreams of being waited on by hand and by foot for the rest of this life, don't you Oliver. He is determined to live a life of leisure, I believe, always has his nose in a book, always reading. For all the good it does him. Are you listening, Oliver?" Mr. Grimwig nudged him hard with a swing of his cane against Oliver's leg. "Mr. Beauchamp is speaking to you."

Oliver felt hot all over and opened his mouth, ready to say something, anything, to make Mr. Grimwig stop.

"Now, I'm just a parson," said Parson Greaves, almost hurriedly, "but if you're looking for work, as Mr. Grimwig states that you are, you could do worse than to gain employment in a factory. They're hiring in factories, such as the mills up north, and perhaps a change of air would assist you on your way with your bereavement."

Oliver kept still, oddly struck by the sudden turn of the conversation. But he did not want to work in a factory and choke his lungs with chemicals and filth. No, he wanted to own a bookshop, pure and simple. It was going to be a nice little establishment, clean and quiet and full of books that he could read any time he cared to sit down and take one off the shelf.

Oliver stepped back a little and clasped his hands behind his back. "I want to own a bookshop," he said, feeling brave by sharing this out loud.

Mr. Grimwig knew this wish of Oliver's; in fact, he had heard it many times over the years. But he'd never supported it, saying that bookshop owners were leeches on society, selling dreams for a price and leading people astray when what they should be doing was applying themselves to good, honest work. He did not say this now, of course, because there was a bookshop owner present

"You'd need to learn that from the ground up," said Mr. Beauchamp. "I'd hire you on as an apprentice in my bookshop in an instant; however, I already have two and have no need of a third."

Oliver felt his body jerk as though someone had struck him from within. This was an idea he'd not really considered before, but it was a good one. Of course, it wouldn't be seemly to simply speak up now and ask Mr. Beauchamp if he might reconsider his position, for indeed, it might be for certain that he had no places available at his shop. But even if he didn't, then perhaps someone he knew might, and didn't booksellers know all types of people, rich and poor, shopkeepers and book readers alike?

"But say, Parson Greaves," said Mr. Beauchamp, patting the brown serge waistcoat over his belly. "Weren't you, in passing, discussing that acquaintance of yours? Surely it was just the other day when he said he needed a likely boy?"

Mr. Grimwig went still. Oliver likewise held himself still and pretended not to be the least bit interested in Parson Greaves's potential response. He examined his toes, looked at the backs of his hands, imagined that he was hungry and how nice a cup of tea would taste right about now, anything but think about the parson's friend's need for a likely boy.

"Oh, yes," said Parson Greaves. "I was at the church meeting, you know, the one regarding the broken windows in the narthex, and he was there. Mr. McCready. You remember."

"Mr. McCready?" asked Mr. Beauchamp, as if searching his memory. "Oh, yes, indeed, Mr. McCready. He owns a small haberdashery in Soho, on Wardour Street."

There were nods in their small circle except for Mr. Grimwig, whose sour mouth turned down in a frown.

"I know no Mr. McCready," he said.

Oliver wanted to say something to point out, explicitly, that simply because Mr. Grimwig didn't know a man personally did not mean that the man didn't exist. But Oliver kept his mouth shut because, for some reason, these two men seemed as though they wanted to help him. At the very least, they were, at present, nodding and smiling, as if Oliver's apprenticeship to the shop owner was a foregone conclusion.

"He keeps a very nice shop," said Parson Greaves. "I've been in there several times in need of a shoelace or a packet of soap powder, a needle, or some such housekeeping thing that you never would guess you'd need until you do. And then, there, in his shop, is the very item you were looking for."

"It's a good, clean shop," said Mr. Beauchamp. His tone was more serious and less playful than Parson Greaves's. The deeper and slower tones lent his words an air of gravitas. "And the boys he hires are well mannered and tidy. He learns them the trade, teaches them. They're very smart boys."

When he looked up, Oliver saw that Mr. Grimwig was looking at him, his brows all beetled down and a tightness narrowing his round face. Oliver knew the second he made a preference, then Mr. Grimwig was sure to combat it with all sorts of reasons why it shouldn't be so, why Oliver should have no say in his own future, why Oliver should be sent back to the workhouse posthaste. The latter of these had been expressed by Mr. Grimwig for years; it wouldn't be a new sentiment to Oliver, but it certainly would sound shocking to Parson Greaves and Mr. Beauchamp.

"The work would be too hard for the boy," said Mr. Grimwig. And just to prove he wasn't saying this out of sympathy or concern, he added, "He's never done a day's worth of work in his life, but spends it reading and walking and begging for money to go to the theater. He wouldn't last a day in a shop."

"Hard work would do the boy some good, I should think," said Mr. Beauchamp, nodding and waving his hand for the girl with the tray of sherry to come closer. "I've never seen a boy, regardless of his circumstance, who didn't benefit from a little hard work."

"Be a good man, Mr. Grimwig, and give Mr. McCready a chance to know about the boy at least." Parson Greaves nodded. "It wouldn't hurt, and the boy's got to make his way in this world sometime. Mr. Brownlow would have approved of McCready, at any rate."

Did Parson Greaves actually know this? Or had he simply guessed it? Probably known it, since Parson Greaves was, after all, the incredible reading parson. And, as Uncle Brownlow had an affection for intelligent, reading men, he might have shared some of his concerns about his ward and made known to the parson just what type of life he expected Oliver would go into. Though as to why Parson Greaves was inclined to use this information for good, to benefit a boy he hardly knew, well, Oliver couldn't bring himself to even imagine the reason.

"He's just there," said Parson Greaves. "Over by the cakes, blessedly good cakes, by the way. Why don't I just go and fetch him and we can be going on with our good deed?"

There was nothing Mr. Grimwig could do, not even make taciturn remarks about upstart young men and the inelegance of being in trade. That Uncle Brownlow had friends not only in banking and in the church as well as in trade never seemed to matter. The fact that Oliver might want to go into trade was enough to make Mr. Grimwig dislike anyone who put on an apron and waited behind a counter.

Parson Greaves didn't even put down his cake plate or cup of tea, but strode boldly over to where a group of men stood, all garbed in black. As he chatted with one of them, that man looked up and over at where Oliver and Mr. Grimwig and his friends stood. Then he nodded and came with Parson Greaves.

The man who came over to join their party was tall and had a clean, tidy air about him in spite of his shaggy sideburns.

"Gentlemen," said Parson Greaves, "may I introduce my friend from church, Mr. McCready, haberdasher extraordinaire."

Mr. McCready nodded his head in greeting, and Oliver realized that while the man might know Parson Greaves and Mr. Beauchamp, he didn't seem to know Mr. Grimwig, and so, perhaps, did not know the story about Oliver's illegitimacy. On the other hand, as Oliver had learned from Mrs. Bedwin, there was nothing people loved to do more than gossip.

"Yes, indeed I own a shop," said Mr. McCready. He had a special little smile that seemed to announce his feeling of both contentment and superiority, as if there were no greater felicity in the world than to own a shop and wear an apron and stand behind a counter all day. "It's a haberdashery."

"There's nothing more pleasant than a well-run haberdashery," said Parson Greaves as he ate his cake with some relish as if, when he left Mr. Grimwig's, there would be no more cake to be found.

"I'd like to think so," said Mr. McCready. "I'd like to think of my little shop as a pleasant respite from the hustle of the street where one can browse for essentials as well as fripperies." He nodded at this statement, seeming well and truly satisfied with his shop and his life. "I've recently added draperies and cloth to my stock, which has widened my clientele a bit."

"That can only be good for business," said Mr. Beauchamp. He patted his waistcoat as he brushed some small crumbs away. "When you widen your scope, you widen your net, and the cash rolls in."

"Indeed," said Mr. McCready with a special glint in his eye. "I am truly blessed in this. My shop might not be a palace lined with marble and gold foil, but is clean and respectable enough for the Queen herself, and I would not be ashamed to have Her Majesty alight on the pavement before my doors."

"Do you still take apprentices, as we were talking of only last week?" asked Parson Greaves, with an abruptness that took Oliver aback.

"Indeed I do," said Mr. McCready. He arched his neck, and Oliver could see the pride there, but perhaps it was based on truth. Both Parson Greaves and Mr. Beauchamp had positively glowed with respect and admiration whilst talking about him.

"I take in apprentices, boys as young as twelve years and as old as fifteen."

"Young Twist is just seventeen," said Parson Greaves. "Just barely too old, though in spite of that, perhaps just right for a shop such as yours. Would you be up for the work, Oliver?"

Oliver tried to think of something to say in reply to this, something that wouldn't reflect anything scathing that he thought about any shop that didn't sell books.

"You waste your breath talking of work, gentlemen," said Mr. Grimwig. "Because here before you is a head that is addled with novels and books and a body that expresses the laziness of a young man upon whom every indulgence has been lavished."

This was true, this was so very true; there was no way that Oliver could make Mr. Grimwig revoke it because since the day Uncle Brownlow took him in, Oliver had had every care in the world lavished upon him. There had been a parade of attendance in the form of private tutors, as many books as he could read, and cake and puddings for his sweet tooth that Mrs. Bedwin had ever despaired of but had never attempted to curtail.

But while it was true that he'd been indulged, it had never been true that he'd not appreciated it. After the first nine years of his living in what amounted to an echo of the dark room at Hardingstone Workhouse—a dark, dank place with no windows and no door—coming into the light under Uncle Brownlow's kind care had created a contrast that he never needed reminding to remember. He knew what it was like to be treated with cruelty and to be disregarded as if he weren't a human being at all, but merely a creature barely deserving to be fed and clothed. But, when comparing his time at the workhouse to the image of Mrs. Bedwin tip-toeing into his room in the morning to open his curtains and bring him a cup of tea, sweet with cream and sugar, well, the contrast was forever drawn.

He could not explain this to the assembled company, for he'd wager that none of them had suffered a day's deprivation in their collected lives. But he could express his mind about part of the question; Uncle Brownlow had always encouraged a thoughtful response, saying it was a mark of a gentleman to speak his mind.

"I intend to work," said Oliver into the small silence that had fallen at Mr. Grimwig's remark. "But I intend to work toward owning a bookshop of my own when I gain my inheritance at twenty-one."

"It's only three thousand pounds," Mr. Grimwig said to everyone, in spite of the comment about money being in very bad taste in such a setting. To this bald pronouncement, Mr. Grimwig followed up with a tart and completely unnecessary explanation, "To be kept by me until he's twenty-one, if he doesn't end up a criminal first."

"I beg your pardon?" asked Mr. McCready, which was indicative of the fact that he was the only one of the assembled company to not already be aware of the stipulation of Oliver's inheritance. His thick, dark eyebrows flew up into his forehead, not only at the crass mention of money but perhaps also at the amount. Three thousand pounds was a great deal and indeed a fortune for an illegitimate parish boy.

"There was some sort of arrangement in the will of the blighted boy's father," said Mr. Grimwig, telling the story that, indeed, was not his to tell, but that he, by all evidence, told to anyone who would listen. "If Oliver Twist can abstain from a life of crime, if his record is clean and unbesmirched by the time he reaches twenty one years of age, then he shall inherit. But if there is one single blot, then he inherits nothing. And gentlemen," said Mr. Grimwig as his chest puffed up, "I would not be averse to laying claim to the fact that the latter is more likely than the former."

"That's a rather odd arrangement," said Parson Greaves. His eyes flicked from Mr. Grimwig's to Mr. Beauchamp's. "Dreamt up during a death fever, I'd dare say."

Mr. Grimwig shrugged as if it were no consequence to him. "Death fever or no, the arrangement is in the will, duly witnessed and signed. A half portion of the original amount of the six thousand pounds was given to Oliver's half brother some years ago, but that gentleman, a Mr. Edward Leeford, went to American directly after, and no one knows what happened to him."

"But I know," Oliver spoke up. He swallowed and made himself say it, although even the memory of Monks and his peering, skulking ways was enough to give him nightmares. "He went to America and squandered the money. Uncle Brownlow said that he died in prison, a pauper."

"Which is how you'll end up, Oliver Twist, if you can't refrain from speaking until you are spoken to."

Mr. Grimwig's voice was loud enough to carry over to the reception in general. A low silence fell for a moment before polite voices took up various conversations again, and Mr. Grimwig's face had a chance to settle back from a sudden puce color into its normal, hearty red.

"Oh, I doubt he'll come to that," said Parson Greaves. "He's got the face of an angel, as it is, and a voice like one as well."

"Yes," agreed Mr. Beauchamp. "No one with a face like that could ever come to crime."

The gentlemen looked at Oliver, frankly appraising him, and Mr. Grimwig did as well, making Oliver want to squirm. Their statements were of the kind that Oliver had heard often, ever since he'd come out of the Hardingstone Workhouse, but the multiple occurrences of that fact never made it any easier to hear. People everywhere—in church, in the shops, or on the street—stared at him raptly as though he were something desirous that they felt they wanted, but he couldn't help the way he looked. At the same time, no one knew better than he what beauty could hide.

"Work is what keeps people out of the workhouse," said Mr. McCready. "Even if that abode casts a long shadow over their lives, having escaped it means that they've overcome their own darkest inner demons."

Oliver tried not to show his surprise at this statement. Because, of course, it might be that if Mr. Grimwig's closer acquaintances knew about Oliver's past, song and verse, it might also be that Mr. McCready knew, at the very least, that he came from a parish workhouse.

Oliver had never expressed his fear of one day ever going back to the workhouse, and he never wanted anyone to know. A true gentleman never worried about going hungry or about being admitted to a workhouse, his body stripped of its own clothes, to be given the grim, threadbare workhouse uniform.

"I do have work, young Oliver," said Mr. McCready. He held his teacup and saucer in one hand but had not drunk from it, not the whole time that he'd been standing there. He'd not taken any cake either, though from the breadth of his shoulders it did not seem that he abstained from eating sweets on general principle. "I could use another apprentice in my shop, someone to work in the warehouse, count the stock, arrange the drapes—"

"Oliver has said that he only wants to work in a bookshop," Mr. Grimwig said, interrupting. The statement didn't surprise Oliver overly much; the protest was merely for form's sake. "He's made that quite clear, though what's to actually be done with him except send him to the mines is beyond me."

Parson Greaves almost choked on his tea. Both he and Mr. Beauchamp tipped their chins low and chortled at the nonsense that Oliver, someone as beautiful as Oliver, would ever be sent to the mines. But they couldn't laugh outright; that would be rude.

"As I was saying," said Mr. McCready as if Mr. Grimwig had not spoken. This gave Oliver a little start of shock because no one had ever ignored Mr. Grimwig. "I could use someone to do general work about the place, to count stock and particularly make deliveries. If you'll pardon me, Oliver Twist, with a face such as yours, you could make plenty in tips doing deliveries to kind ladies who don't want to brave the busy streets and who are full of gratitude for the receipt of their laces and ribbons."

Mr. McCready turned his face to Oliver as he made his offer. His eyes were serious and steady.

Oliver felt his whole body come to a complete stop. His ears rang as Mr. McCready's words faded away, and Oliver, in his mind's eye, saw his future shop, situated at the end of a tidy cobbled lane and made of red brick with two windows on either side of a large wooden door that had a polished brass handle. The shop would be clean and would smell of books and there would be a small iron stove in one corner to keep the books dry, with some chairs for patrons to sit at while they thumbed through books. And over the shop would be Oliver's apartment, with a bedroom with large windows to let the sun stream in when it was shining, and a place, warm and dry, to watch the water sheet down the glass in comfort and safety when it rained.

He did want to own and run a bookshop and had plenty of ideas about what types of books he would procure for it, but he had only the vaguest idea as to how to establish the business itself. If he worked for Mr. McCready, he would be better able to acquire his heart's dream.

"I've an eye for a young man with gumption who wants to make his own way in the world," said Mr. McCready. He beckoned to one of the servants to take his teacup away from him. Then he reached into his inner breast pocket and pulled out a long wallet.

Mr. McCready took out a card, which, in deference, he handed to Mr. Grimwig. "Oliver and yourself might come by the solicitor, Mr. Bond on Oxford Street, if you are in agreement. Then we could sign the papers, and Oliver would work for me, and be a burden to no one."

It was then Oliver realized that for the whole conversation to have come so smoothly to this point, it must have been orchestrated by Parson Greaves and Mr. Beauchamp. As for Mr. McCready, he also seemed very aware of Oliver's predicament. Oliver looked at the three men, and their eyes were kind as they nodded at him. He felt a flood of gratitude and nodded in return.

"I know it is very soon," said Mr. McCready as he watched Mr. Grimwig flicking the edges of the card with his fingers. "So soon after laying your beloved benefactor and friend in the ground only this morning."

"God rest his soul," said Parson Greaves.

"He was a good man," said Mr. Beauchamp. "And as constant a customer that anyone would like to have."

"We should wait some days, out of respect," said Mr. Grimwig. He slipped the card into his breast pocket, mussing up the carefully arranged white handkerchief there. Oliver considered that if Mr. Grimwig lost the card, either accidentally or on purpose, Oliver had only to contact one of the gen-

tlemen gathered there and ask them where the solicitor and
the shop were located.

"But in these modern times," said Parson Greaves
smoothly, "we don't have the leisure to follow traditional
mourning periods of weeks or months. You must make your
way in the world, Oliver Twist, and good honest work is
sometimes the best panacea to a saddened heart."

"Wednesday, then," said Mr. McCready. "Would you be
willing to meet me at the solicitor's in the afternoon, say at
four o'clock?"

"We could, perhaps," said Mr. Grimwig. "If the weather
doesn't turn sour. I'm not desirous of making haste in a sleigh
down London's streets for an appointment with a shopkeeper."

That the recent weather had been icy and cold was true,
with unexpected storms sweeping through the snow-packed
streets almost every afternoon. At the same time, Oliver didn't
figure that Mr. Grimwig would actually let a little bit of bone-
freezing, traffic-snarling weather keep him from getting
Oliver off his hands and out of his sight at long last.

Mr. McCready gave Oliver a kindly nod as if to say that all
would be well. Oliver wondered when he would really begin
to believe that that was true.

"Monday at four o'clock it shall be, then."

"Yes, thank you, Mr. McCready," said Oliver, being his
most polite. If Mr. Grimwig wanted him gone with every
thought in his head, then Oliver wanted to be gone with every
breath in his body. Even if it meant working in a shop that
sold no books.

Mr. McCready nodded again, a little smile on his face now, and his eyes were bright. He was obviously a man who liked making plans and enjoyed seeing them come to fruition. "I'll expect to see you then. Your guardian would be pleased, I think."

"An apprenticeship at this late age should be rather difficult to arrange, I'd say," said Mr. Grimwig.

"I'm only just seventeen," said Oliver before Mr. Grimwig could respond to that and insert a nasty observation about the uselessness of youth. "Turned this January past."

"A rather cold month to be born," said Parson Greaves.

"His mother had fallen on hard times, you see," said Mr. Grimwig almost conversationally, as if he'd been telling this story all along. "She suffered the unfortunate event of giving birth to an illegitimate child in a parish workhouse."

Oliver could see by the expressions on all three of the men's faces that they were somewhat taken aback by the baldness of this statement, as if they'd not heard this particular tidbit before. As if they'd not heard it a hundred times before. Most days it wasn't even noon before Mr. Grimwig had reminded anyone in close company of that very fact. Oliver curled his hands into fists to keep his pounding heart from galloping away from him, but he opened his mouth anyway to try and change the subject.

But just before he was about to speak, one of the men beat him to it.

"From whence came your cake, Parson Greaves?" asked Mr. Beauchamp. "I don't see the girl with the tray."

"She's right over there," said Parson Greaves, waving his fork over his plate, which was picked quite clean. "Raise your hand, she'll see you. Be sure to have her bring you one of the raspberry tarts, they're delightful."

Oliver waited with what he assumed was a polite mien while the servant came over with the tray and busied herself by serving the men various slices of pastry and necessary cups of tea.

Mr. Grimwig did not accept anything, not tarts or cake or even more tea. Instead, he looked at Oliver out of the corner of his eyes, a curl to his mouth, as if daring Oliver to attempt to defend himself and his long-dead mother. Oliver knew that if he said even one word on his own behalf, let alone that of his mother, he might actually start yelling, his temper over-coming him to the point where propriety was well lost and his reputation ruined. And all the while, Mr. Grimwig would smile, as if satisfied that his point regarding Oliver's low birth had been proven right.

Oliver turned away. He didn't want to hear Mr. Grimwig say any more cruel things to these men who were trying to help him. He didn't want to see the sympathy on their faces or witness their attempts to smooth things over. So instead of remaining, as would be most polite to do, he allowed himself a small nod to nobody and slipped out of the circle of wool-clad shoulders, intending to make his escape while he could.

CHAPTER 3

Wherein Oliver Once Again Encounters A Strange Sort Of Young Gentleman

Oliver walked with hurrying steps to the servants' door at the back of the townhouse and grabbed his greatcoat from the rack.

"You shouldn't go out, young master," said the housekeeper from behind him, her heavy skirts swishing over the sound of her footsteps clacking on the tile. "It's not fitting to be out so soon after a funeral."

Oliver buttoned his greatcoat, and tied his red wool scarf around his neck as he pretended not to hear her. When he pulled on his thickest leather gloves, he couldn't bend his fingers enough to pick up his cap, but she kindly gave it to him just the same.

"Thank you," said Oliver. He couldn't remember her name, but that wasn't exactly his fault. Mr. Grimwig had hired all new staff the moment he was able, and since then, the staff, never up to his expectations, came and went before becoming known to Oliver.

"I won't be out long," he said as she opened the back door for him.

Snow swirled across the brick steps that led down to the cobblestone yard that led to the alley, but the drift was thin, as if the snow intended to give up quite soon. The sky above, boiling with low clouds, belied that fact.

"Not long," he said, his heart expanding with a lurch inside of him, seeming thick in his throat as he blinked hard and did not let himself look at her. He could not look at her, or his heart would slip out of him, and his hard-won semblance of calm and control would become undone. Instead, to be polite, he tipped his cap and went down the steps, hurrying, not letting himself stumble or slow, trying to get away before Mr. Grimwig might chance to look about him and notice that Oliver had slipped away.

Oliver walked along the pavement, his chin ducked into his red scarf, the snow almost up to his ankles, until his heart settled in his breast and his rage dulled to a low ache in the shivery air. The row of white townhouses, all neat and tidy, looked cream-colored against the smudged sky, their grey and green painted ironworks hidden by layers of snow. The world was white all around, with a thin swirl about his head and dark flakes coming down from the smoking chimneys, black against the newly laid white. There was, at this hour in the afternoon, yet a gleam of sunlight, slanting over the chimney pots and silver through the clouds.

The street was less busy than it might be, as it was wont to be during the late afternoon hours. A deeper cold was coming on. All the deliveries had been made, orders for tomorrow's milk and eggs made, toast and tea being prepared in houses all up and down the tidy street.

People were inside, as they should be, but Oliver needed to be outside. The townhouse was too full of memories, many of which Oliver knew he'd taken for granted, in a way. Not that he was ever less than mindful of always having a full stomach. Or that his boots were sturdy and without holes, that his stockings were woolen and thick against the cold. And, best of all, he always had books aplenty to read and considerable amounts of time to read them.

It had been Uncle Brownlow that he'd been careless about, and the thought of this felt sharp in his chest, as it had been doing since the day Uncle Brownlow had passed away. Uncle Brownlow had always been old, but uncles lived forever, everyone knew that. Or at least the ones in books did; uncles lived to see their young charges settled in life, happy, perhaps even married. Or if uncles did die unexpectedly or early, it was under mysterious circumstances, which would, and did, eventually lead to a surprise happy ending where the young charge inherited a great deal of money.

Yes, part of that was true, Oliver *had* inherited money. And more, when Uncle Brownlow had become his guardian, Oliver had gained an uncle in Mr. Brownlow, relatives in Aunt Rose and Uncle Harry, along with two fine nephews, and eventually, a circle of acquaintances spreading out from that. But now, living in London, all he had left was Mr. Grimwig, who in no way was going to turn out to be the kindly replacement uncle whose sole purpose in life was to see Oliver settled and comfortable.

Which made the conversation at the funeral reception even more remarkable because it was much like what happened in books. He'd unexpectedly met with three men who were willing to help him out, willing to see Oliver happy. Mr. Grimwig had even grudgingly let all of the introductions proceed and the discussion about an apprenticeship continue, and that without much grumbling. At least not during the funeral reception in front of the guests.

When Oliver got to the corner of Old Church Street, he turned in the direction away from the church and the dark grey workhouse, not wanting to be faced with the reminder of the funeral that morning nor the dark, towering walls that represented his past.

He could go into Elm Street Park where the path was likely to be shoveled and trampled. Though now the rounded, dark treetops were humped in soft white, in the springtime, the path was kept private by boughs of willows and thickets and smelled of green and flowers. Oliver determined that he would think of that, instead of the snow that now bowed branches and lumped over shrubbery. He thought maybe that the snow would forever remind him of Uncle Brownlow, catching a chill, growing weaker, the fever taking him, and then this emptiness. Surely spring would come. Surely the memories would fade into something more pleasant than the ache in his heart.

Oliver walked along the street till he got to the path that ran winding through the park. He faced the wind going out; it was prudent to do this and then be able to walk home with the wind at his back and with his face turned away from the cold as he retreated from his memories. But for now, he walked face in the cold, shoulders back, braced against what might come.

The trail beneath the snow was a little slippery, but there was enough traction from stones and branches and roots of trees to help keep him upright. He had dearly loved to walk with Uncle Brownlow, but in later years, Uncle Brownlow had found that it tired him overly. In the country, during the summers, it was different. Oliver could roam on his own at will, and had, till he was brown from the sun, and bursting with energy, could hardly sit still for his lessons, and ate half his weight, it seemed, each day.

A gust of snow caught an exposed part of his neck, and his cheeks were burning with cold. A group of men with shovels came walking toward him on the path. Their boots were thick and their clothes were thick, but they were bare headed, their faces gleaming with sweat from their efforts to clear snow. As they walked, the heads of their shovels that they carried over their shoulders knocked snow from the upper branches, and they pretended to neither notice nor care upon whose head the snow fell. Oliver hesitated on the path, and then, at the last moment, jumped out of their way, skittering to the edge of the path and shivering as a face full of snow caught him anyway.

Sputtering, he wiped his face with his gloves. He should get back to the funeral reception anyhow before he was missed. Even though there was really no one to miss him now, and the reception was mostly full of conversation of the idle type that he'd never much cared for, there were expectations of propriety and guests waiting.

But as he jerked backward, he felt a hand on his arm.

"Leave me be," he said, low, almost muttering. "I've got it, I say."

"Leave you be, Nolly?" said a voice, using the pet name given to him by Nancy in the old days, the pet name no one had called him in years. "That's all anyone's ever done is leave you be."

The voice was close, and Oliver could smell small beer and unwashed skin and something familiar that made him freeze. He did not know that voice, and yet he did. He shrank inside of his greatcoat, but the hand jerked him again and pushed him against a tree where the snow rattled down and obscured his vision again even as he opened his eyes.

And when he could see, his vision breaking through the curtain of snow, there, to accompany a voice from long ago, was a face from memory, five years on. The face was thin, looking sallow as though his skin were fading from being burnt, bright green eyes snapping, that rough face grown into itself, though sleek somehow, as if with want. It was, impossibly so, the face of the Artful Dodger, also known to his more intimate acquaintances as Jack Dawkins, back from the grave, back, back from wherever he'd been. And he'd found Oliver.

"Oh," said Oliver. "*Oh.*" A prickly feeling rose along the back of his neck and along his scalp, and he was cold all over. He felt as though something had punched him in the gut, a deep blow that sent his whole body reverberating with shock waves that made him reel, unsteady, on his feet.

But in spite of this, all of a sudden a part of him was flickering with the memories of Jack from so long ago. Jack, taking Oliver by the hand on a crowded High Street in Barnet; Jack acquiring a ham and bread sandwich and feeding Oliver with it till Oliver's stomach had been as full as it had ever been, more full than he could ever remember. And then how Jack had pulled him through the streets of Barnet and Islington, to the thickness of London, darting across classy boulevards and trotting down rackety-packety back lanes full of sewage and open doorways with dark figures looming inside.

And Jack's touch in Fagin's den, Jack's hands pulling him back, Jack putting his body slightly in front of Oliver's when Fagin ranted or yelled, waving his iron fork about. Jack, with his hands in Oliver's hair, or patting his cheek, stroking his arm. Jack had been a constant part of those days so long ago.

And then, sometime along when Oliver had been snatched off the streets by Nancy and Bill Sikes, Jack had disappeared, never to be seen again. No one had ever told him what had happened to Jack, and Oliver had never known whom to ask. And yet here Jack was, cutting a bright figure in the snow, dapper in a new greatcoat that was no doubt, *no doubt*, stolen from some fine establishment that was even yet still peering through its racks and crates and boxes, trying to figure out where the coat had gone. They'd probably never even seen Jack, neither coming nor going.

Oliver thought to say a word, and he opened his mouth to say it, but his confusion over whether it should be of welcome or recrimination stopped him. Jack was not his friend; that finely drawn illusion had been shattered some time after Jack had dragged him into a den of thieves. And yet. Jack had been the first person to show him any real kindness. In the midst of Oliver's exhaustion after his walk from Hardingstone and his confusion as to what to do next, Jack had taken him under his wing, fed him, had given him a smile and a pat on the head, and Oliver had been so grateful, so *unbelievably* grateful. It was hard to separate what had happened on the High Street at Barnet from what had come later. Jack Dawkins had found the life of a thief a grand one; in his mind, it was something to be grateful for. So he had not meant—

But now, Jack's eyes were narrow, and his thin face was shadowed and grimy from cold and exposure. With a snap, he shoved Oliver against the tree, sending snow to sift inside the red scarf folded about his neck.

"You're gonna tell me what I want to know," Jack said. His teeth were gritted together, and the accommodating smile that had flitted among Oliver's memories through the past five years was nowhere to be seen.

Lurching forward, Oliver tried to push past Jack, but Jack caught him, the breadth of his shoulders creating a barrier. The group of men who'd been shoveling snow was too far gone, and there was no one else near the little copse in the park, no one to help Oliver. When he'd gotten snatched by Bill and Nancy in the street on the way to the bookshop, he'd shouted, and although there'd been plenty to hear, no one had believed him. This time, there was no one even to hear.

"Let me go, Jack," said Oliver. His teeth were clattering and he wanted to tell himself it was from the cold, only his knees felt as though they'd lost bone and were ready to give way beneath him at any moment. "Please let me go, I won't tell anyone you're here, I won't, promise."

"Tell anyone what, then?" asked Jack. He pushed Oliver hard against the trunk of the tree with cold, gloveless hands, his smile showing the tips of his teeth. "I'm here on orders of the Queen an' all; got papers an' everything. Been hextricated an' that; five years, served me time."

"Extricated from where?" Oliver had no idea what Jack was talking about, and yet it seemed that Jack assumed he did. He didn't correct Jack that the word *hextricated* was pronounced *extricated*; it wouldn't help, and Oliver doubted that Jack would appreciate the difference anyway.

"Got shipped back, by orders of the Queen. Been departed to Australia, to the colonies, haven't I, but now I'm back. On good behavior, no less." Jack smirked, still pressing Oliver against the tree.

"They don't let you come back; they send you there and you never come back," said Oliver, his jaw tight. He couldn't believe that Jack had actually been deported, let alone returned.

"And yet here I am," said Jack, smiling more fully now, showing more teeth, his green eyes flashing.

Oliver's rage during the reception, which had begun to swim into grief, sprang anew in his breast. His heart raced, as it had so many times in the past, pushing against his breastbone in a painful, sharp way, as though battering its way through his chest. But Jack did not notice or care as he held Oliver's shoulders in place. And even though it seemed he did this as if by afterthought, no matter how hard Oliver twisted and pushed, he couldn't move.

"I come to London three days ago an' go straight to the bottom of Saffron Hill. The Three Cripples was there, but no Fagin, no gang," said Jack with a blast of words from his chapped lips. "I asked; no one knows the story. I go to the other hideouts, the perches, the dens, an' then ask around some more. I hang about the Three Cripples till they almost throw me to the peelers. But no one's seen anythin' of Fagin's gang, and no one will tell me exactly what happened, why they're all dead an' gone. An' no one'd ever heard of me neither. It was as if I t'weren't never there."

The words and the grip took Oliver back, right back in an instant, as if the intervening years had never been. As if the last door he'd stepped through had not been the cream-trimmed one at the townhouse on Old Church street, but instead one that led to the room in Fagin's backup den, where Oliver had been kept forever. Kept in semi-darkness and utter silence and fed a meager diet and given books about criminals to read until he'd all but broken.

"Let me go, let me *go*," said Oliver. He could hardly breathe to get enough air in his lungs, and the words came out thin.

Jack laughed a little under his breath and seemed only amused by this rather than moved, though he stepped back and dropped his hands from Oliver's shoulders as if to let him pass. Oliver took a single step, and then in a blur, he was on the ground, shoulders and back pushed into the snow, almost smothering from the weight of Jack on top of him. Jack had Oliver's face between two hands.

"You tell me," said Jack, low, snarling, his breath shocking and warm on Oliver's face. "You tell me where they are."

Oliver could hardly breathe from the weight, and dizzy from lack of air, he could only stare at Jack, blinking the snow from his eyes. He tried to inhale, but his breath throttled in his throat, and Jack still didn't seem to care.

"Who?" Oliver managed. "Who?" He couldn't imagine who Jack was looking for after all these years.

"Them! Everyone! Like I told you! I'm lookin' for 'em." Jack slammed Oliver's head deeper into the snow until the white walls cupping around his ears threatened to collapse in on him and smother him. "Charley, Nancy, even Bill Sikes. And where's Fagin? *Fagin!*"

Oliver's eyes fluttered half-closed; he didn't want to be the one to tell Jack, Jack who had come so recently back to England and didn't know. The papers telling the events of it were five years old, and even if Jack could find them, Jack's reading skills had never been a known thing. But to *tell* him? To be the one? Jack would surely kill him, then.

Oliver shook his head and clamped his mouth shut and was shocked to feel Jack's fist slamming into his face. He inhaled snow up his nose and coughed and thrashed as Jack held him down. His thrashing only shifted Jack's body till Jack's legs were between his own, warm and heavy, shoving, with what felt like an iron brand pressing against the inside of his thigh.

"Tell me," said Jack, thrusting forward. "Tell me or I'll bury you in snow."

It would be foolish to doubt this. Oliver felt the warmth on his face and was sure his nose was bleeding; his jaw throbbed. The press of Jack's chest on his was pushing him further into the snow, and whether Jack buried him or used more of his fists, it didn't matter. Oliver was already marked up, and he was to see Mr. McCready in the next week—

Oliver pushed up, growling, and for a second, this seemed to surprise Jack, who pulled back, only to slam down again as he punched Oliver right on the mouth. Gasping, Oliver sank back, trying to shift his legs so that Jack's weight didn't press so close against him.

Jack brought his face very near Oliver's. He wasn't looking at Oliver directly; it was as if he didn't care what Oliver looked like. He breathed through his nose, and when he spoke, his lips almost brushed against Oliver's.

"You'll tell me," he said. His breath skittered across Oliver's skin. "Or I'll bury you."

"Jack," said Oliver, unable to breathe.

"I'll *make* you," said Jack. He drew back his fist.

"No, wait," said Oliver. He turned his face away. "I'll tell you."

It would be useless to try to explain why Oliver didn't need to look like he'd been getting into street fights. Why it was so important that he get away from Mr. Grimwig and start his new life, start working toward that bookshop he always wanted. But he couldn't tell Jack that because Jack was likely to use that knowledge somehow, to control Oliver and make him turn back into one of Fagin's boys. To make him sink to the level of the street, to the throng and pall of those who barely had enough to eat, and where there would certainly be no quiet corner in which to read. Too much was at stake. He'd tell Jack what he needed to know, and then Jack would leave him in peace.

Jack moved; half his weight was off Oliver now, and Oliver felt the relief in his chest, gasping with it, even though Jack's legs were still tangled with his, sending some humming thing moving through his stomach. But more, he shivered with the touch of Jack's skin, warm against the coldness the snow left behind, the tiny roughness at the end of his fingertips against Oliver's jaw, the heat and pulse beneath the skin.

"You gonna start talkin'?" asked Jack. "Or do I get to shove my fist down your throat?"

"It's difficult to begin," said Oliver. On top of shaking with cold, he could hardly believe that he was having this conversation. It was like being thrown back in time, back to when he'd been a child of the streets, a poor orphan that nobody wanted and could never love. Oh, Fagin had use for him and his pretty face, that was certain, but it was for his own gain and never for Oliver's.

"Try."

"You have to promise—"

"Promise what?"

"I wasn't there, Jack," said Oliver. "I wasn't there for any of this, you have to understand it, you *have* to—"

Jack tightened his hand; Oliver shied back and put his hands up to his face, but Jack's hand was firm. Snow flew up around his arms like white lace, beautiful but cutting and cold.

"I can't tell you more about where they've gone," he said, thinking to take the gentle road, something comforting and soothing, as might be said by a kind woman such as Mrs. Bedwin, even regarding the likes of Fagin and his gang. "Unless it is to the hereafter, and God speed to them."

"What the fuckall does that mean?" Jack spat this at Oliver as if his temper had been frayed by hours of attempting to lure the truth out of him rather than only two moments in the drifts of snow.

"Something happened to Fagin's gang," said Oliver. His lips felt numb. "I don't know exactly, but that's what Uncle Brownlow told me. It was in the papers, but that was five years ago, and they never let me see them, they said it would be too much for me, after . . . well, after everything."

With a shove, Jack pressed close, his fist clenched around Oliver's jaw. "I know you know more, an' you better tell me quick, or—"

"Wait!" Oliver took a breath. Cold air whistled down his neck where the red scarf gaped. "It all happened so fast, you realize, once Nancy was killed and the hunt was on, and the courts, they took it personally, having let Fagin's gang go on so long. So they hanged him. They hanged all of them, as far as I know."

"Where?"

"Where *what?*"

"Where did they *hang* him?"

Then it became clear. Where a criminal was hanged was markedly important; Oliver remembered this from the books on criminals that Fagin had made him read. This, then, was the crux of it, at least for the moment, for Jack.

"Fagin was hanged at Newgate," said Oliver. He said it as plainly as he could. "I went to see him, to pray—"

Jack slammed Oliver in the chest with the flat of his hand then pulled him close again, breathing right into Oliver's face. A low, cold wind whistled around them both, the dark branches stirring overhead, sifting down snow as delicate as though from angels' wings.

"Prayers? For Fagin? From *you?*" Jack looked white, his eyes enormous dark spots, the breath winged out of him as if he'd been struck in the gut.

"I stayed with him to give him some comfort," said Oliver as quickly as he could. Jack wanted the romantic story of it and not Christian platitudes, that was plain enough. Only it had been so long ago, and Oliver had buried as much of it as he could; he couldn't dig up enough of it fast enough. But he had to try. Something, somehow—

"It was one of the most secure cells, guarded over by the warden, an important cell." Some inner core kept him focused on Jack as this news, only slightly false, fell into the cold, raw air.

"Because he was an important prisoner, of course." Jack nodded, some color coming back to his cheeks. "Then what?"

"Uncle Brownlow escorted me there. It was a horrible place, they—there were two guards outside of Fagin's cell—" He stopped thinking what he could recall and instead began to imagine what, exactly, Jack wanted to hear.

"Of course there would be two, for someone as dangerous and canny as ole Fagin," said Jack, arching his neck proudly. "Go on."

Oliver considered the reality of it. Fagin had gone mad with terror, had crouched on his pallet, shivering and shaking and spouting nonsense. He'd continually muttered something about a man who should have his throat slit, someone who had betrayed them all. Someone who had peached. This last was the worst possible sin of anyone of Fagin's ilk, so Oliver could well imagine that the person in question should have his throat slit. At least according to Fagin. And probably according to Jack, who was waiting for more of the story, all of which Oliver had already told. So he swallowed, settled his chin, and determined to make the best of it.

"He didn't want my prayers," said Oliver, the lies, like the words in a heroic story, coming too easily to him. "He waited, upright and strong, for his fate. The major of the guards had questioned him for some time, he told me, wanting to know details and names, but even on promise of a lighter sentence, Fagin never gave anyone up."

That last part at least was true. Fagin had been too busy trying to pretend that Oliver was going to escort him out of

Newgate, as innocent as you please, to even come close to naming names. Except there had been that one name, new and unknown to Oliver at the time. And now, firmly out of reach. It didn't matter anyway. At that point, the guards hadn't cared who Fagin had been able to mention, so in effect, he'd peached on no one.

"Of course not," said Jack. "I always knew he'd go like that." His eyes were blind to Oliver now as if he were miles away, back where he'd come from, back in some moment of his own past. He made a small gesture with his hand toward Oliver as if asking for something.

"What is it?" said Oliver.

Jack focused on him then but didn't say anything.

"That's all I know." Oliver said this as quickly as he could. "Something happened, I don't know what, but Bill killed Nancy. A mob chased him through the streets and he was shot. Along the way, as he ran, he must have led constables to the various hideouts, and they were able to track their way to Fagin, and—"

Jack's hand pulled away and he sat back on his heels in the snow, the edges of his greatcoat digging dark trenches in the soft snow. He pulled Oliver to sitting but kept him close by, hip deep in snow, and banged his fist gently on his own bent knee.

"Hanged." Jack's voice quivered in the sparkled whiteness of snow all around, and it seemed as though he were trembling.

Teeth chattering, Oliver looked up at Jack and tried to shift to a more comfortable position in the snow, but Jack gave him a shove and refused to let him move.

"Stop," said Jack. His face was the color of iced paper. "Fagin was *hanged* no doubt because of you. You an' your snivelin' face an' your stupid, pious—"

Oliver felt the rush of his temper, like flames shooting out of his belly. He rolled to his side and shifted to his feet, ready to be away from Jack and his fists, poised, ready to run. The snow flew about him, and his red scarf fluttered loose about his neck.

"I wasn't there for any of it!" He almost screamed this. He had been there for part of it the night before Fagin was hanged. And he'd told that part of it. But if Jack was going to keep at him like this, then maybe Jack did deserve to know that his precious mentor, his leader, was so mad in the head that he thought Oliver was there to take him away from that horrible place. Kept talking about someone who had sent them all to the gallows, and Oliver hadn't been able to make sense of any of it. "I was in the country, I was at church, I was studying my new textbooks; I simply wasn't *there.*"

Jack bent low and scooped up some snow with his bare palm and placed it on Oliver's jaw. Without thought, Oliver knocked his hand away, making the snow, dappled with blood from Oliver's nose, fly and drift down anew.

"Stay away from me," said Oliver, low, his voice rough from the distaste of having his past, this past, barrel its way into his life just when he was taking a new direction and starting over again. And rough, as well, from his shock at the unexpected but not unfamiliar kindness of Jack's hand. "You stay away from me or I'll call the constable and explain to him exactly who you are and what you were arrested for. And this time?" Oliver could almost taste his disdain for Jack. "They'll believe me and carry you off. This time for good."

For a second, something flickered across Jack's face, and there was a twitch along the edge of his mouth. Oliver wanted to think he'd imagined the hurt there, because Jack had been on the streets most of his life; no hard words could ever hurt him. But Oliver knew that Jack was wounded was because Oliver had threatened to break the code, the one that dictated that none of Fagin's boys ever peached.

Jack straightened up and took a step back, stumbling against the roots buried beneath the white lumps of snow.

"As you wish, Nolly," he said, smirking. "I'll leave you be, but you know, Fagin's boys got to stick together, help each other out. Find good jobs to get to the glittery stuff an' that."

"I'm not one of Fagin's boys," said Oliver, "and I've got nothing for you. *Nothing*. Stay away from me, or I *will* call the law."

"You won't do that, Nolly," said Jack, not at all worried, it seemed. Jack had always been happier in a group, and if he couldn't find his gang, he'd be all alone. But then, it wouldn't be too long till Jack had another gang, would it. Though that was none of Oliver's concern, and bad business besides.

"Good-bye, Jack," said Oliver. He picked up his red scarf that had fallen in the snow and started to push past Jack, stepping back on the path, shaking snow from his shoulders as he went. He could sense Jack standing there, watching him, but he didn't turn back to meet his gaze. Those old days were gone, and Oliver wanted nothing to do with them.

"Hang on, then," said Jack in that voice he had used in the past to distract a pedestrian. The voice he used to direct their attention one way, while the other way he might snatch a handkerchief or a wallet or a pocket watch or whatever he felt was on offer that day. "I'll be takin' that."

With a deft hand, he snaked the scarf from Oliver's hand, where it ran against his dirty, calloused palm like a ribbon of blood.

"Give that back!"

Jack just shook his head and wrapped the scarf around his own neck, tucking it inside his greatcoat in spite of the clumps of white snow that clung to it. It had to be cold and icy wet, but he didn't even shiver.

Oliver leaped toward Jack; Jack nimbly jumped backward and just laughed. "I'll be keepin' this for a while; you look like you can easily afford another'n. Say it's a present from one mate to another, yes, let's call it that. Your welcome home gift to me."

"It's not a gift and you're not welcome!" He tried grabbing the scarf, but Jack was too far away, and Oliver's knees were still shaking. "And you're not my mate!"

Something smoked dark and hot in Jack's eyes, but Oliver refused to feel badly for it. How was he going to explain the loss of a scarf? And with the bells tolling the hour, the very late hour, how on earth was he going to explain his absence to Mr. Grimwig and the rest of the funeral reception?

But Jack had turned his back and was walking up the path, churning up the snow as he went, his shoulders brushing the snow-covered trees, sending a cascade of it to fall around him till finally he was obscured by a misty curtain.

Oliver watched him then turned to spit in the snow, leaving blood-red dapples across the white.

CHAPTER 4

Upon His Return
From A Sojourn
In The Street

When he arrived back at the townhouse, Oliver was still shaking, but he managed to slip up the narrow brick stairs from the back courtyard and hang up his greatcoat and cap in the servants' hall, flipping the snow from his gloves. His skin dripping with melting snow, he turned up the hallway. The back entryway was empty, though he could hear the cook and the girl in the kitchen below. With his heart in his throat, hair dripping on his neck, blood drying on his upper lip, he took off his jacket and hung it up.

By the time he'd gotten himself settled and walked up the passageway to the front foyer, he realized the house was quite empty, and the funeral reception was long gone over.

He rubbed his arm through the cotton of his sleeve, though feeling the length of the scar didn't seem to help him any as he got closer to the front door.

Two servants were in the parlor, clearing up glasses and plates from the tables, dusting and clearing around the black wreath in the corner, and leaving the black cloths draped over the looking glasses and the clocks. They hadn't gotten to the study on the other side of the hall, which meant that the reception was *just* over. Only a moment over, perhaps five. Very soon, but too late to avoid the recrimination he'd so justly earned.

He heard a step behind him, and as he turned around, Mr. Grimwig stood there, unsmiling, which wasn't unusual; it was always the same, whether or not Oliver was considered to be a disgrace. Mr. Grimwig had a glass of sherry in his hand, which, under the circumstance, could go unremarked. But in his other hand, he held an envelope, which he did not quite hold out to Oliver.

"Where have you been? All of your guests have left, you know, each one of them asking to take their leave of you, and you nowhere to be found." Mr. Grimwig barely took a breath, and the diatribe continued. "And what are you doing, coming in like a street urchin all mashed up, blood dripping on your shirt, to track snow and mud on the carpets? Oliver, what have you been up to?"

Oliver shuddered in a breath, fighting against the memories of Jack that swirled in his mind. It wouldn't do to explain what had actually happened, and it wasn't to protect Jack, so newly returned from being deported; Mr. Grimwig would hardly care about that anyway. It didn't have to be Jack that Oliver had been with—any low life or commoner would do; it was Oliver's association and actions that would be seen to be the fault.

"I was attacked in the street," he said, shrugging. "Someone stole my scarf."

"Probably because you were waving it about as though it were banner," said Mr. Grimwig. He finished off the sherry and left the glass on the table, not seeming to care that it might mar the wood, leaving a white ring that would never come out.

He held the envelope in his hand a little way closer to Oliver and shook it. "You received a letter today. From someone in Hardingstone." He peered at the return address. "It's from a Mr. Sowerberry; do you know this person?"

The question jerked Oliver to attention. Sowerberry? The name was from so far in his past it seemed to surface to the top of his memory like dislodged moss from a stagnant pond. He knew the name; the branding of it on his soul had been quick and nasty, as though they were hasty scraps on a plate left for the dog.

He had not allowed himself to think about the undertaker's shop since many seasons ago. But the dark, damp cellar still lingered there, and with it the puffy, cool feel of the casket lining under his hands. The weight of the shutters and the feel of Noah's clammy hand slamming into the back of his head. Mr. Sowerberry had never stopped it, and Mrs. Sowerberry had obviously felt Oliver was a badness she had to control. He'd often felt her switch and her intolerant looks, both of which brought him to heel faster than he would like to remember.

And everything had smelled bad—some dusky, unwashed scent he imagined lingered from the bodies that were brought into the shop to be watched over. When someone died and there was no one to watch over the body, the undertaker was tasked with making sure the person was actually dead and that the body was too far gone by the time it was buried to keep any body snatchers from making off with it. Oliver's own bedding had even smelled of it—some sweet, oily smell—though his nose had gotten used to it. And years later, from time to time, he would recognize it when passing a butcher's alley.

"Yes, I know them, sir," was all he said now. "I worked for them after I left the workhouse. I was apprenticed at an undertaker's." Oliver supposed he'd been expecting that anything would have been better than the baby farm or the workhouse, but the undertaker's shop had been just as bad as everything else. He wondered now how many years before he would truly realize that it would never be better and he would never reach the blue sky above.

"You worked for them? Brownlow never told me this. You have experience at an undertaker's?"

"I was nine at the time," said Oliver, feeling the words of explanation slip out before he could stop them. "But I ran away."

"You ran away? From such a good living as that?"

It was clear that Mr. Grimwig was not only astounded to find out something he'd not previously known but also surprised that Oliver was not still there, rising through the ranks to become an undertaker himself one day. The good living was all that concerned Mr. Grimwig, of course. Uncle Brownlow, on the other hand, had understood that for a sensitive boy of nine, the darkness of the cellar and the black paint of the coffins had been nothing next to the scowling black looks of his mistress and the casual, scathing comments flung at him seemingly night and day.

"Oliver? I asked you a question, and I would like an answer."

Oliver nodded as if he'd just been thinking. "I ran away, it's true. But they were cruel there and were going to send me back to the workhouse."

"Young men's struggles are often overstated," said Mr. Grimwig, pushing out his lower lip. The candlelight glistened on the moistness there, and there was an unpleasant, sullen droop to his eyes. "You ought not to have done that. I wonder if Brownlow knew of your propensity to avoid those duties which were properly assigned to you."

Oliver thought of the way he'd come to the funeral parlor, from the dark room at the workhouse and all those beatings, and of the living he'd barely escaped before that, of a chimney sweep. In Mr. Grimwig's mind no doubt, those who were chimney sweeps or apprentices in funeral parlors deserved their low, grubby status and should remain there till the angels determined they should be called home again.

Breathing hard, Oliver feared that he might start shouting at Mr. Grimwig to keep his ill-spoken remarks to himself and stop making comments about those affairs which were of no concern to him. But the memory of Uncle Brownlow, so recently dead, and how disappointed he would be in such a display of Oliver's temper, stopped him.

He clamped his mouth shut over saying anything and looked at Mr. Grimwig. The room stank of old flowers.

Mr. Grimwig, without asking, opened the folded sheets, tearing through the paper as if the letter were his, and began scanning the contents. He squinted a bit as he read, his mouth moving. The letter must have been short, for he lifted his head and looked at Oliver with an appraising eyebrow.

"They send their condolences," said Mr. Grimwig. "As they should, as is proper, of course. Probably only scouting for business, I suspect, knowing that if there is one death in the family, there is likely to be another. Although this family was shamed by your early departure and your lack of a proper good-bye to our guests."

"I know it was rude," said Oliver, his lips curling in an effort not to scream the words. He regretted not being able to properly thank Parson Greaves and Mr. Beauchamp, to shake Mr. McCready's hand and bid him good-bye until their meeting at the solicitor's office. "You don't have to tell me."

"What I shouldn't have to tell you," said Mr. Grimwig, his eyes snapping, "is how to be respectful when you speak to your betters."

"I would be," said Oliver. A low fire sparked in his breast. "If there were any of my betters here to speak to."

Mr. Grimwig turned white and opened his mouth, and in another moment there would be real shouting. But that didn't matter. If all went well at the solicitor's on Monday, Oliver would soon be out of Mr. Grimwig's circle of influence, gone for good and all. Oliver would remain in Mr. Grimwig's residence as only a story to tell many an acquaintance on a rainy night, with laughter and grievances aired, and no reason to stop, not even out of respect for the dead.

What mattered now was the letter. Oliver reached out and snatched it way from Mr. Grimwig. Without looking back to mark Mr. Grimwig's startled expression, Oliver turned and hurried up the stairs, knowing that his boots were leaving a slightly muddy tread on the swirls and color of the runner. He should take his boots off and carry them at least, to leave them outside of his door for the maid to tend to and not to make her work at cleaning both the stairs and the boots. But to do that would mean pausing and sitting on the steps while Mr. Grimwig watched him, and that he could not bear.

He heard Mr. Grimwig walking away from the bottom of the steps, muttering under his breath, shuffling with his cane, but Oliver did not stop till he'd reached his door on the top floor and opened it. He stepped inside his door and closed it behind him, letting the somber dimness quiet him. Then, with the edges of his fingers pressing open the folds of paper, he read as quickly as he could.

The elegant script was a reflection of Mr. Sowerberry's occupation; undertakers had beautiful handwriting, as if to offset the sadness and grief of their business. Beneath that, the letter was simple, *solemn condolences, respectful regrets*, but nothing personal, nothing for or about Oliver specifically. Mr. Grimwig was right, as he often was in cases of anything to do with money or business. The letter could have been sent to anybody, for all that, but how had Mr. Sowerberry even gotten this address?

The letter expressed, as did so much recently in his life, the carelessness of the world, its attention to business, and whether or not Oliver had some useful occupation—and this rather than any sympathy or condolences sent truly from the heart. At the uncomforting nature of the letter, a raft of bleakness now swamped him. He became overwhelmed with feeling, the realization sinking in his gut. The loss of Uncle Brownlow was a sheer weight hanging overhead that had been waiting for just this moment to rush into the blank spaces of his heart, and he flinched against it.

Instead, Oliver walked over to the fire that was burning in the sparkling grate and tossed the letter into the flames. He watched it till it crisped in the heat, burning down to black curls. Then he sat in his chair by the hearth to soak up the warmth.

The chair was a former occupant of the study, but the old-fashioned silk pattern had been worn and had been considered too old for use there, and so had been given to him. Oliver had barely been able to stop himself from bragging that the chair, though shabby, was well made and so fantastically comfortable that he'd often been able to fall asleep in it. But he'd not wanted Mr. Grimwig to suggest that it was too fine a chair for such a boy, so he'd kept his mouth shut and later had profusely thanked Uncle Brownlow for the gift.

He undid the laces on his boots and got up to scuff in stockinged feet to place them outside the door. Once he'd closed the door and latched it, he let his shoulders sag. Now he was alone with his thoughts and the complete absence of any prayers to bring him the comfort and solace they were said to bring. He'd tried very hard, praying at the church and at the graveside, and once when the local parson had come to tea the day after Uncle Brownlow had passed away. None of it had done any good, and the echoes of those efforts were of even less use still.

All that was left was an emptiness left by the lack of Uncle Brownlow and the lack of anything to do about it. A great, enormous, monstrous lack that rolled into a blankness that filled his chest now, tinged with the gratitude that he'd no longer have to watch Uncle Brownlow struggling for each breath as he attempted to light his eyes on Oliver to let him know it was all going to be all right. Because it was not all right; Uncle Brownlow had suffered for a time, not wanting anyone to know how ill he was. When Oliver had found out, he'd watched his guardian waste away amidst the stone-white bed sheets, the medicine of the bewigged apothecary, the ministrations of the housekeeper, and the prayers of the parson, none of which had done any good at all.

Oliver had held Uncle Brownlow's hand for hours each day. And then once, when Oliver had gone down to the kitchen to get away from the sickroom, just for a moment, when he returned, Uncle Brownlow had breathed no more. The room had quickly been spread with herbs to cover up the miasma of the fever and then closed immediately till the undertaker could come. Horrified, Oliver had struggled with the butler as he'd locked the door, and when unseen hands had pulled him back, he'd raced down the stairs and flung open the front door, gasping in cold breaths as the snow came down thick as cream, filling his mouth and his eyes and slattering against his chest.

Someone had pulled him back. He flushed to think it had been Mr. Grimwig, who struggled even to climb the stairs. But it had been Mr. Grimwig. Though for once, for the only time, he'd not scolded or berated Oliver in any way, even though he'd been standing with the front door full open in his stockinged feet, letting in not only the snow and the cold but the gawps and stares of vendors and servants and everyone passing on the street. Their street was busy, and everyone and anyone had seen Oliver with his mad hair and open mouth and shirt unbuttoned to the waist. They'd stared and then turned away, and he, according to Mr. Grimwig, said later and quite stoutly, he, Oliver, had been the talk all right. From coffee shop to tobacconist, from basket maker to bonnet maker, simply the *talk*.

Not that it mattered. In a short while, peace and God willing, Oliver would be gone from the house where all that had kept him from Mr. Grimwig's derision had been Uncle Brownlow's mild disapproval. At least Uncle Brownlow had had a constant companion in Mr. Grimwig.

Who now didn't want Oliver there, and Oliver didn't want to be there. Which didn't help, the anger didn't help, and trying to use it was like trying to hold up a thin piece of shaved wood to block a flood. He sank onto the bed and struggled to tear off his cravat, which, as he tugged, snapped in his hands. It was rented funeral garb so it didn't matter. In little more than a week, he'd take up the costume of his new position. Regardless, Mr. Grimwig was sure to vent his displeasure at the thought of not getting that deposit back. But as Oliver held the bits of his cravat in his hands, he realized his hand was shaking, and what did it matter?

It was as plain as the black cloth across his palm: Uncle Brownlow was the last person in the world who'd cared about him. Oh, yes, Aunt Rose and Uncle Harry always welcomed him when he came to their home, but Oliver was now only a visitor to them when he came, not a member of the family. Mrs. Bedwin was two years gone, and other than that? He had no one. Everyone died.

He struggled with feeling it, bracing his stockinged feet against the hard iron bedrails and covering his face with his hands. But it was no use, the pain across the soles of his feet didn't even make it up his legs, and however hard he held his jaw, it trembled, and as he shivered all over, it took him, a swamp of blackness that slammed into him hard like a blow to the face. It was like being shoved into a dark room where the only speck of daylight to be had was when someone came in with the lash, ready to beat him, forceful, making him bend to it, the realization that it would always be dark like this. That he was alone. That he couldn't be loved.

His face was hot with tears, but he was shivering all over. He tried stiffening up his whole body to stop crying. But he couldn't by force, so he let the sadness come, soaking his hands and the front of his shirt as he tried to wipe his face with it. It faded in an odd way, growing in his chest and then sinking back, till at last he was left shivering on the bed.

His feet hurt, his face was tired, and his chest ached, so he stumbled to the chair with its pale green and gold-shot silk, and sank into it, curling himself into a ball, bringing his feet to tuck up under him. It was how a young child might sit, not a young man about to embark upon the world, but he didn't care. There was no one to see, and this way the fire in the grate could reach all of him now.

The fire was small, as befitted the grate of an attic room, but it sparkled and flicked its shadows brightly about the room. As his tears dried, he rested his head against one wing of the chair and wondered if perhaps he should go down for something to eat, or if one of the servants might bring him a tray. Though, as to the latter, Mr. Grimwig might take it upon himself to attempt to discipline Oliver by making him come down, instead of being waited upon like a young prince. *That young prince*, Oliver had heard Mr. Grimwig say, more than once. *Prince of the May Dance, he thinks he is, and the world should be better served by making him scrub floors!* Not that this made any sense, it never did, but perhaps after years of derisive remarks, Mr. Grimwig was simply running out of fodder. Not that that had ever stopped him.

This almost made Oliver laugh out loud, feeling an odd relief that he could. As he stroked a hand across his belly, it grumbled down deep, bringing a real and insistent hunger to the surface. Something flickered in his mind then, the idea of being warm and hungry at the same time. He considered the odd juxtaposition of the two. When had that happened? Oh, yes, in the bad old days.

And why was he thinking of it now? Oh, yes. *Jack.* Jack with his whole body next to Oliver's, pushing him down into the snow, their legs tangled together, with a close familiarity as if the last five years had never been.

Oliver shook this off and thought about the old days when Fagin's boys had lined the room around the fire, and even if there had been nothing to eat, at least they'd all been warm, they'd all been hungry together. And in the morning, mysteriously sometimes, there had been sausages and bread and gin, and sometimes even sugar, when Fagin would take the time to heat the gin.

It had almost seemed to make the night of an empty stomach worth it. Especially when the boys would sit in front of the fire, their bare feet stretched out to it, shoulder to shoulder, warm together against the morning chill. It hadn't mattered then, or even later, that he'd been amongst thieves, because there had been those moments of connection, of belonging.

He could almost understand why Jack looked as though he'd been truly grieved to hear of Fagin's death, of the gang disbanded, of all he'd ever known gone. With moments like those, circled around the fire, in company, and the company pleasant if not good, especially with draughts of sugared gin, who would not miss it? Especially when the experience of that had been the best one he had ever known?

Oliver stood up and tried to think more clearly. He needed to wash his face and hands and change his shirt and go down to see if the cook would let him eat in the kitchen. The previous cook had sometimes let him.

Mr. Grimwig was probably locked in his own room now, as the evening came on. With nothing to plan or rent or arrange, he would be at as much of a loss as Oliver was, perhaps more. Uncle Brownlow and Mr. Grimwig had been good friends for many years. Not that that made Oliver feel any more sorry for Mr. Grimwig than for himself, no. But was it better to think upon that than to think of Jack, standing in the cascade of snow, in a stolen coat, with Oliver's red scarf wrapped around his own neck as he laughed?

He couldn't imagine that either would benefit him. So instead, he went to the washstand under the eve in the corner of the room and touched his fingers to the surface of the water in the pitcher. It was still warm. This meant that one of the house maids had taken it upon herself, or had been directed, to bring him hot water, in spite of anything Mr. Grimwig might say. The water which had cooled as he'd wandered the streets, and met up with—

He heard a knock on the door. When he went to open it, he saw it was the kitchen maid. He still didn't know her name, but she carried a tray with a pot of tea, a pile of sliced sandwiches, and a pudding with a small pitcher of custard that was warm enough to steam in the hallway.

She looked at him calmly as if she didn't notice the blood on his shirtfront or the smears of blood on his chin, his rumpled hair, or any evidence that made it clear he'd been in some sort of altercation.

"Here you are, sir," she said. "Thought you might need this after today."

She held the tray out to him and Oliver took it.

"Thank you," he said, almost choking on the words.

"You're welcome," she said. "Things will look better in the morning, I'm sure." She bobbed a small curtsey.

As she turned to make her way down the stairs, Oliver shut the door with his foot.

Mr. Grimwig might have called her bold to take it upon herself to talk so plainly to him, but Oliver knew it was kindness, pure kindness, on her part. It had probably been she that had brought up the hot water, in spite of his never having asked for it.

After a moment's pause, he walked over to the fire and set the tray on the rug in front of it. Then he sat cross-legged near the tray, facing the fire, nodding as the warmth from the hearth radiated out at him. Yes, he would eat like this, though he should not eat like this; young men didn't. But Mrs. Bedwin would approve and know that a young man sometimes needed to eat like this, as close to the fire as he might. The memory of her kind regard was all the approval Oliver needed, at the moment.

Oliver poured himself some tea and brought the thin china cup to his lips. He could smell the sweetness of the tea and see the ripples of fat from the cream, the shadow of the edge of the cup across the brown surface. He took a sip, letting the warmth run through him, and thought of another fire, with a semicircle of barefooted boys around it as they warmed their feet and sipped sugared gin. Of course, he didn't care where Jack was tonight, whether he had a roof to sleep under, but he couldn't help memories of other fires as they crowded around him, now could he.

No. So he drank his tea with one hand and idly poured the custard over the pudding with the other, watching the steam fade as the custard cooled, and let the memories come. They were all he had.

CHAPTER 5

Of Silence And Time Wherein Oliver Imbibes In A Low Tavern

The days until the time Oliver and Mr. Grimwig signed the papers at the solicitor's passed slowly.

Each morning, Oliver woke up, thinking of the bookshop he would one day own. He washed at the washstand, got dressed, ate breakfast. After which, there had been nothing much to do except sit in his green and yellow striped armchair and read. It was either that or take tea with Mr. Grimwig in the front parlor with the green wallpaper that he'd helped Mrs. Bedwin pick out some years ago.

He usually took his tea with Mr. Grimwig. It had felt somehow required and was perhaps expected, even if he and Mr. Grimwig said no more than *pass the cream* or *are we out of cake?* The atmosphere, with or without those polite and short exchanges, was always severe and tense. And, in such stilted circumstances, the tea was not enjoyable, and the cake never satisfied.

Other than taking miserable teas with Mr. Grimwig, Oliver had not much to do, so he dawdled over which books to pack and ended up packing all of them, wondering how much of a scolding he'd receive over having such a heavy trunk. Or, if Mr. Grimwig found out, whether he'd take it upon himself to upbraid Oliver for having the temerity to think he'd even have time to read. Or whether Mr. McCready would be of a like mind and might confiscate his poetry books. But Oliver couldn't bear to leave them behind, so what was he to do? He packed all of them, even his books from childhood, the well-worn *Lessons for Children* and a tea- and jam-stained copy of *The History of Sandford and Merton*.

When he went on an errand once or twice to save the housemaid from having to go out in the frosty cold, he kept an eye out for Jack. Jack had been out of bounds even to talk to him, and Oliver, for his part, had been remiss in allowing the conversation to continue as long as it had. The second Jack had been rough with him, Oliver should have called for the constable, and never mind the trouble and scandal that would have caused back at the townhouse.

But he'd not seen Jack, and none of the servants shared any talk about a stranger skulking about, so perhaps Jack had gone away, out of London, and Oliver would see no more of him. Certainly, in addition, once Oliver had moved to Mr. McCready's, not only would Jack not be able to follow him there but Oliver would be far too busy to partake in anything so unsavory as rude conversations with Jack Dawkins. Which was probably for the best, as he didn't need to get himself into trouble at his new place of work.

And Oliver wanted to go; he didn't think he'd ever wanted something so much. Well, yes, there had been that pony that he'd never gotten, but in the City there would have been no place to keep it, and at Aunt Rose and Uncle Harry's, he'd run in the fields barefoot like a country boy, the back of his neck and arms growing brown as he'd tagged with the local boys and splashed in the creek, chased after crows, made grass whistles.

Now, of course, he was a young man and didn't have time to play. Yet he felt eager to start anew, in a new place, doing something useful, earning money. Many times he'd gone with Uncle Brownlow to buy books or order shelves or a new carpet for the floor. Uncle Brownlow had taken the time to show him the value of the pieces that would soon be on his feet, or beneath them, or along the walls. These were lessons eagerly learned, taken in and absorbed from the gentle hands of his savior.

Anything Uncle Brownlow had wanted to teach him, Oliver had wanted to learn. And so, from Uncle Brownlow, he'd learned to be careful of his shoes, handing them over to be cleaned and polished on a regular basis, walking around puddles instead of through them, and never letting his boots dry without stuffing them with rags first. Oliver felt he knew the value of well-made goods, having been given and divested of several, in spite of what Mr. Grimwig liked to say.

On another day in that slow time, on a wet and chilly day when the snow had melted into a muddy sludge, Oliver had put his on his grey jacket and trousers and gone down to the back landing to get his greatcoat and perhaps find a scarf to keep out the damp. On a peg in the wall next to the coat rack, there happened to be an old, rather taggle-ended grey scarf that looked as though it had no prior claim, and so Oliver wrapped that around his neck. With his gloves in hand and a few shillings in his pocket, he walked boldly out the front door. He was determined to get a breath of air, even though the wind was brisk, making the low clouds cut through the tops of church steeples and foggy, moist air slice through the winter-dark trees.

His feet, naturally enough, took him to the closest bookstore, which was on King's Road, though the wind was in his face the whole way and passing carriages tossed up a great deal of muddy, half-melted snow. The wind was so strong there were not many ladies about, only a shawl-wrapped maid on an errand. Oliver put on his gloves as he walked and held onto his cap with one hand, hurrying along the pavement.

Hillyard's Books, just a few steps along King's Road, was almost too grand for Oliver. It was on a main thoroughfare, and therefore was of the type to have white-aproned clerks with a rather superior air. But he needed, so desperately needed, to breathe the dry, clean air of a bookshop and quiet his mind as looked at the decorated spines, to become lost in the idea of the books and the stories they told.

He took off his cap and gloves as he entered, moving the door slowly to keep from clanging the entry bell too loudly. Politely, he dismissed the first clerk to approach him asking if he needed any assistance. This was always annoying, but in any well-bred shop, it was inevitable.

Oliver had long ago decided that in his bookshop, neither he nor any clerk would interrupt a potential customer's musings. He would greet the customers when they entered his shop, and he would tell them to return to the counter if they had any questions. That way, they would be left alone to dream and ponder as they needed, and never feel the irritation as Oliver did now. Obviously, he could read the titles and the placards on the shelves; he didn't need any assistance. He needed to be left alone.

After a few moments of scanning the shelves nearest the front door, it was natural for him to seek out the new books; he had been so often in this particular shop to know its regular contents. The new books, however, were made up of recent rental-returns or books exchanged for new, and as Oliver came close to the shelf, he saw that there was a slightly-used copy of *The Arabian Nights*. He'd asked for it for his birthday, but Uncle Brownlow had said that it was far too—what was the word he'd used? Far too—provocative, especially for a young man such as himself.

But now there was no one there to restrain him, so Oliver picked up the book, and instantly there was a clerk at his side.

"Will the young man be taking this book today?"

"Yes, please," said Oliver, handing over the book, feeling reluctant to do so when he'd only just found it. But that was the way of this particular shop, the graceful attention, the careful ringing up, and the solicitous handing over of change. By the time the clerk handed him the book, wrapped in white paper with the edges carefully folded in, Oliver knew he could have been well into the first chapter. But there it was. Hopefully, near the haberdashery, there might be a less formal and far less grand bookshop for him to frequent.

"Have a good day, sir," said the clerk as Oliver tucked his new purchase under his arm.

"Thank you," said Oliver, as it was only good manners to do so, though he suspected it wouldn't matter what he'd said as this was probably the last time he'd be at Hillyard's Books.

He left the shop with the bell clanging in his ears, and struggling, kept the book tucked beneath his arm while he put on his cap and gloves. The grey scarf was scratchy and at most kept out some of the damp even while it let in the cutting wind. But there was nothing to be done about it but walk back to the townhouse as quickly as possible. No one would have missed him upon his return, of course, but he was cold, and the thought of reading a new book by a warm fire was a good one.

So he hurried, avoiding puddles when he could, keeping his head down, tucking his chin in the coarse scarf, glancing only slightly at passersby to keep from bumping into them. Black top hats glistened with wet, though a few gentlemen carried black umbrellas, which were stylish but seemed to have the tendency to fold inside out when held the wrong way. Ignoring that, Oliver concentrated on getting back without tracking too much mud and street dirt on his boots and went in the back way in case he'd not been able to manage it.

The back door was already open when he arrived, and the servants' entrance was bustling as the cook and the maid accepted a delivery of meat and eggs and whatnot from a damp-coated delivery boy; supper wasn't for a while yet, so Oliver hung his greatcoat and cap, laid his gloves on the rack without a word, and resettled his book under his arm. It was when he was by the front door and turning to go up the stairs that he caught his reflection in the gilt-edged hall mirror.

Dressed in grey as he was, the wall behind him a soft, al-most-matching color, he felt as though he was seeing an image of someone who was about to melt away. It wasn't merely that the ghost-like properties of his clothes blended in with the wall. More, it was the expression on his face, white and still. And his eyes, in which, were he not himself, he would not have been able to discover a single emotion or uncover any attribute of the type of person he was.

Except, yes, there it was, that flicker that announced that the world was let in and the raw, unhampered feeling of missing Uncle Brownlow came in a rush, all the way from that dark, tender spot inside, flooding him with its misery. Turning away and hurrying up the stairs, he wiped the tears on his cheeks with his cold fingers and told himself he was pathetic to be acting this way. To be thinking that he shouldn't have bought this particular book because Uncle Brownlow wouldn't approve, but at the same time being unable to forget that Uncle Brownlow was no longer around to approve or disapprove of anything Oliver did or intended to do.

By the time he reached his door, he was miserable and crying as hard as a small child, and very grateful indeed that he encountered no one on the way up the stairs. The spate ended, leaving him exhausted as he closed the door behind him and leaned against it. He wiped his face again and looked around the room, as weary as if he'd walked a dozen miles instead of only a handful of city blocks.

Once again, the maid had come—some maid, one of the maids, he would never know which one—and scrubbed the grate and lit a small, bright fire, and even opened the curtains a little to let in whatever daylight might be allowed by the weather. There was a tray on the table next to the green easy chair, upon which had been placed a teapot covered with a tea cozy, the white china full of sugar and cream, and a plate of cookies laced with glaze.

He was about to collapse under the weight of this kindness in spite of himself, but he tightened his mouth and managed to stop it. It was something Mrs. Bedwin had always done, and he was grateful and glad, and now he had no need to go back downstairs until suppertime. He could have his tea and read his book by the fire, and when the cookies were gone, he could lie on top of the quilted counterpane and lean against the pillows and read until he could fall asleep. That was the best option, the easiest option, for in sleep, there were no dreams, no memories nor any grief. At least for now.

By the time the day of the appointment with the solicitor had come, Oliver could stand no more of the solitary silence nor of hiding out in his room, even though, since the funeral, Mr. Grimwig had followed more solitary, inward-looking pursuits and would not be chance met in any room or passageway. Oliver had come upon him only once, sitting at the chess table in the parlor, just sitting there, the pieces half-moved, as if waiting for the next turn, which would never come.

When Oliver checked now, that was what Mr. Grimwig was doing, staring at the chess set again. Therefore, he wouldn't see Oliver making his way into the street, regardless which door he used. So Oliver put on his greatcoat and cap and the old grey scarf and left the townhouse boldly by the front door. He walked east in the icy air and then toward the river, where he soon found himself at Westminster Bridge.

Oliver leaned against the railing, and almost directly below him there was a low skiff with a lone boatman struggling along the sliced ice at the edge of the Thames. Snow had fallen during the previous night, thickening the water, making it an almost impossible task to bank the skiff. Oliver could see that the boatman was trying to get around paying the fee at the dock. But it was too late, the local muscle that collected the rent was already coming for the boatman, and Oliver turned before he could see the tussle in the frozen mud, instead turning his face up to the sky, looking for blue but catching only frosty, sharded clouds.

The City traffic hustled by him on the bridge, people hurrying to or from errands or to home, a pair of dray horses pulling the thick-wheeled carts across the stone, thunder rumbling across the ice that was hardening up as the sunlight waned thin. The smell of the river grew dank as a sharp breeze buffeted over the bridge railing. Oliver clenched his fists around it, realizing that he'd left his gloves behind, thinking that it was probably for the best; the fine leather gloves that he'd gotten on his birthday last year would have been ruined in short order with the roughness of the metal rail.

Oliver stood alone, feeling lost as he traced the patterns of smudged footprints of the mudlarks across the ice.

Death would come to them all someday, he knew that, but it seemed unfair that Uncle Brownlow would be taken too, just as all the others had been taken through the years. Until anyone who he'd ever cared about, who'd ever cared about him at all, had gone, leaving him in the company of the ill-tempered Mr. Grimwig, who at this moment, was waiting upon Oliver's return to go to the solicitor.

Well, Oliver couldn't blame Uncle Brownlow for leaving him with Mr. Grimwig. Uncle Brownlow had been his savior and his guardian, and it was not Uncle Brownlow's fault that Mr. Grimwig had never found Oliver to be a particularly pleasing boy.

In spite of his thick coat, he was cold, shivering as the breeze from the river blew up toward his face, circling around his neck, which felt bare even through the grey scarf. Mr. Grimwig had not given Oliver any money to replace the scarf that Jack had stolen from him, though Oliver assumed that Mr. Grimwig assumed Mr. McCready would cover the cost of a new scarf. Oliver had a small change purse with him, and several coins within, but it was not enough to purchase a scarf.

As he turned away from the wind, he saw the sign for the Green Dragon; the tavern was close enough to the river to be of a slightly doubtful reputation, but the street that it was on was well-trafficked enough to make the establishment more salubrious than it otherwise might have been. So Oliver opened the door and went in.

The tavern was warm with a smoking open fire at one end and a boiler with a fire underneath it at the other. There was a stew being cooked in it, with ingredients no doubt known only to the pot and perhaps the long metal spoon that stirred it. For some reason, Oliver thought he smelled chestnuts, bursting with sweetness and about to explode their skins, but he couldn't see anyone busking any.

The tavern consisted of a few rows of dark wooden tables and scattered chairs, close to the windows for the light or near the fire for warmth. There was some rowdiness going on at the bar, though the majority of the patrons at their tables were quiet and concentrating on their drinks. The low ceiling was dark with smoke and oily with years of sweat and dirt rising up from a type of custom that couldn't care less about the grime and would have been turned away at the door of any establishment Oliver usually frequented. But in this part of London, by the river, where the streets were narrow as though shrunken by time, and the smell of the Thames seeped through every fiber of wood and stone, well, nobody would turn away anyone with a penny to spend.

Oliver kicked at clumps of trash under his boots and ordered a tot of gin at the counter before he could think about how indecent it was to have a drink like this in the middle of the afternoon. But the gin was delivered faster than he could remonstrate himself, and he watched his pennies being swept up with a grime-streaked hand without attempting to stop the exchange. No words were exchanged, no *thank you for your custom, young master*, which Oliver found he missed more than he imagined he might. But then, he'd long ago realized that getting used to something meant that it was much more difficult to attempt to go without it.

He sipped at the gin and thought that it sat nicely in his stomach, sending out pumps of warmth and relaxation. As long as he kept drinking it slowly, the gin would keep him in a nice steady state of not feeling very much. Slow sips would be how he'd spend the next hour or so. If it were true that time flew on wings toward only horrible destinations, the reverse was also true: it dragged itself on broken legs toward a good one. Oliver knew that his good destination was waiting for him simply because he felt like it would never come. It seemed out of reach, like a blue sky, and him in a place of limbo, never moving forward, never arriving.

With the customers crowding around the fire and blocking the heat, it was getting a little cold where he was. He ordered another gin. A sip from the glass warmed him, but only barely. It was, he realized, watered-down gin, not very potent, and it left a slime in his mouth, giving indication of having been served from a not very clean bottle. He sank his nose in the glass to smell the gin and sink in the fumes that way, to warm himself.

Uncle Brownlow would not have approved, not at the second gin, let alone the first, nor at Oliver's sense of relaxing in such a place as his shoulders came down and he sucked back the first large mouthful of his second gin. In spite of the press of late afternoon bodies, the scent and salt of laborers and the frozen snow melting onto the floor near the door, and the drifts of damp dust and spilt beer, he felt somehow at home. Even though he shouldn't.

Uncle Brownlow never liked hearing the story of little Oliver's early life and had listened only once or twice before he'd declared he'd had enough. He didn't even want to hear the part about how Fagin, upon seeing the many holes in Oliver's old stockings, had stolen him a new pair. Nor had he ever liked hearing about how Fagin had stuffed straw around the windows with his own hands to keep his boys warm. None of that mattered, only that Fagin was a fence, a flash man living at the bottom of a very hard world. That he was a thief and a Jew seemed to matter less than that he'd stolen Oliver away.

Uncle Brownlow's disinclination to listen didn't make what had happened not so, however. Oliver knew that. And he suspected that Uncle Brownlow did too. But there'd never been another time that someone had specifically asked to hear of his adventures. Soon, it was as if they'd never happened.

Except in Oliver's own mind. And Mr. Grimwig's memory, of course. For some reason, Mr. Grimwig had not needed to be told the story more than once; he was always able to work it, and the part Oliver had played in it, into any conversation, especially to those persons with whom Oliver was making his first acquaintance. Mr. Grimwig always saw to it that everyone he met knew exactly the low places that Oliver was familiar with. Such as this tavern. Mr. Grimwig would indeed be satisfied to know that all his opinions about Oliver might be more true than he suspected. Not that Oliver would ever tell him.

He took another slug of gin and considered the glass in his hand, smeared with grease and not very clean. He realized quite clearly that Mrs. Bedwin would be shocked to see him drinking out of such a vessel, and that opinion, so dearly missed, was making him feel very badly about being where he was, and on such a day.

"You'll be wantin' better than that, you will, my flash companion."

Oliver heard the jaunty voice from over his shoulder, and it came at him as if pressed through some kind of chamber, sealed at one end so that it echoed back at him without ever having been spoken. The hair on his neck began a creeping dance, rather as if it were trying to slide beneath the collar of his woolen greatcoat. The skin across his shoulders soon joined it, and he turned his head, wondering if there would be something there to scare him or if he would only find the sightless eyes of a beggar wanting a sip of the gin that had turned to ash water in his mouth.

He thought he was very badly drunk, drunk enough to be dreaming, but there Jack Dawkins stood with his heavy brow and that wide mouth that was smiling far too broadly. On top of his head he wore a ragged, once-shiny top hat. Stolen, no doubt, as had been the coat, for it could not have been bought, not by someone with who possessed such talented hands, which were now jammed into pockets, ruining the elegant lines of the coat. Jack was of a height with Oliver, though not quite filling the shoulders of the coat as might have the gentleman for whom it had been designed. But yes, as he wore Oliver's red scarf around his neck, of course, boldly tied, Oliver realized that only Jack Dawkins could wear a scarf that way and call it fashion.

Still Oliver could not speak, could not greet Jack and call him by name, for to do so was to bring the past to the now. Particularly in the now where he'd been caught with his second gin in his hand. In a tavern near the river, in a rough part of town. He saw Jack's eyes take in the ugly grey scarf that Oliver wore.

"Have you been following me?" Oliver asked. His mind froze at this; if Jack could find him on a snowy, ice-crusted day in London, Jack could find him anywhere.

"Why are you always so surprised to see me, eh, Nolly?" Jack smiled that smile that Oliver knew so well.

"Anyway, you're the only person I know in London," continued Jack with a shrug. "Besides, that muck'll give you belly rot," he added, nodding at the glass in Oliver's hand. Jack didn't care, of course; Oliver could sink into drunken madness at that very moment and Jack would only be concerned with what he wanted, with what was good for Jack. Jack Dawkins. The Artful Dodger. Mr. Artful, if you please.

Oliver opened his mouth to speak, and someone bumped into him. Oliver jerked his hand and the gin spilled all over his trousers. The gin oozed down his leg and reeked through the air, and Oliver knew it was beyond him to hope that none of it had gotten on him. And all the while, those eyes, sparkling beneath the brim of that hat, watched him.

"I've got an interview with the solicitor today," said Oliver, his mouth thick over the words. "And no time, not any, to spend in idle talk with a pickpocket. There're more important things than that." His hand shook and he spilled more of his gin on the floor, so that there was only a draught or two left in the glass.

"How much have you had, anyway?" Jack sat down next to him and Oliver shifted back.

There was something sinewy about the way Jack moved, and as Oliver looked at that coarse skin and the fringe of dark hair coming down the hard jawline, he remembered that Jack had told him he'd returned from being deported. That had been five years ago; he'd not heard anything about it and had never braved himself to ask anyone, let alone Uncle Brownlow. But it was from this somewhere that Jack had returned, of a recent date, and his major item, to wit, was to pester his old pal.

But it made sense, in an odd way, though he really couldn't understand why Jack had wanted to find him yet again. Oliver had told Jack everything he knew about Fagin's gang, or at least, what he could say. The truth of the matter was that everyone from Fagin's gang, from the smallest lad to the man himself, had been scattered to the winds. He shoved away the memory of Fagin's last night in Newgate and of Nancy's death.

Though with no details forthcoming, he could only imagine her blood running across the cobblestones, till the street ran red like those at Smithfield. And of Sikes's body, shot, hanged, dead, something like that—

"Some air," said Jack, taking Oliver by the arm as if they'd been in the midst of discussing it and Jack had just decided. He got up and pulled Oliver to his feet and made him walk outside.

The air on the street was painfully cold now that he'd been breathing in the warm funk of the tavern, and his blood was racing through him, courtesy of the gin. The heat of his skin became flecked with frost as it cooled, and he wondered why he'd not worn a different scarf, such as his red one, and then remembered that Jack had stolen it, was wearing it even now, the soft red wool swirling around his ex-convict neck.

Oliver shook his head and let himself be dragged, which was a sad mistake because if Jack meant to haul him into someplace quiet and dark and hold him there till Oliver gave up whatever Jack wanted, well, it would be a short wait. Jack was all bundled up, prepared for the weather, and Oliver was not.

The hand that dragged him into the street stopped and released him. They were still close to the overhang of the sign for the Green Dragon, where people passed in and out of the door, and the snow, as it blew off the roof, slanted away from them. Splats of snow landed on Oliver's neck.

Jack patted the front of Oliver's greatcoat. Oliver found that he was too close to the swath of dark hair that spilled across Jack's forehead in greasy strands from beneath the ragged edges of that hat, and that closeness overwhelmed him. Oliver tried shoving backward, but Jack's hand gripped the edge of his lapel. His own gloveless hands tried for purchase on Jack's thicker coat, but it was useless. He was about to fall on his backside in the snow. Right there in the street.

"Let go of me," said Oliver, feeling flushed, feeling that his words came out indistinct, to be regarded by nobody. He tightened his whole body as if to pull away, but Jack pulled him close, close enough to almost touch Oliver's face with his own. Close enough where Oliver could smell the smoke and sweat on him, see the wreath of grit and beardgrowth on his neck.

"There's no sense in that, Nolly," said Jack, tugging on Oliver's greatcoat to keep him still. "Seein' as I've got you." For a moment, the grit and hardness of that voice erased almost every bit of boy that Jack was. Almost. The street thug was there too, in the husk of air as it pushed out of his lungs. For a moment, Oliver watched the frost of breath and felt himself shake his head as if he were saying no to one of Jack's suggestions. Then Jack laughed and pulled back, twitching his head to resettle his hat, and Oliver sank back against the wall, his boots slipping in the snow, melted ice from the sign dripping down his neck.

Jack grabbed his arm again and pulled Oliver up the street to where it narrowed to a mere lane.

"Let go, I say," said Oliver, trying for force, teeth grit, not wanting to make a scene, not wanting word to get back to Mr. Grimwig for any reason at all. "Let go!"

He threw a punch, wide with his bare fist, hitting Jack in the shoulder. It was ineffectual, but it did stop Jack. Jack bunched up his shoulders as though he were going to strike, but then lowered them. When he reached out his hand, it was to push the moist hair from across Oliver's forehead, and to gently pat Oliver's cheek.

Oliver staggered as though he had been struck, clutching onto Jack's wool-clad arm, dazed and staring, feeling as though he should understand what was happening, could understand it if his head wasn't ringing. When Oliver tried to pull away again, Jack gave Oliver's arm a rough shake.

Jack walked a few paces, pulling Oliver with him. "I'm hurt that you would think I meant you ill," said Jack. "*Wounded*, even."

Oliver rubbed his coat sleeves with his bare hands and tried to be more worried about his soaked and stained pant leg and the tiresome explanation he'd have to make when he got back to the townhouse. Better to worry about that rather than how close Jack was, and how the curve of his mouth and the smell of his skin, warm in the cold, took Oliver right back to a place he'd never thought to return, and from which he'd come so far.

"Here, what money you go? Any change? Hand it over, now, be a good boy."

Blinking, Oliver thought of the small change purse in his pocket from whence he'd brought forth enough for two measures of gin. He'd been a good boy for so long, but with the right sort of people, he might be a bad one. But Jack's expression said, in dark familiar lines, that the kind of boy Jack wanted him to be was an obedient one. One that would hand it over, and that right quick. How much did he have left, and what did Jack want it for? Maybe Jack wanted lodgings and someone to recommend him; Oliver couldn't think straight enough to figure it out. And all the while, Jack's eyes were watching him. As Oliver jerked his hand near his pocket to protect it, Jack reached out and grabbed him by the wrist.

"Pull it out, or I pulls it out for you."

Something warm and dusky was in Jack's voice; Oliver believed he meant to do what he said, though Oliver couldn't imagine anyone doing what Jack was suggesting. To put his hand in another man's *pocket*—

"Just hand it over, Nolly," said Jack, shaking his head, the velvety tones of his voice slipping away to the street-bright ones. "We're gonna get somethin' to sober you up. Here."

Jack made a wide gesture with his hand, and Oliver made himself focus. They were directly near a coffee busker, a cart on wheels with its slanted canvas roof clean from snow, the wheels painted a bright blue, and a little hob over which hung a silver pot. The pot had a short, curved spout. Jack nodded at the man, who tilted the pot and poured out a large dose of coffee into a dented metal cup. Into this he tipped some brown sugar and handed it to Jack.

"Bread as well, then?" asked the busker.

"With butter," said Jack. "Is it salted?" He gestured to Oliver to pull out his money, and this Oliver did, feeling half-stupid and far short of being half-sober. Jack took the change purse, and without asking, pawed through it for a handful of pennies, which he handed to the busker. Then he held out the tumbler.

"Extra sugar in that, if you please," Jack said, pocketing Oliver's change purse so quickly that Oliver blinked. "My friend here likes it that way."

When the busker handed over the slices of buttered bread and the large tumbler of hot coffee, Jack handed the tumbler to Oliver.

"Here, get some of that into you." He even tipped the container toward Oliver's mouth to encourage Oliver to drink.

Oliver took it in both hands and put it to his lips. The metal was hot, but in the cold air, quickly cooling, the steam rose from the surface of the coffee in mad swirls, dissipating somewhere near his forehead. It was occurring to him, through the fog that the gin had created, that Jack meant to help him rather than to hinder.

He took a small sip of the hot coffee. It warmed him through as he watched Jack take a bite of the bread and butter, his lips smacking around the bite as if it were the best he'd ever eaten. It might have been, for all that. Oliver found himself strangely disquieted by the fact that he didn't mind that Jack had spent his money, though he did want that change purse back. Uncle Brownlow had given it to him last Christmas, and the clasp was guaranteed for life.

Jack took the coffee from Oliver and took a large swig. "There's no cream in it," he said. "But it's what you need." Then he handed the coffee back as he ate the rest of the bread and butter, rather as if he were starving, which Oliver imagined he might be. After all, what did an ex-convict, recently *hextricated*, do for a living? Never mind, he had no intention of asking.

"Our own dear Nolly," said Jack after taking another swig of coffee and handing it back to Oliver. He tapped the cup as if to encourage Oliver to drink still more. Which he did, taking a large swallow that was not quite hot enough to burn his tongue.

"Sweet Oliver," Jack said now, still watching him. "Suckin' back a glass of gin from a dirty glass, no less, with his arms on the counter, for all the world like a down-and-out sailor."

Frowning, Oliver handed Jack the coffee, only now realizing that they'd been sharing the same container. But then, what of that? In the bad old days, there'd been fewer mugs and tumblers than there had been boys. Fagin's lads shared what they had, from cups of coffee to slices of bread. Rough pillows and worn blankets. The circle of bare feet around an open fire in a raggedy hearth.

He watched Jack licking his fingers and tucking them around the metal tumbler to warm them. There were new scars along the backs of his fingers, and the bones on his hands and wrists seemed too near the surface. It made Oliver want to ask where Jack had been. What he'd been doing.

Jack tipped his head back, his throat working as he swallowed the rest of the coffee. Then he gave the metal cup back to the coffee busker. He patted his stomach, seeming contented as he gave Oliver a quirky half smile.

"Filled now," he said. "And you're more sober now."

"Yes," said Oliver. His body was beginning to feel the effects of the gin being chased away by the hot coffee. And by Jack's presence, which was, in truth, as good as a slap in the face. It reminded him that if he didn't sign those papers he wouldn't be able to work for Mr. McCready. And then he would end up like Jack, a vagrant in the street, with nowhere to go and nothing to do. Well, nothing respectable to do. "I have to go."

Watching Oliver with an intent expression, Jack reached into his pocket and jostled Oliver's change purse in his hand, up and down as though he were tossing a child's ball. He didn't offer it back to Oliver, and Oliver didn't dare try to grab it, for Jack would just laugh and pull away as if the whole of it were some game. That change purse was as long gone as if Oliver had thrown it into the Thames with his own hands.

"I can catch up with you later," said Jack. "I'll come tomorrow."

"But you won't," said Oliver, saying this before he realized he should just let the comment remain where it was without an explanation. He stepped back from Jack, his boots slipping a bit in the wet snow that had gathered itself around his feet. He had somewhere to be, and though he was an orphan still, he was no longer a small boy to be detained by a street thug. "I'll be moving on, I've got an interview this afternoon, and then I'll be in a different part of London."

"Well," said Jack, tugging at his lapels and tipping his head back to look at Oliver down his nose. "That ain't no matter to me; I'll find you, just the same."

Of course Jack would. He had before; there was nothing to stop him, not when the whole of London belonged to him. Then Jack turned and walked up the slanted street without a backward glance, and in a moment, he'd disappeared around a corner as if he'd never really been there.

Oliver straightened the lapels of his greatcoat and tried to brush the snow from his trousers. He should not have gone for a drink, and he should not have gone with Jack anywhere, despite the fact that Jack had rescued him from where Oliver had been headed, straight into the bottom of a bottle of gin. But it was too late to think about that. It looked as though he'd rolled in a snow bank, and not a very clean one at that. He turned westward to go back to the townhouse.

There was a low sound as the local church began to bong out the hour, and Oliver realized with a shock that it was three o'clock. The wind whisked up behind him, chilling him where his clothes were damp and finding its way into the seams of his collar.

Oliver turned and started pushing past people to get to the center of the bridge, and when he got there, he plowed along, fists in his pockets, cap tilted low over his forehead, wishing the grey scarf were better suited to the wet weather.

When he was almost to the end of the bridge, he realized he was turned around and going the wrong way, and the bells from St. Margaret's church faded away as the cold air started blowing snow in a thick cloud around the portals on the south end of the bridge. There was nothing for it but to turn around and walk very fast and trod on toes and slip in the mud and refuse on the bridge and feel his breath coming sharply in his throat as he hurried, uselessly hurried.

He'd wandered the streets for a good long while as it was before stepping into the tavern, and now Jack had delayed him even further. There was no way he'd be able to stay in Mr. Grimwig's good graces now, if there ever was a chance, which there never was. But he had to get back; the meeting with the solicitor was a pressing matter.

As he headed west toward the nicer part of town, the gas lamps were being lit against the fog and the smoke and the setting sun. The streets were being swept as darkness came, the pavements rushed with people and the streets filled with carriages and horses, the roofline only a smudged, dark cut against the growing dark.

His head ached as the gin faded away and the streets became colder, and he realized his boots were soaked through. His feet were aching with dampness, and there was a large greasy blotch on his trousers that still managed to smell like freshly spilled gin. Thrusting his hands in his pockets, he tipped his chin down and hurried up the street and down the lane and across the park, when it started to snow again.

CHAPTER 6

At The Solicitor's

He was damp through by the time he skirted the front door and took the short flight of iron stairs that led down to the area and the kitchen door. The smell of hot food and grease hit him even before he'd opened it, though the kitchen was empty when he did. He heard the sounds from the floor above, the sound of footsteps and skirts against wood and boots on the carpet and the short bark of an order.

Oliver didn't know if he could make it to his room or even past the parlor, where no doubt Mr. Grimwig was waiting. He looked at the open door that led to the servants' staircase. One of the girls came down in her plain dark dress that reached the floor, her white apron crisp against the black wool. He'd not heard her coming, and she stood there as still as if she'd been there all along.

"Mr. Grimwig has been looking for you. He knows you left the house," said the girl, not smiling or looking him in the eye.

Oliver nodded. It was obvious by her expression what had happened. And it wasn't that Mr. Grimwig had yelled or scolded the maid or threatened to sack her for not stopping Oliver from leaving. If anything, Mr. Grimwig had taken out his watch and looked at it, a sure sign of his agitation. Or his feeling that he was justified in everything he'd ever thought about Oliver. The years had not erased his initial opinion, and no passage of time would do anything more.

"I'll go up," he said. "I'll go up and change directly."

She tried smiling, but it wasn't working, and so he slipped past her to tread up the stairs to the polished landing at the front door. He pushed through to the parlor. Better to have it over with, better to face up to Mr. Grimwig's disapproval.

Mr. Grimwig stood by the front table in the parlor, cane in one hand, his opened watch in the other. The fob and chain against his black waistcoat glittered in the newly built fire in the fireplace.

"Well, young Oliver," said Mr. Grimwig. He was trying to smile politely. But there was no one but Oliver and Mr. Grimwig standing there, and no need for it, so the smile turned into a grimace. Oliver stared hard at the brass fittings on the door. "Are you ready?"

Oliver stared at the looking glass covered still with black crepe and the green silk wallpaper that shimmered in the candlelight from the sconces over the fireplace. The drapes were green too, though they looked black in this light. He chewed the inside of his lip and tried not to think of the gin house he had so recently been in. Tried not to think of Jack, green-eyed and canny, patting Oliver, stroking his forehead with complete equanimity, as if all of this were under his discretion, solely his, and not Oliver's.

"You don't look well," said Mr. Grimwig, entirely without sympathy.

Oliver wasn't going to argue about that. The gin was making him sick; it had been very bad gin, it seemed, not even worth the pennies he'd paid for it.

"You should freshen up now, Oliver." This was delivered in more caring tones that sounded entirely false to Oliver. Mr. Grimwig controlled all now, and it was plain to see he had the confidence of it. "We leave for the solicitor's within the moment."

"Yes," said Oliver. His knees were knocking and there was a sudden slick feeling in his throat. He would walk smoothly out of the parlor and head to the back stairs. There was a dustbin there, an empty one that had, of late, held old rags. He could use that to throw up in. Or maybe he would tear open the door to the back garden and use the hollow beneath the winter-bare rose bushes there. It all depended on which servant was nearby and how fast he could get past them.

"And Oliver?"

"Yes?"

"You will make sure that girl has your trousers to tidy up. In fact, you should change altogether; I can smell the gin from here."

Looking down at himself, Oliver saw again the greasy patch on his trouser leg. He reeked of the gin house, of the street, of coffee, of Jack.

"I'll go up directly and get cleaned up."

"See that you do." Mr. Grimwig put his pocket watch away and wiggled his cane. Tucking one hand behind his back, he pushed out his stout stomach that glistened beneath its sheath of black silk. A threat lingered in his voice, unspoken, and

Oliver knew that his intolerance for Oliver's lack of temperance, long buried, would remain buried no longer.

Oliver found that he wanted another drink of gin very badly. But he'd already done his drinking, and the tears that boiled behind his eyes refused to come to the surface. As a small boy, crying had come at the flicker of an eyelash. Not that it stayed anyone's hand or made the angels come to carry him into the arms of his dead mother. Tears had been like rain to him just the same, affecting no one and making him feel as if he'd been pressed between millstones. Wrung out like a bottle rag.

Now he felt that way, even without the tears. He wanted nothing more than to scream and pound the walls and make Mr. Grimwig's placid, self-satisfied expression explode into shock. His hands pressed against his thighs like hot brands, and the candle flames over the mantelpiece shimmered.

Oliver went up the hallway as fast as he could, knowing he was tracking mud, unable to stop. He went all the way to the end of the hallway to the bin near the back stairs. It was gone. Sweating, he realized he had about two seconds before he spoiled what remained of his good clothes or the woolen runner on the floor. He dashed to the back door, and threw himself into the mist and snow among the bare rose bushes and vomited into the frozen mud with a splash. Fresh gin would taste very good right now, or another cup of coffee. Even some cold water would help.

When he'd washed up and had his trousers brushed for him, Oliver went downstairs. Under Mr. Grimwig's glower, he put on his coat, leaving behind the grey scarf that was far too scratchy. With his cap in his hand, he turned to Mr. Grimwig.

The girl held the front door open and snow swirled in, bits of speckled ice that landed on the black-and-white squares in the landing and winked out of existence in the warmth. Of course, if he got the position with Mr. McCready, then he would, most likely, go to live in residence, over the shop, perhaps, or maybe in lodgings. Either would be hard, mostly in the leaving of a place where he'd shared so many good memories with Uncle Brownlow. But staying would be hard as well; living with Mr. Grimwig, alone, with no one to stand between them, was liable to make one or both of them come to blows.

"In the cab, boy, we can't be at this all day; I've appointments to keep and I shan't let you keep me from making a timely appearance."

Oliver nodded and slipped past Mr. Grimwig's scowling face and the cane held in one gripped fist. Oliver slipped on the pavement and scurried into the cab: a one-horse hansom that would move fast and get them there without too much delay. But it would also mean sitting quite close to Mr. Grimwig beneath the woolen blanket that the coach had supplied. As Mr. Grimwig lumbered to sit beside him, Oliver realized that at least it would be too cold to talk.

Although Mr. Grimwig managed it, just the same. As the driver flicked his whip and the cab lurched off down the street, he said, "Trust you to pick the most miserable day on record for a fool's errand."

Oliver kept his mouth shut and didn't remind Mr. Grim-wig that he'd said the same thing the day they'd buried Uncle Brownlow.

The cab trotted through the streets, which were thick with traffic in spite of the weather. It was cold, Oliver supposed, but the snow coming down covered the black soot on the pavement and the piles of horse manure and the lump at the end of the street that he knew to be a dead dog. Everything at the roofline, however, was white and soft, the slate roofs fur-edged, the church steeples laced with scrolls of snow.

In spite of the weather, they passed a group of quality folk on the pavement. The ladies were in fur-trimmed bonnets, and the gentlemen had fine, thick coats. Maybe they were a skating party, or perhaps a planned trek through one of the parks. They looked merry and warm and probably had hot drinks waiting for them upon their return home. Oliver watched them until the cab was too far past and focused on the front of the interior of the cab.

"We'll be there shortly," said Mr. Grimwig. "Don't go showing off, mind, or acting superior."

"I won't," said Oliver. "I never do." He grit his teeth to keep anything harsh from coming out; the last thing he needed was to alight from the cab with his clothes tumbled and rumpled from an elbow-to-elbow pushing match with Mr. Grimwig.

"That remains to be seen," said Grimwig. Then he thumped the roof of the cab. "Driver, can you hurry? I've some better place to be."

With a flick of the whip, the cab lurched forward and Oliver gripped his thighs with his hands. If he grabbed the rail, Grimwig was sure to mention to one and all what a silly, nervous boy Oliver was. But if he tumbled to the floor, that would be worse. The best he could do was brace his feet on the floor of the cab and try to stay upright and balanced. As the cab followed the curve along Oxford Street, with St. Paul's grey outline looming over the chimney pots, the wind changed direction and came in past the canvas-framed windows. It hit the side of Oliver's neck, and for a moment, he felt as if he ought not to have agreed to this wild choice, to leave the comfort, relative though it might be, of Mr. Grimwig and late Uncle Brownlow's abode. There, it was warm and safe and dry, and there was food, and even though the present company was none too good, it was home. Oliver had to bite his lip to keep from saying it aloud: *Take me home.* Except he hadn't any. So instead, he stared fixedly out of the window, watching the street go by, and determined to keep his mouth shut for the duration of the trip.

"You'll find this a good establishment, I'll wager," said Mr. Grimwig from beside him, leaning forward on his cane as if to catch sight of what had his charge so riveted. He did not add, to Oliver's relief, that if it were otherwise, he'd eat his head. He'd not said that phrase, not at all, in the days since Uncle Brownlow's passing, as if, after all, the point in saying it had passed as well. Oliver had never known whether Uncle Brownlow was laughing to himself or laughing at Mr. Grimwig. He would never know now and didn't really believe he wanted to. Oliver was heartily sick of the phrase anyway.

"Did you hear me, Oliver?"

"Yes," said Oliver, feeling the flatness of his own voice.

"I hear it from Parson Greaves that Mr. McCready only takes in a very few boys. You're privileged to be considered for a position without waiting."

Oliver already knew this. It had been said to him for days since the reception.

"This is a rather good area for a solicitor," said Mr. Grimwig. He had turned the other way now, and Oliver flicked his eyes across the space of the carriage and looked where Mr. Grimwig was looking. Though he couldn't see the whole of each building, they looked as shops and offices ought to look. It was a good street. They'd passed through one or two insalubrious areas, but now the pedestrians looked hale and hearty, bundled to the cold. Out in the sharp weather because they wanted to be, because they had a new cloak to show off and boots that could bear the dampness of snow and ice. And servants standing by later to clean and brush and press and dry.

"Don't you agree, Oliver?"

"Yes." But that was all he could manage without bursting out shouting. When he turned twenty-one, the three thousand pounds left to him by his never-met father would be his. He'd do what he had to at Mr. McCready's because he wanted to buy a bookshop with that money, and he wanted to be ready when that day came. Which was, at present, an eternity of four years away.

The carriage pulled up to a curb, the wheels jumping in the old stone gutter for a jarring second before coming to a halt. The squeak of leather harness and click of metal-clad hooves echoed in Oliver's ears, and then it was still.

Mr. Grimwig was already lumbering out of the cab, handing up money with a tight fist and gesturing with his cane for Oliver to alight also, to hurry and be quick about it.

"Come back at quarter till," said Mr. Grimwig to the cab driver. "If you are late, I will simply hail another cab. But I'd just as soon ride in this one, for I already know that it is clean." The cab driver tipped his hat and flicked his whip to get the horse going in a slow walk down the street. Oliver couldn't have assured Mr. Grimwig that the cab driver would be back. Unless one gave them money first, cab drivers of Oliver's experience did as they pleased.

"They are expecting us, Oliver," said Mr. Grimwig. "Even if we are late, which is your fault."

A gentleman in a dark black waistcoat and jacket, his white shirt gleaming against the wool, came out on the front step to greet them.

"Mr. Grimwig," he said. "I'm Mr. Bond. It's a pleasure to meet you. Let me shake your hand, and that of young Twist. Then come away into the shop where it is much warmer than it is on the street."

Mr. Grimwig shook the offered hand and then tipped his head in Oliver's direction.

"I brought him," he said. "Though he's still not sobered up from his sojourn to a tavern today. The street never leaves the boy, who, I fear, has a taste for the gin."

"Surely you must be joking," said Mr. Bond, his voice thin in the cold air. He took Oliver's hand and shook it.

"I never joke about intemperance," said Mr. Grimwig. "It will be the ruin of our civilization, or I'll eat my head."

Oliver shook Mr. Bond's hand with nerves zipping through him. He was not shocked that Mr. Grimwig had been so bold with Oliver's current state and had voiced sly rejoinders at how horrible Oliver's past was, and how that reflected on how equally horribly he might conduct himself in future. But after today, Oliver would be leaving all of that behind him.

"I had a glass with a friend, in remembrance of my Uncle Brownlow and the time got away from us, is all." Oliver said this looking only at Mr. Bond.

"A friend?" roared Mr. Grimwig. "You have no friends, save that low family of yours in Chertsey."

Oliver could only glare at Mr. Grimwig; if he leapt to Aunt Rose and Uncle Harry's defense, both he and Mr. Grimwig would come to blows, right there on the pavement.

"In remembrance," said Mr. Bond, rushing into the boiling silence. "Which is always a good thing, and time does not matter upon those occasions. But perhaps you should both come in out of the cold and the weather. I have an office where we can conduct our business, and Mr. McCready is already arrived."

Oliver took a deep breath and followed as Mr. Bond and Mr. Grimwig went up the short flight of freshly cleaned stone steps. He let the two men pull ahead and stood back a little as he stepped over the threshold and absorbed the warmth of the solicitor's office, which seemed to reflect the promise of a new life to come.

As they entered Mr. Bond's wood-paneled office, Mr. Grimwig greeted Mr. McCready. After everyone shook hands, they sat down opposite the solicitor, who sat behind a desk stacked very tall with papers. Oliver could feel the stiff cushions beneath his thighs, see the clock with its severe face ticking out the moments, and thought for a moment that he'd made a grave mistake.

The solicitor opened the meeting with some kind words. "Your Uncle was the most Christian of men, and I know that this move to employment would have been what Mr. Brownlow would have wanted."

"I agree, this is the best course of action to take," Mr. Grimwig said, directing his words at Oliver, directly making the kind words into severe ones. "With your past record and your questionable birth—all of these things I've taken into consideration before allowing you to take this apprenticeship."

A silence fell because there was nothing Oliver could have said to that which wouldn't have set Mr. Grimwig off and brought their shared animosity out into the open. It wouldn't do, wouldn't be seemly, to share hard words in an important solicitor's office on Oxford Street.

For his part, the solicitor only regarded Mr. Grimwig from above his half spectacles.

"Oliver Twist is going to be making his own way now, and would be self-guided, and I have every faith that Oliver would do well and make us all proud."

Nodding at the solicitor as if thanking him for his intervention, Mr. McCready leaned back, steepling his hands while he rested his elbows on the arms of his chair.

"You now know most of what I am about here," he said, "You know how I train and what I train in. I take in boys at a young age and keep them until they are twenty-one. At which point they are fit to work their way up in any shop in London. In the world, I daresay, though none of my boys has yet tried it." A smile pulled at the hard muscles of his face.

"Do you have any questions, Mr. Grimwig? Or even you, Oliver?"

Oliver shook his head and was about to politely say no when Mr. Grimwig interrupted him.

"I understand that you give the boys a pay packet each week," said Mr. Grimwig, thumping his cane.

"Indeed. I believe boys need the wherewithal to test their boundaries and independence. Boys work harder for it and spend more wisely knowing how it is earned." Here Mr. McCready paused. Then he said, "I give them a shilling a week."

"An entire shilling? *Every* week?" Mr. Grimwig thumped his cane louder this time. His voice rose so high that Oliver considered it very possible that the next utterance out of him would be a proclamation that if any apprentice boy deserved that much, he'd eat his head. But his astonishment seemed to please Mr. McCready, who dropped his hands and laughed out loud.

"Unless, of course, the shop is doing so poorly that I cannot manage it, as sometimes happens during the slow season. But then the boys learn that their fortunes are tied in with how the market is going. Again, another lesson to be learned."

"*Every* week?"

"And then I give them a penny for the plate on Sunday. Attendance which is, of course, required."

"*Every week?*"

"In addition, I supply all their clothes and smalls. Wear and tear is accounted for unless a boy damages some article or such by carelessness. Then the money comes out of his pocket, which teaches him responsibility."

Mr. Grimwig opened his mouth again, and Oliver thought surely he was going to repeat his statement, but this time he merely shook his head and looked at Oliver. Oliver looked back at him, and for one instant, there was no animosity or veil of criticism left unsaid between them. He felt it was up to him, then, to say something. To make a decision.

For a moment, he looked at the office lined with shelves, crowded with papers and books, but made warm by the fire and bright by two lamps. He heard, from the open doorway, the industry of the several office boys as they went to and fro.

"So then, Oliver," said Mr. McCready, whose dark eyes were steady. "Will you make something of yourself?"

"Yes, sir," he said, not hesitating. "I would like to very much, if I may."

"It is acceptable," said Mr. Grimwig suddenly, as if the final decision rested with him. This surprised no one, least of all Oliver. "It will be a good thing for the boy to make his own way, and have a purpose in life other than sticking his nose in a book. Why his eyesight hasn't failed him with all that reading is beyond me."

With a nod from behind the stacks of books and papers on his desk, Mr. Bond reviewed the paperwork ever so slowly. Time stretched out so long till at last he pulled out a pen and signed. Then he made Oliver and Mr. Grimwig sign and handed the papers to Mr. McCready to examine, and Oliver could see that Mr. McCready's signature was already in place. That he'd done this before they'd arrived meant that Mr. McCready truly wanted him in his shop. Someone handed him a cloth, and Oliver wiped his fingers with it, knowing that the most immediate future of his life was sealed. It felt good.

Mr. McCready stood up, straightening the edges of his frock coat. "Shall we have young Oliver start as soon as may be, Mr. Grimwig? Perhaps on Monday? I'll send him his uniform to be fitted, but I'm afraid I must leave you and get back to my shop, for as you know, the wheels of commerce never stop. Not even for me."

They shook hands on it, and Oliver felt the firm grip of Mr. McCready's fingers.

"I look forward to it, sir," said Oliver. "And I thank you for the opportunity."

He didn't know if that last part was important enough to add, truly, but he meant it. Perhaps it had been to show Mr. McCready that he understood the connections between gentlemen; he wasn't sure. He knew, though, that he wanted to please Mr. McCready. As he had pleased Uncle Brownlow and his Aunt Rose and Uncle Harry. And Mrs. Bedwin.

"Till then, sir," said Oliver.

Mr. McCready hastened out, and after bidding farewell to Mr. Bond, they left the office through the front door, making their way through the crowd of dark-garbed workers, and slowly, for Mr. Grimwig's limp. Monday, and all the days that followed it, could not come fast enough for Oliver.

CHAPTER 7

Arrives Late, Which Is Not Considered An Auspicious Beginning

"If not for the commodious amounts of personal effects that you insist on carting about, you would have been able to walk to this new position," said Mr. Grimwig.

It was snowing again, and one of the servants had ordered the carriage without, quite exactly, asking Mr. Grimwig's permission, but there was a delay while they waited for the transport.

In spite of Mr. Grimwig's rantings, Oliver wasn't taking much with him. Just mementos of his time with Uncle Brownlow: a lace-drawn card from the chapel where Aunt Rose and Uncle Harry had gotten married, the small picture of his mother, wrapped in a small cloth, and of course, there was his collection of books, most of which had been purchased secondhand from the very bookseller where Oliver and Uncle Brownlow had, so to speak, met. And then there was his copy of *The Arabian Nights*, tucked at the very bottom of his case, hidden beneath his nightshirt. It wasn't very much. Surely nothing to express how happy he had been living there.

And Oliver was ready, even though he was running late.

He was dressed in his new uniform, which had been sent to him the day after the papers had been signed. One of the maids had him come down to the kitchen so she could take the trousers in or let the jacket out, as needed. The whole of the uniform was made of a sensible, warm brown wool from his cap to his trousers. Even his waistcoat was brown, as well as his boots. Only his scarf was a different color, a deep, brilliant green; his white green-striped shirt was hidden beneath the layers. The scarf would make him stand out, he supposed, when he went on errands or was anywhere in the City; it would mark him as one of Mr. McCready's boys. And that was all right, wasn't it? A thing to be proud of.

His fingers were numb around the handle of his case, and the staff of the house stood silently in the hall as the carriage arrived. Mr. Grimwig handed him an envelope that contained his papers and the address of the shop for the cab.

"You're to go to Mr. McCready's directly," said Mr. Grimwig. "You're not to make any stops along the way. No loitering and no stopping at any bookshops. The faster you get yourself settled there, the more content you'll be."

And this said as if Oliver had expressed any intention of not going, of not being willing to go. Mr. Grimwig was turning it all around as usual, to make the positive aspect of the whole arrangement his own, thus leaving Oliver to play the part of the reluctant miscreant.

"Yes," he said, his heart thudding.

Mr. Grimwig nodded at the envelope in Oliver's hand. "To pay for the cab, and any small thing you might need before getting your first pay packet."

To send him off with money was for Mr. Grimwig's own benefit, and to entertain anyone who might hear about it. "You'll find exactly five pounds in there," said Mr. Grimwig, a smirk dancing across his eyes. "Exactly the amount you typically like to find yourself holding when you go out and about."

It was a slap, a rude, cruel slap. It had been five years since the incident, and everyone, even the servants, knew the story, knew the truth of it, that Oliver had been *taken*—

That errand, which sent Oliver out into the dangerous streets of the City, had been Mr. Grimwig's idea. It was he who had suggested that Oliver take the books back to the shop for Uncle Brownlow, and a wager had been placed the moment Oliver had left the townhouse. And, as Mrs. Bedwin had told him later, Mr. Grimwig been most insistent that Uncle Brownlow was about to be taken for all he had.

The boy has a new suit of clothes on his back; a set of valuable books under his arm; and a five-pound note in his pocket. He'll join his old friends the thieves, and laugh at you. If ever that boy returns to this house, sir, I'll eat my head.

And while Oliver had not come back, it was because he'd been taken in the street, and he'd not laughed about it, not then, not ever. But it didn't matter now. Any protestations from Oliver, and especially in the absence of taking the time to explain the whole story, would be a waste of time, and he was eager to be on his way.

So he merely nodded his head and tucked the envelope in his pocket. "Yes, thank you."

Mr. Grimwig patted him on the head, which he tended to do when he wanted to show how amiable he was. The cap on Oliver's head padded what was almost a blow, and he ducked his head to stave off any more.

Someone opened the door, and the warmth of tea and toast and the morning fires whisked past him across the polished black-and-white floor and pulled him out into the day. Into the snowy cold of the March morning that, like most March mornings, was cold enough to make him believe that spring would never come. That winter had won, at last, and that the snow-laced branches would always look that way. That it would always snow, the steps coated with some ice that had not been properly scrubbed off. That, as he stepped out and went down the steps to the carriage, he was the coldest he'd ever been. And colder than he'd ever been at Fagin's den.

Ah, now. That was a memory best left alone. Oliver turned back to look at the open door, at the faces that almost did not look sorry. At Mr. Grimwig's satisfied expression, framed by slowly drifting morning snow. Not obscuring it, but taking it into its own memory. Had Uncle Brownlow not died, it would never have been.

"I will be getting reports on you, young Oliver," said Mr. Grimwig, which was obviously his best example of a tearful farewell. "I expect they will be good reports, or we will have to move you, after all. Perhaps a factory up north might better suit you? Or the mines?"

Oliver shook his head. Not either of those, not if he could help it.

The cab took him through the cold morning streets of London, around St. James's Park, past the formal buildings along Whitehall Street, and as briskly as it could through the busy cluster at Charing Cross. At Haymarket Street, where the fronts of the shops and offices clustered in more closely, the cab had to slow down, enough so that as it headed up Windmill Street and then right on the even more-narrow Broad Street, Oliver got an all-too thorough look at the local workhouse.

It was located just along Poland Street, the firm grey brick rising in a wall around it and the even darker brick of the building itself; Oliver had a brief glimpse of the sign that indicated it was St. James's Workhouse, but that was enough to see. Oliver looked the other way and then concentrated instead on the rocking pace of the cab as it went as briskly as the narrowing lane would allow it. Then with a lurch, the cab came to a stop in front of a building with a sign that said: McCready's Haberdashery.

Oliver hunkered in the doorway of the cab; he did not expect any assistance—didn't want any. For one moment, he wanted to be invisible. And it was not that he imagined his life here would be so bad, only that it was, for the moment, so very different.

If Uncle Brownlow had been with him, or even Mr. Grimwig, they would have been very willing to explain to him what he was seeing, but Oliver felt he might be able to see it on his own, concentrating on the details while waiting until two country gentlemen dressed in thick smocks passed by.

The haberdashery was set some streets off Oxford Street, and was only one or two blocks from Soho Square. While the neighborhood was nice, Oliver could see at once that the shop was too near the back streets. The shop itself, however, was saved from being too insalubrious by the fact that it was near St. James's Church, and only one street off a main omnibus line, which made it somewhat more genteel. Street traffic, of the sturdy, industrious, and upwardly climbing type, kept the area relatively clean and safe.

When Oliver alighted from the cab, he pulled out the envelope Mr. Grimwig had given him and paid and tipped the driver out of the five-pound note. The driver grumbled and dug into his pockets for enough change; it took him a moment, but when he gave Oliver four pounds and ten shillings, he was shocked at how much the trip had cost. He resolved to keep closer track of his money and walk when he could.

The driver handed Oliver's case to him and then flicked the reins to trot off to circle around and return to the main thoroughfare. When Oliver's feet met the paving stones, puffs of steam rose from the bodies of the horses drawing other carriages and from the dung steaming in the street. Over the roofline, he could see the grey hulk of the workhouse, and ignoring his dismay at seeing it so close to where he would be working and living, he resolved that when he set out on any errands he would give it a wide berth.

To distract himself further, he looked up at the shop in the bright, cold air. A lad came out of the shop. He was a short, ginger-haired boy and was wearing a white apron, and under that, the same thick brown pants and striped green-and-white shirt that Oliver wore. The lad carried a bucket and shovel, and in perfect silence, stepped into the street and shoveled the manure into the bucket. Then he whisked the remainder with a broom, sending it into the center of the cobbled street, and hurried with his gear around the side of the store.

Of course, he would come out with an empty bucket, but it would be a foolish shopkeeper who allowed his lads to come back through his store with a full or fouled one.

Oliver looked along the street. The haberdashery was at the end of a lane that was filled with shops, all painted in bright, rich colors, with huge windows and drapes of cloth in them. Or bonnets. Or shoes. Or baskets. Whatever was for sale. From down the street, Oliver could smell bread baking, or perhaps it was beer being brewed in a shop nearby.

The haberdashery itself had narrow double doors with three stone steps that led up to them. Though each step that led to the doors sagged in the middle from years of foot traffic, they were free of snow and dust. The double doors were a dark clover green, painted glossy and new with generous strokes, and had bright brass handles and fittings. The tall windows, draped with cloth and hung with articles to buy, were shining clean. The brass handles sparkled; the steps were whiter than snow. Overall, it seemed the sort of shop that Uncle Brownlow would have not only approved of but would have frequented, and it was of the class that he would have been proud to say that he did.

Oliver hesitated at the bottom of the steps and waited, thinking that he was lucky his feet weren't going numb, as it felt as though it had gotten much colder since breakfast. Better these thoughts, mundane and ordinary, than to concentrate on the wild beating of his heart. It was so ordinary, what he was doing, so very, very ordinary, a young man walking into his first apprenticeship. For anyone else, any other boy in the City. But it felt as though he was about to walk over a huge chasm from his bleak situation at Mr. Grimwig's, where his rotten, dark past was never allowed to stray far behind him. From that into a clean, bright place with kind, upstanding and hardworking people, who, while they might know the story, would not, at the same time, be inclined to bring it up every other half hour.

He heard footsteps from within and straightened up, bringing up his chin to look the approaching person in the eye, as he ought, and felt the churn of his stomach. How many doors had he gone through in his lifetime, never knowing what was on the other side, who would be there and if they would be kind. Would this be the last door? Or would it be just the next door in a very long line.

This pair of doors, with a long narrow window in each side and a transom above, opened, and out stepped Mr. McCready, his broad shoulders cutting the air around him. As he looked at Oliver, he was, naturally, standing on the top step and looking down his nose. For a moment, he reviewed Oliver, a haughty downward curve to his mouth, an assaying expression in his eyes.

"You're late, Oliver," Mr. McCready said, his mouth thinning.

"It was the traffic, sir," said Oliver. "It took a good quarter of an hour longer than we—that is, Mr. Grimwig indicated—"

"That's enough, Oliver. But in future, you will not be late; it's not suitable and sends the wrong message to our customers."

Mr. McCready was truly irritated, it was easy to see, from the cold morning, perhaps, and most assuredly from Oliver's lateness. Snow whistled around Oliver's feet as he waited for his orders. Perhaps Mr. McCready would turn him away for this one small slight, though where Oliver would go, he hadn't the faintest idea. Some small part of him thought about Jack and where Jack was and how he was faring with the idea that Fagin's gang was no more. And whether he'd take Oliver in, though the very thought of that was foolish; the last thing Oliver needed at this point in his life was to throw in his lot with a pickpocket.

Then Mr. McCready nodded, holding the door open with one strong hand.

"Come in, then, Oliver," said Mr. McCready as if he felt his point about lateness was both made and taken. "And you will begin to learn."

Oliver followed Mr. McCready into the shop, his large case banging against his knees. It was early, so there were no customers in the shop.

Mr. McCready walked up to the edge of the main counter, long and glossy, and tapped it.

"This is the center of the shop, Oliver, the heart," he said, his loud, clear voice finding its way into every cranny of Oliver's brain. "If you have any question as to what you are about, you come here and ask. But stand at the edges while you wait; I will not have lollygagging in the center of my shop, it presents a very untidy image to the customers."

The shop was set up as many a haberdashery was with shelves all around the walls, in front of which waited a rolling ladder. There was a series of display cases set with glass tops and wooden and brass frames. There were scissors on strings and several small bales of twine and rolls of brown paper, both on brass pikes. Little drawers were set everywhere with labels written in fine cursive script that read *Buttons* or *Pins* or *Hooks*. Open shelves held starched collars or stacks of suspenders.

Oliver's brain was overwhelmed with the array when he realized that the location of each was something he was going to have to learn. Not just admire and select from, but actually know. And the floor. It was polished to gleaming with not a fleck of dust to be seen anywhere. A great deal of work obviously went into keeping the shop as nice as it was. It suddenly occurred to him the amount of work that it was, that the boys who worked for Mr. McCready attended to. That he would be attending to.

The shop boy who had scraped the horse leavings from the street was now waiting on a lady customer who had just come in; the boy barely paused in his attendance to the lady to note the presence of anyone else. He didn't appear like an unfriendly boy; it could be that he was merely busy. Oliver nodded at him just the same.

"The most important thing is that the boys in my shop are known for their politeness," Mr. McCready said. "We open the front doors for customers, whether they are coming or going; we thank them for their custom if they have purchased anything, no matter how small or insignificant, and hand them their carefully counted-out change."

"Yes, sir," said Oliver. This shop, he was beginning to see, was more like Hillyard's Books than he might be comfortable with, but perhaps, if he were one of the lads with a superior air and a clean white apron, it might be different.

"Well, now that you've seen the shop, we shall go see the quarters upstairs."

Oliver nodded and followed when Mr. McCready led the way up the stairs, almost bouncing on his toes on each riser as they went up the two flights of stairs. Oliver had to trot to keep up with him, smacking the heavy case against each step. By the time they reached the top landing, he was almost out of breath and marveled at his new master's stamina.

The landing was small and made up of a short passageway with two doors on the left and one on the right. There was a small window at the far end that let in a vague gleam of light. As with the downstairs, the wooden floor was clean and the window was fairly free of streaks; most of the dirt was on the outside, but then the outsides of windows were always hard to keep clean in winter.

Mr. McCready smiled and opened the nearest left-hand door, which showed a small sitting room with dark, striped wallpaper, and a pair of older but still plush armchairs in front of a fireplace, which was dark without a fire in it.

"This is my private sitting room, Oliver, and beyond it, my bedchamber. I sometimes take my meals alone here, but mostly I take them in the kitchen with the boys. No boy is allowed in here without my permission, and indeed, without my presence, which, I'm sure, only makes sense."

Oliver nodded. "Yes, sir," he said. "I see."

Mr. McCready waved at the other door on the left but didn't open it. "I'm not at liberty to show you, but those are Mrs. Pierson's rooms; she's the housekeeper and cook. And then we have a girl come in most days to help, but she lives elsewhere."

Mr. McCready moved past Oliver to open the door on the other side of the small passageway. His body seemed large for a moment as he shifted to open the door, and so Oliver had to step back. Mr. McCready motioned with a wave of his hand for Oliver to precede him.

Feeling that Mr. McCready was just at his heels, Oliver walked into the room. There were three iron beds, all made up in the middle of the day. The single window at the far end of the steeply gabled room let in only enough light to douse the beds and the floor with gloomy flickers of shadow and light.

Mr. McCready came next to him and pointed to the bed nearest the window and farthest from the door.

"You're the newest apprentice, so it is tradition that you shall sleep closest to the window."

Oliver looked at the bed and walked over to it. He put the heavy case down next to it with a sigh.

"You can unpack later; you may have the pegs on the wall and the chest at the foot of your bed for your own personal use," said Mr. McCready. "Now, take a look at the room here, and tell me what you see."

Feeling a little numb, Oliver did as he was told and turned around. Now that he was facing the room with the window behind him, he could see a little better.

There were three beds lined up like coffins under the eaves, the head of each iron bedstead coming just to the top of where the slanted ceiling met with the wall going to the floor. Beside each bed was a chair with a candle in a small stand, and on the wall a series of pegs; the set nearest Oliver was empty, and from the other two sets hung white nightshirts, and perhaps an extra shirt and a pair of trousers. At the foot of each bed was a small wooden chest. The other side of the room had a washstand with a pitcher stored neatly in the bowl, and beside the stand was a low, battered couch. It seemed rather severe a place after his snug little room at Uncle Brownlow's.

"Well, Oliver, what do you see?"

Pausing a moment, Oliver said, "I see three beds, sir, and three chests. I see—"

"You see order, Oliver. Each boy has what he needs. Each boy takes care of what he is given. Do you see any dirt on the floor?"

Oliver looked, wishing he knew whether or not this was the customary way of things, or whether this was a trick question of some sort.

"No, sir, I don't."

"Do you think the boys clean the floors here?"

"No, sir."

Mr. McCready clapped a hand on his shoulder again, and Oliver wondered if he'd have bruises there in the morning.

"They do indeed but not up here. In the mornings, after breakfast and before the shop opens at nine o'clock, the boys take down the shutters, wash windows, weather permitting, check the count in the change box, and make sure the girl has cleaned the grates and lit the fires properly in the stove in the main room, my office, and the warehouse. At night, the boys dust and polish the shelves, replenish stock and sweep and mop the floor. But up here, the girl comes in and does the cleaning. That way, boys know what it is like to both clean floors and have floors cleaned for them. Do you understand what this means?"

Oliver turned around and struggled with the answer. He could recall Uncle Brownlow talking about something like this. It had been just this Christmas past when they'd discussed what they could do for the poor, and how they could best show the housekeeper and the other servants how much they appreciated them. Mr. Grimwig had thought the whole thing a waste of time, but Uncle Brownlow had enjoyed giving out gifts very much.

"It has to do with…it has to do with knowing your place in the world, doesn't it, sir? Only kings and queens never clean their own floors, only the poorest never have their floors cleaned for them."

"Very good," said Mr. McCready nodding. "You've had good teachers. It is imperative that someone who serves knows what it is like to be waited upon. It is in this way that we can give customers what they want because we know what it might be that we would want. Never forget that."

Mr. McCready turned to go. He opened the door to the hallway and motioned that Oliver should follow him.

"We'll catch up with Tate in the warehouse. He's a good lad, and useful too, for all he's not very easy with customers."

Mr. McCready trotted down the stairs and Oliver followed, his legs already feeling like stumps. How long would it take him to get used to moving so fast?

CHAPTER 8

Oliver Joins With A New Company At McCready's Haberdashery

A t the bottom of the step on the main floors, a short passageway led from the shop to a back hall, and it was there that Mr. McCready took them, the back of his dark, oiled hair set at a confident angle as Oliver followed him.

"The warehouse is this way," said Mr. McCready, opening the door at the end of the passageway. This was said with a smile as Oliver caught up to him, stepping over the slight hump that the floor took as it led through the passage.

As Oliver followed through the doorway, he found himself on an elevated landing of rough wooden boards that had a set of stairs leading directly down into the open area of the warehouse. The ceiling above was quite high, and there were long, horizontal windows on tops of both sides, very high up, letting in the soft winter light. The room was full of shelves filled with boxes and slatted crates that he presumed held more goods for sale, and bundles that looked as though they were waiting to be unpacked. Near the large doors at the far end was a small iron stove, glowing with heat. There were small irons on the top, heating up, and a table with a cloth on it, and a pile of ribbons waiting nearby.

A tall, dark-haired boy stood next to the table arranging the ribbons into long colored strips. He had on a cream-colored apron beneath which peeked sensible black boots. His brown uniform matched Oliver's.

Mr. McCready looked at him. "All nice and tidy then, eh, Oliver? Each boy has a task assigned to him until he is called or directed to another."

Oliver nodded.

"Then, of course," Mr. McCready went on, "each boy is taught how to do each task and is allowed time to perfect the doing of it. Boys must be given time to learn."

Mr. McCready turned to the floor and gave a quick shout. "Tate! Tate Maxwell."

The boy at the table lowered a trail of ribbon and raised his head. "Yes, sir?" he asked, his voice loud enough to carry.

"Come here a moment, would you? I've someone for you to meet."

Tate laid the ribbons down, checked the irons on the stove to make sure everything was to rights, and hurried over to them. His passage up the wooden steps was so quick that he barely touched the rough, unpainted railing.

"Yes, sir?" Tate asked. Though taller, he was some years younger than Oliver, with wide brown eyes and a smear of high color on each cheek of his thin face. Oliver noted the white apron tied around Tate's middle was barely long enough on him to reach his knees. Tate wore a white shirt striped with green, as Oliver did, and it was a green that Oliver suddenly realized matched the painted doors out front. And even though Tate's shirtsleeves were folded up, there wasn't a rip or darn or any sign of wear.

"This, Tate Maxwell, is Oliver Twist, who is going to be an apprentice with us. Oliver, this is Tate."

"Pleased to meet you," said Tate, looking at them with eyes that darted over their faces. He offered his hand to Oliver. Oliver shook it, feeling the faint calluses on Tate's palm.

"And how do you like your work here, eh, Tate?" asked Mr. McCready.

"I like it just fine, sir," said Tate. His voice came out quick and slightly breathless, as if he feared he wouldn't be given enough time to say what he needed to say.

"And you're not just saying that because I'm standing here, Tate?" Mr. McCready winked at Oliver. "Now, be honest."

"God's truth, I've learned ever so much here."

"Ah," said Mr. McCready. "What have we talked about using the Lord's name in such a way?"

"Sorry, sir, it slipped. I won't forget again." Tate blinked several times as if startled by being remonstrated, but he didn't seem to be taking it badly, and in a moment, shrugged his shoulders as if through with it.

"Off with you, then," said Mr. McCready as if he too were done with the issue. "How long till you are finished with that shipment of ribbons?"

"Another hour," said Tate. Tate then waited for Mr. McCready's silent nod and hurtled himself down the steps as if there was nothing more he wanted than to return to his task.

"You see ribbons," said Mr. McCready. "And over there, beeswax candles. Isn't that a bit old-fashioned to be selling those, you might ask? And at such an expense? When paraffin ones are so ready and cheap to buy? So much cleaner to burn?" Oliver didn't know what, exactly, to say to this, but he stopped himself from shrugging. "Old-fashioned?" he asked.

"Indeed," said Mr. McCready, leaning for a moment on the railing, surveying Tate working below. "Old-fashioned it is, and charming, too. There's nothing like the smell of a beeswax candle, and so many who remember it prefer it, even. The chandlers mostly make paraffin candles these days, but I'm offering something special. You see?"

Oliver nodded as if the demands of the consumer and the theories behind offering them one thing instead of another were a subject that he knew all about.

With a satisfied nod, Mr. McCready patted Oliver on the shoulder.

"Go down to the kitchen, and I'll be there in a moment to introduce you to Mrs. Pierson."

Oliver followed Mr. McCready back into the shop, where Mr. McCready went over to a customer and gave a little bow. So Oliver went by himself down the flight of stairs that led to the kitchen. They were steep and split in the middle with a small landing, and as Oliver paused there, he could hear the sound of crockery and felt the warmth of a fire. A second later, he smelled butter and roasting meat.

At the bottom of the stairs was a stone floor, well swept and even. A corridor led to back rooms that looked like they held a laundry area and a boiler. The main room held a table that would not have looked out of place in a farmhouse, but it had been wiped down so many times that it was glossy in the light coming from the windows that led to the area.

At the far end of the room was a stone fireplace. There was no fire in it; it was swept clean. Through a little alcove, Oliver saw an iron stove, glowing with heat, and a woman standing in front of it. In a moment, she turned, her large skirts sweeping the floor, her white apron going from neck to hem and almost free of stains. She had her dark hair done up, as ladies did, eased over her ears in front of the laces of her cap.

"Yes, young man?" she asked as if he'd asked permission to ask her a question. Her skin was fair, though flushed with heat from the stove, and her eyes snapped like dark, shiny buttons. "What might I do for you, or shall I find that you are in my kitchen quite by mistake?"

"I'm—I'm Oliver Twist," he said, worrying his hands together. She reminded him of Mrs. Sowerberry in the way she was so dark, her eyes so severe. He swallowed. "Mr. McCready said, that is, he told me to come down, I'm to—"

"Oh, I see," she said. It had the sound of a box shutting. "You're the new boy. Have you come to inspect my kitchen, then?"

She spoke as if, although he might have the temerity to do so, he would not be able to find fault with her kitchen. And even if he had, she'd have him out on the pavement so quickly that his presence there would be a lost memory. He hated the thought that he'd made her dislike him so soon in their acquaintance; his mind scrambled for a way to set things to rights.

"No, ma'am, no indeed." He bobbed his head just a fraction. "I can see how clean it is, and I know that Mrs. Bedwin would have felt right at home here." His face, unbidden, tightened because he could see, directly and without hesitation, Mrs. Bedwin sitting there at the glossy table with her fussy white lace cap, and her hands, wrinkled and calm, holding a cup of tea, with a napkin in her lap.

"Mrs. Bedwin?" asked Mrs. Pierson, peering at him more closely now.

"My old nurse," said Oliver. "Gone these two years past." His throat tightened and he had to look away.

From behind him came the quick trot of someone moving down the stairs apace. Oliver turned, quite grateful for the interruption of his sad thoughts, to see Mr. McCready, who was not even out of breath as his feet hit the flagstone floor.

"We've come not to inspect your kitchen, Mrs. Pierson, but to allow Oliver to salivate at the thought of eating your good cooking."

The corners of Mrs. Pierson's mouth turned down as if she were, at that very moment, deciding whether to accept his compliment or reject it as insincere.

"Very well," she said, smoothing her apron with both hands in long, broad strokes. "Have him come take a taste of my bread, freshly risen and baked today. And if he promises not to sneeze on it, he may have a quick peek at the chicken stew I am making for supper. Then there's the tea I've got to be getting on."

With a flip of her hand, she bid him to come forward, and looking at Mr. McCready for confirmation, Oliver stepped up to the stove on which sat a large covered pot. Mrs. Pierson took a cloth from her apron waist and lifted the lid. Pungent odors of onion and salt rose up from the golden broth. Just as quickly, Mrs. Pierson replaced the lid. Then she turned to the sideboard and handed Oliver a piece of bread. As he took it, he saw that it was already spread with butter, and that there was an entire plate of buttered bread sitting on the sideboard, covered gently with a thin cloth.

With his mouth already salivating, Oliver brought the slice to his mouth and bit into it. He knew it was rude not to tear the slice in half before he ate it, and he knew that he'd taken off a rather big bite, showing his teeth as he chewed, but he couldn't stop himself. But then, he'd never been able to eat slowly, even after all these years.

"Boys are always hungry," she said, watching him. Though as she handed him another slice as soon as he'd finished the first one, it seemed that the idea of his hunger recommended that he be fed rather than the other way around. Her eyes regarded him as he chewed and swallowed.

"It's very good," he said when his mouth was empty. The last time he'd tasted butter that creamy was last summer when they'd gone to Chertsey to visit Uncle Harry and Aunt Rose.

"Only the finest for Mr. McCready's boys," she said, her mouth curving, pleased.

"Mrs. Pierson, this is Oliver Twist. Oliver, this is Mrs. Pierson, who is my cook, and a fine one too, and my housekeeper as well. We have a girl, as I've told you, but she is out at the moment, I presume, Mrs. Pierson?"

"Yes, indeed, to do the shopping, though whether she'll be back in time to help with the cooking and washing up is another matter."

Mr. McCready *tutted* under his breath; it seemed an old disagreement between them that had yet to see any resolution. "Well, Oliver," he said. "What do you think? The boys who work for me work hard, but they are well fed three times a day. Along with the training I give them, well, more than that you'd be hard pressed to get elsewhere."

"Yes, sir," said Oliver, not sure what sort of reply he might make in the face of such satisfaction on Mr. McCready's part. The ginger-haired boy with the white apron that he'd seen in the shop, and the one he'd spoken to, Tate, had seemed well enough, with faces brighter than most of those he'd seen in other shops he'd been to.

With a smile, Mr. McCready turned to the stairs, calling after him as he went up. "Come along, then, Oliver, don't dawdle. I'll show you the office and then you will have seen all there is to see before we put you to work."

Oliver followed Mr. McCready up the narrow stairs, trotting to keep up, his face cooling as he left the warmth of the kitchen for the more chilly air of the shop. There were no customers at the moment, and the boy he'd seen before was standing at a glass-topped table near the door, folding cloth and stacking handkerchiefs, his eyes intent on his work.

Mr. McCready walked up to the boy and Oliver followed. The boy stood up straight and stopped his work, but he looked at Mr. McCready directly, without the sullen expression of many shop boys toward their master, and in fact, without the least bit of fear.

"All right then, my lad. This is Oliver Twist, who has signed on as a new apprentice. Oliver, this is Henry Poulton."

As Mr. McCready pointed to him with all apparent fondness, Henry dipped his head and Oliver did likewise. Henry Poulton was slight and compact with fair ginger hair. For all the cravat on his neck was slipping to one side, he seemed tidy, and looked at Oliver with still brown eyes.

"Henry is my senior boy," said Mr. McCready, slapping Henry generously on the shoulder. "He's almost too smart for his britches, but I don't know as how I'd manage without him. When you're ready, he'll teach you everything about the front shop duties. Tate will teach you the back shop duties, and will move up to help Henry. That'll leave me a free hand to work on expanding my stock." Mr. McCready seemed to sigh then, as if Oliver's arrival was a relief he didn't know he'd been waiting for.

"Am I not to work in the front shop directly, Mr. McCready?" asked Oliver, thinking too late that perhaps he should have asked permission to speak before he spoke. Or that his question was altogether too bold for the new boy.

"No, indeed, Oliver," said Mr. McCready. "But it is not any slight against you or any apprentice, new or old. I have a system, you see. I've had many boys work their way through it, and all of them have started in the back shop, learning the business from the ground up. Then, when they are ready, the boy comes to the front shop and learns to interact with customers and learns that end of the trade."

"Don't worry, Oliver," said Henry, with a slightly musical up and down rhythm to his voice. "It won't take you long till you're working in the front shop."

"That's right enough, Henry," said Mr. McCready, again smiling fondly at Henry. "He's been here long enough to know how things work. Why, if I took off on holiday tomorrow, he'd be able to run the place without me for a fortnight."

Henry nodded and seemed unabashed at the compliment.

"Boys are trained by me in all aspects of running a business such as this. For example, you'll not only know how to receive stock, but how to keep track of it and order more. My boys do everything from the most common tasks, such as taking down the shutters in the morning and cleaning steps, and then waiting on the ladies and gentlemen of quality who come through those doors. All tasks are tended to; eventually everyone performs some of every duty, every task."

"I see, sir," said Oliver. The numbness he'd been feeling all morning, and indeed since the funeral, seemed to be fading away a little. This was a good place, he could see that. It was a fine shop, with well-trained, well-treated boys who could eventually make their way in the world when they left the confines of Mr. McCready's establishment. Though it was not exactly as he expected, surely it was a good start? He wanted to own a bookshop, didn't he? And wasn't knowing how to run a business a part of that?

"Besides, young Oliver," said Mr. McCready. He looked at Oliver appraisingly in a way he'd not done, not even at the funeral. "With that face and your knowledge of the streets, I think I'd do best to put you on deliveries almost right away. You'd bring in extra custom, and, as you know, my lads keep their tips."

Oliver flushed and opened his mouth to protest. Yes, he'd been told he'd had the face of an angel so many times, but he'd never really been asked to use it to make money. And he hadn't known many ladies nor talked at length with them, nor did he know the streets as well as one might think, given his background. Yes, he'd assisted Bill Sikes with breaking into the Maylie house, but that didn't make him a criminal! And it certainly didn't make him the type of lad who—

He felt hot and flushed, and his collar felt tight as his chest swelled with indignation, but a customer came in, and Henry turned away to attend to the gentlemen.

At the same time, Mr. McCready waved Oliver back to his office and Oliver followed, swallowing his spark of anger; it really wouldn't do to say what he felt, not when this was the best offer going. And now that he'd moved across town, Jack would be hard pressed to find him. At least not very easily. And being a part of a respectable shop such as this might keep Jack away, and help to rid Oliver of some of the tarnish he was apparently still carrying around. Furthermore, perhaps most important of all, he would be busy, too busy to spend any more time grieving over Uncle Brownlow, which tended to tear him down to his very bones, making it almost impossible to get through a day, let alone a single moment.

When he got to the door of the office, he saw that it had a desk against one wall so that Mr. McCready could sit at it and see anyone passing through the small corridor. The walls were lined with shelves and a series of cubbyholes that were labeled with slips of paper that said things such as *Incoming, Ordered, Special Order, Arrived, Outgoing.* Toward the middle of the room was a small fireplace with a comfortable chair and hassock, presumably for when Mr. McCready felt he needed a break from the hectic swirl of his shop.

"This is my office, Oliver. If you need anything, and I am here, simply knock at the door, whether it is open or closed."

"Yes, sir," said Oliver. "Thank you."

"Then we'll begin." Mr. McCready stepped out into the small hallway.

"Henry, come here." Mr. McCready gestured to Henry, who was just finishing up with his customer. Then with the aplomb of confidence, Henry smoothed his apron and came over to them.

"I'm handing him over to you now, Henry. Show him the outside tasks and then give him to Tate, who will show him the warehouse duties. Can you manage that before Mrs. Pierson calls us for dinner at noon?"

Henry nodded, sage and sure in his knowledge and his position in the shop.

As Mr. McCready moved behind the counter to wait on a lady customer who had just come in, Henry turned to Oliver.

"I've been at the shop for two years," he said, even though Oliver had not asked him anything. "And in a few more, I aim to be the best shopkeeper in the City."

Henry was shorter than Oliver and was younger in years, yet he had such a voice of conviction that Oliver didn't doubt him.

Henry led Oliver down the back hallway, away from Mr. McCready tending to customers, past Mr. McCready's private office, and down the back steps into the warehouse. Tate was sitting on a high stool next to a long table against the wall, having left the ribbons in a heap. Now he was sorting through a box of what looked like buttons, carefully writing down amounts on a slate. His mouth moved as he counted, isolated and alone in the chilly warehouse, but seeming content, for all that.

In the snowy morning, the large wooden doors to the courtyard were shut, so the warehouse was bare and dark in the light from the high windows. Henry took Oliver around the stairs to the cupboard against the wall where the supplies were kept. He drew out the bucket and brooms, the cleaning cloths and the polishing stones for the stone steps that led up to the shop's front door.

"Here's an apron for you as well. It's a little worn, but it's for outside work. When we make deliveries, which I imagine Mr. McCready will have you doing mostly, we take them off, of course. Use a clean one if you are working in the shop at all, either in the warehouse or out front." Henry pointed to two large hooks that stuck out of the wall.

"Clean aprons are on the left, of which you get two a week. And when they are too filthy to be worn, you hang them on this peg; Mrs. Pierson sends most of the laundry out once a week on Monday, and the rest the girl does. Do not put any soiled laundry in the basket or the mice will get at them." Henry gestured to an oval wicker basket on the floor, which was empty except for a few scraps of metal, perhaps being kept for the dustman. "For now, leave your coat and jacket on that peg. And your cap."

"Of course," said Oliver, slipping his greatcoat and brown jacket off and ducking his head to pull the yoke of the apron over it. He kept his scarf on, but even so, he was chilled without his jacket and his cap. Henry, on the other hand, seemed unconcerned that his lips were already blue, so Oliver shrugged it off.

"I see you got your scarf. We all heard some street thug stole your other one." Henry was almost smirking, but it was the fact that the story of it had gotten so far, so fast, that shocked Oliver the most. Of course, it had to be Mr. Grimwig's doing. Trust Mr. Grimwig to take one last, dashing stab at what was left of Oliver's reputation. It was in tatters already, and added to his being late on his first day, would it have troubled Mr. Grimwig overly much to keep his mouth closed for once?

But there was nothing to be done about it now, so when Henry picked up the bucket and the bag of stones and cloths, Oliver picked up the broom and followed Henry through the small door in the big door, out of the warehouse and into a small, high-walled courtyard.

"Never take this gear through the shop," said Henry over his shoulder as he led Oliver into the alley. "Mr. McCready won't like it. All gear, all deliveries, come through the back door."

"Yes," said Oliver. It made sense, of course, but the instant arrival of tight rules that seemed to have unspoken but dire consequences made him feel fatigued before he'd even begun.

They made their way down the ice-bound, cobbled alley. Once on the walk in front of the shop, Henry laid his bucket and broom down and placed the sack with the cleaning stones on the ledge that the empty flower beds made.

"It'll be your job to keep this area clean and tidy," said Henry, scanning the pavement in front of the shop that was bare except for a dusting of snow. That there were piles of snow elsewhere, in the gutter, in the center of the street, on other pavements in front of other shops, hampering passersby as they stood there, did not seem to concern him.

"Every day, you will need to give the pavement a sweep and a cleaning, or shovel snow and cast it with sand. Depending on the weather, you will scrub the steps each morning and whiten the stone. Not today, though, the washing soda and water would only freeze."

This seemed obvious, and Oliver had seen this logic being applied to many shops over the years. The clean shops, the ones with swept pavements and scrubbed steps, attracted the better type of customer. He could see that there were long, narrow iron bars nailed above the windows that could, at various times, be hung with banners and colors draped over the glass to give the shop a festive air. Surely Uncle Brownlow might have come to this shop had he been in the neighborhood. *A good shop,* he would have called it.

To stave off pangs of loneliness, of home, Oliver turned his attention back to Henry, who was still talking and instructing.

"In warm weather, you'll wash the windows daily. In cold, you'll carefully scrape the ice and dirt off."

Henry pulled out two slats made of iron, each with a razorsharp edge. "Don't break the glass when you do it. We'll start with that."

He handed Oliver one of the slats, and demonstrated a curved-wrist movement that tucked beneath the edge of the ice and popped it off to clatter to the pavement. Together he and Oliver scraped at the ice, leaning over empty flower beds, moving the slats over the bottom and edges of the window where the melted snow and water had hardened into ice the night before. Oliver tried to keep up with Henry, who was fast and efficient, wiping the ice off the slat with his apron, and working with a little hum under his breath. Always moving, always pointing out spots that Oliver had missed.

Within a short period of time, Oliver was warm, and he realized why he didn't need his jacket. But his hands were numb, stiff as pieces of chalk, and his ears felt as though they were tipped with frost. When they were finished with the windows, they wiped the pieces of iron down for the final time and slipped them in the sack. Then Henry took the broom and showed Oliver how to sweep the ice and any other debris into the gutter, what the most efficient strokes were.

"We'll come out after the dinner break to check, but there's not much that can be done in such cold weather."

But a little more they did, picking up the odd stray piece of paper, staying out in the cold, snappy air for a good ten minutes or more. They even assisted a lady from her carriage as it stopped in front of the shop. Henry held out his hand to her in an almost obvious way with his other arm tucked behind his back, as if showing Oliver how it was to be done, as if suspecting that Oliver had never helped a lady from her carriage before. Which, truth be told, he hadn't. Henry was so quick that he even beat the footman at this task, though Oliver wondered at the entire exchange as the lady only nodded at them both and walked up the street a ways to a different shop.

Before Oliver could point out the wasted effort, Henry smiled at him. It was a real smile this time, giving Oliver the decided opinion that Henry enjoyed working at the shop, liked doing what he was doing.

"She won't soon be forgetting us, that's what Mr. McCready says."

What Mr. McCready knew about keeping a good shop, Henry was, apparently, willing to learn and take to heart.

They were picking up the broom and tools when from the alley came Tate, his dark hair flying around his white face as he ran, slipping on the icy cobbles in his haste. "Henry!" he said. "Mr. McCready wants you for a delivery. Bring the new boy; you're to show him how it's done."

"You'll be taking over for me in no time on those deliveries, I expect," said Henry.

Oliver followed Henry through the alley and into the courtyard and tried to remind himself that being a merchant was more like being a bookseller than anything else he could be doing, and being a bookseller was what he wanted to do. Although, at this moment, chilled through as the sweat from the cleaning dried on his brow and the back of his neck, what he really wanted to do was find a soft couch somewhere and curl up on it till Uncle Brownlow came home. But it was too late for that, too late for couches and cups of tea and soft chats until the girl came to call them for supper. That life was forever behind him now.

Henry showed Oliver how to put the supplies away in the cupboard, and they both hung up their aprons on the pegs in the wall. Pulling on their coats, caps, and Henry his scarf, they met Mr. McCready coming toward them in the hallway.

"You took your time," he said, almost snapping. He held out a parcel wrapped in brown paper and string. "These are the silver buckles Mrs. Acton has ordered; you need to take them to her quickly. Do you remember the address?"

"Yes, sir," said Henry, who had finished buttoning his jacket and took the package with two hands.

"Take Oliver with you. And don't take the omnibus; I've no pennies to spare you. Then come back and hand him over to Tate."

In the narrow passageway, with no pennies to be spared, Oliver felt the sudden rush of urgency and matched Henry's movements and speed as he grabbed his scarf.

"Here, Oliver, you should be tidy when you are in the streets representing the shop."

As Oliver turned, Mr. McCready tugged on his neck, tying his scarf so that it was warm and plush around his neck and draped just like the scarf Henry had on. Mr. McCready didn't mention the stolen scarf or the street thug that Oliver reported had taken it off him, but it might be there in his eyes, hidden away behind the sudden display of kindness, along with his barely checked temper at the need for haste.

Oliver tugged on the scarf to loosen it a bit then followed Henry and the packages and bundles out the front door and into the street.

He took a deep breath as he kept up with Henry's quick pace. Being out in London, on his own with another boy, without Uncle Brownlow, was like breathing new air. Not to mention that he'd have someone with him, if they chanced to cross Jack's path. Then Jack wouldn't be able to say anything more than hello or good-bye. But even so, as Oliver walked at Henry's side, he cast an eye about him, looking for the shape of the figure that his brain would never lose the memory of. And, in spite of himself, listening for an echo of the long ago high dog whistle and the snap of a command barked out to all that instantly cowered and shrank from it. But Mr. McCready was no Sikes, he was sure, nor no Fagin either. Though why Oliver was making this comparison, here on this snowy street, he had no idea.

Henry tugged at his sleeve. "Come on, new boy. We aren't to dawdle, you know."

Henry didn't say this with any meanness or with any implied threat to report him back to Mr. McCready. He just meant for Oliver to hurry so that they could both perform this task to Mr. McCready's satisfaction. Which was quite different than the last time Oliver had worked with another boy, back at Sowerberry's. With Noah, who would as soon have tripped him up as looked at him.

CHAPTER 9

In Which Oliver Makes His First Delivery

They walked through the brisk streets, avoiding the crossing sweepers by hurrying quickly behind a carriage as they headed out to the main thoroughfare. Luckily, Henry led them up Wardour Street, which was in the opposite direction from St. James's Workhouse and its hard angles and dark, rising brick walls. The entire way to Oxford Street, Oliver kept his eyes on Henry and pretended he didn't see the beggars at the corner—two men, one with a hideously scarred face, the other with only one leg. He had no money in his pockets, and if Henry had any to spare, he was moving too quickly to be parted with it. Oliver wanted someone to come and shoo the beggars away, but Henry walked fast and Oliver trailed close behind him; the beggars never had a chance.

Mrs. Acton's residence was a good way uptown, and they had to hustle up Grey's Inn Lane till they got to the turnoff to Doughty Street. When Henry allowed them a breather on the pavement, Oliver looked at the residence that was his first delivery on his first day of his apprenticeship. It was a townhouse, tall and narrow in the middle of a tidy block of town-houses just like it. The front steps were clean and well scraped, but Henry led the way down the slanted iron steps that led down to the kitchen area.

"You make deliveries at the side door or the back or the front. Whatever they say, right?"

Oliver nodded.

"If you don't know, use the side one or one like this till they tell you different."

The door opened, and a lady's maid stood at the threshold in a striped dress and clean white apron. She looked severe until she saw who it was and then she had a smile, for Henry at least.

"Who's that, then?' she asked, looking at Oliver as she held out her hand for the package.

"That's the new boy," said Henry. "He's Oliver Twist, and he'll be making deliveries from now on, I reckon."

She stared at Oliver, almost out of the corner of her eyes, as if she were trying very hard not to stare. "Mrs. Acton doesn't want mud on the walk, so scrape your feet next time, you."

Oliver looked down at his boots, which had tracked only the faintest of dirt on the clean stone. "Sorry, miss," he said anyway, just to stay within her good graces.

"Ah, we'll forgive you, with a face such as yours." She reached into her pocket and handed Henry a penny. Then she held one out to Oliver. "Go on, take it. It's only a penny, but they add up."

Henry jostled him with an elbow, and Oliver took the penny, still warm from her skin, and put it in the pocket of his trousers. He would find a box to keep his tips in, and he would never spend any of it. All of it would be to purchase his bookshop one day. He wouldn't even spend it on books, let alone gin. And, perhaps, though he had no idea how, he'd be able to get his change purse back from Jack.

"Tell Mr. McCready she wants a dozen of those beeswax candles next time you come this way. She needs then for her prayers."

"That's fine, missus," said Henry. "I'll tell him."

Then he tugged at Oliver's sleeve and led them up the stairs and onto the pavement. From an upstairs window, Oliver saw the curtains twitch and a woman in a white morning cap and robe as she looked down at him from her higher perch.

"And that's it?" asked Oliver, looking away from the woman. He'd expected it to be somewhat more complicated than that from the way Mr. McCready had talked about it. "She didn't pay us."

"She's on account," said Henry, shoving his hands in his pockets to keep them warm. "Some are, and some aren't, and it's up to you to remember which."

Oliver nodded again. That's how it was complicated; it sounded as though nothing were written down. Or perhaps Mr. McCready had it written down and his boys were simply expected to remember everything. His head was aching from the cold and the activity and the overwhelming sense that he was never going to catch on, never be as adept as Henry. For surely Henry was the high-water mark at the haberdashery; Tate was the youngest and—Oliver ground his teeth and made himself stop. He wasn't, didn't want to be, in competition with his fellow apprentices. He wanted to learn what he needed to learn and then he wanted his own bookshop. And that was it, full stop.

"That was Mrs. Acton's, at any rate," said Henry. "She's a very particular customer of ours."

Then Henry trotted ahead as the snow started coming down in little whispers. "Come along, Oliver. We must get back as there's plenty to do at the shop, as Mr. McCready likes to say."

Oliver hurried and was able to keep up, but he wondered how long it would be before he felt as tireless as Henry seemed.

The warehouse windows, fogged from layers of moisture and dirt from the alley, let in very little light. The little doorway was opened to let the light in somewhat, but the cold air came in and battled with the heat of the potbellied stove.

Oliver had witnessed the short, heated discussion between Henry and Tate over opening the big doors. Henry insisted the day's delivery from their supplier was to come soon, and Tate insisted it wasn't till after dinner, in the afternoon. But Henry won out, and now he marched to the double doors and flung them open. The sky looked as though it was going to shrug down more snow, and Oliver knew he'd be chilled through quite soon.

He was only paces away from the open door, watching Henry's retreating back as he marched up the steps to the shop. Tate tiptoed over and closed the big doors most of the way.

"They're still open," said Tate, almost in a whisper. "But there's no sense catching our deaths simply because he thinks he owns the place."

Oliver didn't let himself smile, but it was nice to be included in Tate's small act of rebellion. Tate didn't know him from Adam; how was he to know that Oliver wouldn't side with Henry? But Oliver wouldn't. He wouldn't side with anyone; he would be on his own side.

Tate shifted the next box of stuffs to be unpacked and sorted. When he opened the box, Oliver saw that it was yet another box of spooled silk ribbons. Only the ribbon had become unspooled and had traveled in a mangled, twisted mass, causing creases in the silk and winding all the colors around each other.

"Don't cut them apart," said Tate. "No matter how much you are tempted. Here, we spread this old cloth on the table—"

He shook out a faded muslin sheet from a burlap bag beneath the table, spreading it on the table with quick hands. Then he upturned the box and let the ribbons tumble out. With deft hands, he began to untwist the ribbons; there had to be yards and yards of the colored silk: pale yellow, bright pink, green, blue, purple—

"How long will this take?" Oliver managed at last.

"Oh, probably a good few hours. Mr. McCready would rather we take the time here than to make a lady wait for her ribbons. He calls them impulse buys, bright things such as this. A lady cannot resist when she sees them, and often doesn't. And just wait till you see the buttons."

Tate smiled and nodded, as if this was very exciting, and Oliver supposed it might be if one was stuck in a warehouse all day. Shiny buttons coming out, all a-tumble, might be the very thing to brighten up your day. He hoped the time would never come when a bright button would be all that was needed to make him smile.

"We'll heat up the stove," said Tate. "And iron them, probably this afternoon. But for now, we twist and untwist, and lay them out in their proper colors."

Oliver nodded. His stomach began to growl, but he moved to stand next to Tate at the long table and reached out for a hump of twisted colors. The silk was soft and easy under his fingers and rippled like snakes as he pulled the mass toward him. At least the work was fairly easy; at least he wasn't in the mines, as Mr. Grimwig had threatened.

When the chimes from St. James's Church echoed through the streets and alleys to sound the noon hour, Tate put down the spool he'd been working on, and Oliver followed suit.

"We'll go to dinner now," said Tate. "We can leave the ribbons, as long as we shut the door." He seemed to find this funny, probably because he'd been right about the delivery not coming till the afternoon and Henry had been wrong. Oliver watched him close the door and wondered how long that particular battle had been going on.

Then he followed Tate up the short staircase and into the passageway, past Mr. McCready's office, and down the stairs to the kitchen. At the bottom of the steps and against the wall was a small table with a basin and towel. Oliver did what Tate did, rolling up his shirtsleeves only a little way to his elbow, as there was no sense flashing his scar about, and washed his face and hands and wiped them on the towel that Tate had just used.

Mrs. Pierson waved them both to sit down; Oliver noted that he was to sit on the bench seat away from the warmth of her stove. It was obvious that the head of the table was reserved for Mr. McCready, and the seat on the other side was for Henry. The division of superiority was no doubt perpetuated downstairs as well as up.

"Mr. McCready will be down directly," said Mrs. Pierson, checking everything on the table as the boys sat down. She spoke in a clear voice; the kitchen was her domain, so of course, she was in charge. When her eyes decided that everything was just so, she went to the bottom of the stairs. "He's just locking up, I expect."

Tate didn't serve himself, so Oliver didn't. But he watched while Mrs. Pierson brought over the kettle of soup, and the hired girl, who seemed to have popped out of the scullery, carried over a hefty plate of buttered bread. Then she darted out to bring a bowl of buttered and boiled potatoes.

Oliver kept his hands in his lap. He felt slightly ill from standing for so long and then from sitting as the smell of food poured over him. Was he as weak and useless as Mr. Grimwig had always seemed to think? Even without always expressing it, those wide-apart eyes and the scowl of disbelief had said it: that Oliver was not truly kin, did not belong, and should be put out on the street before anyone was forced to eat his own head.

And why did he have these mean thoughts now, when he was being served a dark, rich stew, and was being handed a plate of bread and butter from which he could take as much as he wanted? The girl poured cups of tea for everyone at the table, and then Mrs. Pierson went to the sideboard and fussed with what looked like a large pudding.

A wind whipped through the front area, banging the windows in their panes.

"Not another storm," said the girl, rather boldly, since no one had asked her. She tucked up her hair under her cap, but the cap was askew and so her hair slid down her neck.

"This one will bring ice, mark my words," said Mrs. Pierson.

Tate and Oliver waited in silence. Oliver watched the steam of heat curl off the platters of food until finally Mr. McCready and Henry came down the stairs. They washed at the basin, and Mr. McCready took off his suitcoat and hung it on a peg. Henry hung his apron and the two of them took their places at the table.

"Good afternoon, boys," said Mr. McCready, dipping his head. His brown eyes flicked around the room as if looking for something amiss. But they found nothing and he smiled at them all. He seemed calmer now that the day was underway, and Oliver began to think that Mr. McCready's irritation had passed. "There was a good bit of work done this morning, which I am glad to see. I hope those ribbons won't take too much longer."

He looked at Tate as he said this, and Tate nodded, seemingly unworried.

"A few hours, Mr. McCready," he said.

Oliver nodded his agreement.

"Good. Let's continue that. Are we ready, Mrs. Pierson?"

"It's all on, Mr. McCready," said Mrs. Pierson. "And I hope the new boy is well satisfied; it's not cooking he's used to at home, to be sure, but I do my best." She wiped her hands on her apron and stared at him as if daring him to disagree.

Mr. McCready bowed his head, and the boys, Mrs. Pierson, and the girl did likewise. Oliver followed suit and listened as Mr. McCready said a quick grace.

"Amen," said Mr. McCready, raising his head. "Well, tuck in, then."

"Yes, sir," said Tate and Henry at once.

Oliver opened his mouth to echo the agreement, but he was seconds too late, and his voice hung on the empty air. Tate seemed to smirk, but no one paid any attention to him as they picked up their knives and forks and began eating. Oliver cut his piece of bread and butter in half and dunked it in his stew. The first bite told him that it was delicious, with just enough salt to make his stomach jump up and down and demand more. He had yet to make it through his first afternoon, but this meal just might see him through. Besides, didn't it take a fellow a bit to get used to work when he'd not been doing it for a while?

When they were all mostly through their stew and bread and butter, Mrs. Pierson cut them each a large slice of pudding, putting each slice in bowls. The hired girl poured the steaming yellow custard over each slice and then handed them around.

"Pour more tea for the lads, girl," said Mrs. Pierson.

"They've got enough; they've got full cups already." The girl's tone was sullen.

Oliver kept his attention on his plate and didn't look up. No one he knew would have permitted themselves to be talked to by a servant. But it wasn't his place to determine;

perhaps the rules were more lax here; perhaps Mrs. Pierson liked it when—

"Just pour it and then you can go check the fires, make sure there's enough coal on hand."

Oliver made himself not pay any mind as the girl slopped the tea in the cups, picked up the coal scuttle, and stomped past the scullery to where a little door led to the coal closet.

Chewing on the last of his slice of bread and butter, Oliver picked up his spoon to attack the pudding. It was a yellow sponge with some jam swirled in. The pudding was good; it was heavy and moist, and though Mrs. Bedwin had preferred to make light, airy puddings, this one was just fine. It filled the corners of his stomach and let him know that he'd make it till supper.

"Looks as though the new boy enjoys your cooking, Mrs. Pierson," said Mr. McCready from the head of the table. Oliver looked up to see Mr. McCready wiping his mouth with a napkin.

"Nothing like honest work for a healthy appetite," said Mrs. Pierson. She looked as though she was trying to appear stern, and if Oliver let himself, he might think that she meant to say the word *honest* to make a point. As if a boy such as Oliver wouldn't know the first thing about honest work. But there he went again, imagining that Mr. Grimwig had gotten to each and every person in the household. Mr. McCready might have told her about Oliver's past, but then again, as he'd thought before, Mr. McCready didn't seem the gossiping type. He wouldn't feel the need to explain why he'd taken an orphan, ex-pickpocket, member of a thieves' gang into his house. No, he would make his decisions and expect Mrs. Pierson to accept them.

"Was it enough, then?" She was looking at Oliver as if her greatest enemy was a hungry boy and she the only soldier in the ranks to combat it.

"Yes, Mrs. Pierson, it was very good." His voice sounded small and meek to his own ears, and he mentally kicked himself. If he wanted to make a new start, he had to start acting like a young man brave enough to be on his own with a job to do. Not some milksop orphan who had barely enough backbone to stand up with.

"You spoil these boys," said Mr. McCready. He put his napkin on his plate and pushed back his chair to stand up.

"And why not?" she replied, jerking her chin at him but in a friendly way, as if this were an old, comfortable argument. "With mine fully grown and all?"

"No reason at all," said Mr. McCready in kind. "You boys bring up your cutlery and plates. Put them in the right place; no tossing, do you hear?"

"Go on, then" she said, making motions with her hands. "I've got to get that girl on the washing to take down to the laundry and a joint to get on for supper."

Oliver's mouth began to water all over again. Uncle Brownlow's cook had done well enough, but with an invalid in the house and Mr. Grimwig not being the most active of men, their evening suppers had been light, soups and toast, perhaps some cheese. To be able to look forward to a proper meal was good news indeed.

Henry and Tate did exactly as they were told, and Oliver did as well. A full belly made him feel very obedient. Or perhaps it was Mrs. Pierson's stern eye and manner, standing eye-level with the boys' collars and breast buttons. Checking them over before they went upstairs. She stopped Oliver when he came up in the line to place his empty plate and bowl and utensils in the correct location.

"You've got a bit of potato, here," she said, taking the edge of a cloth to wipe it off. "There, that's you, then. Off you go with the others."

Oliver nodded his thanks and washed up in the basin. He used the comb and the looking glass to neaten his hair, without really taking time to look at his own reflection, and went up the stairs to the warehouse where Tate and the ribbons waited. His stomach was full, and although the back of his legs ached a bit, he found he could keep going for a while.

He joined Tate in putting on his apron, looking up at the windows, which were whitish grey with snow. The warehouse felt even colder than it had before dinner.

"It's only till teatime," said Tate, tying his apron on.

"Beg your pardon?"

"Until teatime. Mr. McCready doesn't like it when boys drag their feet at the end of the day. So Mrs. Pierson, she makes us tea. Puts in extra sugar."

"Really?"

"Keeps us on our feet, he says. For those end-of-the-day customers, we're all bright and bushy-tailed, ready for them. Instead of dragging about. That's what Mr. McCready says."

It sounded sensible and even kind. So maybe, with the good food and the work not being overly difficult, except for all the information to remember, this might be the best decision he'd ever made. For all he was so exhausted and his feet ached and his wrists hurt, like someone had twisted them, this would be a good place for him. He knew it.

Even with the nicely hot and sweet cup of tea that Mrs. Pierson brought out to the warehouse at mid-afternoon, by the time supper was served, Oliver's eyes could only see objects and people through a blur; it was as though he were looking through the plain glass windows of an old church. Windows that had been in place for centuries so that they sagged at the bottom of the frame, leaving bubbles and a thinness so stretched it could not be seen through. Yellow light, or grey, depending on the weather, might ooze through, but it was all shapes and blobs and the hiss of the fire in the stove.

He heard someone speaking to him.

Oliver blinked and looked up. He realized he was hunched over his plate, both hands on the edge of the table, and that Henry and Tate were bustling to the counter with their plates and knives and spoons. The girl was grumbling as she poured a bucket of water into the large kettle, and Mr. McCready and Mrs. Pierson were both staring at him.

"I'm—" He jerked his head up, not sure what he'd been going to say. "Sorry?"

"Are the ribbons done?" He was asking Oliver directly now, and not Tate.

Oliver nodded. They'd worked at it for hours, and halfway through Henry had come in and reminded them to spool the ribbons on the new wooden spools. Which meant that he and Tate had had to unwind and then rewind all the ribbons all over again. But they'd looked very nice on the new spools, and even Henry had been well satisfied when he'd come to check on them.

"Yes, sir," he said now.

"Well, on with you," said Mr. McCready, waving grandly. He took a sip from his cup of tea and then said, "The lads and I will shut up shop, and tomorrow you may learn that as well."

"Thank you, sir," said Oliver, standing up. He reached into his pocket. "I got a penny today," he said. "As a tip. Mrs. Acton's maid gave it to me." Too late he remembered that Henry had gotten a penny as well, and would Henry think that Oliver was trying to get him into trouble? Henry had not mentioned his penny at all.

"You keep that," said Mr. McCready. "Mrs. Pierson, get one of those empty boxes, you know, the one that matches come in. Oliver can have that for his tips."

"But I'd give it to the church on Sunday." Oliver stood steadfast, wanting to make his point clear. He wasn't the sort of lad to take off with money that didn't belong to him, but he was too tired to think it through clearly.

"Oh, for heaven's sake, Mr. McCready, give him an early night. The boy's done in." Mrs. Pierson shook her head as if at the foolishness of overworking a poor lad on his first day. "Here's a box for you. I'll take your plates."

As Mrs. Pierson handed him a small rectangular wooden box that smelled slightly of sulfur, she gave him a pat on the arm. Then she took up his plate and cutlery. "The girl will bring up some water for you to wash; you go straight to bed, mind."

Oliver climbed the stairs, eyes half-closed, clutching his box to his chest. He could hear the girl stomping up the steps behind him. Once in the room, he hung his apron on one of the pegs near the bed nearest the window and watched as the girl poured the steaming water into a tin pitcher that sat on a table opposite the beds. She lit the three candles, one by each bed, then she growled at him and slammed the door behind her. He could hear her angry steps down the stairs and wondered blearily if she hated him or the position. He couldn't imagine anyone turning their nose up at working in a good household such as this.

He sat on the bed, putting the box on the floor, and struggled with the laces on his boots. He caught the vague scent of soap and boiled onions and felt the odd whistle the wind made against his neck as it snuck in through the thin panes. It didn't resemble his old room back at Uncle Brownlow's; that seemed years away now. But it was nice enough, though cold; the candles burning by each bed made dappled shadows across the slanted ceiling.

Unpacking as quickly as he could, he put the case under the bed and his books and letters from Aunt Rose in the box at the foot of his bed and closed the lid. He hung his nightshirt on the peg on the wall and lay back across the bed. He looked at the shadows and felt the thin pillow behind his head and thought about his old bed. He folded his hands under his head and let his stockinged feet loll on the woolen blanket. It was thick enough, but nothing compared to his silk counterpane on his old bed. He could feel the rough cotton of the sheet, durable but nothing fine. Nothing such as he was used to.

But he was not in his old bed. In fact, his old bed would probably never be made up for him again and, in essence, no longer existed. If it ever had. He'd never been kin to Uncle Brownlow, a fact that Mr. Grimwig enjoyed reminding him of as often as possible. *You're on loan to us,* Mr. Grimwig had said once, *and as soon as we're able, we'll be sending you back.* As though he'd been a book from a shop or a rented seat in a park. To let, for hire, return for deposit.

He made himself stop and turned his head to bury it in the pillow. There was only one pillow and one thick grey blanket. Oliver enjoyed having two pillows, three if he could get them, with a few little ones thrown in lest his head ever think of touching the mattress. He wanted a fluffy eiderdown and soft flannel for his bed. Though he could do with one pillow and had slept many years without either, was it a sin, then, to want more?

It wasn't. Besides compared to his first ten years, his current residence was a palace. He had a whole bed to himself and his own chair next to the bed, a box for his books, his own pegs on the wall. He shared a washbasin with only two boys, and there was a couch to lounge on that they might share with him. He had hot meals during the day and water to wash in and a job to go to. Clothes to wear. Sturdy boots. A window that, mostly, had no holes. A penny in his pocket, and four pounds, ten shillings as well. He had a brand new scarf: bright green. Why should he complain?

Because for five years he'd lived as a young princeling, and he had only to voice a whim but to have it answered. Or, at least, seriously conferred upon until he could be convinced that, indeed, sliding down the banister was not an occupation for a young gentleman. Nor was playing with the tinker's children. Or that eating a hot roll in the street was any way to set an example. All imparted to him in Uncle Brownlow's soft tone, a brown-eyed smile, and a pat with a large, gentle hand. A hand, which never, not in all of the days that Oliver had known it, had ever been raised in anger. Only in love.

Do you miss me, Uncle?

They had never been apart. Except for that time, that short by the sun but long in Oliver's memory. The time he never wanted to think about again. And he certainly didn't want to think about Jack—

He screwed his mind shut to the memories and threw his arm over his eyes. If he could cover himself to the light, then he could cover himself to the memories and hold them at bay. Till his death day, if need be.

Too tired to wash up or even read, he breathed in and out, watching the flicker of candlelight from under half-closed eyelids. In and out, till his breath seemed to flow as though it were a river, solid and slow, focusing his mind on it, on the stillness beneath the push. On the current pulling him into darkness. Wondering if it would ever take him someplace good. Toward the blue.

He woke sometime later with the candle beside him guttering out all on its own; the other two candles on their respective chairs were already properly out. He could see the humped shapes of Henry, closest to the door, and of Tate in the middle bed nearest Oliver. He wondered for a moment if Henry had made Tate sleep in the bed closest to the window, or if it had remained empty until Oliver's arrival.

Well, that was between Henry and Tate, wasn't it? Oliver made himself let the thought go and stood up, the floor almost icy beneath his stockinged feet. He slipped off his waistcoat and made a quick wash with what was left of the cold water in the pitcher and dried his hands and face on the much-used towel. He fumbled around on the wall where he'd hung his nightshirt and wondered how much noise he was making, and how grumpy that would make Henry and Tate if he actually woke them up.

Standing there for a moment, he heard the snow slapping against the windows and realized he was shivering. As he took off his trousers and shirt, he folded his clothes roughly and placed them on top of the box, knowing that he would have wrinkles. But the wrinkles would be covered by his apron, and in the morning, Henry and Tate would thank Oliver for not waking them up with his bumbling about, trying to hang things on pegs in the half dark. He bent to blow out the candle then he slipped between the sheets, which were clean and thick and heavy.

He'd gotten lucky. Mr. Grimwig probably hoped that Oliver would be miserable, but so far he was not. He tipped his head back; the pillow was thin, but what of it? That he'd ended up here, someplace nice, was almost a miracle. The river came. And then sleep took him.

CHAPTER 10

A Cold Day To
Offset Grief

The next morning, Tate had to shake Oliver awake, and with muscles protesting even the smallest movement and eyes half-closed, Oliver struggled into his clothes and boots. But when he was buttoning up his waistcoat and rolling his sleeves halfway up his arms to wash, he saw that Henry and Tate were waiting for him at the already open door.

"There's no hot water to wash up here," said Henry, in a tone that indicated that Oliver should have known that.

"Sometimes the girl forgets," said Tate, giving Henry a piece of his elbow. "So we wash downstairs. Sometimes."

His throat was still too closed from sleep to reply, so Oliver only scrubbed at his eyes with the back of his hand and followed Henry and Tate downstairs to the warm kitchen. There, they washed at the basin on the stand against the wall, with Oliver last in line, as was the order of things. He didn't want to look at himself in the mirror, but in spite of that effort, he caught a glimpse of his hair pressed to his skull and large circles beneath flat blue eyes. It was to be expected, perhaps, as yesterday had been his first day. He knew he could catch up to Henry and Tate's energy and speed, if given the chance. But as the god of beneficence would have it, when Oliver turned around, there was Mrs. Pierson in her dark, wide-skirted dress and a bright, clean apron and cap. She was busy at the stove, stirring something on the stove while she added what was perhaps sweet milk from a pitcher. The kitchen was warm and smelled wonderful, and as Henry and Tate sat in their usual places, it occurred to Oliver that there was, indeed, a place for him at the table, and he felt the shock of the change in his life all over again.

And when he sat down, he realized Henry and Tate were, really, only half-awake themselves. Henry yawned at him, and Tate slumped on an elbow as if he were a young boy at home and not really expected quite yet to behave with good table manners. Breakfast was more relaxed altogether, it seemed, as Mrs. Pierson came over and ladled them each porridge in their bowls. The porridge was golden with some spice, and heaped high, and on the table was a pitcher of cream, a yellow bowl of butter, and a blue bowl with lumps of sugar in it.

"You boys start with that," said Mrs. Pierson, observing to make sure they took at least their fair share. "I've got to be finishing making the eggs and sausages myself, after having built my own fire and heated my own water on top of everything else since the girl didn't show today."

"Can we help with anything, Mrs. Pierson?" Henry said this just as he was shoveling in the first mouthful of porridge.

As Tate straightened up to attend to his breakfast, he nodded to show his agreement with this idea, and so Oliver nodded as well, though his mouth was watering and he felt as if he might strike someone if they attempted to take him away from the bowl of porridge in front of him. He piled on the butter and sugar and laced the whole of it with plenty of cream.

"Well, you're a good lad, that's what you are. All of you are." Mrs. Pierson put down the ladle and pot from which she'd served the porridge and looked about her at the kitchen. "After you've eaten, if Tate would carry the slops down and wipe the stairs, and Henry could help me with the bedding, perhaps Oliver could get coal and take care of the fire in Mr. McCready's office and in the warehouse?"

It was a lot of work for one person, and he was glad to help if Mrs. Pierson needed assistance. And while Oliver didn't relish getting his hands black with coal dust, at least he wouldn't be carrying slops or making up other people's beds.

"I'd be most willing, Mrs. Pierson," said Tate brightly, as if the occupation, while beneath him, didn't bother him in the least, though Oliver knew it had to.

"And I as well," said Oliver, watching while Mrs. Pierson bustled at the stove to finally bring over fried eggs and sausages, which she piled on the plate in front of each boy.

"Very well and thank you, and mind, here comes Mr. McCready now; he'll be wanting some fried bread with that."

The heavy tread sounded on the steps, and when Henry and Tate straightened up to more polite postures, Oliver did likewise. It wasn't as if they had been being disobedient, more, it was apparent that there were different levels of decorum for different occasions: one for Mrs. Pierson at breakfast and another one for when Mr. McCready was present.

"Ah, there we are, Mrs. Pierson, thank you for the fire this morning. I'm dreadfully sorry about the girl; you should give her a good talking to about her punctuality or she will lose her place." Mr. McCready sat down and pulled his napkin into his lap as Mrs. Pierson served him tea and fried toast all at once.

"Good morning, boys," he said.

"Good morning, Mr. McCready," said Henry and Oliver. Tate's mouth was full, so he nodded in place of that, and Mr. McCready went on with his breakfast as if everything was in good order.

When the boys had finished, they excused themselves and went to attend to their morning chores while Mr. McCready dawdled over his tea and flipped through pages of the newspaper from the day before. Oliver went to the short door that led to the coal cellar and grabbed a bucket full of coal. He knew he should have gotten the proper copper scuttle, but he didn't know where it was, and he wanted to keep up with the other boys as well when they started on their proper shop-related chores.

He went up the stairs to Mr. McCready's office first, trying not to scatter coal dust on the stairs as he went, but then Tate would be following soon behind to wipe the stairs down. Still, it wouldn't do to make extra work on his first—no—second day. Mr. McCready's office was narrow, and it was by lifting the bucket up high that Oliver was able to avoid leaving black marks on any of the furniture.

As he knelt down and opened the stove, he knew he should scrape out all the ashes and then blacken the stove before he lit a new fire. And while he could easily put the ashes in the bottom of the bucket, the stove being a small one, he didn't know where the blacking was nor the stove brushes. Besides, the girl would black the stove next morning, so perhaps it wasn't up to Oliver to set everything to rights, but only to light a good fire.

This he did, getting smudges of black on his skin all the way up to his wrists. He managed successfully to open the damper before the smoke started to fill the room, and afterward, as he stood up brushing his hands together, he felt well satisfied with himself.

The stove in the warehouse was much easier since the opening was bigger, and there was a vent in the bottom of the stove for the ashes. Oliver placed the large pieces of coal on the floor and then put the bucket beneath the stove and pushed the ashes through the vent. Clouds of dust flew up, but that couldn't be helped.

There was plenty of room in the stove for coal, and the fire was easy to light and didn't smoke at all. At the very last moment, he remembered the vent, and had to push the coal away to pull the lever to let the ash fall into the bucket, after which he had to poke at the coal with the iron poker that stood next to the stove to make the fire more even. Then he closed the front of the stove and stood up, looking down at himself while at the same time praying that he'd not gotten any ash or coal dust on him, as he'd quite forgotten his apron.

There were no black streaks, luckily, so he went over to the pegs in the wall to pull down an apron that looked slightly used, tying it on to be ready for the regular shop chores. Henry was soon there, putting an apron on as well, and together they went outside into the icy air. The clouds hung low and the morning air was so still that when he and Henry breathed out, the puffs of air coming from their mouths wreathed around their heads, dappling bits of beaded frost in their hair.

"It is cold," said Henry, as if agreeing with Oliver's unspoken observation, while he demonstrated how to take down the shutters. "But it's only for ten minutes or so on a day like this."

Oliver nodded, gasping at the weight of a single shutter that Henry seemed to carry with such ease. He followed Henry, slipping a bit on the icy stones in the alley, then staggered across the yard, quick as he could on Henry's heels, following him into the warehouse where the shutters were placed.

"These go just inside the warehouse, so no one can take them and they won't get smashed by horses' hooves in the yard."

"I see," said Oliver, shivering in the stillness of the warehouse. The fire he'd lit seemed to have gone out, and indeed, none of the heat had reached as far as the doorway.

"Two more trips, then," said Henry, going back outside, though again, his lips were blue with cold. "Tomorrow, it'll take you six trips in all instead of three, since you'll be doing this on your own."

Oliver could only nod; his whole face was stiff, and his shoulders and back shivered up and down until they ached. The air outside in the yard was now coming down with frost that settled on the top of the tall brick fence and the open wooden gate, looking like sparkles of frozen diamonds on every surface. Grabbing the next shutter that Henry handed to him, Oliver almost ran through the clouds of glittering air to be done with this part of his morning chores; it was dreadful, so dreadful, that he longed to be back in bed, at home, under his comforter, waiting for the maid to bring him hot tea.

But no. Henry insisted they perform their usual duties of scraping ice from the windows and sweeping the steps to the front door, and clearing the walk of any snow and scattered debris. By the time they returned to the warehouse to change out of their dirty aprons into clean ones, Oliver was shivering from head to foot, his teeth clacking in his mouth so loudly that Henry turned to look at him.

"You'll get used to it," Henry said, and he didn't seem to be completely without sympathy for Oliver's plight, perhaps because he had recognized how hard Oliver had worked. Or at least it was to be hoped.

"Go on down to the kitchen," Henry said now, as he led Oliver out of the warehouse and into the passageway to the shop. "Mrs. Pierson will let you warm yourself by her fire and perhaps, if you look pathetic enough, she'll give you a cup of tea. After that, go out and build the fire in the warehouse again, and help Tate for the morning. We might go on deliveries this afternoon, if there are any."

Oliver did as he was told, his brain feeling numb from the realization that he had a whole day of working and he was already exhausted, and it wasn't even noon. But Henry and Tate seemed contented enough, so the situation had to get better, it must get better. He would just have to keep putting one foot in front of the other and keep moving, doing as he was told and stopping for a breath when he could.

As he clomped down the stairs into the beautifully dry warmth of the kitchen, Mrs. Pierson called to him. "Is that you Oliver? I rather imagined you might be down."

When Oliver's feet hit the flagstones, Mrs. Pierson was there, guiding him to sit in Henry's chair, which was nearest her stove. "You sit down now, and drink this. It's always hardest on the first few days, I know that. But Mr. McCready doesn't want his boys to look at any moment as if they might collapse; it's important to keep up appearances, you see."

Oliver sat down and curled his fingers around the mug of tea in front of him. The mug was hot in his palms and steam rose from the tea. His legs vibrated against the edge of the chair, blood pounding through them, making him glad of the waves of warmth that oozed from the stove and began to soak into him.

"You finish up that tea, Oliver," said Mrs. Pierson, turning back to her stove. "And tell me whether you fancy pudding with jam or pudding with currents for dinner? Or both?"

Taking a long gulp of hot tea, Oliver sighed. There was only one apparent answer to that question. "Mrs. Pierson, whatever you make will be fine, I'm sure of it." And then, feeling a dash of boldness amidst all of the comfort and warmth running through him, he added, "Though, you might want to make extra, as I'm sure to be rude and ask for seconds."

Behind him, he could almost hear her smile.

The morning spent with Tate in the warehouse followed much the pattern of the day before. Tate showed him how to open the damper in the stove just a bit more, to make a better draw and keep the fire from going out. He demonstrated the use of the poker and the cloth that hung on a nail in the wall to open the stove when he was going to put more coal in. Then he walked Oliver through the shelves, pointing as he demonstrated the way the shelves were organized, not alphabetically, but by content—buttons here, ribbons over there, collars in the middle where the dust was less likely to seep in to befoul them, and the beeswax candles, as far up the shelf as was possible to go and tightly bound with canvas and rope.

"Why with canvas?" asked Oliver. It wasn't likely that the candles might spill out, not when they were packed in solid wooden boxes.

"Well," said Tate, brushing his hands on his apron. "Truth be told, the mice might like to eat them, but especially rats, if they can get at them."

"Rats?" asked Oliver, somewhat stunned. The townhouse had never had a single rat nor mouse that Oliver knew of, and any that had managed to creep in would not have lasted for long. Not with the standards of cleanliness that was kept there.

"Perhaps a few," said Tate, shrugging as though this were completely ordinary, though Oliver could hear a small bit of mirth in Tate's voice, as if he were amused by Oliver's shock. "And don't mind the noise if you hear them scratching in the attic. There's far more filth and dirt outside for them to scrabble through, so they are never up there long."

"I see." Oliver tongued the inside of his teeth, struggling to keep his mouth closed, to keep from bragging that he'd never known of any rat or mouse under any roof where he'd abided, but that wouldn't be fair, at least not to Tate, who was doing his best to be informative.

"There you go," said Tate. "That's the spirit. Now over here is the pole that we use to open and close the windows as need be. They're closed at night, but sometimes, even if it is cold, we open them in the afternoon, to keep the air fresh. That

keeps the mold from growing on silk ribbons and woven patterned shawls and the like. Do you see?"

"Yes, I see," said Oliver again. He struggled to focus on
what Tate was saying and prayed for the noon hour to come.

The morning, gratefully enough, sped by, and Mrs. Pierson's dinner was as filling as breakfast had been, with the
added benefit of jam pudding with custard cream to pour over
the top. As promised, Oliver asked for a second helping, which
Mrs. Pierson was serving to him even as he was requesting it.
The indulgence she paid him was kind; indeed, her kindness
was given to any at the table who wanted more pudding. If
nothing else, the food was excellent.

And the afternoon seemed somewhat easier than the day
before. Oliver was able to help Tate sort through more boxes
and to sweep the warehouse for Tate, and though he had to go
and wipe the stairs as Tate had been unable to get to them,
Oliver didn't grumble. Besides the fact that Tate had not mentioned that Oliver had not correctly lit the warehouse stove
the first time, the work appeared to be shared as was needed,
with a sense of fairness and balance that made him feel easier
about doing someone else's chores.

Then, just before supper, as Oliver was carrying in a box of
hat pins for Henry to stock the shop with, he heard Mr.
McCready in the hall.

"It's so cold and icy, we'll shut up shop now, I think. Don't
you agree, Henry?"

"Yes, sir," said Henry from around the corner. "There's barely anyone on the streets right now, so no one will be coming in the shop unexpected."

Feeling joyous, Oliver assisted Henry with the brisk job of hanging shutters in the half dark of the street, shivering the whole while but concentrating on Mrs. Pierson's cooking and the hot supper to come. He helped Tate lock up the warehouse and bank the warehouse stove and hurried into the shop to help Henry sweep the floor and wipe the counters. Then he hurried down the stairs to wash up in the kitchen with Henry and Tate before sliding into place for Mr. McCready to say grace.

After the *amen* was said, Mrs. Pierson served up a thick stew with noodles in it, which was accompanied on the side by stewed tomatoes and rice, which Oliver appreciated even more, seeing as how she'd been on her own all day without any help. Dessert was a baked crumble, filled with pie plant and served with hot custard. Oliver ate until his stomach was quite full, and he thought he was as content as ever he could be, even if part of him longed for the familiarity and comfort of the townhouse.

"Would you boys care for any more? Mr. McCready?" Mrs. Pierson held out the remains of the pan of crumble as if loathe to save it for another day.

"No, I am quite replete, Mrs. Pierson, as you well know, because the colder it gets, the richer your food, for which I know we are all entirely grateful."

With a sense of satisfaction swirling in the kitchen around him, Oliver smiled to himself. Boldly, he took his finger to make a last swipe for a bit of custard that lingered on the rim of the empty bowl in front of him. Sucking on the taste of custard on his skin, Oliver looked up. Everyone was watching him; he'd quite forgotten where he was and had lapsed into manners that befitted a stable hand.

But Mrs. Pierson only smiled as she patted him.

"I'm glad to see that at least *someone* enjoys my cooking," she said as if peeved at every one else's collective lack of appetites and appreciation.

"We all do, Mrs. Pierson," said Mr. McCready, accompanied by Henry's and Tate's nods. Then he added, "We'd starve without you, you know that."

"Well, that's good then," said Mrs. Pierson, mollified. "Now up you get, clean your places, and bring down your letters and lessons and whatnot. It's far too cold to linger up there, isn't that right, Mr. McCready?"

"Yes, indeed," he said. "Now do as Mrs. Pierson says, and come back down with your things. We'll keep the fire going down here till bedtime."

Somewhat befuddled, Oliver did as he was told, but as he followed Henry and Tate up the many flights of stairs to their room, he determined to make a clean breast of it to them.

"But I don't have any letters or lessons; what do I bring?"

"Oh," said Henry as they got to the top floor and he opened the door. "You finished with lessons, then? Well, bring whatever you have, books or whatever."

As Henry and Tate preceded Oliver into the room, the still air icy and chill from being unoccupied for the entire day, he stopped. He was being told to bring his books down so that he could read in the warmth of Mrs. Pierson's kitchen. He was being told to do it, and it was like a gift, a miracle, to be told to do the very thing he actually *wanted* to do. Without a moment's more hesitation, Oliver walked straight to his box and pulled out the thin volume that contained Boswell's biography of Dr. Johnson. That had been another gift from Uncle Brownlow, and though Oliver had read it twice already, it would make comfortable, familiar reading in such a new place. With the book under his arm, Oliver followed Henry and Tate back down the stairs to the warm kitchen, where Mrs. Pierson had wiped the table and made a pot of tea, which she casually placed on a thick mat in the middle of the table. In small bowls, all set in a row, were the remains of the crumble, slightly cool now with the custard thickening on top, but Mrs. Pierson had put them out as if she'd known that no one would be able to resist having just one more bite. And she was right.

Oliver settled in his seat and accepted a mug of hot, sweet tea. And as he began to read, he absently reached for a bowl of pudding, putting the spoon in his mouth as he leaned over his book and absorbed the words.

Across from him, Henry was reading letters and asking Mrs. Pierson for some sheets for reply, as the paper the letter was on had already been crossed. Tate was sitting next to Mr. McCready, using a slate to make notes on from the book he was studying. It looked like history, and even then Oliver didn't envy him one bit. He had his book and a hot drink, and his stomach was full, and he was warm all the way through. Perhaps, since today hadn't been as difficult as the day before, tomorrow would be even better. All the activity of the day pointed to it, so he was hopeful and sank into his book until Mr. McCready announced it was bedtime.

This sent the boys washing hurriedly at the bowl in the kitchen, in the cold leftover water, and hurrying up the stairs to the icy, dark attic room to change as fast as they could into their nightclothes.

"Leave your stockings on," said Tate, pointing at Oliver as he struggled with his boots.

Oliver took this advice gratefully, and wished he had the light of a candle so he could put his book in the right place. But there was nothing to be done about it at this point except place it all anyhow in the chest at the foot of his bed and to change for bed as fast as he might and slide beneath the woolen blanket. And then, as soon as his head was settled on his pillow and Henry's and Tate's were settled on theirs, he heard a scratching noise from overhead.

"Is that—?"

"Yes," said Tate, in rather dark tones. "There must be hundreds of them up there by now, coming in from the street on account of the cold, you see."

"Don't mind him, Oliver," said Henry, his voice somewhat muffled from beneath his blanket. "There are two or three at most; Mrs. Pierson wouldn't hear of rats in her attic, so there simply aren't that many."

"Maybe thousands, Oliver," said Tate, his voice coming through the dark in a way that made Oliver's heart pound. "All scrambling around up there with their yellow teeth clicking and their sharp claws scratching."

"*Tate*," said Henry. "Honestly, sometimes you are so full of nonsense I cannot understand how you make it through the day."

With a small laugh, Tate turned in his bed so that his voice was close to Oliver's ear. "I'm only messing, Oliver, it's just for fun."

Fun as may be, but the thought of rats running along the beams over his head kept Oliver up for some time after the other boys had fallen asleep. But though he heard one or two sounds which might have been rats, the other noises were merely the familiar groans and creaks of wood shifting as the building around him settled into the cold night. He fell asleep eventually, somewhat tense, but willing himself to not be, mindful of his new situation and the luck which had come to him in getting it.

CHAPTER 11

Relates How Oliver, Hard At Work, Is Distracted From His Tasks

Halfway through the next morning, Oliver felt as though he'd gotten the rhythm of it. After breakfast, Oliver was sent to clean the steps, and again before dinner. These tasks were interspersed by jobs of counting and sorting with Tate. The work was never-ending, it seemed, but Mr. McCready had given him a nod or two, and a *well done, there*, so Oliver imagined everything was well and that he was doing a good job.

Then, in the brisk, grey-lit afternoon, with the cold turning into a light snow, he and Henry bundled up and delivered packages. They walked all over London, to the river and back, going through Newgate and Cripplegate and Aldgate, each one of lumbering grey stone grown even darker with wear and time and coal soot. They even delivered to some of the fine houses around St. James's Park, where Henry was courteous enough to explain to Oliver how each residence preferred their deliveries.

Sometimes, Henry would stand back and let Oliver have a go at it, to later tell him what he'd done wrong or right, in perfectly reasonable tones so that Oliver felt courageous enough to ask him a question or two. Without Tate around, Henry was still acting as though he were in charge, which he was, but he was less bossy and snappy, so the afternoon went well.

And at night, he could sit with the boys and Mr. McCready in Mrs. Pierson's kitchen, with candles lit and the stove banked and warm, to look at his geography book and thumb through the poetry he'd also brought down. And though Henry and Tate raised their eyes at his selection, they didn't ask what he was reading nor did they mock him.

After dinner, when Oliver was replete with roast chicken and roasted potatoes, he washed up and followed Henry to the shop. Henry was busy tying on a clean apron, looking quite settled in his plans to attend customers at the counter that day.

"Beg pardon, Henry?" asked Oliver. When Henry looked up at him, tying the last knot behind him by feel, Oliver said, "It's good weather out and there are plenty of deliveries to make; I see the list there on the counter."

Mr. McCready, who was opening the door to let some lady customers in, seemed to hear Oliver's question and he nodded at Henry.

Henry turned to Oliver. "Today is the day, Oliver. You're to make deliveries on your own today. I've watched you;

you're efficient with customers, and have a good sense of direction. Here's the list, get the deliveries together, and do your best."

There was nothing to be gained by protesting that it was too soon, besides which, Oliver felt a flutter of excitement at the thought of it. He was going to be trusted to perform shop business on his own, and on his third day; it was quite an accomplishment, and he wished, suddenly, that he had Mr. Grimwig right there so he could very carefully explain just how wrong Mr. Grimwig was.

"Do Mrs. Acton's delivery first, mind you," said Henry. He pushed several small bundles across the top of the counter at Oliver. "It's only candles and soap, some needles, and a pair of garters, but she's asked for you specially, so do be on your best behavior. Remember, it's your job to keep our delivery customers happy, and she's one of our best."

It was with his chin held high and a sense of pride that Oliver took the list and gathered and bundled the items together, putting them in the basket with Mrs. Acton's purchases on top of the rest. Then he went downstairs to doff his apron, put on his cap and coat, and let Mrs. Pierson fuss over him a bit as she arranged his scarf around his neck and tucked it into the collar of his jacket so it would be warm and look nice. He even let her pat his cheek as Mrs. Bedwin might have done on such an auspicious occasion.

Then he went back upstairs, grabbed the basket, and practically sailed out of the front door. It was blustery and cold, but not overly so, and for once, it wasn't snowing. Besides, he was well wrapped up in his coat and scarf and on his own in London. He felt well prepared for his first solo delivery; he was a real apprentice at last, so he barely felt the weather.

As he walked along the lane to the corner where Oxford Street would take him to Mrs. Acton's, he noted that some shopkeepers weren't as alert to the niceties of scraping snow and ice from their windows nor of laying grit on the pavement in front of their shops. It was this common courtesy, as Mr. McCready had repeated often, that allowed potential customers to linger in front of the shops, and then, finally, most likely, come in.

Oliver had seen it demonstrated in the shop. If customers came in, they browsed. And if they browsed, they purchased. There was not one lady in a hundred, Mr. McCready had intoned, who could resist a lilac sachet nor a set of brass buttons or anything refined that her eye fell upon. Mr. McCready, it seemed, was well convinced of the fickleness of a woman's mind and insisted on arraying his shop as if he were waiting for a blue jay, or any bird who liked to gather bright things.

But Mr. McCready's insistent practice of keeping the front walk clean, well, Oliver believed it now, for he found himself hurrying, head down, watching where he walked on the slippery, un-gritted pavement. Others as well, top-hatted gentlemen and ladies with sloped bonnets, even the beggars—and there were a few—scurried past untended pavement in front of empty shops and lingered in a convivial throng in front of those whose pavement had been cleared. Who knew so much could be manipulated by the deft removal of a little snow and ice?

Oliver hurried, stopping on Oxford Street for only a moment to linger at the window of a bookshop, where the spines of books were arrayed on a small table through the frosty window. There would be time, perhaps later, do tarry and touch the pages, though he did spy a few books that looked good: some he'd read, other's he'd heard about. In particular, there was a new French version of *The Arabian Nights*, though he couldn't imagine why anyone would want to read it in French when the English version was already so handy.

There was also an old copy of *Dr. Johnson's Dictionary*, a book of poems by Byron, which he'd never been allowed to read, along with poems by Thomas Grey, and even a battered version of *Moll Flanders*. Not that most apprentices would be spending their pay packets on books, but as he was to own his own bookshop one day, there was no better time to start collecting his stock of books. The bookshop's location on Oxford Street promised to bring with it fairly dear prices for books, however, so Oliver shuffled past it without going in and thought to find a better place more suited to his current salary.

Besides, the day might be nippy, but it was glorious to be out and about among the movement of the City. Even when Uncle Brownlow had been alive and they were in the City, he and Mrs. Bedwin, truth be told, had flinched against any idea of Oliver being on his own. Even though the danger of being snatched off the street was well past, lo these many years, he went out with someone, always, either Uncle Brownlow or Mrs. Bedwin with her shopping or his tutor if there was no one else. Otherwise, he stayed at home.

It wasn't that he himself couldn't be trusted; it was the City that couldn't. So really, this was his first encounter of a taste of freedom in the City. Except for the trips to the taverns, and those didn't count, because he had always been afraid of getting caught. Oliver shook his head, clearing it of unproductive thoughts. He was well on his way to a future that wanted him, a future that any respectable person would approve of.

It took him a good twenty minutes to make it across London, with views of frost-covered spires and the smoky tip of St. Paul's from time to time, to where Mrs. Acton lived, all the way up past Russell Square. As to why she couldn't have taken her purchases with her when she paid for them had been explained to him in quiet tones by both Mr. McCready and Henry. *A lady does not want to be burdened with packages. Especially a lady of some rank and breeding.*

Unsaid, of course, was the idea that for a lady of such breeding, and of course, wealth, having such fripperies delivered at some cost—to be seen having such deliveries made—only elevated her status even higher. Oliver knew to be thinking such obvious thoughts was crass, so he didn't speak of them aloud. But he thought them, just the same.

When he arrived at Doughty Street, he stopped a moment to admire the row of townhouses made of cream-colored brick, the tidy stone pavement swept of snow in front of each house, and neat, narrow rows of chimney pots, all pouring out a fine, black trail of smoke. The carriages that passed had no less than two horses each; the drivers were brisk with their whips, and the wheels made only the faintest of clatter on the cobblestones as each passed by. No milkmaid tarried anywhere, no sandwich men, no street sweepers holding out grubby hands, waiting to be tossed a penny for their labors. There were no geese or cows being driven through the neighborhood on their way to Smithfield, and there certainly weren't any remains to mark their having passed this way in many a day. The whole street, at least two blocks in either direction, bespoke of a place inhabited by a higher quality of people who expected the best and were able to pay for it.

As Oliver walked up the stone steps at Number 14, he noted with new awareness that the steps were not only white and gleaming, they were entirely stone dry, which bespoke of recent, perhaps hourly, cleaning. Had he been delivering meat or milk, he would have gone down the stairs to the kitchen area, but Mrs. Acton's request had been clear: deliveries from McCready's Haberdashery were to come to the front. So he walked directly up and clapped the well-polished knocker against the brass plate, and heard, in short order, footsteps within.

When the door opened, he saw it was a maid, different than the one before, dressed in afternoon black with a white apron and cap, as befitted a good house such as this one.

"Can I help you, sir?" she asked, looking up at him.

"I have a delivery from McCready's Haberdashery, miss," he said. "It's the items Mrs. Acton ordered."

The maid stared at him a moment, her mouth open. And just as Oliver began to wonder if he'd mumbled, she blushed hotly from cheek to ear. Taking a step back, she ducked her head, exuding clumsiness where only a moment before had been grace.

"Won't you step in a moment, young master, while I get the mistress."

Oliver stepped in, and as the maid turned away, kept himself from frowning by sheer dint of force. Surely he'd not been actually flirting with her? But no, he'd kept his voice as level as he could, hadn't held her eye in any bold manner, hadn't done anything to incite such a reaction. And yet, there it was. That blushing, girlish reaction he often got, that made Mr. Grimwig call him vain and accuse him of causing it on purpose. But he never had; he could swear to God he never had. At least not on purpose.

As he waited, he examined the front parlor through the open doorway. It was thickly done in a red wool carpet and severely dark furniture. He'd hardly started on his examination of the ornaments on the mantelpiece when Mrs. Acton came down. She was dressed in an afternoon gown with plaid flounces that were trimmed with black velvet. Her hair was done up as if she were planning to go out, though Oliver didn't see any other evidence of her outdoor things being prepared for her.

"So you are the new boy, Oliver Twist, at the haberdashery?" she asked. When she reached the landing, she stopped, though her hands remained on the banister, arrayed as if she were posing for him. "I saw you from my window when you were last here, when you were kind enough to deliver my silver buckles."

"Yes, miss," he said with a little bow. "I've come to deliver your order. Beeswax candles, I believe, and other items as well." He held out the package, which was tightly snug with string. She'd need a penknife to open it, though he supposed her maid would have one.

She came down and took it with fluttering hands, barely glancing at it, and held it out for her maid to take. "Take these, Jane, and see that they're set out and properly trimmed by prayer time." Then she looked at Oliver with a little smile such as he was unused to receiving except from the likes of Mrs. Bedwin, and now, recently, Mrs. Pierson.

"Did I order any ribbons, young man?"

"No miss," he said with what he hoped was a responsive and responsible air. "But if you had, they'd be all ironed and organized, per Mr. McCready's instructions."

"What a good lad," she said, coming down off the last step to stand quite close to him. "You must be chilled from your walk. Won't you stay and have some tea? Or tea and cake, young men always want something hot and sweet after a cold walk. Jane, go and make some tea and bring it into the parlor. Leave the door open, please; it'll be more proper that way."

Jane hurried off and Mrs. Acton placed her hand on Oliver's arm, prepared to draw him into the parlor. He could feel the warmth of the fire, see the silver teapot set out, the silver creamer, and a bowl of white sugar. There were even sweet cakes, and—

Well, it would be rude to refuse a lady, now, wouldn't it? Mr. McCready would say so himself, and Oliver very well knew the direction of keeping the customer happy. So he nodded his head and tucked his cap under his arm and loosened his scarf as he followed where Mrs. Acton led.

Her parlor was very grand, done up in the latest style with dark red walls and a thick red rug on the polished floor. There were ornaments all around, a group of china shepherdesses and a brass dog by the fireplace, a large painting of a country scene over the mantel, and a large peacock feather fan spread out behind a vase of fresh roses.

Over on the sideboard was a large collection of silver plates, arrayed to show how shiny they were, a platter that leaned against the wall, a pitcher, a set of knives, all of which were carved in loops and swirls in the old-fashioned way. There wasn't a speck on them, shining as if they'd recently been polished, for all it seemed that they were too grand to ever get used. And underneath every object was a circle of lace or something crocheted to add an additional elegance, though Oliver wondered how long it took the maid to dust such a room.

"Come now, and sit beside me," said Mrs. Acton. She sat on the small floral settee and patted the seat next to her. "Jane will be along soon, I hope you have a taste for sweet things."

Oliver did as he was asked, putting his cap and scarf on the seat next to him. He was puzzled that if he was asked to tea why no servant had offered to take his cap and scarf. But this curiosity was outdone by the fact that Mrs. Acton shifted closer on the settee and patted his knee. Her eyes were bright, the pupils enormous, and a hectic flush colored her cheeks.

"You do enjoy sweet things, don't you, Oliver?"

She was close enough that he could smell her breath. It was sweet, as though she'd recently drank something that contained floral water. Or maybe it was her hair that had the scent of attar of roses. He only knew that it smelled like flowers all around his head, and he thought if he could just shift away, even if only for a moment, he could get a clear breath of air.

"Yes, ma'am," he said. He felt hot under his collar, as though he were suffocating from the force of her attention.

Luckily, Jane came back in the room carrying a large silver platter and silver tea urn. A footman came behind her, and with a smart bang, unfolded a little wooden table in front of Mrs. Acton and Oliver. As he went away, Jane placed the tray on the table, and Oliver saw that it had a complete tea set of silver, the cream and sugar jugs of the same scrolled silver that was on the sideboard. Then his attention was on the plate of sandwiches and the plate of cakes.

"I'll serve, thank you, Jane," said Mrs. Acton, and she was silent for a moment as she watched Jane depart. Without asking him his preference, she poured a cup of tea for Oliver, putting in two lumps of sugar and a large dollop of cream. When she handed it to him, Oliver tried not to jerk backward when he felt her fingers linger on the backs of his hands as he took the cup and saucer from her.

"It's so nice to have a young man to tea," she said with a bright smile that made Oliver think that there was definitely something amiss. No woman would take on so, not with a lad much younger than she. And even if age weren't the matter, the fact that she had a wedding ring on but the husband was nowhere to be found—and Oliver was only an apprentice boy. It suddenly occurred to him as to whether or not he should even be having a cup of tea, let alone such an intimate interaction with her.

"Drink up, now, Oliver, and tell me how you're getting on at the haberdashery. Is Mr. McCready as good a master as I hear tell of?" She curled her fingers under her chin and coquetted up at him through her lashes.

To keep from speaking, Oliver took a quick gulp of tea. He liked sweet things, that was true, and while the tea was sweet enough, it was not very hot, and the taste was weak, as though it had been hastily brewed. Which he could put down to Jane, trying to answer to her mistress's instructions to make tea and quickly. Oliver took another swallow and didn't let his eyes wander to the plate of sandwiches or cakes.

"Well?" she asked.

"Mr. McCready is a very good master," said Oliver. "I'm learning many things as an apprentice."

"I'm sure," said Mrs. Acton with a little curl to her lips that Oliver couldn't even begin to understand. "Have a sandwich, Oliver; you must be hungry after that long walk all the way from Soho just to bring me my candles."

There was something in her tone, her manner, that made Oliver want to fidget, and as he caught sight of Jane, passing in the hallway outside the parlor. Her expression was fixed but disapproving, though whether that was of her mistress or of Oliver, he didn't know. Yes, it was very easy to determine that the whole interaction was somehow inappropriate. Should Mr. McCready hear of it, he was sure to be sacked.

Oliver put his cup and saucer, with half the tea still remaining, back on the silver platter. "I must be going, Mrs. Acton. I have other deliveries to make, though it was quite kind of you to—"

"Must you go?"

Oliver stood up, and Mrs. Acton stood up also, clutching at him, pressing her bosom against his arm. He was almost made immobile by this action, never having been so close to a lady, or any female for that matter, before. She smelled good and was soft, as all ladies must be, but there was something wrong with the way—

"Mistress," said Jane from the doorway. "Is there anything else I can get you?" Jane was speaking to Mrs. Acton, but her eyes were on Oliver—large, enormous eyes. Oliver knew that this was his chance, perhaps his only one, to make a graceful exit.

"I must go, Mrs. Acton. Thank you for the tea. It was quite nice. Let us know if you need anything else from the shop."

Oliver snatched up his cap and scarf, and without putting them on, strode out of the parlor, brushing by Jane, giving her a grateful look as he did so. He grabbed his basket and let himself out the front door, not wanting to tarry, to hear whatever other unpropitious things Mrs. Acton might say. She should not be saying them, and he didn't want to hear them.

He hurried down the stairs, and once on the pavement, paused only a moment to put on his cap and wrap his scarf around his neck and adjust the basket on his arm. The wind was cold, and he started down Doughty Street, away from Mrs. Acton's and on to his other deliveries, wherever they might be. On the corner of Doughty Street, he paused only for a moment to scan the list of addresses and determined his next delivery. It would be a good ten-minute walk to Craven Street, an address that he knew to be by the river and sounded vaguely familiar somehow. Best of all, it would take him well out of the neighborhood and force him to walk very fast, which would help clear his head and settle him down. And so he began to walk briskly, head held high as though he were— as he was—a valuable, responsible apprentice with very important deliveries to make.

His delivery to a bonnet maker on Dean Street—his last— confused him somewhat, as there were two Dean Streets on the map of London in his mind. He was easily able to figure out that the first Dean Street was near St. James's Park, and the address actually was to a church; the second Dean Street was quite close to the shop and the address was that of a bonnet maker who had urgently needed new pins for the bonnets she was making. That she could have easily walked to the shop to get the necessary articles was less important than the display of having the owners of nearby shops getting a good view of her having them delivered to her. Oliver held his tongue about this and only inquired as to whether she'd need anything else delivered, and when she said no, Oliver walked back to the shop, faintly out of breath and very glad to be on what was beginning to seem like more familiar ground.

On Thursday morning, after breakfast, and after he'd already taken care of the pavement in front of the shop, Mr. McCready sent Oliver out again to brush the dusting snow from the pavement and to make things as tidy as could be, given the weather. Oliver wanted to linger in front of Mrs. Pierson's kitchen fire first, but he did as he was told without balking, using the broom to push the snow into the gutter, the bustle of the street bumping past him as though he weren't even there. Though the day was snapping with cold, Wardour Street and on into Broad Street was full of shoppers and buskers and dogcarts, their wheels bumping over the refuse poking up beneath melting clumps of snow, with everyone getting out as though there'd never be another day where it didn't snow. The bells from St. James's Workhouse bonged out the hour through the fog that was already thick across the rooftops, the air thick with the smell of sulfur and sending nits and spots of black coal soot down on Oliver's newly cleaned stairs.

Oliver picked up the bucket and cast the grit around. He'd have to sweep it up again in the afternoon, once if not twice, but in the meantime, potential customers would enjoy the sensation of walking without sliding on ice, which would then draw them into the haberdashery. Or so Mr. McCready often said.

He was just gathering his gear, gripping the cold handle of the bucket in one hand when a passerby bumped into him, hard, with a sharp, rude elbow. Oliver tightened his face as he looked up to determine what he should say, whether it should be *pardon me, madam, miss,* or *sir.*

But instead of any of these to be spoken to, it was Jack Dawkins, resplendent in a short top hat and a thick coat, different from the one he'd worn before, with a double row of shiny buttons down the front. And of course, Jack wore Oliver's scarf of brilliant scarlet red around his neck. Oliver did not doubt for one second that the rest of Jack's get up, in addition to the scarf, was stolen, or at the very least, acquired by less than legal means. Oliver's heart sped up and his breath caught, not sure whether he was surprised to see Jack, angry about it, or rather, if he was pleased to see a familiar face.

"Hard at work, I see," said Jack, already laughing, eyes alight, his teeth sharp. "Like a proper servant."

Oliver's potential spark of pleasure died as quickly as it had come and gave way to the heat that rose behind his eyes. Jack was there, unwelcomed and unannounced, and what's more, mocking him. Oliver had hoped that the wretched meeting in the park by the townhouse would have been the only time, but here he was again. Just like a bad penny.

Two customers, quality ladies with fur on their cloaks and bonnets and all over their muffs, came out of the shop and looked out of the corners of their eyes at Jack and then hurried past as if he were something dangerous. This was dreadful; if Mr. McCready caught Oliver lollygagging at his duties, that would be bad enough. But to have Jack spotted, there at his side, making conversation with him as though they were a pair of idle gentlemen?

"You don't belong here," said Oliver, low. "You should go back to wherever you came from." He wished he could pretend to keep working, but he'd already cast the grit, and so now the task was finished.

"That's what I come to tell you," said Jack saucily. "Where I am these days, an' it's at the Three Cripples, now."

Though Jack's presence was disruptive, he was vibrant as he stood there in the street, and more alive than anything Oliver had seen in days. In comparison, he made the newness of being at McCready's Haberdashery seem worn and dull. Oliver had to fight against the flash in Jack's eyes.

"It ain't much, but it's home, an' I'm signed up for some jobs, an' I got a fence an' everythin'—"

It was with this declaration from Jack that fighting the draw of Jack's bright plumage became much easier.

"I don't care where you are," said Oliver, determined to make Jack go away. "And what's more, I don't care what you do there. Now you need to leave before my master sees me with the likes of you."

Rather than being injured by this, Jack just showed his teeth in a smile that wasn't truly a smile, his eyes looking Oliver up and down. "It's a free country, ain't it? I got as much right to be here on this pavement as you, ain't I?"

As benign as this remark seemed on the surface, there was something in Jack's tone that made Oliver clench his fist around the handle of the bucket. He hefted the broom as though it was a spear, ready to strike if Jack came closer.

But Jack didn't move. He eyed Oliver, taking in the tenseness of his hands, looking at Oliver as if examining him for flaws. Then he cast a glance over Oliver's shoulder, at which point he stepped back and tipped his hat, that shiny new top hat with a low crown that he couldn't possibly have actually *purchased*—

"Looks like someone's lookin' for you, so I'll come back another day, and why not? I'll have more to tell you then, show you my takings, share it with you, like we did in the old days."

Oliver heard the door to the shop open and turned to see Mr. McCready look at him and then over his shoulder. Oliver looked around, and to his dismay, saw what Mr. McCready was seeing: Jack, sashaying down the street, with a flicker of red scarf and all the dash of a man who owned the earth he walked upon in spite of the worn-at-the-heel boots Jack wore.

Mr. McCready gestured for Oliver to come closer, rubbing his hands together to stave off the cold. Oliver did, holding his tools in his hands so as not to leave them in the way of any ladies or gentlemen who might want to use the pavement.

"Who was that?" Mr. McCready asked from the top step, looking down at Oliver. And while he looked comical with puffs of air coming out of his mouth, his forehead was wrinkled, which made him look grave.

"No one," said Oliver, shaking his head. He swallowed. "Just someone looking for directions; he wanted the nearest bakery, I think, or some—"

"You don't want to be hanging out with the lower orders, Oliver," said Mr. McCready, idly rubbing the brass edge of the door with his fingers as if attending an invisible spot. "It brings down the tone of this establishment and everyone who works here, and we can't be having that. Are you finished here?"

"Just about, sir," said Oliver, casting a glance to see that all was done. Yes, the steps were scrubbed and polished, the trash pushed into the gutter, and grit spread about. "Yes, sir," he said.

"Then bring in some coal for Mrs. Pierson; the girl's gone early, someone sick at home, I believe, but then, when isn't there? She's entirely unreliable, that girl."

"Yes, sir," said Oliver. The task was actually beneath him, but he'd hauled coal for Mrs. Pierson before and was willing to do so again.

"After you take Mrs. Pierson some coal, be sure to wash up before you sit down to dinner; she won't appreciate her good cooking being flavored by coal dust," said Mr. McCready. Then he shut the front door behind him, only to turn and open it with a little jangle as a pretty miss and her black-garbed governess hurried up the stairs. "In you come, ladies, where it's nice and warm and out of the wind."

Oliver watched them go, tracing their outlines through the wave-patterned windows.

Henry came up to them, his apron gleaming through the glass as though it were made of snow, and tipping his head to the ladies with a little bow. Henry was perfect at the job, that was plain to see.

Well, that was all right. Oliver could learn a great deal from all at the haberdashery; it might not be books, but it was buying and selling and dealing with customers, and counting up money and going to the bank. It would work out well. All he had to do was pay attention, mind his temper, and do everything that Mr. McCready asked of him. Then, one day, not too far off, he could start making inquiries as to how one started a bookshop. Then, on that day, he would really be on his way.

Oliver quickly brought some coal from the cellar for Mrs. Pierson and washed up at the basin along the wall just as quickly. At the noon hour, after Mr. McCready said a quick grace, Mrs. Pierson served up boiled beef and potatoes, and bread and butter. It was simple and plain fare, but Oliver ate through the pile of his first helping and then looked hopefully at Mrs. Pierson. She *tut tutted* a bit at him but dished out some more for him, trying not to look pleased that he was enjoying her cooking so much.

"This afternoon," said Mr. McCready between bites of beef, "I need Tate to attend to the pavement out front while Henry shows Oliver how we do the count up. I want to make a deposit in the morning and to be able to rely on more than one apprentice for that task."

"That's quite an honor, Oliver," said Mrs. Pierson. She was stirring something in a pot on the stove; when she brought it over, Oliver saw that it was only stewed pie plant, but at least there was warm custard to put on it.

"Tate's helpless with money," said Henry around a mouthful of potato. He didn't say it with true meanness, but Oliver knew it could have gone unsaid. "He can't remember the difference between a pound and a guinea, and he wouldn't know a halfpenny if it bit him."

Tate just rolled his eyes at this.

"But he is good with keeping track of stock," said Mr. McCready. "He's got a memory longer than Moses; he can remember what anyone bought, when they bought it, and in what part of the small warehouse anything was stored."

"He still can't even remember how many shillings in a pound," said Henry boldly, trying to make his point. Or as if he was trying to maintain his status as being more useful than Tate.

"That's not a concern, seeing how he works mostly in the warehouse." Mr. McCready shook his fork at Henry. "So just never you mind; he's good at what he does, and I know I can leave him to it, to handle the incoming stock, and in making orders to the tradesmen."

The argument was one that Oliver sensed was an old topic that bestirred Henry to speak out in that way or to make Tate ignore Henry. But Mr. McCready felt he had it well in hand enough to get up from the table without another word about it. And Mrs. Pierson bustled about as if the matter were all settled.

CHAPTER 12

An Inauspicious Second Visit From A Certain Low Acquaintance

After dinner, there were no deliveries to be made. Instead, under Henry's watchful eye, Oliver helped with the count up. He enjoyed the feel of the coins under his hands as they thunked on the pad of leather that Henry had put down to protect the glass. Oliver wrote amounts on a scrap of paper and then added them up, double checking as he went. Henry looked at the final total and gave Oliver a nod.

"This is to the penny," Henry said. "And you've a nice hand as well; Mr. McCready will be pleased."

As was Oliver himself.

Later in the afternoon, Mr. McCready and Tate went with Oliver out to the high-walled cobbled yard that abutted the warehouse and that led through the gates to the alley.

"This," said Mr. McCready with a wave at the yard and the small shed against the brick wall, "is where the flats and carts and delivery wagons come to unload. It is also where the drivers watered their horses, and unfortunately, where the horses relieve themselves. Though no customers come back here, it must be kept spotless."

He turned to look at Oliver and Tate, but mostly at Oliver, who was still the new boy.

"Go get the shovel and bucket, Tate; show Oliver where they are kept."

As Tate raced to do this and brought back the large broad-bladed shovel and a heavy wooden bucket, Mr. McCready continued.

"The tone of the establishment must be kept," he said. "It is not an elegant task," he said now, handing Oliver the shovel and bucket. "But it is a task that must be done. Henry has been elevated above it by dint of his being a full-time front shop boy; you and Tate must share this task now."

Oliver looked over at Tate, who shrugged his thin shoulders as an invisible wind tufted at his thin hair. He made a face, a not unkind face, because though it was still his duty, it was not, at present, his turn. Oliver determined not to be thrown off course; as a gentleman who owned a bookshop, he would never be called upon to perform such a duty. But as the newest apprentice in the lot, he could be asked to do any number of things. Shoveling horse manure was one of them.

"Don't forget to sluice the cobblestones with water, Oliver," said Mr. McCready. "And carry the muck into the alley."

"Yes, sir," said Oliver. He took the shovel and bucket and hefted them in his hands as Mr. McCready and Tate headed into the warehouse where they would no doubt review stock and determine what the next week's order should be. Except for counting money with Henry, which had, ostensibly, been to test Oliver on his arithmetic, Oliver had yet to be a part of what it really took to run a shop, and he was itching to do it. Shoveling manure and rinsing horse urine wasn't what he'd had in mind for the day's tasks.

But he began it, keeping his face still, not showing his disdain for the lowness of the task. First he shoveled the leavings in a bucket, the cold air racing down his neck. He grimaced when splats of urine and manure got onto his apron, but there was nothing to be done about that except mutter under his breath in dismay. But at least it wasn't on his trousers.

Then he carried the bucket through the gates and into the alley, tossing them in the small ditch in the middle that carried an ever-present trail of water that came from a dripping pump at the end of the alley. Even in the coldest weather, the ditch ran and steamed, cutting through the ice and iced mud, smelling dank and fulsome, like a dark bite of something rotten.

Most of London smelled that way; he was used to it. But typically it had been from a distance in his old life back at the townhouse, where the girl, or sometimes the lad who tended the fires, carried slops and dumped them where they ought to go. Oliver had only to avert his nose whenever a fulsome smell chanced his way. Only now he was right in the thick of it, doing his best not to get any on his boots, for he had no doubt that neither Mrs. Pierson nor the hired girl would be called upon to clean them. No doubt Mr. McCready would consider the boys doing their own boots a task that would teach them responsibility.

It took three trips with the bucket out into the alley, and four buckets full of water to get the cobblestones looking somewhat less fouled, though there was never a way to get horse manure from the cracks and dips in the earth, where his too-large shovel could not go. He tapped the cobblestone with the edge of his shovel and considered it. No, he would not be scooping that out with his bare hands.

"Here's the lad, the very lad I come to see."

Oliver whirled, shovel and bucket in hand, to see Jack standing there between the open wooden gates to the courtyard. He wondered how it was that Jack not only seemed to always catch him off guard but with a bucket in his hands as well, working as though he were a common laborer.

"What do you want; what are you doing here? I thought I told you this morning—" He snapped this with anger at being startled and caught with the brightness of Jack's ease, standing there, a bright spark in a grey and cold afternoon.

"It's no use," said Jack. He was dressed as he had been that morning, with Oliver's red scarf tucked high under his chin, demonstrating the same bright air. "You know I'll always find you, and anyways, I'm stoppin' only on my way to the palace, to have tea with the Queen, you see—"

"Jack, stop it. Just please go away." Oliver's heart was pounding with wondering when Jack would start tormenting him about the dark splats on his apron. Jack acted as though he were a feathered bird from some hot place, flitting about, free to wing from place to place, nothing to do, no responsibilities—

"Actually, I just wanted to say thanks, as one mate might to another." Jack pushed his hands in his pockets and tipped his head back jauntily, but he seemed somewhat more diffident now, as if needing less to impress and more to simply be there with Oliver in his sights.

Oliver wanted to send him away, directly, before Mr. McCready came out wondering at the delay in Oliver finishing his assigned task, whereupon he would spot Jack. And not just on the pavement where he might have a right to be, a simple passerby, but in the yard, on haberdashery property? Besides which, what on earth would Jack want to thank him for? There was no need for Jack to linger, no reason at all.

"Say what you have to say and go." Oliver said this low, trying to be threatening. It wouldn't do to encourage Jack.

"For not peachin' on me earlier."

"What on earth are you talking about?" Oliver cast a look over his shoulder at the doorway to the warehouse, at the windows above the courtyard. No one was watching, so he had about a minute. He turned back to Jack, who was bundled and warm against the snow and smiling at Oliver, and who had missed none of Oliver's covert glances.

"I listened to you talk to Old Grumbly, I heard. Or didn't hear."

"*Jack.*"

"You never mentioned my name. You'd never call no peelers, now would you? If you were serious about it, you would have. So thanks for that."

Oliver felt himself start all over. Yes, he'd done that, protected Jack, but why on earth would he do that, when with one shout it would be all over? For Jack was surely lying about being here legally; he'd never heard of anyone returning from being deported, so Jack must be lying. But Oliver had done it, that very thing, had lied about Jack and who he was, as Jack said, lied while explaining it to Mr. McCready, never mentioning at all that he knew Jack.

"I knew you wouldn't break the code," said Jack satisfied.

"I didn't do you any favors," said Oliver, keeping his voice low, wanting Jack to understand this. "And next time, I'll shout it out at the top of my lungs, so will you stay away? Otherwise, I will have the constable, I *swear* it."

Jack just smirked. "I might come by an' I might not," he said. "But I've been lined up for some jobs at the Three Cripples, like I told you, an' all the while waitin' for the gang to come back. I'm pretty sure that if they were to come anywhere, they'd come there. So you should—"

Now, instead of just thanking him for a favor between old friends, Jack was trying to pull him through a doorway, into Jack's world, where Oliver simply did not want to go. Oliver felt hot along the back of his neck. He did not want this; he did not *need* it.

"Look, you," said Oliver, pointing the handle of his broom at Jack. He was almost close enough to touch Jack with it, but not quite. He didn't know what Jack would do if Oliver actually hit him. "I told you. Bill Sikes died while trying to escape the law. Nancy died by Bill Sikes's hand. Fagin was hanged at Newgate. The gang is scattered to the wind, gone."

"Well, they might come back," said Jack, nonplussed. "They might do, if—"

"They're not, Jack, will you listen to me?" Oliver knew he was raising his voice, that it echoed in the yard, that surely someone in the shop might hear him. But it was as if he couldn't help it. Just the sight of Jack was enough to make him feel hot inside and out, anger boiling up into his head, filling his lungs with a shouting animal that for so long he'd kept locked up inside. His astonishment battled with his frustration; why wouldn't Jack see reason?

Jack was frowning, something a little hurt and lost in his eyes, but Oliver didn't let that stop him.

"Fagin and his people are not going to come sashaying into the Three Cripples. They are dead, gone, and scattered, and the sooner you realize that, the sooner you can move on with your life. Take advantage of the reprieve given you, if indeed it has been given you."

"Got nowheres else to go," said Jack. He swallowed and straightened up and narrowed his eyes at Oliver. "An' neither, from the looks of it, do you. Besides, there's nowheres else I'd rather be, so you better be good to me."

The door from the warehouse was partly open, spilling a little bit of light from the glow of the potbellied stove onto the cobblestones of the yard so recently tended to by Tate. Oliver turned to check, but no one was standing at the door as if looking to see the source of the shouting that echoed off the bricks in the alleyway. In a moment, if Jack left and no one had seen him, then Oliver could step into that relative warmth and continue on with his pretty good life. While Jack would have to trek back to the Three Cripples, where Oliver was sure he'd never been, but of which he was also sure he could picture in his mind—a filthy, decrepit huddle of a building, where only thieves and pickpockets and the dregs of the street would hang out.

When Oliver turned back around, in a swirl of snow, with the last flickers of the red scarf, Jack was gone, with only traces of his footprints in the snow to signal he'd been there at all.

"Oliver."

Oliver whirled. Mr. McCready stood inside the warehouse, just at the steps that led into the back hallway of the shop. He was only an outline in the relative smudge of the daylight, but he must have seen Jack. *Had* seen Jack as he scampered away, leaving Oliver to deal with the mess Jack had left in his wake.

"Come here, Oliver," said Mr. McCready. His voice was stern, but then, it had a right to be.

Carrying his tools, Oliver walked over to the doorway to the warehouse, through which he could see Tate, busy with his counting, his *never-ending* counting, working away; Oliver didn't think he'd run telling tales to Mr. McCready, as he didn't know about Oliver's injunction against speaking to lower orders. But then, Tate might simply have said something to Mr. McCready based on the odd fact that Oliver had been seen talking to a strange boy. In the yard, no less.

"Well, Oliver," said Mr. McCready. "Do you have something to say to me?"

Standing there, Oliver felt a tad faint, and cold, now that he wasn't moving.

"You have been spoken to about this, Oliver, and I have asked you a question that you are beholden to me to answer."

The snow was starting to flurry a bit and Oliver shivered. He opened his mouth, but there was nothing he could say, nothing to hold on to about who he'd been in his past and why he would even consider tarrying with the likes of Jack Dawkins.

Mr. McCready's brows began beetling together, and Oliver realized he had to say something.

"It was a young man," he said. "He'd lost his way; I was giving him directions."

"And is this the same young man with whom I saw you talking this very morning when you should have been working?"

Oliver felt hot now, the whole of his neck under his collar hot as a steam house, the smells from his stained apron thick in his nose. "It was, but—" He could not even begin to create a story around this; he'd been warned, and now it was too late. "He came by again; I don't know why."

"You will cease letting him hang about the premises, Oliver, do you understand this? I am running a business, not a boy's home, and he looked quite disreputable, and do you actually want to bring down my shop in a way that will send away customers who don't wish to mingle with the lower orders?"

Mr. McCready loomed tall and angry; his mouth was bunched up in a scowl, and Oliver knew that he himself was in the wrong. It wouldn't do, at this point, to explain that Jack Dawkins recognized no boundaries drawn by God or man; he came and went as he pleased. And should Jack be confronted by Mr. McCready, Jack was less likely to listen to him than he was to Oliver. It wasn't Oliver's fault that Jack had come by, but he couldn't say it, couldn't explain it that way.

"Do you have nothing to say for yourself?"

"He's an old friend," said Oliver, finally. "We lost touch long ago. I don't know why he's coming around now, but I'll tell him to stay away." He shrugged his shoulders with a sigh; Mr. McCready was a decent businessman, and as such, had probably never been even slightly known to the type of street person with which Oliver was very much acquainted. "I'm sorry, Mr. McCready."

"If I see you with that young man, or any person of that ilk, and believe me, I will know it, then I will have to punish you. It will mean a whipping, is that clear?"

"I won't let it happen again."

"See that you don't," said Mr. McCready, still stern but mollified. His anger died away so quickly that Oliver realized that Mr. McCready wasn't a cruel man. Just, it seemed, one who was very invested in being an honest shopkeeper; he was steady middle-class and he didn't want anything to disrupt that.

"No, sir."

"Finish up here, then, and help Tate with the new shipment; it's arrived in a muddle as usual."

Mr. McCready left him in the yard, in the white curtain of light snow, closing the door to the warehouse behind him, blocking off the light and the streaks of warmth. The next time Oliver saw Jack, and he knew he would, he needed to tell Jack to stay away. But Jack was not only persistent, he did not care what Oliver wanted. Were Oliver to explain it with even the slightest bit of increased force, it might very well make Jack just that much more insistent on coming by. There was almost no way Oliver could win this.

CHAPTER 13

Descriptions Of Jack's Delight Regarding Occurrences At The Three Cripples And The Repercussions Which Oliver Must Bear Alone

Wren business picked up on Friday, there were again deliveries to be made in the afternoon. Pleased, Oliver bundled up for the cold as he waited for Henry to fill the basket. He was eager to be out and about, even with the frost thick in the air and the dark smuts from smoking chimneys making the snow black and grey.

The deliveries took him from Soho down to the river straightaway, where fine carriages on Prince's Street attempted to run him over as if he weren't even there. The packages for the white townhouses along Weston Street by

Hyde Park were small and carefully wrapped by Henry. Oliver got a penny at almost every door, with the copper weighing down his trouser pocket and jingling about, making him wish he could have at least gotten his change purse back from Jack before he'd sent him away that last time.

For his last delivery, he walked boldly up the Strand, amidst the hustle of black-coated business men, or the groups of bewigged lawyers standing just outside a tavern, and past the sweet young miss in a bright blue bonnet with a cloak to match, who smiled at him as she tucked her hands into her fur muff. He paid none of the sights any mind, but got through the deliveries quickly, making his way up to Oxford Street, and finally, past Russell Square. By the time he'd gotten to Number 14 Doughty Street, his face was numb with cold.

When he trotted up the snow-dotted steps and tapped the brass knocker, it was Mrs. Acton herself who answered the door. She was dressed in an outfit that looked as though it was made of white froth, something like Mrs. Bedwin might have described as her morning dress, even though it was afternoon.

Mrs. Acton floated as lightly as foam through the doorway to Oliver. With a start, Oliver realized that Mrs. Acton was outside, on her own front step, out of doors dressed in that way, with her cheeks as rosy as though she were already next to the fire.

"Are those my deliveries? Are those my ribbons at last?" she asked. "One can never have enough ribbons, so I'll be sure to order more that you can deliver to me."

Oliver nodded and took out the last string-tied brown parcel to hand to her. With a start, he realized that her fingers were curling around his arm in a possessive way and that she was attempting to pull him inside.

"Come, take off your coat and tarry a while. Mr. McCready surely won't need you back at the store so soon?"

Oliver stepped back as lightly as he could, keeping his smile painted on. Her hand fell away from his arm as he did so, and though it felt as though a weight had fallen away from him, his chest felt tight.

"I'm sorry to say, Mrs. Acton, that I must get back, even with such a kind invitation."

Mrs. Acton frowned, her pale white skin pulling as she did so, and it was then that Oliver noted how she smelled like fresh flowers, and how her hair was done up loosely in a trailing pink ribbon, as though she were just preparing to go to bed, rather than to meet visitors in her front hall. Then as she saw him looking at her, she smoothed her features and tried again, petting his arm and leaning in close.

"Oh, won't you stay, young man, just for a while, a quarter of an hour—"

"No, ma'am," he said, trying to make his voice stern as he had with Jack, hoping that this time around it would have more of an effect. He pulled away far enough so that her hand was forced to drop from his arm, though her fingers seemed to leave traces of perfume in the chill air. He saw the sparks in her eyes, though they couldn't be tears, not with her mouth in a smile again.

"I'm so very sorry, but I must go now." As he said this, his face felt tight. With a tip of his head, he put his cap back on and backed up on the front step. The maid was off making tea, he presumed, so unfortunately there was no one to witness his refusal, regardless of how firm it had been. With a parting glance to her, he dipped his chin. "Good day, ma'am."

The air on the street was icy after the warmth of her doorway, so he tightened his green scarf around his neck and tucked his hands in his pockets as he strode down the pavement, his empty basket banging against his hip in his haste. That wasn't the way it was done, of course; a gentleman made his way along a street with dignity and grace. But he felt rattled, knowing that he shouldn't have gone in and had tea with her that first time. He wasn't a gentleman of leisure to be consorting with ladies.

Oliver reached the corner, ignoring the crossing sweeper with his thin body, valiantly sweeping the street against the falling snow, his thin boots flopping around his feet, mud ground into his trousers up to the knees. Oliver looked the other way, and just as he was about to step into the street, he careened into a body.

"Such a rush you're in, Nolly," said that voice.

Oliver looked up. It was Jack. *Again.* He looked bright and warm, his green eyes sparking, replete with that smile and sharp teeth, that low top hat tipped back on his head as if it wanted to fly off at any moment. He made a complete contrast to the highborn pedestrians on the tidy street, and the clean, white rows of townhouses upon whose slanted roofs not even the smallest smut ever dared land.

"I told you to leave me alone; what are you doing here, how did you find me?" Oliver asked, half-glad for a moment before irritation set in. The last thing he needed was to get another scolding about meeting up with Jack. He was trying not only to make a good impression but to keep it. But who knew how long that would last, with Jack coming around— Mr. McCready had already threatened a whipping over this;

the only thing saving Oliver was that they were far enough from the shop so that Mr. McCready might never hear of it.

"I followed you, of course," said Jack, his smile getting more broad, as if he enjoyed the teasing almost as much as he enjoyed Oliver's reaction to it. "An' anyway, I've come to bring you news, news that couldn't wait."

"I don't wish to hear any news you might carry," said Oliver with what he thought was haughty dismissal, even though talking to Jack was preferable to ruminating on his own thoughts about the street sweeper.

Oliver looked across the street where the sweeper had just finished, and leaning his broom against his thigh, was holding up a soot-blackened hand for the penny that he had just earned. But the gentleman whose path had been cleaned for him held his head high and walked on as if the sweep wasn't even there. Oliver fought the impulse to give the urchin a penny from his own collection of change jingling in his trouser pocket. So instead he turned back to Jack and looked at him with what he hoped was haughty implacability.

"It's just that—" Here Jack stopped and there was something in his voice that Oliver had not heard, not recently. And not in five long years; not since the day they'd met in Barnet. The memory teased him, and he wondered, not for the first time, what Jack had been doing so far from Fagin's hideout, as Barnet was some miles from Saffron Hill. "I've been lookin' for some of Fagin's gang—"

"I don't care who you're looking for!" Oliver felt his shoulders go up; talking about Fagin's gang was bad enough, but looking for them? It was beyond his ability to comprehend why it would be important. Besides, passersby were starting to look at them, confusion evident that a well-dressed apprentice lad was standing in the middle of the pavement in earnest discussion with a person of such obvious ill repute. "I don't want to know anything about that, can't you understand? Please go away, Jack, *please.*"

"*Please*, is it now?" Jack asked. His eyebrows twitched as if he were keeping himself from laughing outright, but only barely. "Such fine manners, you have, when there's somethin' you want."

"I only want you to go away." Oliver lowered his voice and stepped closer to Jack in the hopes of making their conversation more private and perhaps more effective. "To leave me alone and quit following me!"

"Such an ugly frown on such a sweet face." Now Jack did laugh, tossing his head back, giving his hat a little jerk to keep it in place. "So I'll tell you quickly and save your face from freezin' that way."

Oliver turned on his heel and started walking away. "Get out of my way, or I'll call the constable and have you arrested." He meant it this time, he really did.

"I'm at the Three Cripples, havin' my dinner," said Jack, calling after him. "An' in he walks, one of Fagin's gang!"

Oliver froze at the corner of the street. All of Fagin's gang was dead or disbanded, either of which, to hear Jack tell it, was tantamount to the same thing. "And what of it?" he asked over his shoulder, waiting for the carriage in the street to move past him so that he could cross. He had no desire to remember anyone from that time.

"Don't you see? How grand this is? You said that no one would ever come, an' now they have! His name's Morris Bolter, an' he says he knows you."

Jack's voice, so bright and charged with energy, was right over Oliver's shoulder now. Oliver turned, barely missing Jack with the edge of his gloved fist.

"I told you," said Oliver, through gritted teeth, trying not to think of where he'd heard that name before. "I don't *care* about anyone from Fagin's gang. I don't *know* anyone named Morris Bolter, and I wouldn't care if I did."

"He knows all about you," said Jack, so close his breath brushed across Oliver's cheek. Jack smelled like onions from his diner and the stale beer he must have drank. "Told me about those blue eyes an' that rosy mouth of yours, told me about your thing for washing up an' how you had an appetite like a sailor, an' how you once attacked—"

"I don't care, don't you understand that?" It was beyond him to be able to figure out why Jack simply wasn't listening. Not to mention that Jack's closeness was prickling on his skin. "Those days are long in the past, and I've moved on. You need to move on, and why aren't you off stealing silver and picking pockets, or whatever it is you are doing these days? Or really, I shouldn't wonder, you've already got small boys stealing *for* you—"

He meant to hurt Jack, and maybe he had, for there was a pause before Jack burst out laughing, right there on the street, where anyone could see the raw display of his wide-open mouth. But it was of no concern to Jack that anyone might see a fine young gentleman such as Oliver Twist consorting with a street thug such as Jack Dawkins.

"You know me too well, Nolly," Jack said, shaking his head, causing his hat to slip a little. He straightened it with one bare hand and then smoothed his lapels, tugging on the edge of

Oliver's red scarf. "I'm lookin' to start a new gang, although, right enough, that might take some time. There's a couple of lads at the Three Cripples who are lookin' at me with interested eyes, I don't mind tellin' you, but it's Morris, he's the one, he's got all these *stories*—"

Jack's voice rose on the last word as if this fact, associated with that particular person, were the shining star in all of this, as if any of it had any merit at all, and Morris the best thing about it. Jack's remark and his admiration for someone with such a sullied reputation snapped Oliver's patience right in two, and he actually grabbed Jack by the lapels and gave him a good shake.

"Don't you understand? I do not care. Not about the Three Cripples, or this Morris Bolter, and especially not about *you*." His voice was rising to a pitch, enough so that passersby were looking at him, watching with widened eyes that told Oliver exactly what they thought of two lads coming to an altercation in the street. One of those lads was going to end with his backside on the pavement, and it wasn't going to be Oliver.

"You keep on and I'll call the constable, right now, I'll do it, I swear." He put his hand over his heart to emphasize his intent that he, Oliver, was going to do this thing.

But Jack just smiled and put his hands—bare, cold, knuckle-scarred hands—over Oliver's brown gloved one. Jack held on tightly, fingers curved, pressing Oliver's hand against his own chest. Oliver looked down, closed his eyes, and tried to jerk away from the pressure of Jack's hands. Oliver opened his mouth to shout—yes, he was positively going to shout for the nearest constable.

"Young master," came a voice.

Oliver's eyes snapped open, and he turned his head just as Jack let him go, and he in turn let Jack go to look at the owner of the voice. It was Jane, the maid from Mrs. Acton's house, only three doors down. The door to Mrs. Acton's townhouse was closed, but there was the maid, without even a shawl to keep off the afternoon chill. She had an envelope in her hand, which she held out to Oliver.

"It's from the mistress; she wishes you to take it to your master." Jane was blushing again and looking at Oliver. She purposefully did not look at Jack, not that Oliver could blame her. He'd do anything at that instant to not be associated with Jack; perhaps Jane felt that if she didn't look at Jack, the meeting between the three of them had never happened. She only need report to her mistress that she'd delivered the note and that was the end of it.

"Thank you," said Oliver. He took the envelope, which seemed weightless in his gloved hand. Both he and Jack watched the maid scurry off. Then Jack smacked Oliver on the shoulder.

"She's a pretty one; been flirtin', have you?"

"You can just shut your mouth."

Jack took a step back, eyes widening with a bit of surprise. Then he smirked. "Yes, sir, young master, sir." He doffed his hat and curved his other arm around his waist, bowing low, oily hair spreading out, the hat and the hems of Jack's coat almost sweeping the ground. "I only live to be at your service."

With his mouth pressed tightly against anything else he might say, Oliver stuffed the envelope in his pocket and marched off. He didn't look back to see if Jack was following. It wouldn't matter. Jack knew where he lived and would come around, and then it would turn into a disaster. The only hope Oliver had was if he managed to stop Jack before he came in the yard again, or God forbid, came into the *shop*—

"Till later, then, Nolly," said Jack in the retreating distance.

Oliver didn't look back. He marched along, head down, concentrating, trying to pretend that the meeting had never happened. There would be no one to tell Mr. McCready about it, no one in this part of town, and he certainly wouldn't mention it. God willing, that would be the end of it.

The light was growing pale and blue and the shadows long as Oliver hurried back to the shop. That his path was downhill most of the way did not help, for ice had formed, freezing the runoff from the noon melt. He had the note from Mrs. Acton, and he'd mention to Mr. McCready that Mrs. Acton had mentioned perhaps wanting more ribbons. That might make a future sale, something Mr. McCready would approve of.

He checked his pocket with his hand and slipped down the cobbles as he stepped away from the Strand. Now he had to duck between carriage wheels and the wide skirts of ladies on their way home from taking an airing with their maids, showing off their fine skirts. They rather enjoyed walking slowly and grandly, and with far too much skirt and not enough hustle; they were making him later than he already was. Surely it was coming on to suppertime; he could not imagine what Mrs. Pierson would say, let alone his own stomach, were he to miss out on her good cooking.

Somehow, he made it in time, slipping in through the yard and the warehouse door just as the bells from St. James's Workhouse started tolling. As he came up the stairs from the warehouse and opened the door to the shop, he heard footsteps leading down to the kitchen. He hung his jacket, scarf, and cap on the peg in the hall and stuffed his gloves in his coat pockets. Rubbing his palms on his trousers, he took the note from his jacket pocket and headed down the stairs with as much calm as he could manage.

The kitchen was warm, and the smells of cooking filled his nose almost immediately. Mrs. Pierson moved from the stove to the sideboard, her skirts swirling. The girl was nowhere to be seen; Henry and Tate had already taken their usual places. A second after he realized that Mr. McCready was also not among them, he felt the step on the stair behind him. He had a sense of those broad shoulders and then Mr. McCready's voice.

"Running late, Oliver?" he asked. "Never mind, those streets can get treacherous and busy this time of day. Is that a note for me?"

Oliver turned slightly to hand it to him and then slipped onto the bench seat next to Tate. He held his breath as he did this, hoping no one had noticed that he'd not taken time to wash up. But Mrs. Pierson was busy handing around the platter of fried cod and potatoes, and as always, the bread and butter. This time, there was a dish of pickles in the center of the table. His stomach growled and demanded that he hurry and start eating.

"I'd have gotten to the peas if that girl hadn't taken off early," said Mrs. Pierson, scooting the hot dishes around the table, making sure that each boy had some food close at hand.

"No need to worry, Mrs. Pierson," said Mr. McCready. "The boys have plenty to eat here and should learn to eat what's put before them."

"Are you saying I spoil these boys?" she asked, holding her hands to the apron over her stomach as if quite shocked.

"As is your duty, Mrs. Pierson, as is your duty."

"And in doing my duty," said Mrs. Pierson, "there's apple pudding for dessert."

As Oliver looked up, he could see the pudding on the sideboard. As always, there was a pitcher of pouring custard next to it. It was probably full to the top, and she could make, as she always said, more very quickly if need be. He waited for Mr. McCready to say grace then pulled his full plate to him and picked up his knife and fork, preparing to dig in.

He barely noticed Mr. McCready standing up, Mrs. Acton's letter in his hand, but when the whole table froze, Oliver forced himself to pay attention. He had his fork halfway to his mouth, but at the expression on Mr. McCready's face, he put it back on his plate with a clink. Mr. McCready glared at him, eyes narrow, his face turning white, and in his hand, the letter almost shook. Almost, for Mr. McCready put it on the table next to his plate. Oliver could see the careful dark script that seemed to go on for quite some time. He couldn't imagine an order for ribbons and lilac sachets or anything else Mrs. Acton might want could take that long, or require that much close writing.

"Oliver, put your knife and fork down and look at me."

Oliver looked up as he was told, but he didn't understand it.

"Why, whatever is the matter, Mr. McCready?" Mrs. Pierson stared at him, hand half over her mouth, the other on her bosom. She could see the letter in his hand as well as Oliver could, and the way Mr. McCready was holding it, it was easy to see that this was the source of his agitation.

"I don't wish to—" Here Mr. McCready stopped. "It is not right to keep secrets, not when it affects my business. This is a letter from Mrs. Acton. It concerns Oliver's meeting in the streets near her home. A meeting with a young man she describes as wearing a half top hat, a greatcoat, and red scarf. She states, Oliver, that you were talking with him as if you knew him. She describes him as a low, disreputable person, exactly the one who I specifically stated you were not to have any dealings with."

Everyone in the kitchen turned to look at him. Tate and Henry looked wide eyed, as Oliver supposed that not much of this type of drama ever happened in the kitchen at McCready's Haberdashery. Mrs. Pierson, however, looked mortified, as if on Mr. McCready's behalf.

"Are you quite sure?" she asked, her voice coming out faintly. "Perhaps she misunderstood the meeting, perhaps Oliver—"

For one moment, he felt he loved Mrs. Pierson, perhaps almost as much as he had, and still did love Mrs. Bedwin, for coming to his defense as she had, even though she'd only known him a short time. Perhaps it was because of the fine manners Mrs. Bedwin said he'd always displayed, or maybe even because of his pretty face. Or his appetite for her cooking, it didn't matter, because—

"Do you deny it, Oliver?" asked Mr. McCready, breaking into Oliver's thoughts. "Did you meet with some person you did not know, and Mrs. Acton mistook it for an acquaintance?

Or was it truly, as I have forbidden, the same young man as has been coming around to detain you from your work?"

Here Mr. McCready stopped to fold the letter with quick, angry motions of his hand. He placed the letter on the table, as if not caring that her fine writing paper might get smudged with grease. Then he looked up at Oliver with blazing eyes.

"Is this the young man, the *same* young man, who your dallying with will most *assuredly* bring down the tone of this shop and send customers away, just as Mrs. Acton says she will take her custom elsewhere, for as she says—"

Now Mr. McCready unfolded the letter again, just as quickly, and scanned it for the exact quote he wanted. "That she cannot bear to associate with a shop that allows its workers to mingle with . . . And then she almost comes to state that you were *impudent* to her, though I imagine she's just trying to add insult to injury there. No, I believe she saw what she saw, and what I'm waiting for you to do, Oliver, is to either deny or accept these accusations."

Oliver could hardly breathe. He'd had no idea that Mrs. Acton would take his refusal of a cup of tea and a slice of cake so badly. Of course it was more than that. He'd refused her the second time because she'd pawed at him the first time. But then, after refusing her, Oliver had marched right out into the street and gotten into a heated discussion with some lowlife, an ex-convict, no less. In comparison, that would make Mrs. Acton feel very insulted indeed, so no wonder the letter.

As well, the crux of it was that the real accusation was quite true. Though he couldn't have imagined it getting reported this far, this fast. Then again, he'd carried the accusation in his pocket and delivered it with his own hands. He might have well as willingly put his own head on the block; ice filled his lungs with a sense of despair that he'd engineered, though unwillingly, his own doom.

"Do you deny what she states, Oliver?"

Mr. McCready was quietly standing there, at odds with the terror climbing in Oliver's breast. Why had he not called for the constable the very first time Jack had come up to him, at the very first words out of Jack's mouth? *Leave you be, Nolly? That's all anyone's ever done, is leave you be.*

Well, he was paying for it now, that laxness, that acceptance and allowing Jack to stand there and talk to him, wasn't he? That and his own vanity at Mrs. Acton's attention.

"Oliver, don't add sullenness to your list of sins; I only want you to answer me."

This made it worse; Mr. McCready had warned him. If only Oliver had stopped Jack that first time or run in the other direction when he'd met up with Jack or something—

"I see you are not denying it. Well, then, come with me now. Mrs. Pierson, make sure the boys eat and help you clear the table afterward."

Mr. McCready began walking around the table, and when he got to where Mrs. Pierson was standing, he gestured with his hand. Oliver, feeling numb all over, let Mr. McCready grip the back of his neck and push him up the stairs and down the small passageway to the warehouse. It was freezing cold and dark, and Mr. McCready only let him go long enough to light a candle, the one that stood at the end of the long table where Tate worked.

Mr. McCready took down a switch that had hung on a handle from one of the long beams. Oliver had seen it there but had not thought anything of it. It would never be for him, he'd been sure, because he was going to do well here. At least that's what he'd thought; now he knew differently.

Looking at Oliver gravely in the half-light, he said, "I will give you one more chance to say what needs to be said. Your apology will take you a long way in my good graces. But you must apologize, ere you lose that way."

He felt as though he was already lost. Mr. McCready had helped to place him here, in this house. His intentions had been good, and Oliver himself had agreed to it. He had felt, even at the time, that it had been a good choice, and he knew now that only he himself was to blame for the predicament that he was in.

"Do you have an apology, Oliver? Or even an explanation?"

"No, sir," said Oliver, low.

Mr. McCready started as if Oliver had struck him.

"I mean, that is, I'm sorry for today, but I don't have an explanation." He wanted to add that he deserved what was coming to him, but he didn't quite have the voice for it. Mr. McCready had been reasonable and generous, and Oliver had only let him down.

"Then I'm afraid, Oliver," said Mr. McCready, looking somewhat cross, "that I'm going to have to deliver punishment, as promised."

Oliver's stomach dropped as though it had fallen down an old well with no water at the bottom.

"You will come to the table, now," said Mr. McCready. He stood to one side and swished the switch once in the air, checking to make sure that the damp had not softened it.

Oliver walked to the table and bent himself over it. Part of him hoped that this would impress Mr. McCready; the other part hoped he could distract himself from the squirming of his gut by clenching the edge of the table. He hadn't been beaten in years; it was hard to breathe.

A hand landed in the small of his back and pressed down, and Oliver had to open his mouth to get in enough air. The snow spat against the windows in the silence, and somewhere a door opened and closed, leaving an eternity between.

The whipping started with three quick strokes across the backs of his thighs, and Oliver cringed away from the switch. The blows vibrated all the way down to his bones. He felt Mr. McCready's body blocking his way and tried to force himself to stop quivering. He failed.

"Do not make this more difficult by trying to get away, Oliver," said Mr. McCready.

Oliver did not answer this; prolonging the whipping by being openly defiant, when he'd already brought enough shame on the shop, would make it worse.

Mr. McCready started again, bringing the switch down on two or three spots only, six more times, making it feel like Oliver's skin had split in a burst of heat, as though someone were pressing burning iron against him.

Then Mr. McCready stopped without ceremony or announcement, and Oliver wanted to cry; he was shaking so hard his teeth rattled. Hot lines vibrated in an uneven path in his brain. He clenched and unclenched his fists as his arms curled around his head. He wanted to stay there forever and sink deep, deep into the cool, scarred wood of the table.

But Mr. McCready yanked him up by the collar, jerking Oliver so hard that stars flashed in front of his eyes.

"You will go to bed directly," said Mr. McCready, releasing him with a shake. "And you will not get any supper. And on the morrow, we will make a new start. The matter is done now, and you will no longer consort with—"

Mr. McCready paused, and in the light of the single candle, his face was soft around the edges with concern. "Is he someone from your past, Oliver? Is that it? Someone you knew when you were—?" Mr. McCready stopped himself and began again in more confident tones of instruction. "You should know that he will only hold you back. Your past is an angry, monstrous thing; you must do your best to escape it. And this person, this friend of yours, is really not your friend."

Oliver's knees felt weak and his thighs throbbed. The care and comfort Mr. McCready lavished on his boys was worth a great deal. And he was right, of course, in that hanging about with the likes of one Jack Dawkins would do Oliver's business prospects no good at all. But how Mr. McCready had sussed it out that Jack was well-known to Oliver was beyond him. There had been three brief meetings, only two of which Mr. McCready had seen with his own eyes, so how had he guessed it? He wanted to confess it all, tell the whole story, but Mr. McCready was already waving Oliver off, hanging up the switch, and moving toward the stairs.

When they got to the main landing, Mr. McCready motioned Oliver to go up the stairs.

"You'll go to bed without supper, young man, and perhaps you'll be able to think upon the direction your life had better take." Then he went down to the kitchen, leaving Oliver in the darkness of the closed shop.

Oliver trod slowly up the stairs, finding his way amongst the gloom and into the slanted dormitory. There, he used his hands to find the matches and candles and lit one and stood there, smelling the sulfur and the sparking wax. Mr.

McCready supplied only paraffin candles for his apprentices, not that any of them expected more. As he watched the paraffin start to melt beneath the golden sliver of light, he realized that he'd let Mr. McCready down today, and himself. And as to why he had not called the constable on Jack each and every time, he could not fathom. His brain was too tired, and the backs of his thighs ached with every move he made.

There was no water to wash with as both pitcher and basin were dry. With the lack of the girl to help, Henry and Tate would most likely wash in the kitchen before they came up to bed, so Oliver would have to sleep as he was, coated with sweat and the dust and ash from the street. And with Jack's touch, the mere brush of his hands, having left the faint smell of beer, still pulsing through the back of his hand.

He didn't want to look down at his legs, so he shifted out of his clothes as fast as he could, his teeth chattering in the chilly air. But, just as he put on his nightshirt, he did look, and could see that the backs of his thighs were a swarming red, with darker lines across the swellings. There'd been nine blows in all; none of them had broken the skin, but even so, he had to look away.

He thought about reading till the boys came up and the lights went out; his books would help relax him and make him feel more as if everything was as it should be. But exhaustion fell on him like a blanket of wet clay. The candle guttered as he moved to his bed. He yanked back the sheet and the two wool blankets and got into bed and lay down on his left side. Pulling the covers up to his chin, he looked at the light flickering shadows on the wall and the panes of glass in the window.

Yes, he had to roll back over and blow out the candle; Mr. McCready didn't want the boys to leave anything burning.

Wincing, he rolled over and blew out the candle sitting on the chair beside his bed, and then rolled back, clasping the scar on his left arm to settle himself in the dark. A darkness into which leaked Jack's voice. *I'm at the Three Cripples...one of Fagin's gang has come an' he says he knows you. He's the one, he's got all these stories.*

Oliver shut off the thought as fast as he could. But something echoed there, something, a memory that he couldn't quite pin down. Of course Jack would want to know stories; he was always ready to hear those. Ones about great criminals dying nobly or getting away with it, which was even better. He could imagine Jack's glee at finding a member of Fagin's gang, but except for Charley Bates, Oliver couldn't remember any of their names, and certainly not anyone named Morris Bolter. Who, evidently, knew Oliver well enough to know about his penchant for cleanliness and his great appetite for food. No, Jack was teasing him, making it up for his own amusement on a lark. Which was Jack's way, and always had been.

He sank his head into the one pillow and tried to breathe slowly and not think of anything. But this absence of thought allowed the pain from the whipping to seep in, the great throbs echoing as his heart beat. He'd deserved the beating, almost as assuredly as if he'd asked for it. Which didn't make it hurt any less; it hurt a great deal. Had he grown so soft, then? Although, when he was little, a whipping like this would have sent him sobbing into a howling ball on the ground, so maybe he was tougher now, could stand it more. Or, which was more likely, the switch that Mr. McCready had held in his hand was not as harshly felt as was his disappointment.

Oliver sighed. He could only do his best to do better in future. He would do everything that Mr. McCready said. The instant an order was given him, he would obey it. And if Jack came around again, Oliver would be hollering for the constable and marching right up to Mr. McCready to report the incident. Yes, that's what he would do. He swore it. This whipping would be the last he would ever receive at Mr. McCready's hands.

CHAPTER 14

Less Drama And Violence Are Called For But Are Difficult To Achieve

Getting dressed, through wincing, Oliver followed Henry and Tate down to the kitchen. He felt sore all over, and the visits from Jack and Mr. McCready's disapproval nagged at him. But in the midst of this wash of emotions came the confusion of watching Henry and Tate line up in front of Mr. McCready, who was already seated at the table for breakfast.

Henry, as usual, was first in line, and he held out his hand, into which Mr. McCready unhesitatingly pressed a shiny shilling. Tate was next, his fingers curling around the coin with a smile, and then, indeed, Mr. McCready nodded that Oliver was next.

"Well done, lad, keep up the good work," Mr. McCready said, handing Oliver his first week's pay of one shilling.

In that small moment, with the coolness of the shilling in his hand, Oliver received his first pay. In spite of this small victory, Oliver felt the remains of the previous day's whipping as well as the glimmer of temper that Oliver imagined was still in Mr. McCready's eyes.

Oliver put the silver coin in his pocket, meaning to tuck it away in his tip box when he had a chance. But as the girl had not brought up any hot water, the boys lined up to wash in the kitchen. Since Oliver was the last boy in line, by the time he'd washed his face and hands, splashing water and soap all over the washstand and the slate floor, and as he dried his face on the towel, he looked up to see the entire of Mr. McCready's household already seated and waiting for him. No one said anything as he limped to his place beside Tate on the bench seat. Then Mrs. Pierson began serving up hot toast and butter, honey and bowls of porridge, and a tray of baked eggs.

Pausing before she served, she said, "I don't know as yesterday's doings have brought this house down forever." She stopped to scowl at Oliver, her eyes a little moist, as if she weren't quite sure whether or not she was angry. "But it seems to me that a good deal less violence and drama would be better to be getting on with. Wouldn't you agree, Mr. McCready?"

"Yes, indeed, Mrs. Pierson, and thank you," said Mr. McCready. "Would you happen to know if the tea is ready yet?"

Mrs. Pierson nodded and shoveled a baked egg onto Oliver's plate, plus an extra one for good measure, and then quickly walked to the stove where the kettle was only now just boiling.

This almost made Oliver feel worse than the night before; he'd upset Mrs. Pierson, and *still* she was feeding him. Which only fed his resolve to shout at the top of his lungs the moment Jack again turned up. Which he would, knowing Jack.

After breakfast, Oliver followed the boys up the stairs to put away their respective shillings and quickly followed them back downstairs where Mr. McCready was already behind the counter. Henry went to unlock the doors as Oliver hustled to rush outside and take down the shutters. While he was grateful that he'd actually received his pay, his heart was pounding with the thought that Mr. McCready might still take it upon himself to send Oliver packing.

And indeed, upon his return inside, Mr. McCready was waiting for him with his hands on the glass countertop.

"And you, young Oliver. You were quite indulged this morning. Mrs. Pierson thinks a great deal of you, I'd say."

Oliver didn't know what to say to that. So he nodded and tried not to look prideful. Which was hard, when his stomach was comfortably full of Mrs. Pierson's good cooking, and he'd gotten the extra piece of buttered toast.

"I do feel, however, that some extra work is what you need to keep your mind and body occupied."

Extra work was not what Oliver needed, not when every movement of his trousers brushed the backs of his legs, irritating the welts and bruises there. But he nodded his head and kept his mouth shut. Whatever Mr. McCready had in mind, it wouldn't be beyond his ability to bear, surely.

"There's a delivery due this morning; you will unload it yourself, without assistance."

"Yes, sir," said Oliver. Anger bloomed in his belly. He'd already taken his punishment and apologized, so why the additional workload? Perhaps it was because he'd not been able to explain away his meetings with Jack, or perhaps it was because he'd not begged to be let off or appeared with as much meekness and contrition as was called for. But it was hard. He'd spent so much of his life standing up and facing his misfortune, without letting anyone know—No, he had to stop. Mr. McCready wasn't the enemy; Mr. McCready only wanted the best for him.

"Yes, sir," said Oliver now, instead of everything else he wanted to say. "I'm sorry about yesterday, sir."

"I know, Oliver," said Mr. McCready. "Now, to your work, and we'll speak no more about it."

Then, to prove how normal a morning it was, Mr. McCready turned to Tate, who was standing close by, pretending very hard that while he was eavesdropping, he was really only waiting for his orders.

"Tate, would you double check that box, the one with the spools of thread that came yesterday?" Mr. McCready consulted a list on the counter. "I feel almost certain the count is low, but before I talk with the manufacturer, I want to be sure. Can you do that?"

"Yes, sir," said Tate, and he hurried off, ducking down the stairs to the warehouse like a rabbit disappearing into its burrow, and Oliver took a grateful deep breath and hurried out to the warehouse.

The gate was hooked wide open to admit the delivery wagon, and Oliver stood alone to greet it. Normally, there would have been at least two boys to attend to this particular task, but now there was only Oliver.

With the horses' shod hooves striking sparks on the cobblestones, and with creaks of wheel and harness, the wagon finally stopped, half-turned in the yard, with the back end of the wagon sticking out in the alley and taking up a great deal of room all the way around. The driver covered the two dray horses with a blanket each, and as Oliver began unloading, the driver climbed up on his bench behind the horses' rumps, watching him. He had a flask in his hands that he sipped at from time to time. Oliver imagined it was gin, but far be it that he would be the one to object. Although, at the same time, he wouldn't lower himself to ask for a dram to help keep him warm while he hustled.

The work carrying each box from the wagon to just inside the door of the warehouse made the morning almost warm enough that in the weak sunlight trailing through the mist Oliver soon doffed his jacket but kept on his apron and cap. He still felt cold and cross about it, with sleeves rolled up in the cold air, with the driver watching and no one to help him. There seemed to be hundreds of slatted boxes with rough edges and splinters everywhere, leaving wooden flecks on his apron and under his skin. In truth, he knew there to be only about twenty or so boxes, although, yes, the splinters were real enough.

He'd jabbed himself with a splinter along the fleshy part of his palm and it ached with each trip through the open door, the little one, so as to keep the chill off Tate, who was at his counting next to the long table. Oliver wondered if he could chance to go into the workshop and ask Tate if he might use the gloves that Tate wore when there was rough work at hand.

The gloves went with a workman's coat, a rough, stained thing of heavy wool that he'd seen Tate burrow into when he'd grown cold during his counting. The coat was so ugly that Oliver did not even want to touch it, but he was thinking about it differently this morning. The wool of the coat might protect his arms, which were now scratched and red and bleeding in streaks on his left arm. But each time he went into the warehouse, he didn't look at Tate, and Tate didn't look at him.

There were several boxes at the far end of the wagon, so Oliver ducked through the gates and walked closely along the wet and dripping brick wall of alley till he could reach them. And just as he did, he felt a movement behind him and casually looked, thinking it was some pedestrian with the foolish notion that walking through the alley would provide a better passage than walking along the street.

"Ho, there, Nolly," said Jack. "You look like you're limpin' a bit. Been in an accident, have you?"

Oliver froze. He saw Jack there, and in spite of all his promises to himself, simply froze, with a slatted wooden box in his hands, though at least it wasn't a bucket this time.

"Go away, Jack." His voice held no inflection, and his lungs felt as if they had no power. "You're not wanted here."

"But I've more to tell you," said Jack, moving close. Oliver's red scarf was still in evidence around Jack's neck, although it was now becoming smudged along the fine woolen edges. There was a flash of blue silk inside of Jack's coat, which meant that Jack had managed to procure a new waistcoat, by stolen means no doubt, and suddenly Oliver was sick of thinking about Jack and how he took everything and anything he wanted without working for it.

Now Oliver moved. He threw the box down to the cobbles and watched out of the corner of his eyes as it exploded against the mud and ice. Then he slammed into Jack, pushing him against the far wall of the alley, smacking his head hard enough against the icy brick to send that fine hat of his tumbling into the mud. He brought his face close to Jack's and thought about yelling for the constable, of alerting the driver so that he could go and fetch Mr. McCready. But first, he wanted to make his point, that he wasn't afraid of Jack, and moreover, didn't want anything to do with him.

"Now, you're going to listen to me, Jack Dawkins," said Oliver. He wanted to be fierce, he felt so *fierce* with his anger, and he wanted Jack to cower, to shrink away from him and listen. He grabbed Jack by the lapels of his jacket, and shoved hard, holding Jack there, looking into his green eyes, shaking Jack till his dark hair sprawled across his forehead, making him listen. "I don't *care* where you've been or where you are or who you've been talking to. I simply don't care, and I want you to leave me alone. Do you understand? Leave me *alone*."

Jack chuckled, though Oliver sensed he was trying to catch his breath, that he was not quite comfortable, and maybe his head ached a bit. "But it's a funny story, an' don't you want to hear it? The things Morris has to tell about you—and about me, he was there when I was arrested!"

"No story about any friend of yours would be funny, Jack. No one is laughing. I'm certainly not."

Oliver was about to release his hold on Jack and shout at the driver for assistance, for he knew there was nothing that

Jack would listen to better than the shrill of a peeler's whistle. When Oliver did let go, Jack shoved at him with the flat of both palms against Oliver's chest, and down Oliver went, his feet slipping on the ice as he fell with a slam into the ditch in the middle of the alley. He was soaked through with icy mud; the clawed edges of the ice cut into him, into his bruises, making him yelp as he tried to roll free.

Jack was over him, pulling him up to press him against the near wall of the alley. Oliver shivered, dripping and cold, blood pounding under his skin so hard that for a moment all he could see were black spots in front of his eyes. He clenched his hands at his sides, not wanting to reach out for something to hold on to, feeling at any moment that he was going to topple over, right back into the icy mud. And then he grabbed on anyway, to the first thing his hands could find.

When he could blink enough to clear his vision, there Jack stood, standing close but not touching him, even though Oliver was clutching Jack's lapels. There was something overly still about the way Jack looked at Oliver, watching him, as if waiting for Oliver to move as an animal waits for prey. His eyes darted to the open gates to the yard, his ears listening to voices on the street. Wary for any movement that might spell danger to him. Of course. Jack was always on the lookout for danger, and never mind what trouble he'd caused Oliver.

Jack must have taken the pause for hesitation on Oliver's part because he smiled and stepped closer. He pressed his bare hands over Oliver's with a sudden, quick movement that jostled Oliver all over. He tried to cover his wince as best he could, but Jack's eyebrows came together.

"Just come an' meet him," said Jack. "I promise I'll stop coming round an' getting you into trouble with your master. He won't whip you anymore."

It was too much to imagine how Jack so quickly got to the heart of the problem when Oliver had never told him.

"Don't squinch," said Jack, taking one hand up and rubbing his thumb along Oliver's brow. "It makes you all bumpy an' ruins those pretty looks of yours. One visit an' all," he said now. "Upon my word as a gentleman."

"For what *that's* worth." Oliver let go of Jack's lapels, trying to calm his breathing, and smacked Jack's hand away as he cast a look up the alley. The passage from the yard into the alley was blocked by the wagon; for Mr. McCready to find Jack there, he would have to come out the front door of the shop and walk all the way around.

From the cobblestone yard, Oliver heard a shout, sharp in the misty air. "Oliver! What's keeping you?"

It was Mr. McCready, who at last, alerted to the delay in the delivery being unloaded, and no doubt, the presence of a wagon for so long in his yard, had come to look for his newest apprentice boy. If Mr. McCready came out to the alley, he'd find Jack; Oliver needed to get Jack to go away.

"Get out of here, Jack, for the love of God," said Oliver, his jaw feeling tight. He knew that Jack might keep his word if it suited him, and then again, he might not. But for the time being, it would keep Jack away and Oliver out of trouble. "I'll come, I'll meet him. But after that, no more, Jack. No more visits, no more pennies, and give me back my scarf! And my change purse!"

Oliver reached out but Jack danced back, his eyes laughing as he brought his hand up and held it over his scarf as though he were holding his hand over his heart. "Yes, yes, an' no," said Jack. "It's mine now. Nine out of ten of the law an' all that."

It was ridiculous the way Jack misquoted everything as if he'd heard it and deliberately turned it around to annoy Oliver. It was as if he knew exactly how to do this, as though he liked watching Oliver get riled and seemed always to know exactly how to get the desired results. It made his head hurt; he pushed his palm hard against the side of his head, trying to stem the low throb that was developing.

"Am I giving you a headache?" asked Jack, trying for innocence as he picked up his hat from the damp stones and shook it off before he put it on his head.

"You *are* a headache," said Oliver. He swung backward, freeing himself of the pull of Jack that he didn't understand.

"Oliver! Oliver Twist!"

Mr. McCready sounded closer now. Oliver looked at Jack, who had not moved.

"Please," he said. His voice sounded as pleading and tremulous as a child's, and he didn't like the way that made him feel. So he swallowed, and tried to gather some air in his lungs, to make it come out stronger. To make it come out as though he meant it. "I need to get back to work."

He turned away from Jack and heard noises, as if there were booted feet making their way out of the yard and into the alley. But as Mr. McCready appeared around the corner, in the space between the wagon and the gate to the yard, Oliver didn't dare look back to make sure. Either Jack would be gone and there would be no need to speak of it, or he would not be, and no explanation that Oliver might offer would be enough.

Mr. McCready stopped, mouth open to speak, and for one instant, Oliver thought that Jack had not left. But then Mr. McCready came up to the mess of the box that Oliver had thrown on the ground. It contained many narrow paper boxes of hat pins, now spilled all over the ground, and of those, some had opened and spilled their bright, colorful contents into the icy mud.

"Whatever has happened?" asked Mr. McCready. He wasn't really talking to Oliver, he was already bending down and reaching for a pile of pins that had come loose from its box. Then he looked up at Oliver. "Why is the box smashed?"

"I slipped, sir," said Oliver, taking the easy road. And it felt easy, so incredibly easy, to lie about this. "It was the ice, and I, well, I'm sorry sir."

Mr. McCready straightened up, pins in his hand, mud dripping from his fingers. As he looked at Oliver, Oliver knew he would see what was most obvious to see. That the box was broken, and Oliver was quite rucked about, muddy, soaked, and dripping. Anyone in the world would conclude the truth of what Oliver had just said.

"Get these pins, Oliver, and I'll get Tate to do the rest of the boxes. We need to get this cart out of here; there's another delivery due any moment."

The disaster of having to pay one driver to wait while another backed out of the yard was, of course, very much to be avoided. Oliver gritted his teeth and kept his mouth shut.

"And you're bleeding. Never mind those pins now. Get Mrs. Pierson to bandage up your wrist, and brush off those trousers before they are permanently stained."

Oliver looked down at his hands, palms up. His left wrist had been sliced by the ice. Not deeply, but enough to leave a jagged tear that had bled to cover the heel of his palm. Now that he was looking at it, it began to sting, blood oozing in the cold air to drip down to his boot tops. All at once, his head began to weave back and forth and his body followed, obediently, spiraling into a sense of what he had done to himself. He'd cut himself wide open so that he was bleeding in the street, smashed a box of perfectly good hatpins, and *still* had not called the constable on Jack.

"Oliver." The voice came from some distance. "Oliver, are you all right? Here, we'll get you inside first. Tate. Tate!"

He felt a warm arm around his shoulder and the sudden shield of Mr. McCready's chest. Then he heard the scurrying footsteps of Tate, running but trying not to slip on the ice. As Tate rounded the corner into the yard, Mr. McCready let him go, motioning to Tate to *hurry now, hurry.* Out of the warehouse door came Mrs. Pierson, her hands over her mouth at, presumably, Oliver's state.

"Oh, *no*," she said. "Whatever have you been up to?" She held up her apron and skirts above the mud in the yard and gestured to him, almost violently, in the cold. "Come away in, this instant. What a disgrace you are! And you're bleeding all over those trousers."

But her voice sounded only mild and scolding rather than that she was truly angry with him. Not to mention the look on her face bespoke of her intention to straighten him up, to get his trousers brushed. And moreover, to *feed* him. And for the first time in what seemed the whole morning, Oliver felt his chest and shoulders relax. This he could bear up under; a little clucking and fussing would not come amiss right about now.

With his wrist bandaged, Oliver stood in his nightshirt, waiting with a thin towel as Tate finished his bath. Henry had already gone up, and being the senior boy, had had the first go at the cleanest, hottest water. Though Oliver was shocked when Tate had stripped to bare skin and had gotten into the slightly grey water that Henry had just used, he pretended it didn't matter. Because even though he was used to having hot water brought up to his room for his own private Saturday night bathing needs, at this point in his life, it couldn't matter. Apprentices were lucky to have any water at all to wash with, and sharing bathwater was only to be expected.

So he kept his mouth shut and rubbed at his scar while he waited for Tate to finish and thought about whether or not he should take off the bandage Mrs. Pierson had wrapped around his wrist. It would be better, perhaps, to give the wound another washing, and so, while Tate got dressed, seeming to be unembarrassed by his mostly naked state, Oliver concentrated on unwrapping the bandage.

By the time Tate was thumping up the stairs, Oliver had slipped out of his nightshirt and was in the fast-cooling grey water. It wasn't that anyone was there to see his scar, or stare at his state of nature, it was just that it was easier to jump in the water fast enough so that he did not have time to think about how it had so recently been swirling about other bodies, other naked limbs. At least there was soap, and he had his own towel. More sharing than that, he could not have borne.

The early bedtime of Saturday night was followed by a slow Sunday morning, with Mr. McCready and the boys showing Oliver how it was done. They ate, mostly in silence, the cold breakfast Mrs. Pierson had prepared the day before, which was followed by attendance at St. James's Church just down the street. Mr. McCready took Henry, Tate, and Oliver with him to St. James's; Mrs. Pierson, who was off for the day, went to her own church, St. Anne's, where apparently her family all went.

Oliver sat on the hard bench of the pew, turning the penny that Mr. McCready had given him for the collection basket over and over in his fingers. It was nice to be able to sit in a pew and listen to someone talking without feeling as though there was something he should be doing or worrying about. And, as well, Jack was hardly likely to come to church services, whatever the provocation.

Then, in the afternoon, when church services were over and Mr. McCready and the boys shared the cold lunch that Mrs. Pierson had left for them, Oliver was left on his own. He went upstairs and took out his book of poems by Dr. Johnson. He read on his bed on his stomach, turning the pages slowly beneath a vague patch of sun that came and went through the window as the clouds tumbled past.

CHAPTER 15

Oliver Keeps His Promise To Jack And Finds The Three Cripples Insalubrious

It wasn't until early the next week that Mrs. Pierson determined that Oliver's wrist could be unbandaged. Up till then, she'd insisted he be kept close by, so any deliveries were local and quick. But Mr. McCready insisted, with equal force, that Oliver do his regular tasks around the shop, and so, for a few days, the warehouse was always swept and the coal bins by each stove kept full, even though the girl was being entirely unreliable again. Oliver was willing to pitch in, not only to keep himself busy but to be useful enough to make up for his, as yet undiscovered, dalliance with Jack the week before. In addition, he was grateful to hear, while listening to Mr. McCready talk to Mrs. Pierson, that, as she was the shop's most particular client, Mrs. Acton's upset had been taken care of.

"Mr. McCready wants you to make deliveries today, Oliver." Henry handed over a list, which Oliver took and scanned. Then he looked at the basket, full to the brim with string-tied brown paper parcels.

"These addresses are as far as Russell Square," Oliver said, and then he realized what it meant, and of which part of London his deliveries would take him near. He couldn't believe that he actually meant to keep his promise to Jack, but he was a gentleman, and he'd given his word.

"No," said Henry. He tapped the string-tied parcel at the top of the basket. "That's *Regent* Square, and it's uphill all the way, so you better hustle."

Oliver nodded as he hefted the basket. He tucked the parcels in the basket so they wouldn't fall out, and indeed, it now looked as though there were more packages than there actually were. He needed the time, and Henry would support that he sent Oliver off with a full basket, were anyone to ask.

At Henry's nod, Oliver, with jacket and cap and scarf firmly in place, was out the door, pushing past customers in a rude way, turning abruptly away from St. James's Workhouse to avoid going past the high iron gates. He used his shoulders to slip through the traffic on the street, dodging carts and barrows, and hurrying past the beggars and the coffee vendor. He made his way up Oxford Street then went into the dodgy back lanes and muddy alleys off Tottenham Court Road, where he ought not to go, not if he wanted his pocket to remain unpicked or his person to remain unassaulted. But he must have been too early for most who would do him ill, and he managed to slip through to where the streets widened out, and Regent Square appeared, tidy and quiet, before him.

He went as fast as he could to get the deliveries all made before it got too late to go to the bottom of Saffron Hill, where Jack said the Three Cripples was located. When he was through and his basket empty, he headed down Grey's Inn Lane. And when he got to the bottom of the slope at Holborn, it started looking as though it would lead to somewhere less than amiable. Completely ill at ease and not a little bit lost, he stopped at a corner tavern and asked for directions to the Three Cripples.

The proprietor did not even pause as he continued to pull mid-afternoon beer and ale.

"What you want is to go across to Field Lane, and take a left, and when that ends, then up you go on Saffron Hill. It's right there."

"Saffron Hill?" asked Oliver. He couldn't imagine that Field Lane simply ended up being Saffron Hill.

"You follow this bit," said the proprietor with a sigh as if Oliver were the most troublesome of fellows. He pointed out the window, gesturing the way the street went uphill, "and then, when you get to Field Lane, keep going up; the Cripples'll be on your left, you can't miss it."

With the directions all dizzy in his head, Oliver backed out of the shop. As he walked along, the street started being lined by row upon row of handkerchiefs, hung on strings, an all too familiar sight, even if the memory was long in the past. He followed the directions, feeling blind, feeling as though he would miss it in spite of, or perhaps because of, the directions. When he got to the downward slope of Holborn, with the sounds and smells of Smithfield Market just beyond a street or two, there was a dark, narrow lane to the left. Of course, it would be the very direction he needed to go that looked nasty and bad, where the light went dim and the smells combated with those of the market.

But he went up. In spite of the fetid scraps in the street and the gutter of mud, he passed a pie shop, which was a bustling spot of activity. There was even a short line out the door and the wafting smell of hot meat and onions almost smacked him in the face. But he kept walking, and suddenly, it was there, the Three Cripples. It was almost at the near end of the lane, somewhat tall, with narrow windows peeking out from beneath the rough-edged roofline. The last coat of fresh paint had been years past, and the window casements were sooted dark and had not been cleaned within recent memory. The sign that hung below the eaves was a rough shield shape with faded green paint. The three figures on it barely resembled anything approaching three figures, let alone crippled ones.

Snowfall tended to bring coal dust down in thick layers, so if the tavern keeper had not enough hands to fortify against it, then layers of grime was the result. But other shops and doors and windows looked in far worse shape; at least the Three Cripples looked as though it had active customers, upright ones, rather than the skulking, filthy shapes that he tried to ignore out of the corner of his eyes as they passed behind him or lounged in doorways that looked like they'd not been passed through in years.

It began to occur to Oliver that he ought not to be here at all, not here in this neighborhood, and especially not with the goal of visiting Jack Dawkins. He should be able to deal with Jack's stories and threats another way, shouldn't he? But he didn't have another way, and anyway, here he was, at the Three Cripples.

As he opened the door, the smell of beer and damp hit him along with the thick reek of an untended cesspit. He stepped into the large room, which had a sleek wooden bar taking up most of the center, with a scatter of tables and chairs along the floor. The windows had short seats and low tables attached to the wall beneath them, windows that would barely let in any sunlight at all, were it shining. A small fireplace was jutting out from the far wall, and beside it were two doorways, one that led to a small room, and perhaps other rooms beyond that, and the other that led down a dark corridor.

While no one was looking at him directly, he sensed that they were looking at him askance. He was dressed too fine to be where he was, and while he thought he had the right Three Cripples, perhaps he didn't. Maybe there was another one? Besides, Jack was nowhere to be seen. Oliver felt the stirrings of panic at the thought of actually going up to the bar to talk to one of these rough men to inquire after Jack.

The door opened to admit more customers, all roughly garbed in stained woolen jackets and thick boots, their caps and hats all tucked low over their eyes. A small wind whisked around his heels, carrying the scent of their labor, the odor of long-since-unwashed grime on their skins.

Oliver wondered if he should stay or go.

Go. He should go.

Oliver walked up to the door and pulled it open; it sagged badly on its hinges, and he struggled to keep it open so he could slip out just as more customers came in.

"Come in, then, if you've a mind to."

Oliver turned around, and there was Jack. His face, dirtier than Oliver had last seen it, was streaked with old sweat, and his eyes were narrow, as if speculating the reasons why Oliver had given in to his threats. But he looked pleased somehow, somewhere behind his green eyes, as if content that Oliver had come to see him at last.

"Close the door, then," said Jack, coming up to do it for him. Casually, as if Oliver's visit was not his first, as if Oliver showed evidence of having been born in a shed and did not quite know how to close a door.

"Want some cider, then?" asked Jack. "It's on the house. Or gin, you'd rather that, I reckon."

Oliver looked at him, holding his empty delivery basket between them, standing in the flow of working men that continued their passage, snaking like a river, in and out of the door. The voice was overly friendly, but those eyes appraised him, not ready to be truly welcoming until Jack was good and ready.

"Been making deliveries, Oliver?" asked Jack now, moving in close, and with both his hands, reaching out to run over the trim of Oliver's lapels. It was a move that felt familiar, and Oliver stepped back. "They'll be missin' you, them that gave you them togs, you think?"

"No," said Oliver shortly, though the statement didn't surprise him. "They won't. I'll be going now." Of course he would be going back; even Jack wouldn't dream of stopping him. Even if the men with their elbows at the bar were starting to eye him as though he was a prize bullock at a fair.

"Comin' all this way just to leave your card, eh?" Jack tipped back his head with a laugh then settled for giving Oliver a rough pat. "You're here; you might as well wait as Morris'll be along any time now."

Jack led Oliver into the first room off the main room, a small alcove that had a table and pair of bench seats in the corner near a small coal fire. From the rooms down the corridor beyond, Oliver could smell yeasty bread and grease that said something was frying. Jack sat with his back to the wall, near the fire. Oliver saw the clay pipe sitting in a small dish, oozing smoke, and the sight of it brought back a rush of not altogether unpleasant memories from the past.

As Jack pulled Oliver to sit down across from him, Jack gestured with wide arms, smiling honestly now.

"Sit down, Oliver; there, that's better, isn't it? And there he is, the man of the hour. Come, Oliver, say hello."

Oliver couldn't imagine who Jack might know that knew him and had also been in Fagin's gang, it just didn't make sense. But his curiosity overrode his irritation, and so he turned slowly in his seat and looked.

The man coming through the low doorway had long arms and legs that poked out of once well-made jacket sleeves and trousers. His hat was off, but he touched his forehead to Oliver, those fingers brushing straw-dark hair above glittering eyes. He came close, standing near enough to Oliver so that the tin-smelling cologne and the sour smell of unwashed linen overpowered the smoke of the coal fire. Oliver's mind formed a question as though it were trying to solve a puzzle he'd forgotten he'd set it to.

The man smiled, showing an eyetooth lapped across a fore tooth, and with a lopsided grin said, slowly, "'Ello, Work'us."

"Noah," said Oliver, not believing it, though his stomach felt as if it had warded off a blow, and he cringed inside, imagining that more blows were to come. "Noah Claypole."

"His name's Morris Bolter," said Jack, almost laughing as if Oliver were playing a joke on him. "Like I told you. Morris Bolter from Fagin's gang. The one I told you of—"

"Yes, I know," said Oliver, not heeding his own rudeness as shock ripped away any semblance of manners he might hope to hold on to. "Morris Bolter, as you said, but this is Noah Claypole, for all he's anyone else."

"Same as was," said Noah, his voice the same as it had been many years ago, mocking, slippery, but much deeper now. He had the breadth of a man across his shoulders and towered over Oliver as he always had. "One in the same, actually. Bolter is me workin' name, as it was when I worked for Fagin."

"Then it's true," said Oliver. One look at Jack told him that Jack had no problems with not knowing all of Noah's aliases; he was too dashed with pride that he'd been right and that Oliver had been wrong about one of Fagin's old gang having come back. No doubt he'd be rubbing it in with much salt later.

"Of course it's true, Oliver," said Jack. "And here I was tellin' Morris, I mean, Noah, all about you, and that you'd already met. What a laugh it is!"

"Work'us and I met, right enough, and you an' I, Jack, almost met that day in the courthouse, though you probably don't remember it."

Noah looked a little smug at Jack's pleased expression. Oliver had the impression, right away, that Noah had a great many of these little story tidbits that he had been, and would be, feeding to Jack, little by little, to keep him hanging on.

"'Course, I don't know as what the record books say, but I was there, right enough, an' didn't I run straight to Fagin to tell him all about it? I reckon I did, an' he was as pleased as he could be."

"You'll tell me the story, won't you?" said Jack. "We'll have drinks an' talk around the fire; that's what gentlemen do, ain't it, Oliver?"

Jack reached across the table and gave Oliver a generous smack on his shoulders, and Oliver jerked away, gritting his teeth, not saying it, but wanting to. Jack was falling in with this lout who professed to know Jack's story as well as his own, and that was something that Jack would not be able to resist.

"How do you two know each other?" Jack's eyes were on Oliver now, fully, glinting green and brown all at once in his excitement. "I'll wager you never expected to meet each other here, then, eh?"

Oliver felt his eyes grow hot at Noah's smile, which always had, now that he recalled, the ability to get him worked up with a mere twitch. Then, when Oliver's feathers were well and truly ruffled, he'd throw on a comment or two and watch the fire explode into temper, which would always get Oliver into trouble.

"Work'us," said Noah, as a tear rolled down Oliver's cheek. "What's set you a-sniveling now?"

"Not you," replied Oliver, hastily brushing the tear away. "Don't think it."

"Oh, not me, eh?" sneered Noah.

"No, not you," replied Oliver sharply. "There, that's enough. Don't say anything more to me about her, you'd better not!"

"Better not!" exclaimed Noah. "But you must know, Work'us, your mother was a regular right-down bad 'un."

"What did you say?" inquired Oliver, looking up very quickly.

"A regular right-down bad 'un, Work'us," replied Noah, coolly. "An' it's a great deal better, Work'us, that she died when she did, or else she'd have been hard laboring in Bridewell, or transported, or hung: which is more likely than either, isn't it?"

Noah's smile now showed that he'd not forgotten this power he'd once had, and Oliver made his heart settle in his chest and vowed that he'd not let Noah get to him. Not yet, anyway.

"We met," began Noah in the wake of Oliver's silence, "at Sowerberry's undertaker shop, back in Hardingstone. Oliver was the workhouse boy brought to tend to the shop while I learnt the funeral business. Then, after he was promoted to mute, ahead of me, mind you, Oliver ran off, an' I figured, soon after, that dead folks were of no interest to me, in spite of the money to be made. We're both shet of that place, ain't we, Work'us?"

"What?" asked Jack.

"'E's a workhouse boy, ain't he?" said Noah, nodding in Oliver's direction. "But 'e was such a mite of a thing when he came in, I 'ad to shorten the word just to match his stature. But didn't he grow!" Noah tossed back his head to laugh. "Just like the missus said he would, grew right out of his station, an' that's the last we saw of him. Won't they be surprised to know I found you 'ere."

"You won't be writing to him," said Oliver, the words clipped off. "Besides, they already know."

"No, no," said Noah, reaching out in what he was probably sure would be calculated as a friendly gesture, thumping Oliver on the chest. "If I was to tell them where you were, I'd have to tell them where I was, an' I'm afraid I can't do that."

"Why?" asked Oliver with a snap. "Because you made off with the master's silver?"

Jack roared at this. Roared as loudly as Charley Bates would have done, and at something completely illegal, and for one moment it was as if the spirit of Fagin's gang was alive and dancing right there around them.

"What a treat," said Jack, gesturing across to them with his hands as if to draw them close to each other. "I propose we toast this with a round of beer!"

"My friend, you are too generous," said Noah. "But I must be away, as I am expected in court soon to bear witness to some horrible, though not capital, crimes."

"Come by later, then," said Jack in return, giving him several stout pats. "The beer will be as cold as ever it lasts. An' you an' your old mate Oliver can catch up an' tell me stories of your adventures in the coffin business."

"Indeed, I shall, an' I shall look forward to it." Noah gave Oliver a slanted smile and a wink. "You an' me in front of the fireplace; just like old times, Work'us?"

Oliver had clamped his mouth so firmly closed that he could not speak. But Jack was watching, so hopeful and expectant, that Oliver made himself nod. He didn't know why he was staying even this long; perhaps Jack's world was so different from the haberdashery shop that it invited, by mere curiosity, further inspection.

"Don't mind him, Noah," said Jack, emphasizing the new name with a nod. "He's a little wound, comin' in here, steppin' lightly as if he were a thief comin' into a den of peelers and traps, instead of the other way around!"

This lively statement earned Jack a roar of approval from Noah and more thumping of Oliver's shoulders. Oliver could only scowl and didn't stop, even though something flitted across Jack's eyes, and surely he knew that all was not right? That he and Noah were not friends, never had been. Never would be.

Jack shook Noah's hand and watched him go, turning to Oliver with a broad smile.

"Fancy you knowin' him, Oliver; why did you never say?"

"You said his name was Morris Bolter," said Oliver. His mouth felt stiff; in fact all of him did with the shock of Noah's return. "I only ever knew him as Noah Claypole."

This made Jack nod as if the sense of it were all very clear to him now. "Still, it's strange, ain't it? That our paths seem to all cross here, at the Three Cripples?"

It did seem rather strange, though Oliver let this though distract him for only a moment. The immediate concerns of whether or not this visit with Jack and Noah would suffice outweighed the comfortably distant, philosophical question of how different rivers of time could carry twigs from different mountains to the same gritty pond.

Jack moved to wave over a serving of beer, still smiling as though pleased about the fact that Oliver was wrong, that Fagin's gang was coming back to him.

There was a movement in the crowd, and Oliver sought to use it as an excuse to leave but was stopped as men shifted aside to let someone through, and a man came into the alcove to stand beside their table. He was tall, his broad shoulders stretching the thick cotton of his shirt to the breaking point. His stained vest gaped open from a missing button. He had a scarf around his neck, as many working men did. But what stood him out was his mass of curly, dark hair that hung low over his eyes, and a broken tooth when he smiled.

"Who's this, then, dear Jack, as you have come visiting amongst us?" His voice was ragged, as though he'd been punched in the throat one too many times.

"This here's me mate, Oliver Twist," said Jack, and while Oliver wanted to object to the term, he didn't; the man was looking at him too hard, with sharp eyes, eyes that probably saw Oliver as he twitched and tried not to shift away. "I've known him since before I was hextricated, you see, and now, well, he's come by to visit, haven't you, Oliver?"

Oliver nodded. He didn't hold out his hand to shake be-cause, in this sort of place, with these sort of people, it simply wasn't done. Greetings were done by shouts and slaps on the back, an elbow in the ribs. At least that's what he'd seen in his travels, such as they were.

But the man held out his hand; there were calluses along his fingers and the edge of his palm that spoke of handling hard tools. "I'm Cromwell, they call me. Never had a first name, so I might pick one someday."

There was nothing for Oliver to do but shake the hand in return; the skin felt like worn wood left out in the sun, and he pulled his hand away as fast as he was able. The feeling re-minded him of the time he'd been with Bill Sikes and Toby Crackit on a job to rob a house of all its silver plate.

"Well, I'm off, then," said Cromwell with a toss of his curls. "Jack, you come by later about that job. An' bring your friend, if he's interested. There's plenty we could do with a pretty face such as that."

Jack nodded his assent and smiled at Oliver as Cromwell left. "One for you?" he asked. He seemed to take it for granted that since Oliver was there he might stay awhile.

"No," said Oliver, all at once feeling the boundaries between their respective lives as clear as daylight. "I've got work to do. For unlike some, I've a job, and a station in life that I aim to keep."

Jack took the pot of beer that was served to him, but he was scowling now, and Oliver realized he might have made a mistake in making Jack angry. And just when he was on the verge of getting Jack out of his life forever.

"And I'm sure you have more important things to do as well," said Oliver. He tugged at his scarf and adjusted his cap. "More important than entertaining the likes of me. It's just that—" He broke off, not knowing quite how to put it. Though he questioned his own gentleness with Jack, he could not afford to have Jack stomping through his life, breaking it apart just as Oliver was building it up.

"You're not to worry, it's my word," said Jack, after a swallow of beer. "I've given it. Won't go back on it, even if you are an arse."

Oliver nodded, and turned to go. But Jack tugged on his jacket, just once, as if to make Oliver stay. Picking up his empty basket, Oliver made himself pause to hear what Jack wanted to say. It wasn't his fault that Morris Bolter turned out to be one of the few people that Oliver hated with every breath in his body.

"You're always welcome though," Jack said, and for once he seemed in earnest. He evidenced no winking or smirking or larking about as though the whole thing was one big joke. "For some hot gin an' sugar, a break from that fancy life of yours. I could show you my tattoo an' we could be swappin' stories, an' that. You reckon?"

"I doubt it," said Oliver. He kept his voice low. "But thank you."

He tipped his cap at Jack and then turned to plow his way through the crowd that had assembled in the main room. The faces in the throng of men all turned to watch him as through surprised to find him there. And if that was so, then they were as surprised as he was. For though he must have been in or near the Three Cripples at some point, when Fagin held him, he did not remember any of it. And now, he felt he might not forget it.

CHAPTER 16

The Consequences Of A Broken Stove

For several days, Oliver felt something sharp in his chest at the memory of Noah Claypole and his oily smile, and Jack, so happy that Fagin's gang was, in his mind, getting back together again. Everything at the shop, however, and in spite of Oliver's distracted thoughts, went on as usual, with work in the warehouse, cleaning the front steps and pavement, and making deliveries. Each night, at the table in the warm kitchen, with Mr. McCready and the boys and Mrs. Pierson bustling about, he would try to read from his book of poems, or even one of the children's books, but his eyes would close as the candlelight started to gutter while Tate and Henry muttered at each other and Mr. McCready scowled at the newspaper.

When it started to get cold again, and his chance to get out of the shop abated, he worked with Tate in the warehouse, making up new record books by lining ledgers with a piece of lead and a ruler to make the lines straight. Tate admired Oliver's workmanship, though he wouldn't yet let Oliver write in any of the record books regarding the stock. That was Tate's job, and he was very jealous of his position.

Oliver looked at Tate and thought, suddenly, how different he was from Jack. Or from himself. Or from Uncle Brownlow, for that matter. Uncle Brownlow, who was unfailingly polite to one and all and who never reflected even the slightest bit of jealousy toward his fellow man.

It came at him, a slamming weight, and almost seemed too much to bear. He hadn't felt this way for days, so why now? Why this sudden, dark grief? He had to pause at the bottom of the warehouse stairs as though he was adjusting his apron and turn away toward the wall, to take a deep breath and tell himself that now was not the time. To cry over Uncle Brownlow and that life he once knew was to lose it; while the memory hurt, it was still fresh. And mixed with that was the recent dredging up of Noah Claypole, someone who Oliver had never expected to see again in his life. And then there was Jack; Oliver had no idea what to do with his uncertain feelings about Jack.

He took a deep breath and turned back toward the warehouse, toward the balm that untold hearts before him had found, that of industry. Thankfully, there were always shelves to dust, floors to sweep, and the pavement in front of the shop to keep clear of snow and litter and dirt. Stocking tape had to be rushed to Henry in the shop, and the lady patrons who deigned to brave the cold, as always, needed something desperately, something they could have done without, but would never suffer themselves to do so: corset strings, a new hat pin, garters for their husbands.

For all of his deliveries, either quick and close by or most of the way across London, Oliver took particular care for any

deliveries to Number 14 Doughty Street. He did not want to
see Mrs. Acton again, let alone be put in a position where he'd
have to detach her claws from his arm. Mostly, he did not
want to give her any excuse to complain to Mr. McCready
about how he'd behaved with her. She'd proven herself to be
flighty and cruel, so when there were packages that needed to
go to her townhouse, Oliver ensured that Mrs. Acton wasn't
at home, even if he had to go back two or three times and thus
be delayed finishing up for the day.

And ever, with relaxing regularity, deliveries came through
the tall gates at the back of the yard, and the goods were accounted for as they came off flat-bedded wagons or high-sided
carts. Horses stomped over the cobblestones in the yard, chip-
ping edges and leaving their droppings and puddles of urine.
Oliver poured himself into tending to all of it, wanting to be
exhausted at bedtime.

At the end of the week, Oliver woke to the cold and the
sound of rain smacking on the windowpane. He got up and
washed his face in the cold water, not rolling up the sleeves of
his nightshirt as far as the scar, as always, so that neither
Henry nor Tate would have any questions to ask. Then he
hurriedly dressed in the chill air and tagged behind Henry and
Tate down the stairs to the kitchen to find Mrs. Pierson red-
faced, hair trailing in wisps against her cheeks, quite unlike
her. There was dust on her chin and on her white starched
apron. The stove was boiling with smoke that filled up the
room. Standing next to her, Mr. McCready pressed his mouth
tightly together as he listened to her through her tears.

"Last night was bad enough, with that girl taking off the way she did. I let it go and did the washing up myself. But *today?* She never even showed up, so by the time I came down, there's no stove lit, no hot water going, no breakfast set out for me to cook, and so now it's only me with all the shopping and cooking *and* cleaning!"

"I'll get you a new girl," said Mr. McCready in a tight way that told Oliver that he was struggling to keep his voice calm. For if he lost his temper then Mrs. Pierson would surely lose hers, and they would lose a cook and a housekeeper, something Oliver couldn't imagine was easily replaceable in the middle of winter.

"It won't be enough!" Mrs. Pierson's voice rose in a way Oliver had never heard it. "I've been struggling with stiffness and aches and pains this past year, so it's not enough! You may sack me if you will, this moment if you must, but I cannot abide those stairs another day. Let alone carrying coal and cleaning three fireplaces and hauling hot water, day after day—" She broke off, clutching her handkerchief to her mouth.

Oliver looked at Henry and Tate and they at him, and none of them dared move, let alone laugh, not while smoke loomed over the room. Presently, Oliver determined to open the door to the kitchen area, which he did. The smoke eased out while the colder air from the street rushed in.

Mr. McCready looked like he wanted to comfort Mrs. Pierson somehow, but one didn't actually touch a housekeeper, let alone hug her. At least not in Mr. McCready's book. Had this been Mrs. Bedwin sobbing into her handkerchief, Oliver would have run to her without a thought and wrapped his arms around her and begged her not to cry and for her to tell him what was wrong and what he might do to fix it. The memory was so strong he could almost feel Mrs. Bedwin's pillowy bosom beneath his cheek, and the edges of her white muslin pelerine against his skin. *Tell me what I can do to aid you, my dear Mrs. Bedwin, and I shall fix it at once.*

"Oliver."

Oliver snapped to attentiveness, focusing his eyes on Mr. McCready, though it took him some seconds longer to force the image of Mrs. Bedwin back into that of Mrs. Pierson. Who, though just as respectable and as kind, would never have the creamy, grandmotherly softness of Mrs. Bedwin.

"Oliver, pay attention and close that door. It is quite fresh in here."

Oliver blinked a few times and then did as he was told, all the while sensing Henry and Tate shuffling from foot to foot, seeming to be at a loss as to whether or not they should sit down or depart.

"My dear Mrs. Pierson—Henry, make her a pot of tea—do sit down, Mrs. Pierson."

Mrs. Pierson sat down, something Oliver had rarely seen her do, even in her own kitchen. As she sat in a chair at the end of the table, her respectable black skirts fanned out around her, and her apron crumpled in her lap. She wiped her eyes with her handkerchief and seemed to compose herself.

"There won't be any tea, because the stove won't light. 'Tis broken!"

"The stove won't light?" Mr. McCready seemed astonished by this.

"It's been broken for weeks now," said Mrs. Pierson in a cracked voice.

"But it's been working all this time."

"That girl had a knack, which is why—"

"But why did you not tell me the stove was broken, Mrs. Pierson? And how long has it been thus?"

Her handkerchief now soaked, Mrs. Pierson buried her face in her apron and sobbed anew. Henry and Tate inched toward the stairs; Oliver remained frozen where he was, mesmerized. He'd never seen anyone collapse in this way.

"Because I broke it just after Christmas, and I didn't want you to dismiss me."

Mr. McCready's mouth flew open, and for a moment, no one said anything. Indeed, Oliver didn't know what could be said. But the situation was desperate, even he could see that. Mrs. Pierson was the best cook, bar none. Even Mrs. Bedwin hadn't been able to find someone with such a sure hand at roasting a chicken or making a crust for an apple tart that melted on the tongue. If McCready's Haberdashery lost her, they would be hard pressed to find another like her.

Mr. McCready sat at the table next to Mrs. Pierson, and reached out to pat her arm, but then, at the last moment, pulled back.

"My dear Mrs. Pierson," he said as gently as he might to one of his most timid customers. "That stove is not the youngest of its kind, I'm afraid, and even the stoutest of metal can suffer wear and tear."

Mrs. Pierson used the edge of her apron to dry her eyes. She looked at him, a little color coming back to her streaked face. "But who will fix it? And what about—"

"I will send for a blacksmith to fix the stove."

"But what if it can't be fixed?"

"Then we shall get a new one."

"And the stairs? What about them? I can't take all those stairs any longer."

"We'll get you a hired girl. A respectable one from the Collins Agency, you know the one."

Oliver wondered if there had ever been a risk of saying good-bye to those mouthwatering pies or if this had been a ploy of Mrs. Pierson's all along. For there seemed to be a small glint in her eyes; the cold kitchen and lack of anything to eat— the whole of it was too grand a tableau for a woman who planned her day's cooking and cleaning as though she was an army general. It was a grand scheme indeed to get what she wanted, if not a new stove, then a working one. And not just some help, but a reliable girl, a top-notch girl from a top-notch agency.

"Those types are too haughty for words," said Mrs. Pierson. But she was sitting up straight now, tucking her dark hair back under her cap. She almost seemed to smile as she said, "Too haughty to take orders from a common housekeeper and cook, and with hands too fine to clean a stove, let alone light it. I've seen girls from that agency; too haughty for words, I tell you."

"We'll get you a boy as well," said Mr. McCready. "He can take care of the lower sort of work."

Oliver could see it as if it had already been done. If Mrs. Pierson had a hired girl from the Collins Agency, and a boy as well, she would be able to lord it over her friends and other housekeepers along the lane. Not only that, she would be able to drop it in casual conversation after church.

"Then I shall put it to you, Mrs. Pierson. You shall dress in your best, this very day, and with a clean face, go to Collins and select the girl yourself."

"But what about breakfast?"

Mrs. Pierson looked up as if suddenly seeing the three apprentice boys standing there amidst the wreck of the cold and ash-dusted kitchen. Apprentices she looked after going hungry? *Perish* the thought. Mr. McCready looked up at them also, regarding them each with a solemn eye.

"We have a reputation to uphold, Mrs. Pierson. No girl is too fine for this establishment. You go and sign up whomever you please. And in the meantime, Henry and Tate and Oliver shall have—"

"There is no food, Mr. McCready," said Mrs. Pierson. She stood up, tucking her handkerchief into her apron pocket, from which she pulled out a piece of paper. "There is only what can been cooked, which nothing can be, and the last of the loaf of bread went at tea time yesterday, and this is my shopping list. There is simply nothing to eat."

She held out the scrap of paper as though it were a ticket of admittance.

Mr. McCready stood up at this, almost smiling. He reached into the pocket on the inside of his jacket and pulled out his change purse, from which he counted some coins. "Boys, come here."

When they did, he handed them each a tuppence.

"Coffee and bread on the street till the stove is fixed today."

To Mrs. Pierson, he handed a five-pound note before putting his wallet back in his inside jacket pocket. "To put on the account and for groceries. You have the girl help you with the shopping on your way back from the agency."

"And the coal?" asked Mrs. Pierson smartly as she folded the bill in her hand. "Who will carry that?"

Oliver's mouth was watering at the thought of coffee and buttered bread from a street vendor. Mrs. Pierson's bread was, of course, miles above the rest. But there was something about sipping hot dark coffee from a metal cup while standing in the street as a cold wind whistled past. It made the coffee warmer and more darkly rich somehow. And the buttered bread, slightly coarse and so sweet between sips of dark coffee. Then of course, the last time he'd stood at a coffee vendor's was with Jack when he'd stolen Oliver's pennies.

Jack had smacked his lips over that stolen repast, his mouth glistening with butter, puffs of coffee-flavored steam exuding from his mouth with each chomp. He'd only laughed when Oliver had reached for his red scarf; Oliver had known he'd never get it back. But the memory of the smell of the hot coffee and Jack's still-new presence had struck him all the days since.

"Henry and Tate will put a sign in the window, keeping the shop closed till noon. And then they will go to Mueller's down on Broad Street and tell him of the stove and hire his services. Mrs. Pierson will hire a girl."

Again Mr. McCready's words broke through Oliver's reverie. His empty palm reflected the fact that Mr. McCready had not given Oliver a tuppence as he had Henry and Tate.

"And what shall I do, sir?" he asked, thinking that Mr. McCready might have him sort through the new stock in the warehouse. The little box stove there worked, at least, and the peace and quiet might be nice.

"You and I shall tend to the matter of a boy," said Mr. McCready. "We'll go over to St. James's Workhouse over on Poland Street; they'll like as not have something."

Oliver nodded. It didn't even take him a moment to recall that the workhouse at St. James was the closest. He'd passed it sometimes when making his deliveries, and when he couldn't avoid going past it, he averted his eyes. His only picture of the place had been through mere sideways glances: the severe, dark grey edges of the roofline and the dark green paint on the pointed iron gates, the semicircular sign above the gate, iron letters spelling out the name.

His feet felt cold as if someone had dropped him in the icy water of the Thames. He looked up at Mr. McCready, mouth working as he tried to come up with a single thought that he could turn into an utterance that might excuse him from such an errand.

"Caps and coats and scarves, boys," said Mr. McCready. He gave Mrs. Pierson a slight nod. "Get the finest girl you might hire, Mrs. Pierson. Come along, Oliver, we've a boy to find."

Feeling numb from the waist up, his feet frozen and heavy, Oliver followed Mr. McCready up the stairs to the small back hallway. There he gathered his cap and his brown coat and green scarf, which still felt new and a little bit stiff against his neck, but at least it was warm.

As they stepped out the front door and shut it firmly behind them, the day was quite rainy and almost cold enough for now. With the rain beating down on the top of his cap, Oliver shivered. A low dread began to fill him as they headed toward the lane where St. James's steeple broke above the sharp, slate-covered roofline. The bell began tolling nine o'clock, and with each tone of the bell, Oliver shuddered. He'd lived all of his life within the sound of one bell or another, but this was the first time he'd felt a sense that the sound was something fearsome, marking, rather than the hour or a call to prayers, a call to some more awful fate.

"You look a trifle pale, Oliver. Shall we stop for a bite to eat?"

They were passing the Crown and Miter, a higher class tavern than the Three Cripples could ever hope to be, and just then the door opened to push out the smell of something hot frying, pork perhaps, and the smoky warmth of pipes being smoked. Mr. McCready led the way in through the push of people, mostly gentlemen in dark coats, not waiting for Oliver's reply.

And perhaps he did not need one, for it appeared that if one was with the master, one didn't breakfast on mere coffee and two slices of buttered bread. Perhaps, also, it was the emptiness of Oliver's stomach, which was filling him with such unease. Usually by this hour, he was well finished with his breakfast. His unusual sense of fear, then, was hunger and nothing more. He told himself this.

A pleasant woman in a starched apron and cap led them to a table near the fire and brought two bowls of coffee without being asked. Oliver lifted the bowl with both hands and took a tentative sip. The coffee was new; it was early in the day, so it tasted sweet with sugar rather than bitterness.

Mr. McCready ordered some cold meat and whatever hot bread was just come out of the oven. Then Oliver and Mr. McCready both sipped their coffee, holding onto their bowls with both hands, warming their fingers. They shared a silent moment, enjoying the cheer of the fire and the convivial company of the warm room.

The food came, slices of cold ham and twisted, crusty bread so warm the butter dripped off the slice that Oliver prepared for himself. As he stuffed it in his mouth, he thought that this surely was much better than standing in the street drinking from a metal cup. Better and warmer and surely more respectable. But he was enjoying almost none of it.

"This workhouse boy," said Mr. McCready, cutting up slices of ham with a clink of his knife on the plate, "he can do the rough work so you won't have coal dust all over you when you go out for deliveries. What do you say to that?"

Oliver tried to keep his face a complete blank and to keep eating. But he felt the blood rushing around inside of him, doing something harsh that made him want to spit out what he had in his mouth. His fingers and toes had gone numb besides. There was no way he would ever want to step foot inside of a workhouse, let alone to go to one to acquire a boy to do the rough work. He knew how it would go, *exactly* how it would begin, and afterward, how it would be. Workhouse boys were grimy little creatures, despised by all and pitied by none.

Mr. McCready was a genial enough man when things were going as he wanted them, but Oliver knew the truth of it. The orphan they acquired would be scrawny to begin with. He would do all the drudge work and be subject to the most basic of care, if that, and Mr. McCready wouldn't think anything of it. That's just how workhouse boys were treated, and after all, the workhouse always had plenty of them to spare. Not to mention that Oliver would be required to look at that face, where he would see his own past, twisting along a long, scarred string, leading right back to Hardingstone and Mrs. Mann's baby farm, and to Dick, who he last saw weeding in a garden. He'd done his very best to forget about Dick with his angled face and thin shoulders and a heart so good it shone from beneath his rags. Oliver shuddered all over.

"Oliver, I'm speaking to you."

Oliver could only look at him as he forced himself to swallow the tasteless mass that was in his mouth.

"I must say, I would have expected you to be more excited about the prospect, for it will, in a way, take you up a notch up in the shop. You'll no longer be the newest boy, eh?"

"Yes," said Oliver, though his voice sounded faint to his own ears. "It's just that—"

He paused, thinking of a way to explain how he felt about all of this, which was, even now, a twisted mass inside of his brain. He could not explain how he felt every time he passed the gates of a workhouse. Or how it made him tense up to see a small boy or a young girl in the street, who were, by their clothes and demeanor, instantly recognized as being very poor and probably hungry; each time, Oliver had to fight against the hope of doing anything about it.

And it wasn't just the chimney sweeps or the crossing boys or boys hauling carts way too large and heavy for their skinny arms. It wasn't just the beggars, or those faded, grey-faced girls selling useless trinkets from trays slung from their necks. It wasn't even what they did or didn't do—it was *all* of them, the looks in their eyes, their sunken cheeks and unwashed faces. He didn't want to be around it at all, and up till the time of Uncle Brownlow's death, he'd been able to do that. To avoid anything that smacked of it. Until now.

"I sense that you are uncomfortable with workhouses, Oliver," said Mr. McCready. His gaze was steady and his eyes solemn as he put down his knife and fork. "Mr. Grimwig indicated to me that you suffered badly at the workhouse you came from. And I imagine you still suffer mental anguish at the death of the guardian who took you from that life."

Mr. McCready took a sip of his coffee and scanned the room with its dark-coated customers. They were mostly men, but there were two black-garbed women at the table near the window, partaking of a small meal of meat pies and sliced fruit.

"I am coming to realize that you are loathe to have anything to do with our business this morning, the way your brow looks as though it were lowered by some oncoming doom. But not all workhouses are fully bad, Oliver. Don't you see? They do a great deal of good for the indigent and the poor. And if we take a boy, surely he'll be treated better among us, and with food and useful work, will be a more productive member of society?"

Oliver wanted to stand up and shove the table back and let his rage be expressed with his words as he shouted that Mr. McCready didn't have any idea what he was talking about. Because if Mr. McCready thought that workhouses did a *great deal of good*, then Mr. McCready might as well be living with his head in a barrel. Workhouses, any workhouse, did nothing good, nothing of the sort. They stripped the soul and beat any hope out of the body, and starved and smacked and locked up any gentleness till all that was left were the bones and some rude, leftover animation to keep those bones going till they dropped.

And though his heart was beating fast, Oliver kept his hands in his lap and his jaw stiff. He looked at Mr. McCready as steadily as he could.

"Must I go, sir?"

"Yes, Oliver, you must. For who knows more about workhouse boys than you? I need your keen eye. Finish up, and then we'll be off."

Oliver felt Mr. McCready's eyes on him. He made himself eat and respond to a polite request for the salt.

"All is well, Oliver?" asked Mr. McCready at one point.

"Yes, sir," said Oliver, trying for an assuredness that would stop Mr. McCready from looking at him in that way and asking Oliver questions he couldn't possibly respond truthfully to. "It's just a little strange, going back like this."

"Indeed, it must be," said Mr. McCready.

CHAPTER 17

Treats of St. James's Workhouse And The Orphan

Oliver wanted to drag his feet as he walked along beside Mr. McCready, but it wouldn't do. If Mr. McCready noticed Oliver's reluctance, it would give a lie to Oliver's assertions that he wasn't troubled at all by going to acquire a likely boy. Workhouses were scattered all about the City, and he'd passed the very one they were headed to a time or two, so surely going inside would be no more troublesome than any delivery he'd been on for the shop.

What was more disconcerting, at any rate, was the fact that Mr. McCready and Mr. Grimwig had exchanged words about him, and he'd not known until now. Whether that exchange had been by post or in person didn't matter because either way Mr. McCready knew whatever Mr. Grimwig had seen fit to impart that would have cast Oliver in a less than sterling light. However slight or great Oliver's fears, it was to be sure that Mr. Grimwig would have described them as badly as possible. And now Mr. McCready knew something Oliver had been only dimly aware of until that very morning.

Even more unnerving than that was the fact that Mr. Grimwig had seen this in Oliver. Enough to take it, understand it, and communicate it to another person. And all while Oliver had been himself blithely unaware.

Yes, he was conscious of having crossed over to the other side of the street, however broad or narrow, rather than having to pass directly in front of the gate to *any* workhouse. And yes, he'd skirt quickly past blind beggars. He had ignored the ragged woman, there was one on every corner it seemed, who held out her little one, raggedly bundled, tiny bare feet exposed, stained with mud and blue with cold, and begged with a loud voice devoid of shame and broken with worry. Or the little girl in her shabby broken bonnet who he'd seen often by the haberdashery; he'd ignored her too. Ignored her proffered silk flower drawn from a basket of them, a tumble of purple and pink against the grey snow where she'd set it down.

Besides that, all the beggars smelled—of dirt from the streets, from barefoot walks through overflowing basement cesspits, with mud dried on every edge of their sparse clothing, and they all had the dark tang of unwashed skin that was spotted with sores. A week's worth of good soap and hot water would have done miracles for many, but Oliver had none to spare. Never did, never would. But still, they all looked at him, speculative and with hopeful eyes, begging him to search his pockets, his heart.

He'd rushed past them all, never handing out so much as a farthing; he'd been in the same circumstances, and look how far he'd come. Let them all pull themselves out of their respective gutters as Oliver Twist had.

St. James's Workhouse loomed in front of them before Oliver was properly ready. The building rose, grey and hard, above the walls surrounding it and the wrought-iron gate, which was spiked with a half circle above proclaiming the name. There were more iron spikes that embellished the top of the stone wall that ran all the way around the workhouse grounds, walls which were there to keep people out or in at the parish's pleasure, it didn't matter the reason why. The spikes made a boundary between the two worlds, maintaining the distance between hopelessness and hope, though with the sounds of industry and of protest from inside along with the dark low bell that was forever ringing, the hopelessness continually oozed into the street, reaching Oliver in a way that he'd known for nine years of his life before leaving it behind.

Mr. McCready rang the bell pull at the gate and waited, looking down at Oliver with a benign smile. All was well with Mr. McCready, of course; in his mind, he was performing a duty that had a dual benefit to the world around him. The first was relieving the parish of its obligation to a pauper, and the second was providing his newest apprentice with a trial by fire that could only prove to be to his benefit. Oliver could see this in Mr. McCready's eyes, with the cordial way he greeted the stiff-collared porter at the gate, in the polite way he announced their business there.

"We've got a number of likely lads," said the porter. "Come away into the office and we can discuss the particulars."

Oliver's whole body felt tight as he followed Mr. McCready and the porter along the cobbled walk through the stone forecourt, his eyes briefly alighting on the female paupers all around. They were dressed as he once had been, in brown uniforms, but it was not the same as the rich, deep, warm brown he now wore. No, the pauper's brown was faded, as if even the dye used had been too meager of strength to do more than stain the cloth. Their faces were thin and pale, their unwashed hair covered with grey caps.

Oliver raised his eyes to look once into one face, and even that was way too upsetting. After a fleeting second of seeing that hopeless, *hopeless* hungry expression, he had to look away. Thereafter, he kept his eyes down, looking only at the hem of Mr. McCready's greatcoat or the steepled clasp of his own hands. It was safer. It provided no chance for anyone to look back at him.

Once inside the building, the porter led them down a short, dark hallway to his office, which was a small room with two high windows crossed with bars on the outside. There was a shelf with around ten books and a large table that served as a desk. The porter invited them to sit in the two chairs across from him.

Once seated, Oliver pulled off his cap and let—no *forced*—his mind to wander. He didn't want to participate in the exchange of conversation for a boy. *A likely lad*, the porter was saying, *of about ten years or so, the going rate, five pounds, of course.*

Suddenly, the whole outing felt more as though it resembled the descriptions of the slave trade such as he'd read about in America. He clamped his jaw shut, feeling his stomach roll. Not wanting to think of it now, not wanting to thinking of it as it had happened then.

"Dear me, he's very small."

"Why, he is rather small; he is small. There's no denying. But he'll grow, Mrs. Sowerberry, he'll grow."

"*Ah! I dare say he will on our victuals and our drink. I see no saving in parish children, not I; for they always cost more to keep than they're worth. However, men always think they know best. There! Get down stairs, little bag o' bones.*"

The memory felt as though someone had slapped him right across his face, bare skin stinging with the echo of those words. Mrs. Sowerberry had never liked him, and while it seemed at the time that nobody had, she was so intent with her hatred and scorn that she had never hesitated in letting him know it.

The porter clapped open a ledger and Oliver started in his chair. His eyes were riveted as the porter ran his finger down the page.

"Yes, this is the one," said the porter. "Martin, aged ten. Christian name, Gregory, and the parents, well, the mother, dropped him off last summer and never came back for him. He's not as rough as most; he should do for you very nicely."

Mr. McCready took his wallet out of the breast pocket of his suitcoat and unfolded it. He crinkled the five-pound note between his fingers a moment before he handed it over. The porter took it, laid it on the desk, and pulled out a sheet of paper. He picked up his pen and dipped it in ink then looked at Mr. McCready as he tapped off the excess.

"We'll make it for three months to ensure he suits. Will that do, Mr. McCready?"

"Will that do, Oliver?" asked Mr. McCready, breaking through the cloud around Oliver's head. "Oliver?"

Oliver blinked and ran his fingers across the brow band of his cap. Telling himself that he'd not lost all feeling in his hand from clutching the cap too tightly.

"Looks as though he seems a bit reluctant, sir," said the porter.

"Oliver? You have been asked a question, and you would do well to answer it."

Now, Oliver had to look up and focus to take in the expectant face of the porter and Mr. McCready. To see the five-pound note, a shining, gold-edged white thing on the dark blotter on the porter's desk. To see the sensible, plain wallpaper framing the large casement of a window that looked out into a small yard, cobbled with walls of grey stone. And beyond that, another wall of stone. The meager light that could barely get in through the glass, the stone walls through which no one could get out.

His throat went dry, and the two faces in front of him began to swim in a hazy way, back and forth. He felt Mr. McCready's hands on his shoulders, and realized Mr. McCready was standing in front of him. He felt a light tap on his cheek.

"Oliver! What's wrong with you, are you ill?"

Oliver heard the question from a distance, as though his whole body was rushing through air, toward the sound of Mr. McCready's voice and then away from it at the same time. Then he felt the rush of cold as wood slid against wood, and he realized that the porter had opened the window. Oliver took a deep gasp of air and tried to narrow in on Mr. McCready's voice.

"I had the windows closed against the morning chill," said the porter. "It does get somewhat stuffy in here; I do apologize."

"It's nothing," said Mr. McCready. "Oliver, are you all right now?"

Oliver sat up and nodded. "Yes, sir, it was just the close air. I'm all right now."

Indeed he was, his face turning hot at the thought that he'd almost fainted simply because he was sitting in the porter's office of the St. James's Workhouse, waiting for an orphan to be brought to them so they could take him home and put him to hard labor. Starve or feed him as they would. Cheap at any price.

The porter stepped to the door and opened it, bringing another push of air, this one washed by the smell of dust and damp and laundry soap too strongly applied. Oliver wanted to itch as he remembered that feeling, of prickling stiff wool after the semiweekly laundry was done. But he didn't; young gentlemen didn't scratch themselves in public, so he sat, stiffly, hands clamped on the edges of his seat.

The workhouse matron appeared; Oliver knew it was the matron from her enormous starched cap and broad white apron. By her hand she pulled a small boy, dressed in workhouse brown. Oliver had a glimpse of untidy dark hair and enormous brown eyes before he made himself look away.

"This here's Martin Gregory," said the matron, her voice curling stiffly around what she probably presumed were cultured tones. "He ain't got much to say, but he should be of some use to you."

She let go of the little boy's hand and shoved him in their direction. The boy came right at Oliver it seemed, for the boy's thin garment brushed Oliver's knee and the tiny hand almost rested there. Oliver lunged to his feet and stepped away, shuddering, brushing imaginary dust from his cap.

"Go along with the gentlemen, Martin, and do as you're told, for I certainly don't want to see you back here."

The little boy, Martin, nodded, eyes wide with trepidation, Oliver assumed, and no wonder, for the world was a big, noisy place. Then Martin held out his hand, held it up for someone to take.

Oliver's eyes grew hot, and it was then that he looked away and promised himself he'd just pretend that the orphan wasn't even there. Orphan? What orphan? There was only the shop and Mr. McCready and the lads, Henry and Tate. And Oliver himself, working hard at being the best apprentice shopkeeper London had ever seen. And Jack, there was Jack of course, causing trouble as he always did. Oliver focused on shared moments with Jack, and they sprang brightly in his mind. Jack and his snapping grin were a perfect distraction, and they allowed Oliver to follow after Mr. McCready and the small figure he towed by one hand. Out of the porter's office, across the yard, and through the gate. It was only then, when his boots hit the paving stones outside the yard, that Oliver felt he could draw a deep breath once more.

They arrived at the haberdashery just as Henry and Tate did, and Mr. McCready motioned for them all to go down to the kitchen. Mrs. Pierson awaited them, motioning to the newly fixed stove. Then, with several *tut tutts* and *my mys*, she called for the new girl. The new girl came forth, a round and rosy-faced, sensible thing with a dark blue dress covered with a white apron; her shining golden hair was tucked up under a starched white cap.

"This is Lucy. She's as stout as a mountain pony," said Mrs. Pierson, politely trying to hide her smile and failing. "Go along now, and let me know if you can't find that cleansing soda."

The girl went down the corridor to the washroom and fetched the tin bath to place it near the stove, went out again, and carried back two buckets of hot water in no more time and with no more effort than she might have taken to lift a sheet of paper to write a letter.

Then Mrs. Pierson's eyes alighted on the orphan, and she pulled him close.

"Come along, you," she said and began unbuttoning his shirt collar to divest him of his garments. "Let's get this lice and dirt off of you before you track it all through the house."

Oliver escaped up the bare wooden stairs to the ground floor. He took off his jacket and cap and pulled on his apron. He went out to the chilly warehouse and turned to Tate, who'd been following him.

"It's my turn to clean the yard from where yesterday's wagons and horses have been," said Oliver, grabbing the shovel and the bucket.

"What?" asked Tate, his mouth open, not hiding his surprise that Oliver was volunteering for the most loathsome of tasks, even though it wasn't his turn.

"Yes, I'm going to do that and sweep the warehouse, and then I'll help you count stock."

"You're going to—but what about—?"

"I'll do everything else, but I won't go past the kitchen for more coal for the warehouse, Tate, you understand?"

Tate nodded. He didn't look as though he was going to protest, let alone question Oliver's demands. It had been an easy day for him already, Oliver knew, and no apprentice worth his salt would be likely to grouse against more of that continuing.

Oliver scrubbed and swept and counted and did not allow himself to think. By the supper hour, when Mrs. Pierson actually had to come out to the warehouse to call him in, Oliver felt he'd worked off most of the tenseness in his shoulders. He followed her in obediently and doffed his apron before clattering downstairs. But as he washed up in the basin by the wall, he caught sight of everyone already seated around the table, looking at him, somewhat puzzled at his tardiness.

As Mr. McCready said grace, Oliver bent his head and clasped his hands. Out of the corner of his eyes, he saw the orphan, sitting on a tall stool next to the sideboard with a plate of food at his elbow that not only looked meager but that he hadn't yet touched. His face and his hair and brown clothes were much cleaner than they had been, but his eyes were still wide. He did not involve himself with grace but instead was looking at Mr. McCready's back with some apprehension. It was certain it had been made clear to him his standing in the haberdashery.

When Mr. McCready said *amen*, Oliver spared a glance at Mrs. Pierson, noting that her mouth was downturned with displeasure. She served them her good, hot food, apron twitching, serving ladle clanging against china, and it was then Oliver realized why the room was filled with nothing but silence.

First, there was a spare seat at the table next to Henry, but it was obvious by the rigid line of Mr. McCready's back that the orphan wasn't to be allowed to sit with the master and his apprentices. Fair enough; Oliver didn't know of any master, fair or cruel, who would allow such liberties to a mere pauper. But second, the orphan wasn't to eat as the rest of them did. The orphan had, Oliver could see, a single slice of unbuttered bread and a bowl of the stew that Mrs. Pierson had served to them all, but other than a mug of plain water, that was it. He had no boiled potatoes, no buttered peas, no steaming pile of carrots. Likewise, it was easy to presume that the orphan would not and would never be allowed to partake in the pudding and custard that were always the delight of everyone who'd ever been privileged to sit at Mrs. Pierson's table. Hence Mrs. Pierson's displeasure. She lived to feed, and to be denied that, especially to one who could benefit so greatly from it, well, that was tantamount to her having to go hungry herself.

Oliver made himself concentrate on his own plate and on the good food there and not on the orphan, who although he was apparently trying to be as unobtrusive as possible, his skinny elbows tucked at his sides, nevertheless, tore into the plain bread and drank the stew from his spoon noisily, in big gulps, as if he'd not been fed, not properly anyway, in years.

When the orphan finished, he set the bowl down next to him on the sideboard with a rude clunk. Mrs. Pierson jumped up, spoon at the ready to give him a second helping. Oliver felt something in his chest loosen as he watched her.

"No, Mrs. Pierson," said Mr. McCready, holding up one hand firmly. "He will eat what he is given and nothing more. He is only a workhouse boy, after all."

"What about scraps?" asked Mrs. Pierson, her voice sharp, as if the orphan had been begging for hours and she only come to her last reserve of politeness. "Surely we can spare those; there is only so much I can sell."

Mr. McCready studied the table, looked at the plates and cutlery. "If the boys leave anything on their plates," he said carefully as if wanting to make himself quite clear, "then the orphan may have that. But nothing else, mind."

"Very well, Mr. McCready," said Mrs. Pierson. She nodded, smoothing her apron as she laid down the serving ladle she'd not been allowed to use on the table next to the soup tureen. By her frown and crinkled brow, it was apparent to everyone at the table that she was not happy about it.

Oliver looked down at his plate. His stomach was tight even at the thought of the sweet pudding to come. Beneath his carefully laid cloth napkin, he was shaking. But in spite of this, he picked up his knife and fork and proceeded to eat everything in front of him. Every bite. Even the peas, and he loathed and despised peas.

When it was time for bed, the new girl, Lucy, had left enough hot water in the pitcher in the boys' attic room that there was no squabbling over the basin. They each took their turn, and Oliver went last because he was still the new boy. But for the first time since his arrival, when Oliver poured Tate's leavings into the slop bucket, there was enough hot water for him to have an entire basin to wash with. He used it all, and a great deal of soap besides, and dumped that in the slop bucket, and saw that there was still more water available.

The lack of hot water had never been anything that any of them had ever wanted to complain to Mrs. Pierson about. Not only were they mere apprentice boys, and as such, not obliged to expect anything so luxurious as enough hot water, they all knew, unspoken, that with the aid of only one unreliable girl, not to mention all those stairs, Mrs. Pierson had been doing her best. Plus, as Oliver had once or twice surmised, Mrs. Pierson's cooking was far too good to risk complaining about anything else.

Oliver sat on the edge of his bed and took off his boots as he looked at the box where his books were stored. But he was too tired to read, so, shaking his head, he undid his suspenders and took off his trousers, pulled on his nightshirt, and crawled into bed with his stockings on. He listened to Tate and Henry, who were disagreeing, albeit drowsily, about something that had happened that day, but to Oliver's gratitude, nothing about the orphan. Of course not. To them, the orphan was beneath their notice, worthy of little regard.

He would do the same; he decided this as he shifted on his narrow bed, pulled the blankets up, and began his nightly ritual of ignoring the skinny draft of cold air that whispered past the window casement.

It seemed that sleep would never come, but eventually Oliver found himself starting awake and sitting straight up in the dark. His head pounded and the memories of a nightmare clung to him with ragged fingers. Thin, underfed fingers, and the image, startlingly clear, even after all this time, of Dick's face. Dear, sweet Dick, that large collar flapping away from his workhouse-thin neck. That sparse auburn hair, that narrow face, thinned from want. Spindly fingers clutching at Oliver's arm as they both crouched in the dark, backsides sore from a recent thrashing from Mrs. Mann. Both of them too weak to stand, the space too cramped for them to be able to lie down.

"I'm so hungry, Oliver. Tell me that you spared a bit of dinner in your pocket."

"I don't have anything for you," the dream Oliver had said, with his teeth gritted against the bear's claws ripping the inside of his own stomach.

Then the images had shifted, as they did in dreams, to that morning when Oliver had run away from Mr. Sowerberry. Dick had been in the garden, weeding at an ungodly early hour, probably as punishment. Stick thin, face grubby, fingers turning into skeleton fingers as he reached for Oliver's bundle that he carried in one arm. That he knew was full of thickly buttered bread and sweets and a jacket potato and bowls of porridge, hot and drizzled with honey. But Oliver said no to Dick and broke off his finger bones, one by one, prying Dick off him, breaking the small, thin bones of Dick's neck—

Oliver gasped and clutched at the bedclothes, trying to focus on the darkness above him. For that had never happened. Yes, he'd stopped to see Dick and had said good-bye; he should have asked Dick to come with him, but hadn't. Dick had assured Oliver he was dying anyway, and the much younger Oliver had left it at that and walked off to seek his own fortune and never mind Dick's fate. Then Dick had died, and it was, at least partly, Oliver's fault.

He should have insisted that Dick come along, should have dragged Dick behind him. Maybe it would have slowed Oliver down to the point where he would not have met up with Jack

Dawkins, and the whole nasty sordid business with Fagin and his gang never would have happened. But then, perhaps Oliver would not have been nearby when Jack and Charley had picked Uncle Brownlow's pockets, and he, Oliver, might not have ended up as Uncle Brownlow's cosseted ward and discovered that fate would have its grand, unpredictable way by the fact that Uncle Brownlow was an old friend of Oliver's dead father. Such was the turn of the wheel that circumstance begat circumstance. But did that mean that Dick had had to die so that Oliver could be given his inheritance? That Dick's life had been the prize for Oliver's current good fortune?

Oliver pitched forward in his bed and scrambled out from beneath the bedclothes. His whole body was so hot, as though with a sudden rush of fever, that the floor felt like solid ice beneath his stockinged feet. But that was good, the chill shiver that went through him; it helped clear his head. He leaned down to rip off his stockings and paced in his bare feet, willing the icy boards to distract him.

He went over to the washstand and plunged his hands in the last of the water in the pitcher, now quite cold, and splashed his face with it. All of this in the stone-cold darkness, breathing through his teeth, desperate not to wake Henry or Tate, either of whom might exclaim in surprise, which would bring Mr. McCready from his peaceful, law-abiding slumber across the hall to inquire about the disturbance and who was the cause.

Perhaps he might not be overly surprised to find Oliver as the source of disquiet in the middle of the night. And that dis-covery, perhaps, might encourage him to send Oliver packing, into the street without so much as a reference, and leave him there to starve, to turn into a ragged beggar with skeleton-thin arms and sores on his face and a belly full of nothing. Fit for the nearest workhouse and nothing more.

Gasping out a cry, Oliver froze, his hand grabbing his left arm, clamping on the scar so hard it went numb. He had to quiet himself before he woke Henry and Tate; he had to shut everything off before he might come apart in bleeding, sobbing pieces. How could the presence of a single orphan under the same roof be so disquieting? It shouldn't be. It wasn't. Oliver couldn't let it. *Wouldn't* let it.

He took a deep breath and pressed his hands, now drying in the chill air, to his hot eyes. Took another hot breath, feeling fully now the cold rising from the floorboards. His teeth were chattering. He clamped them tightly and did not let them chatter. Did not hop from foot to foot to ease his freezing skin. Did not hurry as he climbed back into bed, which was now cold with the lack of any body warmth remaining. There was nothing the matter now, he knew that. An orphan was only an orphan, after all, and it had nothing to do with the likes of Oliver Twist.

CHAPTER 18

Oliver's Treatment Of Those Who Are Beneath Him

In the morning, after he'd received his second week's pay, he galloped upstairs with the other boys to stow it away. When he raced back down to the kitchen for breakfast, Oliver didn't see the orphan during the meal, but that didn't matter to him. If the orphan had already been dismissed and sent back to the workhouse, then that was a good enough way to start the day and not question anyone about it. But when he went out into the yard to open the gates to the alley for the delivery wagons, there the orphan was. Shielded from the cold by one of Mrs. Pierson's oldest shawls, the orphan was picking up bits of smashed crockery from the cobblestones and putting them in a bucket.

It happened sometimes, on a Friday night, when men were drinking and spirits got high, that they tossed things about. It amused them to hurl items into yards of unknown contents simply to, Oliver assumed, listen to things crashing against stone. It was probably similar to the feeling he'd gotten in the country when he'd thrown rocks down a gully or shied stones at the water, listening to the smacking sounds. So he understood that it was just that these men, drinking, didn't care what or whose property they destroyed.

At the same time, it left the orphan, on a cruel, frosty morning, picking up shards of very sharp pottery with his bare hands. Oliver felt his lips curl, and as the orphan looked up, he turned his face away. He had to concentrate on his own morning tasks and open the gate. So he walked forward, more warmly dressed than the orphan in thick stockings and the warehouse coat that hung by the doors to the warehouse. He even had a scarf around his neck for the brief jaunt into the cold weather. With eyes averted, he walked past the orphan as if he weren't even there. And truly, he wasn't. An orphan was nothing, amounted to nothing. Was of no account.

When Oliver got to the gate, he pulled his hands out of his pockets and tugged the scarf away from his neck to wrap around his hand. Bare metal was cold, and any dampness might be likely to freeze his skin to it, so he was careful. He pulled the bolt up from the rivet in the ground then undid the upper cross bolt and then, finally, the latch in the middle. He swung both gates open, pushing them apart. He did up the left side first, as he always did, attaching it to the iron bolt through the eye bolt in the high brick wall, and then he did the right one.

He turned around, and the orphan was right there, not two feet from him, mouth open as if to speak.

Oliver couldn't even begin to imagine what the orphan would have to say to him. And in fact, the orphan shouldn't even deign to speak to him at all. Oliver was a working lad, on his way up in the world, and the orphan was at the bottom of the heap.

So Oliver held his head high and marched right past the orphan and his too-heavy bucket full of broken crockery, thinking somewhere in the back of his mind that the orphan only meant to ask what he might do with the leavings from the night before. Well, it was none of Oliver's concern, was it. His boots clicked on the cobblestones as he hurried into the warehouse with an eye out for the sort of the work that would keep him out of the way of the orphan.

During the noon meal, Oliver kept his eyes on his plate and ate everything that Mrs. Pierson served him, even though his nerves felt jangled and sore. What with attempting to help Tate in the warehouse without it also looking as though he were more concerned with anything else, and not jumping out of his skin when, more than once, he would come around a corner of shelves to find the orphan there, with a broom in his hand, or a cloth, or whatever it was he was working with. And with big, scared eyes, he would look up at Oliver as if with fright that Oliver might not see him there and walk right over him. As if Oliver could do anything else but notice that the orphan was there.

Right after dinner, Oliver went upstairs to grab his coat and cap, and tossing his scarf about his neck, hurried out to the warehouse where Mrs. Pierson said Mr. McCready had gone. He intended to inquire if there were any deliveries that needed doing right away, for he needed to be out and about in the City. He needed to be away.

As Oliver pounded down the warehouse steps, Tate was already bent to the stove, poking at it and eyeing the coal scuttle with Mr. McCready at his side.

"Oliver, come here, lad." Mr. McCready waved him to come closer, which Oliver did with as much haste as he could without actually running.

"Yes, sir?" he asked.

"Here," said Mr. McCready. He held out a long sheet of paper with Henry's writing on it. "Evidently, Henry took a length of orders yesterday while we were out and only now saw fit to tell me. I want you to tend to this directly and collect the order for each delivery and wrap it. Can you do that? And then deliver them before it snows today."

Oliver took the list, trying to hide his pleasure. The list would keep him busy all afternoon and would put Oliver in places that the orphan would never dare to go. Oliver would be out in the streets of the City, free as a bird in his green scarf and his brown jacket and cap that announced to the world that he was the delivery boy of a very important shop.

"Yes, sir," he said, "I'll get on that right away."

He heard a hesitant step behind him, more of a shuffle, and a clang as someone put down a too-heavy bucket.

"Sir," said a very small voice indeed, and Oliver heard Tate's start of surprise.

Shaking this off, Oliver hurried into the narrow room off of Mr. McCready's office where the delivery basket was kept. He'd gather the items from the warehouse himself, that would be quickest, and then he'd wrap them in brown paper and string. Then he'd be off. With luck, he wouldn't have to talk to anybody at all.

Alone at the long table in the warehouse, gathering and packaging all the bits of ribbon and pins and collars and sweet soap powder and samples of cloth for their regular customers, and a bobbin stand for a new customer who lived way out in Burton Crescent near Tavistock Square, took Oliver the good part of an hour. He tucked all the paper-and-string bundles in the covered basket; there was enough to make both lids stand up, and the basket was quite heavy.

He took down his green scarf and wrapped it carefully around his neck. Then, as he put on his cap and was shrugging on his coat, Mrs. Pierson came up the stairs from the kitchen. She came up to Oliver and helped him with his buttons.

"It's such a cold afternoon," she said, snugging the scarf higher under his chin. "We don't want you frosting that pretty face of yours, now do we?" Her voice sounded stern, but she helped him set his cap on his head, fussing over him as if he were one of her own. "There, now. You hurry back, and don't be late for supper. I'll have apple tart waiting."

"Yes, Mrs. Pierson," said Oliver, trying not to grin too broadly at her. She might think he was mocking her for fussing over him, and he didn't want that, for Mrs. Pierson's apple tart was so good it might have been made by the angels themselves.

"Now then," she said, turning to look behind her. "Get along with that, you, in Mr. McCready's office as quick as you can; why are you just standing there? Get along, now."

To his dismay, Oliver saw the orphan. He had the coal scuttle in his hands. It was full to the brim, and way too heavy for those small shoulders to balance. Oliver hefted the wicker basket in his hands; it was heavy too, but no one saw him complaining, did they.

In order to avoid brushing past the orphan, Oliver hastened out the front door, leaving it open to bang behind him, but he couldn't stop to check it and see that it didn't. He needed to be very far from the shop just now. It was better to be out of the shop, even if it was starting to spit icy rain; he didn't think it would turn to snow, but it was cold, just the same. Thank goodness he'd have a hot cup of tea and a nice meal, not to mention Mrs. Pierson's apple tart, waiting for him when he got back. And perhaps, as sometimes was the case, one of the nice maids he saw along his delivery route would take him into the servants' kitchen and offer him a hot drink as well. He'd be fine; the day would turn out fine, in spite of the weather.

When he finished with his deliveries, absently thinking of the meal that Mrs. Pierson would hold warm for him even if he was late, Oliver absently headed down Doughty Street, his basket swinging empty on one arm. When he got to Grey's Inn Gardens, he could smell the dust heaps along the side streets. He took a left since that way was more free of pedestrians, and when he got to the street where all the leather shops were, selling their wares of boots and belts and harnesses, he realized where he was. All this way north, to one of the nicer parts of London, to discover himself to be only two streets over from the warren of Saffron Hill, where the windows went unwashed, and the steps were rarely scrubbed, even though they were tracked with mud all the year round. Where rooftop tiles went slipping into muddy, fetid gutters in which bare-legged children searched for scraps. One more block would take him directly there, to the exact place where he ought not to go.

He kept going in that direction anyway, thinking that maybe, perhaps maybe, he could inure himself to the sights and sounds of the less well-to-do, indeed, the poorest of the poor. So that by comparison, the orphan might seem very well off. He would try it. It might work.

At the top of Saffron Hill, he headed down into the streets of dank air where the houses and questionable shops almost met across the street at their rooflines, and where crumbling walls were sometimes held up with the shaved trunks of felled trees. Where, if the cold didn't freeze it up solid, a narrow river of water ran constantly in a ditch in the middle of the lane. The smell of cesspits overflowing into the ground below rose up and smacked him in the face. Covering his nose with the back of his hand, he hurried down the hill, passing filthy shops where dark-coated men lurked and open doorways displayed strings of handkerchiefs, both tawdry and silk. He kept walking as fast as he could past the old bone-and-rag shop with its mildewed piles and stacks of rust and iron until he at last came upon the door to the Three Cripples. The door banged open as someone exited, and then three men went in. Oliver slipped in with them, hoping to use them as cover, not that it was likely that anyone he knew would be there to witness what he was doing.

For it was one thing to visit Jack upon the threat of Jack coming into the haberdashery, but it was another to do it of his own free will. As if his time were his own and this was not the very worst thing he should do. But there was the orphan and all the beggars and sweepers, with their grimy hands reaching out for the smallest coin, passing just at the edges of his vision. And they wouldn't *stop*.

The air of the Three Cripples was, as it had been before, close and still and dashed with smoke, as if no one ever thought to clean the grate of ash and soot, let alone open a window. The walls, once light colored, were patchy with smoke stains and streaked with damp. The mantelpiece over the main fireplace was cluttered with unwashed glasses and pots, with candle wax dripping down in slow, off-white streaks.

Oliver skirted the crowd of men at the bar, who were hastening to order their mugs of beer that served in place of a meal, and made his way to the open door that led to the warren of rooms for the better type of guest.

He got lucky, for there was Jack Dawkins, sitting where Oliver had seen him last, in the bench seat nearest the fire. Though Oliver's red scarf was nowhere to be seen and his coat was off, Jack was fully resplendent in his silk-embroidered and grease-spattered blue waistcoat and his shiny, worn low top hat. He had his sleeves pushed back and his clay pipe in his mouth, for all the world like a gentleman at home, warming himself beside a coal fire.

Indeed, there was a coal fire glowing in the grate, sending out waves and waves of warmth that Oliver was drawn in by. He realized his teeth were chattering and his hands couldn't feel the basket that hung from his fingers, but he didn't think it was the cold alone, no. Not just the cold.

As he came close, Jack looked up and fanned a deck of cards between his fingers in an almost graceful way. His hat slipped forward and he sent it back on his head with a jerk and then smiled at Oliver. His lips curled as though he were smirking, ready to mock Oliver at the first opportunity.

"My eyes," said Jack, his eyes sparking, amused. "Will you look at this. Of his own free will, yet, the great one comes to visit us."

When Oliver didn't say anything, Jack tipped his head and doffed his hat, waving it over the seat opposite him. He placed the hat on the table because, of course, he knew that it would irritate Oliver. "You are most welcome, Oliver Twist." Which did sound mocking, but in that funny, shaded way that Oliver remembered as being only one flicker away from being either kind or mean, as determined by Jack's mood and the circumstance.

Oliver sank into the bench seat opposite Jack and laid his cap and scarf and basket on the plank beside him. He figured he'd draw less attention when it didn't look so obvious as to how out of place he was. And in spite of himself, it was good to sit still for a moment, in the warmth, to not be moving. He watched as Jack took a draw on his pipe, holding it with one hand, then laid it aside in a little clay dish as the smoke twirled up from his mouth.

"All this way, then, just to see me?" Jack asked, his eyebrows going up.

"No," said Oliver, knowing that his presence needed some explanation at least. "I was a few streets over, making—" He clamped his mouth shut. It was none of Jack's business what he'd been doing. "I was in the neighborhood, is all. It was raining."

He saw it in Jack's eyes, even though Jack didn't say it aloud: *It rains all the time, and you're all over London every day. So why today?*

But instead Jack shouted for two beers, and when the drinks were delivered in plain tin pots, he looked at Oliver as if he expected Oliver to refuse to imbibe at such an hour of the day. And in such a place. With a hot feeling in his breast, Oliver picked up the pot nearest to him and took a large mouthful, rude as a sailor, swallowing a great, greedy gulp. The beer stung his throat, but he kept it down anyway, looking at Jack, his eyes narrowed.

"So, then," said Jack, shuffling the cards in one hand while he took a drink of beer, bringing the mug to his mouth, with the other. "Care to join me in a game? Somethin' simple, whiskey poker, perhaps, or there's a new game out called black hearts. Shall we have a go? We can play for pennies, or sticks, if you haven't got any pennies."

It was on the tip of Oliver's tongue to say it, *playing cards is a sin*, but then, so was being in a place such as this when it was still before evening, and truly, as an apprentice, his time wasn't his own. That he was sitting there, lollygagging on what was his master's time, that was the sin; playing cards would just make it worse. His thighs tightened as he attempted to get to his feet, but he overbalanced and tumbled against the edge of the table, tossing his mug enough to make it spill beer in shiny circles on the black-scarred surface of the table.

"Steady on," said Jack, his hand going out as if he meant to keep Oliver from falling over. "The beer got to you, then?

Don't drink much of it, I reckon, being the teetotaler that you are."

Which was a lie. Jack had seen him quaffing back the gin not so long ago, so Oliver knew that Jack was now, truly, mocking him. But the expression on Jack's face said something different. His dark brows were lowered, and he looked thoughtfully at Oliver. He took another puff from his clay pipe and laid it by again in a small pot and slowly, as though tasting it, let the smoke go out of his mouth. As though it were nothing that Oliver were here, with almost no explanation at all, in the middle of a working day, as jittery as a high-strung horse. As if Oliver in a tavern, spilling his beer, were an ordinary, everyday event.

"This here's patience," said Jack, shuffling the cards twice before putting them in a stacked pile between them with their worn edges all lined up, the gold and black pattern shining up dully. "It can't be much of a sin because you don't play to bet, or even to win. You plays it just to pass the time, like. When you're on your own an' waitin' till the time is right to meet with your fence or the fella who's gonna melt down all that silver you just stole into a nice, sellable blob. Like I been, but you don't want to hear about that, eh?"

Oliver frowned, but Jack just smiled as though teasing Oliver was something he did every day, and that talk of fences and stolen silver and how to melt and sell it was a common conversation between them.

He watched Jack's hands, deft and black-knuckled, turn up the cards, one-two-three, and pull out the aces to lay them in a row when they came up, placing the other cards, as the numbers and colors, black and red, came up so as to be in sequence as Jack laid them on their respective piles of spades, hearts, clubs, and diamonds. The pattern was simple and somewhat mesmerizing, and surprising even, that Jack didn't cheat, not even when Oliver could see the necessary card directly beneath the one that showed on the top of the pile.

"It's just to pass the time, see. Do you see, Oliver? Not quite so much the sin as you might like to think."

"No," he agreed. "I guess it isn't."

"You want somethin' to eat?" asked Jack, shuffling the cards again. "Somethin' to help you keep that beer down?" Without waiting for an answer, he waved his hand, presumably at someone behind Oliver, and presently, one of the servants brought over two bowls of stew and a plate of bread and cheese, which she placed between them.

"Eel an' potato," said Jack, picking up a dented spoon, starting in on the oily looking broth in his bowl without waiting for Oliver.

Not that Oliver would eat anything made of eel, not that Jack knew that. Instead, he picked up a corner of cheese and brought it to his mouth. He could tell, without even tasting it, that the cheese was old and dry, fit only for hog swill. He didn't quite know what to do but found his hands crumbling the cheese back onto the plate.

"Typical," said Jack, shaking his head. "You and that fancy taste of yours."

Of course, Jack was right. There was many a mouth that would be willing to eat cheese like that, even if it was old and moldy. Or who would take the dented spoon that now rested on the table in front of him and eat the stew, whether or not it contained bits of eel. He ducked his head, feeling ashamed; he knew what it felt like to be so hungry you could eat dirt. Jack, of all people, didn't need to remind him of that. Shouldn't have had to. But it made him a little cross as well; he'd come up in the world and was above having to eat what was put in front of him if he didn't enjoy the taste of it. He had money in his pocket, tips from his deliveries made that very day, and he could walk into any shop and order a real meat pie, if he fancied it.

He opened his mouth to give Jack this very return and found himself saying something quite different indeed.

"Mr. McCready bought an orphan, yesterday," said Oliver, low, as though to himself. And so very glad that Jack kept his attention on his food. In fact, Jack was practically slumped over his bowl, both elbows on the table, one hand propping up his head, and the other using the spoon to shovel the stew in as fast as he could. He had the worst manners Oliver had ever seen, and the spark of anger at seeing this felt better than the feeling of shame from a moment before.

"An orphan," said Jack, not looking up but only pausing in his shoveling to take a large drink of beer.

"From a workhouse," said Oliver. He wanted Jack to look up at him, to understand what Oliver meant without him having to explain it; he could barely explain it to himself. But Jack just kept eating and didn't look up, so Oliver had to manage on his own. "And I can't stand the sight of him."

"Me either," said Jack with a grunt. He picked up the bowl and tilted it to his mouth, using the spoon to scrape the last bits in. Then he set the bowl down, and with a sigh, wiped his mouth with the back of his forearm, looking at Oliver while he did this. "Can't stand their skinny little faces an' their dirty hands clasped in prayer, lookin' up at me like I'm the last stop before hell's fires." Jack's eyes glittered as he finished saying this, and Oliver felt he was being told something he didn't quite understand but should. "Makes me want to smack 'em right into next week."

"And then I had a nightmare about Dick." He hadn't meant to say anything about it to anyone and couldn't believe he was attempting to tell the story of Dick to Jack.

"Who's that, then?"

Oliver's face flushed, and he told himself it was the heat from the coal fire finally getting to him. "Never mind." He shoved the bowl of stew at Jack. "You eat it, then," he said, trying to stand, and finding the table getting in the way. The bench seat was nailed to the floor, and he couldn't shove it back at all. He grabbed his cap and basket and began to slide out sideways, fingers grasping the edge of the table, tucked back so that his fingers wouldn't go into the pool of beer and quickly cooling stew.

"Hey, now, Nolly, don't be cross. You know I'd never be so mean as that. Why, I'd give 'em a penny, if I had it, you know I would." Jack stood and put his hand on Oliver's arm just as Oliver had gotten his basket free from the confines of the bench seat. He clapped his cap on his head and glared at Jack, willing him to let go. But Jack didn't, and so Oliver had to yank his arm free and try to push past Jack, who stood up and let him pass, though not without some attempt at delay.

"Say, did I ever show you my tattoo?" Jack started unrolling his shirt sleeve to peel it back. "I got in on board the *Bertha May* when I was exported, an' you know what it's of?"

"No," said Oliver, gritting his teeth and shoving Jack out of the way. "No and I don't care. Only thieves and whores have tattoos." Although, truth be told, he himself had a tattoo of sorts, if one counted scars left by a servant's bullet. Not that he was about to tell Jack about it; Jack would just want to see it.

"Well," said Jack, letting Oliver get by him as though it were of no consequence to him. "I'm not a whore, by any stretch, but I *am* a thief, ain't I? An' an ex-convict, I'm proud to say, so, you might amend your list a bit there, don't you think?"

Fury exploding in his stomach, Oliver pushed past all of the customers at the Three Cripples and wondered, as he slammed the door open, why on earth he had thought this had been a good idea. Not only was the thought of eel stew making him feel like vomiting into the nearest gutter, he'd gotten black smudges on his trousers somehow, and his scarf smelled like dank smoke. Mrs. Pierson was sure to fuss over him when he got back to the shop, and how was he going to explain his tumbled state to her, let alone catch sight of the orphan without wanting to burst out shouting? He had no idea.

He was late for supper; there was no way around it. By the time he'd wrestled open the large back door to the warehouse, climbed the steps to the shop to take off his outdoor things, and then clattered down the wooden stairs to the kitchen, the smells of hot food were strong, and everyone was already seated at the table. As his feet touched the stone floor, everyone stopped, spoons and forks halfway to their mouths, which were open in surprise, even though, by now, Oliver's lateness to meals was becoming a commonplace event. Even the orphan looked taken aback, in an almost comical way, as if

Oliver's keeping him from his bread and broth were the worst sort of manners.

"Oliver," said Mr. McCready, wiping his mouth and laying his napkin back in his lap. "You're quite late. I'm assuming you have an explanation for this? Regardless, I'm quite tempted to make you go without supper, to teach you—"

"Oh, dear me, Mr. McCready," said Mrs. Pierson, coming up to the table without waiting for his leave. "On such a cold day as this, can't you see the boy's had a struggle, making all of them deliveries this afternoon? Henry said there was one as far as Burton Crescent; he's done in." She paused to dish up a bowl of something that resembled potato and cheese and onion, all melted together. She plunked that down on the table at Oliver's empty chair and then got slices of cold ham and boiled celery. "Bread and butter's just there, Oliver; now you wash up and catch up with your supper, so we can all start on the pudding together."

Oliver looked carefully at Mr. McCready, but it was obvious even to him that the decision was already made.

"The streets were very crowded today," said Oliver, generally, to no one, as he washed up. When he sat down, he put his napkin in his lap and tried to pretend that he wasn't aware that both he and Mrs. Pierson were, essentially, disobeying Mr. McCready and doing as they pleased. She to feed him, and he to eat.

Another glance told Oliver what he already knew and didn't care to think about. That the orphan had finished his allotment of bread and broth and stared at Oliver's plate as he ate. Which he did, as quickly as he could, determined that there'd be no scraps for the orphan. But he did this so fast that by the time Mrs. Pierson served up the jam tarts, his stomach hurt. Still, he ate his share of pudding anyway, telling himself he needed the food and that his stomach wasn't uncomfortable. And that no one in the room could smell the smoke on him or could tell by the smudges he saw on the edges of his palms. He'd washed up very carefully, so his only hope was that everyone was concentrating on the tarts and not on him.

That night, before bedtime, he lit two stubs of candles and ignored Tate's remarks to Henry about it and tried to read one of his books while lying in bed. He had picked out *Aesop's Fables*, but he knew all the stories by heart, and the words merely danced on the page as though they wanted to take flight. Attempting to concentrate even more didn't help; his stomach ached, and in his mind's eye, he could see the orphan, on a coarse blanket on the kitchen floor. Perhaps he was pressed close to the warmth of the cast-iron stove; even as the heat faded away, it would be better than nothing. Perhaps he had two blankets. Perhaps he had none.

Oliver got up to put his book away in his chest, ignoring Henry's irritated sigh and any remark that Tate might make, and blew out the candle. The smell of burnt wax lifted in the cool air; Oliver inhaled it, thinking of sleep now, concentrating on that.

The dream came again, of Dick, in the garden, his thin garments hanging off white bone, and his hair falling across empty eye sockets. When Oliver woke up, he was sitting, breathing hard, staring into the darkness. He had tried to forget about Dick in all those years since he last saw him, forget about the thought of it and how he had left Dick behind. But it seemed that the idea of Dick, and what Oliver had failed to do, was not about to be left behind.

CHAPTER 19

Of Cruelty

After the dank dreams with images of Dick crowding into his sleep, going to church with Mr. McCready and Henry and Tate on Sunday was hardly enough to manage the twisted feeling in Oliver's breast, however peaceful the service might be. The rows of pews, with their graceful glow, and the smell of fine candles, the dim light coming in colored streaks through the decorated, lead-lined windows—none of it made even a dint into Oliver's unsettled state. Sunday afternoon, though, it allowed for the leisure of reading and resting by the kitchen fire, left Oliver troubled enough that by the time he'd reached his bed, his sleep was as unsettled as though he'd spent the day in battle.

By the time Oliver was dressed and in the shop on Monday morning, he was exhausted and heavy-eyed. Then he heard the voice behind him.

"A moment there, Oliver."

He stood at the edge of the long counter in the shop, searching with his eyes for Henry's list, desperate to not be in the warehouse where the orphan was sweeping. The broom was far too long for the orphan's tiny frame, and Oliver had lasted all of five minutes watching him before he had left off sorting boxes and crates and snuck up front.

"The deliveries can wait, Oliver, my boy," said Mr. McCready coming up behind him. "I know the sun is peeking through the clouds and fog, but it'll be more worth your while after dinner, yes?"

Oliver tapped the glass on the counter, watching his prints smear across the glass. Henry would have to take vinegar and cloth to those later, but it would make him look busy and efficient, so perhaps he might enjoy it. The shop was quite quiet, as though with the weather picking up, every customer had somewhere else to be. Subsequently, there was almost nothing to do. All the work was in the warehouse today, where Tate was the king of his roost, counting boxes and buttons and sorting through starched collars and ordering the orphan around. Tate wasn't cruel, necessarily, but he was lordly, pointing and commanding in a way that had the orphan scampering and stammering.

"Why don't you go back and help Tate? I fear he's determined to start spring cleaning early."

Spring was weeks away yet, but Oliver was feeling the same restlessness that Tate probably was, the push of some energetic sensation that had Henry buffing the brass, almost needlessly, with puffs of his breath and a brisk cloth.

"Oliver?" Mr. McCready's hand clamped down on his shoulder.

Oliver didn't let himself jump under the touch but instead gripped the edge of the counter to tap his irritation.

"Yes, sir," he said, making himself let the counter's edge go. He turned and Mr. McCready patted him with some heartiness.

"You can make deliveries after dinner, Oliver," said Mr. McCready kindly. "And that's a promise."

"Yes, sir."

Oliver made himself step from the relative warmth of the shop and into the sunnier albeit chillier warehouse. The sun came and went as wafts of cloud scudded along and whispers of fog fought and tumbled against the glass before being burned and blown away. For a moment, Oliver stared at the high, narrow windows before focusing. Tate could be heard beyond the set of shelves, muttering to himself; Oliver imagined that at any moment, Tate might start barking out more orders to the orphan.

As for the orphan.

Oliver scanned the room, the high windows, the brick walls, and the long wooden table along the one wall, piled with the half-sorted boxes he'd abandoned, with ribbons spilling out, corset tapes stacked awkwardly as though ready to fall, given even the slightest push.

"*Martin*," came Tate's shout, finally. "Put some more coal on the fire, damn you, before my arse freezes off."

It wasn't as cold as it had been the week before, so Tate probably didn't really need more heat. But even though there were bits of red glowing gently through the slits in the stove, Tate was too far from the stove, trapped in the box of cold air between the shelves, was all. Had he been near the stove, he would have been warm enough. He merely sounded as though he was enjoying giving orders.

The orphan, for his part, was under the table with a narrow blacking brush and a cloth, taking the grit and cobwebs from the space between the wall and where it almost met the floorboards. It would take the orphan a good few moments to extricate himself from between the wall and the footboards of the table, so when Tate shouted Martin's name again, Oliver strode over to the stove, intending to perform the task himself.

But the orphan, as if seeing Oliver's boots go marching past him, scurried out from beneath the table and ran to the coal scuttle, reaching out for the door of the stove with his bare hands. There was a charred cloth on a nail in the wall next to the stove or, indeed, the door could be opened with the fire poker, with the curved end shoved under the latch. Perhaps the orphan hadn't been taught this, but knowing Tate's tendency to over-speak things, the orphan had been taught and had just forgotten.

The orphan's skinny, chapped hands were just at the handle when Oliver grabbed the orphan's collar and yanked him away from the stove door. With the back of his hand he landed a good, solid smack on the side of the orphan's face, so hard to the bone that a bruise blossomed there, even as the orphan went sprawling to the stone floor. Arms and legs spread, crying piteously, the back of his jacket torn by Oliver's tug on the cloth.

"Mind what you're doing, you," said Oliver, his voice storming out of his chest, his eyes hot, "or I'll smack you right into next week."

Crying in earnest now, the orphan attempted to sit up, looking up at Oliver with big, dark, teary eyes. The orphan's hand went to his mouth, and shaking, came away; there was blood on his chapped lips. Tate had meanly ordered the orphan about, but only he, Oliver Twist, had sent the orphan to his knees. And had struck him so hard, he was crying. *Bleeding.*

Oliver was no longer the newest boy in the shop. And now he was no better than Noah Claypole, who would, if he were here, howl with amusement at Oliver's fall from grace.

Tate came out from between the shelves and approached slowly, looking at the orphan and then at Oliver, his eyes wide and wary as if Oliver might strike him next.

"On your feet, Martin," said Tate, and while he pulled the orphan to a standing position with some confidence, his voice was shaking. "There's work to be done, eh?"

"Where's the shovel and bucket?" asked Oliver, trying to stand firm against the waves of white that swam past his eyes, the way the brightness of a sudden shard of sun made him feel blind.

"'Tis already done, Oliver," said Tate from somewhere beyond the white.

"The broom, then, and I'll sweep." He felt the desperation of his plea rising in his chest.

"Martin's already attended to that, just now. As you well know."

Oliver sensed rather than saw Tate push the orphan in the direction of the shelves and then he came up to Oliver. Close enough so that Oliver could see his face, tucked in lines of confusion.

"Will you sort collars, then, as you started? While I clean the shelves." Tate sounded almost gentle, and Oliver had to bite the inside of his cheek lest he burst out shouting at Tate as well, as that behavior Mr. McCready would definitely not tolerate.

"Yes," said Oliver, biting the word off. And without saying anything else, he pushed past Tate and marched on numb feet to the table and stood there for a few breaths till his head cleared. As Tate fussed with the stove, Oliver let the clanks and clunks of iron against iron and coal against iron pull him back to the very spot where he was. In the warehouse, sorting collars, tucking the corset stays back away from the edge of the table. To help Tate avoid additional work, Oliver's fingers grabbed the first stack of collars, and he cleared a space on the tabletop and began to sort.

Oliver kept his head down while he worked and didn't allow himself to listen to Tate and the orphan working some feet away nor to lift his head or to stop working till Mrs. Pierson called them for dinner. Then he washed up, last in line, and didn't dare look anyone in the eye. Not even when Mrs. Pierson *tutted* over the orphan's state.

"What have you been tumbling in, then?" she asked.

"Nothing, miss," said the orphan in a voice very small and soft.

"Leave him be to eat his dinner," said Mr. McCready, setting his napkin in his lap. "Workhouse boys are used to hard work, and he'll not thank you for softening him up."

Oliver felt himself flushing hard and couldn't tell if Mr. McCready was looking at him markedly or not. Didn't want to find out. Didn't want to eat Mrs. Pierson's good cooking. But he didn't want her to start *tutting* at him either, so he made himself take a bite and keep it down.

The afternoon had turned windy, but it was still bright, so after Oliver had swept the melted snow and dirt from the front steps and pavement, the order of the day was deliveries. And as Mr. McCready handed him the delivery list, Oliver felt that he himself had been delivered. For if Mrs. Pierson kept the orphan close by, or if Henry felt he needed more coal, then Oliver would be far, far away, and would not have to reconcile him to any of it.

Mr. McCready helped him gather the packages and tie them up.

"Unless you are unwell; you look unwell," said Mr. McCready stuffing yet another brown package wrapped in string into the basket. "If you are, I will select one of the other boys to go."

"No, I'm all right," said Oliver, putting on his coat and cap and scarf. He pulled the basket over his arm before Mr. McCready could make any more remarks that might keep Oliver around the shop. "Some fresh air will do me good, I think."

Fresh air, indeed. Being out of the confines of the shop would be almost like being free of the insistent cloud hanging inside of his head. It might follow him out of the shop, but the streets of London would afford him a great deal of distraction. Oliver almost ran out of the store.

The air moving on the street, in the scattered sunshine as it struck the snow-clad streets, was almost overwhelming. Oliver breathed it in and hurried up the lane into the main thoroughfare. Cabs and carts and butcher's floats clattered against the cobblestones, spraying slushy snow and mud as they went. He dodged between them, heading toward his first delivery just on the other side of the Strand with as much haste as he could muster. But being an apprentice boy from

McCready's Haberdashery did not mean he could shove and push his way through the crowd. The clothes he wore stood out and resembled a uniform, the brown trousers sensible, the brown jacket thick and well made. With the green scarf, he was a walking advertisement; any ill usage of potential customers on the street would not reflect well on the shop.

He made his deliveries quickly; they all seemed to be clustered around a group of grand hotels just where the Strand turned into Fleet Street. His last delivery was at a fine house where he could see through the open curtains a gathering of well-dressed folk and a woman in a flowing dress and veil that indicated that there was a wedding party going on. Oliver handed over a small brown parcel to the woman who answered the door. She was the mistress of the house, it was easy to see by her silk gown, and with her hair coming out of its bun, she looked quite distracted but happy.

"Here's a shilling for you," she said, handing it over to him just before she closed the door. His attempt to hand it back to her was met with a quick slam of the door.

Oliver stood there for a moment, money in hand, listening to the sound of happy chatter and voices and laughter coming from beyond the door. He would only disturb them if he were to attempt to return the shilling; it was far more of a tip than he'd ever gotten and seemed out of measure with the amount of work he'd done for it.

But Mr. McCready said that tips could be kept, so he slipped the shilling into his pocket and hurried down the steps. He cast his eyes up and down Fleet Street at the thronging crowd, the hustle of skirt, the brisk pace of the sandwich men. It was early yet, and he wasn't wanted back in the shop. What's more, no one was expecting him.

He could go back, of course, and hang about, hoping for more deliveries. Or he could face the disaster that had become the orphan, hoping all the while that no one had told Mr. McCready what he'd done. Or that the orphan himself had not, though Oliver didn't think that was likely. He knew himself that masters believed the hired help over any pauper.

With a finger, he traced the edge of the shilling in his pocket and felt the wind skiff around his head, the blowy smells from the river, which was not some streets off. Beyond the direction his feet were pointing lay some disaster, but he could hardly go back and face the confusion he'd mentally left behind at the haberdashery. He was hungry anyway, and he knew of a pie shop, one with good smells and lots of bright customers, just on Dean Street. He would go there, get a pie to eat while he stood in the street, and then he would go home. He refused to allow himself to remember how close Dean Street was to the Three Cripples.

The pie shop beneath the bright sign saying *Abigail's Pies* was as busy as when he'd last seen it, and it took him a good five minutes of standing in line before he was at the counter. A slightly frowsy older woman with her hair straggling from beneath her mostly clean cap slapped the counter in front of him with a flour-dappled hand.

"Sixpence," she said. "Cheese and onion, or sausage and onion, or egg, leek, and onion. We're all out of sausage and cheese."

"Sausage and onion," he said, his mouth watering. He handed her the shilling and she handed him back sixpence change, which, as he shoved it in his pocket, would make a better story to Mr. McCready than to say that he'd been tipped an entire shilling.

The woman behind the counter shoved the pie at him.

"Next!"

Oliver stepped away, out into the damp and windy street, with his empty basket over one arm and the pie in both hands. He took a bite and the flaky crust fell over his lips almost lovingly; the filling was still warm. He only hoped, as he chewed and swallowed, that it wasn't actually made of horse or cat or something; the neighborhood around the shop was dodgy at best, but Uncle Brownlow had shown him a shop like this a time or two, and they'd always had something nice to eat or to look at.

Within minutes, the pie was finished and his stomach felt more settled than it had in hours. Oliver licked his lips and wiped his hands on the sides of his trousers. When he resettled his basket, he realized where he was. Of course he'd known, he'd always known, right where he was. Just a turn to the left and up the street and there he'd be, at the Three Cripples. Though why he imagined he might want to go there was beyond him.

But as he thought about going back to the shop, where he worked for a respectable man and made an honest living and had hot water to wash in and a clean place to sleep, his whole body stiffened up. The *orphan* would be there, with half of his face blotted dark by a bruise delivered by Oliver's own hand. Tate would be there, with looks out of the corner of his eyes, as if he didn't quite know what Oliver might do next, but that it wouldn't be anything polite. As for the rest of them—

Oliver shoved his hands in his pockets and marched up the lane, making the brief left and marching right up to the door and opening it before he could think twice. The smell of beer whapped him in the face again, and the skuff of wind he brought with him turned the customers at the bar to look at him as they had when he'd visited the last time, as though he didn't belong.

He stood there a moment, refusing to let his out-of-place feeling send him back out the door, but then Jack strode through the door at the far end of the bar with two pots of beer in his hand. His hat was, for once, not upon his head while he was indoors, and he'd doffed his blue waistcoat as well, leaving him only in his muslin shirt with the buttons opened at the neck.

"Nolly!" Jack gave a jerk of his head. "We're just havin' a drink, so come on then. I'll get them to bring some gin an' sugar for you."

Oliver nodded, wondering who the *we* was that Jack spoke of, and as he stepped through the door to the little room with the coal fire, he saw that, yes, of course, it was Noah. He had shed his coat to reveal his stained plaid waistcoat. Rolling up his sleeves, he was just sinking back in the bench seat when he caught sight of Oliver.

"Nolly, me lad!" said Noah heartily as if they were the best of friends, and Oliver's whole body jerked.

"Only I calls him that, mind," said Jack in a way that had Noah blinking at him in surprise.

"Work'us it is, then, come an' have a sit. We're celebratin' my pay packet, an' we invites you to share."

Of course, someone such as Noah would think to celebrate getting paid by spending it instead of putting it by, as any sensible person would do. But then, perhaps for Noah, there was always more where that came from, so Oliver didn't say what he wanted to. It was none of his business anyhow where or how Noah made or spent his money.

Instead of saying anything about it, Oliver merely took the bench seat across from Noah, and since he had stolen Jack's spot, Jack shoved Oliver in toward the wall to take his place on the outside. This placed Oliver in the corner, somewhat trapped, but this was probably a good thing as he couldn't be seen from the door or the window. Not that anyone he knew would come through the doors of the Three Cripples, now or anytime soon.

"Bring us some gin!" shouted Jack, turning his head away from Oliver. "Warm gin an' sugar, for my friend Nolly, here!"

"Gin, is it?" asked Noah with a smirk. "Never thought I'd see the likes of that, our very own Work'us drinkin' gin."

"Yes," said Jack, turning back around to grin at Noah. "He likes it best of all, an' mind you," here Jack leaned toward Noah, giving Oliver a wink as if it were all fun, "he can put back many a tot, as many as a sailor, before he starts any singing."

Where Jack had gotten that idea, Oliver didn't know, as Oliver couldn't even sing a note, but it made Noah and Jack laugh very hard indeed, almost spilling the beer in front of them.

The gin arrived in a tall tin tumbler, accompanied by a small pitcher of warm water and a little bowl with clumps of sugar. It was a strange feeling to have had this ordered for him and to be prepared to drink it while Noah and Jack looked on, but he'd had the worst day possible, the worst day in his experience at McCready's Haberdashery. Not that he was about to tell Noah and Jack that, but he wanted this drink. He wanted the relaxed feeling in his bones that it would bring him.

So, pretending that they weren't even there, at least for the moment, Oliver plopped a bit of sugar in the gin, grabbing it with his fingers since there were no tongs to be found, and then swirled the gin and sugar around, waiting for the lump to melt a bit. Then he poured in a little of the hot water and swirled it around some more.

He took a sip and saw that Noah and Jack were watching him, Noah with that sneer he wore when thinking about how to bedevil Oliver, and Jack, his brows quirking down as if something confused him. Oliver looked away, took another big swallow, and felt himself loosen from the inside.

"You'll be wantin' fried onions an' potatoes with that," said Jack, and as he shouted for the order, Oliver didn't stop him. He had sixpence, and lord knew how much Noah had in his pockets, and yes, he was hungry now, very hungry, if you please, in spite of the pie he'd just eaten. Fried onions and potatoes would be perfect with the sweet gin.

"So tell us the story about me," said Jack. He grabbed the plate of potatoes and onions from the serving girl and plunked it in the middle of the table.

"You mean the one where you was announced to be hextricated," said Noah. "Where I saw it all, 'cause I was there, right an' proper like, on Fagin's orders?"

"That's the one."

"But I've told it *three* times already."

"But not to Oliver." Jack looked straight at Oliver, and Oliver could see that Jack was proud of this event, that he wanted to brag on it as though it were something right and proper. The fact that Noah had actually been there, in the very courtroom, on the very day, seemed only to add fire to the fuel. "C'mon, Noah, be a dear lad an' tell the story."

"Fine, but this is the last time, you hear me, Jack? The last time!"

Jack nodded, though Oliver had a feeling that to keep Jack close, Noah would tell the story as many times as need be with as many embellishments as were wanted to keep the story fresh.

"So there I was," began Noah, spitting a bit, "in the back row, keepin' low like, behind some old dame who smelled like a tannery, an' along comes Jack Dawkins, as ever there was, resplendent in his gentleman's top an' tails, struttin' like a peacock, wavin' to one an' all."

"Tell the part where I demand me rights," said Jack, leaning forward on his elbows. His muslin shirt became half-rucked on his shoulders, exposing the naked skin of his chest, which he seemed not to notice. Though, even if he had, he wouldn't have cared.

"I'm gettin' to that, if'n you'll shut the hell up."

Jack just smirked, and Oliver took another sip of his gin and sugar and let the warmth of the liquor do its work. He was fairly sure half the story would be untrue, but as it was, it was beginning not to matter nor he to care.

"'Where are my privileges?' I shouted to the magistrate!" Jack almost shouted this now.

"Yes, yes, you shouted it an' then you lectured the court on their responsibilities to you an' to your schedule that day, an' if it would please them, could you have the names an' records of all of them who were on the bench accusin' you."

"An' then the whole place busted up laughing!" Jack pounded the table, eyes sparkling. "An' all of this for a twopenny-halfpenny snuffbox."

Jack was laughing so hard at this, at the recollection of it, even though Noah hadn't yet finished the story, for surely there was the judgment and sentence to come, that Oliver couldn't help but smile himself. There was just something so quirky, almost amusing about the whole affair, that he could almost imagine the Jack that he knew then, much younger but just as cocky, demanding the attention of one and all and imposing his will on them. Or trying to; Oliver couldn't imagine that the magistrate had been much amused, however much anyone in the bench seats had been laughing.

"An' the witnesses," Noah continued. "They brought the very gentleman in to testify, an' a high toff he was too."

"Could have bought another snuffbox easy," said Jack. He shook his head. "What was it to him, then, eh?"

Oliver opened his mouth, thinking just then to remind them both that private property was protected under the law, whether it be a snuffbox that cost twopenny-halfpenny or whether it be the crown jewels themselves.

"That's when you told them that you wouldn't besmirch yourself talkin' to the witness an' announced to the place that you was to breakfast with the Vice President of the House of Commons that very mornin', an' could you be on your way. Which is when they committed you!"

Now both Noah and Jack pounded the table and roared and ordered more beer to make up for what they had spilled. Oliver allowed them to order him another gin and sugar, which he politely sipped while they swilled their drinks, getting it over their collars and cuffs.

"C'mon, Nolly," said Jack, giving him a shove with his elbow. "You're all long in the mouth like someone's just pulled a tooth from you. Tell old Jack what's wrong with you, an' I'll cheer you up, quick as you please."

"It's the orphan," said Oliver, feeling it slip out of him before he could stop it. "They're being cruel to him at the shop, and I—" He was about to mention Dick one more time, to see if by explaining it to Jack he could understand it himself. The guilt was eating at him, and maybe it would be good to say it out loud.

But Jack interrupted him.

"Why are you so worked up about this lot? Is the poor, wee mite bein' buggered?" asked Jack. "You'll not want to worry about that, my pretty, boys get buggered every day."

This sent Noah to snickering into his beer, and Oliver felt as if the gin were starting to wear off. Still, the room was warm and close and exactly what he needed to chase the images of a skinny-faced orphan from his mind.

"But what's buggering?" he asked, hating it that he didn't know.

Now Noah spat up a whole mouthful of beer, mostly on himself, as he howled and pounded the table.

Jack, ignoring Noah and his spasms of laughter, was serious and almost kindly as he looked at Oliver. "You can't save the world, Nolly," he said.

"I can, my little corner of it," Oliver said. He gripped the edge of the table and fought off a sudden light-headedness. He shouldn't be at the Three Cripples at all, let alone drinking, let alone having this conversation. Let alone visiting with Jack Dawkins, ex-convict. Let alone sharing a drink with *Noah Claypole*, of all people. But the worst of it was the lie; he couldn't save the orphan because he himself was the one being cruel. But he couldn't confess it now; Noah was wiping his eyes about whatever buggering was and shaking his head as if he couldn't believe that Oliver didn't know.

"I should get back to the shop," Oliver said. He began scooting out of the bench seat, looking around for his basket, when Jack grabbed the sleeve of his jacket and did not shift in his seat so that Oliver could go.

"But you'll come again?" said Jack. "I'll show you my tattoo next time. I got it durin' a ceremony; them blacks're awful clever with a needle."

"I thought you said you got it on board the *Bertha May*?" asked Oliver. He stood up and moved along the bench so that Jack would have to lean back. He was sure that he'd heard it differently last time.

Jack just shook his head. He looked up at Oliver with a little smile as he leaned back, but not far enough to give Oliver a clear space; their bodies pressed close for a moment, thighs and knees bumping. "No, no, it was them already there, in Australia, that did it. You couldn't get a tattoo as clear as mine on a movin' ship, now could you?"

Oliver nodded, pretending not to be irritated as he lurched free of the bench, beyond the reach of Jack's hand as he bent to grab his basket. He supposed that what Jack said was so, but why on earth Jack couldn't stick to the truth the first time was beyond him.

"Good day, gentlemen," said Oliver, tipping his cap at them.

Noah was shaking his head as Oliver pulled himself together. "Always with them airs an' graces o' yours, eh, Work'us?"

"What's it to you, then?" Oliver asked, his reaction breaking through the ease the gin had created.

"Nothin', as always," said Noah, smirking at him.

For a second, Jack looked confused, as if he couldn't possibly imagine that Noah and Oliver were not friends. Oliver could see how in Jack's mind they were all one big collection of Fagin's boys, and surely, being such, they would want to band together and hold down the fort until more of them arrived. The likelihood of that was very small, but Jack had proved Oliver wrong once before, and so might again.

Tucking his basket in the crook of his elbow, Oliver made his way out of the throng that had collected in the Three Cripples and into the street. It was much later than he had supposed, with the sun now fully behind the clouds that were building over the rooftops of the City. Bells started clanging the hour; it was five o'clock, then, and Oliver began walking as fast as he might, given the traffic and the slippery streets. If he didn't make any wrong turns, didn't get held up at any crossings, then he'd be back at the shop within the half hour. No one would know where he'd been or who he'd been talking to. But only if he hurried.

CHAPTER 20

Considers His Impetuous Actions And Past Regrets

It took several days before the bruises on the orphan's face began to fade, though no one asked any questions or seemed concerned in any way. The orphan himself had not said anything about it, though, truly, he never said much of anything at all. Oliver told himself that Martin was getting used to the hard work and that everything would work out before too long.

In the middle of the week, there was another delivery to yet another new customer on Charlotte Street. Oliver left this delivery for last as a kind of treat; the area was a newer, fancier neighborhood than the one where the shop was, and just a little bit more elegant, with wider streets, and newer paving stones. There were a great many street sweepers, as well, who were just as dirty about the face but were, perhaps, a bit less fractious about their task of sweeping the walks as there was plenty of stately traffic and well-dressed gentlemen for every sweep to attend to. Even as Oliver crossed the street, a penny flipped past his head, and the sweep caught it. Not that Oliver had ever paid for a sweep in his life, but a penny was all it took to have the street free of debris, to save the staff at home from having to spend too much effort cleaning one's boots.

The delivery of the shawl was at a very fine townhouse, but then Oliver had expected that, given the address. What he didn't have was any information about whether deliveries should be made to the front door so as to make an impression, or down to the kitchen area in a more circumspect fashion. Since the townhouse was in the middle of the block, there was no side door for him to linger by while he attempted to figure it out. He stood there, right on the pavement, with the basket over his arm. He studied the sparkling windows, the newly scrubbed steps, the fresh paint on the railing down to the kitchen area while the rain soaked into his cap.

Just then, the white cap of a parlor maid peeped out from behind the thick curtains. The front door opened and the maid stuck her head out, just a little way.

"Go down," she said. "I'll meet you there."

Oliver nodded and then hurried down the iron stairs to the kitchen area, and tapped lightly on the wooden door. It opened to admit him to the wide, clean kitchen. The parlor maid came up to him and took the package, opening it with the cook's knife to examine the silky, patterned cloth of a shawl before she refolded it to take it up to her mistress.

The cook, who was talking to someone who looked like a housekeeper, gestured to Oliver to sit and warm himself by the fire, and Oliver did so, doffing his cap and loosening his scarf, reaching out for the hot cup of sweet tea that was urged upon him. The parlor maid, the cook, and the housekeeper all flitted about him as if they'd nothing better to do than urge another cup of tea on him after he'd drunk the first one, and then a slice of yellow cake. As if he'd just crossed some frozen tundra and would surely perish without some sustenance.

The cook even patted his face, saying, "How your cheeks are, you're as fair as an angel."

But this attention wasn't the same as those paid to him by Mrs. Acton, with her fingers curled around his arm, expecting him to say or do something a bit more daring than he usually did when making deliveries. No, the cook was more like Mrs. Pierson or even dear Mrs. Bedwin, cooing and petting and mothering as though there were no tomorrow. As if he were the dearest, sweetest creature on earth, very precious, and so worthy of their prayers. He dropped his chin and smirked a little bit, then held his cup out for more tea.

Then he saw the scullery maid coming from the washroom with a basket full of lumps of white cloth. She was thin in the face with straggles of hair coming out from beneath her none-too-clean cap. He could tell it was an effort for her to hold the basket of white things away from the soot-dusted fold of sacking she had tied around her waist. He'd heard Mrs. Pierson complain a time or two as to how getting clothes clean got the ones being worn so very dirty; it was obvious that the scullery maid was having the same problem. Being so very thin, her arms were shaking under the weight of the basket, and in a second or two, she was going to drop it and spill the clean linen all over the stone floor.

Then it happened. Just as everyone's back was turned, Oliver saw her shift forward as if to heft the basket a bit better on her hip, and three white lumps fell to the floor. She looked at him from beneath her straggles of hair, her eyes wide. And he didn't know whether she was ill-used or just having a bad day, but he had only a brief moment to decide what to do. Did he draw the attention of the parlor maid, the cook, and the kitchen maid to the incident? Or did he distract them? But why should he help a mere scullery maid? What was it to him if she got smacked around and had to wash the whole lot over again? Henry and Tate would have fallen about laughing had they been there, as would any apprentice.

But before he could do either, the cook caught him staring and turned before the scullery maid could scoop up the washing and put it back in the basket.

"What are you after?" snapped the cook, getting red in the face as she advanced on the scullery maid. "Flouncing about as though you weren't the least scrap of flesh in this kitchen? Pick that up and get back to your work before I have a good excuse to lock you again in the coal cellar for the night." Then the cook slapped the girl in the face, leaving a red mark, dark beneath the streaks of grime on her cheeks, and bringing quick tears to her eyes.

The scullery maid trembled as she bent to get the once-clean laundry, crying hard enough to leave silver-white splotches on the brick floor. Her hands shook as she tucked the cloth in, and were white as they gripped the edges of the basket. Without lifting her eyes, she turned and hurried down a small white-washed corridor, where, he assumed, there was a room strung with rope for drying before the ironing.

Unsettled, Oliver put the tea cup back in the saucer and stood up, holding his hands out for his cap, his scarf, and his basket. The back of his throat tasted bitter, not because he hadn't been able to help her but because he'd not been able to decide. And in the end, he might as well have announced her mistake, as he had done by looking her way so intently. She wouldn't be thinking kindly of him, and all the attentions of the rest of the female staff wouldn't change how badly that made him feel.

But what should he care? He took his coat and scarf, now mostly dry from being next to a warm, coal fire, and put them on. Then he took up his basket and put his cap on and said thank you to the ladies. With their waves and good-byes, he made his way up the stairs, telling himself he wasn't shaking. When he got up out of the kitchen area and onto the street, it was as busy as before, even with the slanted, freezing rain coming down, causing the gentlemen to hurry to their carriages or under their umbrellas, pushing past him as if he weren't even there. Standing, as though he were a dolt, in the middle of the pavement, his empty basket under one arm, hearing the chimes sound the hour from a nearby steeple.

As Oliver tucked his chin into his scarf and scurried through the back lanes to Oxford Street, he realized that he could have taken the time to go to the Three Cripples to see Jack, but he wasn't going to. He was soaked through, and besides which, Jack would not only be completely unaffected by Oliver's struggle, he would laugh and slap Oliver on the back as if the whole thing was a lark performed for his amusement. But it wasn't.

None of this was amusing, not any of it. That Oliver's hand, in temper, had struck Martin to the floor, and whether it had not been as cruel a blow as the cook's to the scullery maid, didn't matter. A blow against someone who was not only defenseless but who would be punished even further for fighting back—well, it didn't matter. A blow was a blow, and through his cruelty to Martin, Oliver was no better than a common cook. Worse, even, far worse, for Oliver had been through it himself, and knew, *knew* what it was like to be on the receiving end of that sort of senseless, blind brutality.

To finish matters off, Oliver had, since the orphan's arrival, been pretending, when he could, that the orphan wasn't even there. To be treated as though invisible? That was the height of cruelty. No one deserved that. Oliver certainly never had, no matter what the man in the white waistcoat might say, and the orphan—Martin—certainly didn't. He and Martin were both workhouse boys, bundled and tossed into the world without a hint of caution. They shared that, even if between them there had not been anything else; under the skin, they were of a kind. In realizing that, he could no longer go on treating Martin as he had. If he did—if he did—

At the corner of Soho Square where the streets started bending toward the river, Oliver stopped, feeling somewhat light-headed. Normally, he would have put it off to hunger, though certainly his body was accustomed to far worse than the emptiness that the mere hours between dinner and supper might supply. But Martin—so small for ten years of age. Oliver had seen him at mealtimes, more than once, trying not to stare at the amount of food on the table once he'd finished his own food, and failing. With all the work he was doing, as much as any boy in the shop, he must be—he was starving. And it wasn't right, Oliver knew that, knew it inside, feeling it right alongside the loss of anything kind and good inside of himself, which would happen if he didn't change his approach to this. Yes, Martin reminded him of uncomfortable memories better left forgotten, but he did not deserve to go hungry for it.

Oliver swallowed and took a breath, collecting his thoughts as the rain dripped from his cap. It was pouring now, and ice was starting to come down like shards of silver, slipping down his neck through his sodden scarf. It was time to go back to the shop, and he started walking, heading directly there instead of delaying along the way as he normally would have.

Upon his return, he hung up his dripping coat and scarf and hat in the warehouse, and went straight down to the kitchen to wash, wanting to be the first person at the supper table. Which he was, and he felt slightly warmer as he slid into his seat and accepted the cup of hot tea that Mrs. Pierson gave him to drink while waiting for Mr. McCready and the boys. She didn't give Martin any tea; Oliver felt himself flush, cheeks red, and wished he could put it off to the warmth of the kitchen versus the damp cold of outside. But it wasn't. No, it was Martin's small glance his way, and his obedient stillness on his tall stool, which wobbled a little as he balanced his thin elbow on the sideboard. Waiting. Just waiting.

Oliver looked away, even though he told himself he wasn't going to, and ignored the hard press of a fist in his empty stomach. He tried sipping his tea instead but found that it had gone cold, or maybe there wasn't enough sugar in it, he didn't know. It didn't taste as good as it ought to have done.

Tate and Henry soon came quickly down the stairs, squabbling about the warehouse door, as usual, much to Oliver's relief. They washed up, bumping each other to be first at the basin, and then sat at the table, loudly, drowning out anything Oliver might think to say, and particularly, anything he might want to say about the fact that Martin was still watching him. Normally, Oliver would snap at him, even with an audience, to mind his own business, but he only tucked his head down and kept his mouth shut.

When Mr. McCready arrived, washed his hands, and sat down, Mrs. Pierson stood by the table and bent her head as the boys did while Mr. McCready said grace. Then as soon as he said amen, she hurried to serve them their supper, even more eager to feed them, perhaps, on account of the cold weather. Oliver picked up his knife and fork and began to cut open one of Mrs. Pierson's perfectly baked cheese and onion pies, salivating before even a single crumb of it was in his mouth. As he chewed, he watched Henry and his perfect manners, as he usually did, then looked up. The orphan, with a bowl of something cold and leftover, was eating with both hands, and though he was looking at Oliver, he didn't say anything. But then, he wasn't supposed to, not at mealtimes.

Oliver looked at the wall, at Henry and Tate eating, at Mrs. Pierson fussing over their plates, anywhere but at Martin. Then he looked at his own plate. In addition to the pie, there was a pile of buttered peas, which Oliver had never cared for but made himself eat for Mrs. Pierson's sake. He'd seen the orphan and his thin sallow face just that morning scrubbing the stone floor that led to the larder and boiler room, soaked to the skin, his wrists and thin arms red from the washing soda. It was obvious, even from where he was sitting, that there were no peas in Martin's bowl.

As Oliver paused in eating, putting his cutlery down, Tate looked up, knife and fork in each hand, and watched Oliver push his plate back.

"I'm quite full, Mrs. Pierson," said Oliver, slowly. "Or would you see that as a ruse to leave more room for your sponge pudding?"

Mrs. Pierson preened a bit at this then jumped up to grab Oliver's plate as if he might, at any minute, change his mind. Before anyone could say anything, she scraped the remains of Oliver's plate into a low-sided bowl and handed it to the orphan.

"Waste not, want not," said Mrs. Pierson. She watched for a moment while the orphan grabbed the slice of pie with one hands and scooped up the peas with the other, and then turned back to the table where everyone was looking at her. Mr. McCready looked a bit thunderous, but there was nothing he could do, not really. Leftovers were to be given to the orphan.

She took all their plates and handed out the sponge pudding. Across from him, Tate took a few spoonfuls that were dripping with custard. Then, looking at Oliver, Tate pushed his bowl away from him.

"I cannot understand it, Mrs. Pierson," said Tate, his mouth quivering as if struggling not to smile. "I am so full, even your pudding can find no room."

Henry only shook his head when Tate looked at him, and Oliver imagined this game was too foolish for such an up-and-coming young man as Henry.

Now Mrs. Pierson's eyebrows flew up, and she grabbed Tate's plate and rushed it over to Martin, who was looking at her with a small, shocked expression. But it was too late for Mr. McCready to object to this, the portion of sponge was gone in the orphan's mouth before Mrs. Pierson barely had time to make it back to the table.

Oliver finished his pudding, not letting himself look at Tate. He felt shivery and hot inside at the realization that Tate was doing this to amuse himself. It might be fun for a while, but then again, it would be bending Mr. McCready's rules to the point where they would break, the rules would change, and the orphan would again know hunger and want. It would be the orphan who would be the one to pay for it, even though it wasn't his fault that Tate enjoyed a good joke. Or that Oliver's soft heart could no longer be guarded while the orphan looked so pale and shivered as he went about his daily tasks.

"That's quite enough, Mrs. Pierson," said Mr. McCready. "Back to the shop, boys. And you, Martin, bring more coal; I cannot imagine why you think there is sufficient to supply each fire."

They returned to their tasks, Henry and Mr. McCready to the front shop and Oliver and Tate to the warehouse. It was colder today, and so Oliver poked up the stove and added coal to the fire, putting in bits of coal with his bare hands, using the charred cloth to close the door tightly. The orphan came at some point with a scuttle of coal to fill the box next to the stove and went away quietly. Oliver tried not to think upon it and instead focused his efforts on drawing up more ledger books for Tate using a square piece of lead and the edge of a ruler to make the lines straight.

"No one does it the way you do, Oliver," said Tate as he took the prepared ledger from him. "You've got quite the hand, ever so tidy."

"Thank you," said Oliver. When he owned a bookshop, he would be able to do more of that, sitting at a desk keeping records than sweeping and dusting and picking up horse droppings from the yard. A man who owned his own store had workers to do that for him; he never had to dirty his hands with the more mundane work.

It was just before the supper hour on Friday, a day that had turned quite cold, where the snow began to come down in thick flakes, cutting through the fog and making the ground quite white within minutes. Oliver had just finished loading boxes onto the shelves and was looking at his finger where a splinter had gone in. He worried it with his teeth for a moment and then thought about leaving it in place and pretending it wasn't there.

"Splinter?" asked Tate as he walked past Oliver, untying his apron.

Oliver nodded, halfheartedly thinking about getting a penknife and digging at it, and watched as the orphan came from the shop, carrying a bucket of ashes down the stairs.

For the past few days, Oliver, at most meals, had explained to Mrs. Pierson that he'd been too full to finish what was on his plate, so, subsequently, Martin had had more to eat. Tate had joined in for the joke of it, giving Martin his pudding both at dinner and supper, he'd stopped, probably because going without a sweet at the end of the meal wasn't as funny to him as he'd thought it would be. And though Oliver had wanted to punch him, he didn't. At the very least, that was more food for Martin, who, indeed, had a bit of color in his face and more energy in his walk.

Still, Martin was now leaving a trail of ashes behind him as he walked down the wooden stairs to the warehouse, but it was easy to see that he wasn't aware of it. Without considering it, Oliver straightened up from his lean against the shelves, his mouth open to say something, trying to think quickly so that it didn't come out harsh as it had before.

But then there came a roar from the shop, and Mr. McCready was on the heels of the orphan, smacking him to the stone floor before Oliver could get a single word out.

"Blast you, leaving hot ashes to burn a wooden floor, have you no sense?" Mr. McCready stood over Martin as he curled up on the stone, holding the side of his head where Mr. McCready had boxed him. "I'll teach you to be so careless."

Mr. McCready grabbed the switch from beside the door and hauled Martin up by his collar, much in the way that Oliver had done, but Mr. McCready's grip was sure and the collar stayed true. Which meant that Martin was half choking as Mr. McCready held the orphan there, and began thrashing him. Oliver could hear the switch whistling through the air, and the cold, sharp sound it made as it cut through skin and cloth. The orphan, through low-pitched cries, couldn't even breathe enough to scream out loud, and the switch kept coming down.

"Stop." Oliver heard this coming out of his own mouth, more of a croak than anything else, with Tate standing nearby, eyes wide in astonishment.

Oliver cleared his throat and tried again and heard himself say it again, in clear, ringing tones that belonged to someone altogether quite different than the person he felt himself to be. "*Stop*. Stop *hitting* him."

The switch froze in midair, and Martin hung from Mr. McCready's grip, a dark, black bruise on his face and livid stripes of red pushing through his thin garment. The switch had torn the cloth as much as the skin, and Oliver saw the lash marks and counted them, vivid pulses of switch marks his own skin had so often felt.

"What did you say to me? Are you speaking to me, Oliver?" Mr. McCready's voice thundered as he pulled Martin to a standing position. "How dare you? I run this shop, and the boy is in my care. You will apologize at once, do you hear?"

"When heaven's trumpets sound," said Oliver.

"What?"

"I said I will apologize *when heaven's trumpets sound* and not before." The words came out as a roar, as though a wild animal had been woken by seeing the orphan being thrashed with such violence unbefitting his small stature.

"What on earth—" Mr. McCready's mouth fell open, shock coloring his cheeks.

"He's only little," said Oliver, swallowing, feeling some of the fire die away inside of him. "And it was an accident, him spilling the ashes. The bucket's too big for him to carry, and it's been filled to the brim. What else would happen but that he would spill it? You shouldn't treat him so cruelly."

Now everyone in the warehouse was looking at him, their eyes wide, frozen in place as if Oliver had begun speaking in tongues or had grown an extra head. Because either of those would be more likely than that he would speak up on the orphan's behalf. Oliver knew this; he'd been nothing but cruel to the orphan since the day he'd arrived, the gift of the leavings from his plate notwithstanding. To see him now, thus, in defense of Martin, he could understand their confusion. But to stop Mr. McCready from doing what he saw as his duty? He must be mad.

Mr. McCready let the orphan go with a shake. Martin shuddered, wiping his face with the back of his hand, and looked up at Mr. McCready with wet eyes.

"You sit over there on that bench beside the steps and don't get up until you're given leave, do you hear me? And you will stay out here until I give you leave to come inside."

Martin nodded and went to sit down, wincing with each movement, sitting there with the weight of his body on the welts. It was a cruel thing to do, but of course, Mr. McCready never did anything by accident.

"And you." Mr. McCready turned on Oliver, pointing the switch at him. "I will give you one more opportunity to apologize. You are *not* the master here and you will *not* dictate to me, you—now apologize at once!"

"No," said Oliver. He could see the anger suffusing Mr. McCready's face with color, could see the confusion in his eyes, the wrinkled brow. He was a disappointment, he knew that, and Mr. McCready's trust in him probably felt like it had been misplaced; any warnings Mr. Grimwig might have shared were probably coming to the forefront of Mr. McCready's memories.

He could not apologize, not for this. The orphan was a tiny mite of a thing, put to tasks that would have left Lucy, the sturdy hired girl, breathless. And Oliver could no longer stand aside and see it done. Not even if, particularly not if, he'd been party to it from the beginning.

"No," he said again. "I will not. And this cannot go on."

This stopped Mr. McCready; the switch lowered in his hand. "What are you on about?"

"He needs more food; he needs more rest." Oliver could hardly believe he was saying any of this out loud, let alone to Mr. McCready. Yet something insisted on being said from his heart. "Let the girl take some of his tasks; she can manage those buckets better than he."

"Are you telling me how to run my shop?"

Mr. McCready's brows lowered and he went white, and Oliver knew he'd said the worst things. It was one thing to defend the orphan, the most important thing, but to give Mr. McCready direction? He was an upstart orphan himself, who, in Mr. McCready's eyes, had overstepped his station. But it was too late to back out now.

"Yes," said Oliver. He jerked his chin up, stood his ground.

"Get over here. I've spent my last ounce of compassion on you, thinking you'd shape up to be a proper clerk, but no. In spite of my best efforts, the workhouse has left its stamp all over you. Now, get over here."

Mr. McCready gestured with the switch to the table. As Tate scurried out of the way, pressing himself against the wall on the other side of the stair from the orphan, Oliver walked over to the table. He wanted to think he marched up, proudly, head held high, but he knew he barely lifted his feet. The whipping he was about to receive was the least of it. Oh, yes, it would hurt, for days, perhaps, but he'd let Mr. McCready down in the worst way, and that hurt more than anything.

His face quivered as he bent over the worktable, and he hid his head in the circle of his arms. There was trying to save his little corner of the world, and then there was this. When the switch came down, Oliver's whole body jerked as if he was being ripped apart from within, but he did not make a sound. Would not, clamped his mouth shut over it, pressed his forehead against the rough boards as the switch came down, cutting through the air, whistling, feeling like a knife on his skin. Finally, at the tenth blow, he was gasping, sweat on the back of his neck, as Mr. McCready hauled him up by his collar.

"You," said Mr. McCready through gritted, bared teeth. "You will go to bed without supper while I think of reasons not to dismiss you." He let Oliver go with a shake, much as he had done with the orphan, to whom he pointed with the end of the switch. "And *you* will stay there till I give you leave to get up."

With dignified steps, Mr. McCready replaced the switch on the hook and pushed his hair back from his forehead. He gestured for Oliver and Tate to precede him up the stairs. When they reached the landing, he stopped.

"There will be two less for supper," he called down the stairs to Mrs. Pierson. Oliver could hear her confused voice as she replied but could not make out the words.

Then Mr. McCready cuffed Oliver on the back of the head to send him up the stairs to the boys' dormitory. "I don't want to see you until morning."

"Likewise, I'm sure," said Oliver, shocked to hear himself, but he kept his voice low, almost a whisper as he limped up the stairs. The risers seemed interminably steep, and the narrow walls seemed to press in upon him as though to stop him on his way. Halfway up, he paused on the landing, leaning against the wallpaper to breathe slowly, in and out, waiting for his heart to slow down. Waiting for the hot, burning layers all along the backs of his legs to stop feeling as though they'd just been shifted into action with stern jabs of a fire poker.

By the time his lungs had stopped heaving and the feeling in his thighs had abated only a little, he made his way up the stairs to his room. He went to the washstand and used the leftover cold water from yesterday to dip his hands right into the pitcher and pressed his palms to his face. Had he been in anyone's good graces, let alone Mrs. Pierson's, she might have *tut tutted* over him and given him some sweet honey to distract him from his ill-usage, and maybe a cold cloth, drops of lavender pushed in, for his forehead as he lay on his bed.

But he had none of this, only the cold water, which he drank, lifting the pitcher straight to his mouth. When that was gone, he put the pitcher back in the bowl and turned to face the row of beds. They were neatly made up, as they had been every day since Lucy and the orphan had been hired. The floor was shining, the bedsteads dusted. The room was a model of industry and comfort, at least, the type of comfort an apprentice shop boy could come to expect. From below came the smells of supper, wafting up, speaking of boiled potatoes and butter, meat frying, and something sweet for afterward.

Shaking this off, Oliver thought about getting a book, but this would mean bending down, and he was not up to that. There was nothing for it but to shed his clothes, put on his nightshirt, and struggle under the covers. He had to lay on his front, with his arms tucked under the single pillow, so he did this, clasping his left arm with shaking fingers, blinking against the semi-gloom of the late evening room, some reflected light coming through the curtain, from a link boy perhaps, or a fire from the alley, lit by some squalid street person, made up of old crates that Oliver and Tate had left there.

He had thought he would have to deal with Henry and Tate when they came up after supper, answering their foolish, probing questions. But when he next opened his eyes, the room was dark and he could sense the breathing dark humps that were Henry and Tate, tucked in their beds, already asleep. For hours, it seemed; it was so dark and still and cold, Oliver knew it was the middle of the night.

He'd woken up from another dream about Dick, with tangled, messy images of bone and hunger and a sharp wind whistling through his clothes as he tried to find his friend. The feeling of hunger lingered on a smudge of memory right behind his eyes. Oliver was cold all over, and the backs of his legs hissed at him whenever he tried to move at all.

Would Mr. McCready send him packing in the morning? Or would he have some kind though disappointed lecture for Oliver, one that would make Oliver feel worse than he already did? Would he again demand an apology, and could Oliver give it? He couldn't change the world, but surely he could do something to protect this one orphan. Just this one.

He imagined what Jack might say if Oliver were to tell him the tale of the night's happenings. And the look of confusion that Jack would give him, as if to ask, *why should you care? Why would you go to such ends?* Because he knew it was true; one orphan or a thousand, the story was the same. They all lived hard lives, and were loved by no one. It was his own story, and the fact that he'd escaped it to start another life was a miracle of coincidence and dumb luck, all carried on a river of circumstance, such as the one that had carried Noah to the Three Cripples just in time to help Fagin with his machinations. How odd was that, how improbable?

Noah, for his part, would just shake his head. Not only did he not care about any humanity save his own, he, from Oliver's experience, couldn't understand why anyone else would feel any differently than that. Looking out for himself had always been Noah's credo; to do anything else was to cause his own soul too much expense and bother. Let the other man fall on his face, for what did Noah Claypole care? He would only mock Oliver if he knew what Oliver meant to do. To stand up to Mr. McCready in the morning, to ensure that Martin, at least, was not overworked. That he be treated better.

What would Oliver do to gain that aim? Would he then apologize?

It would be a burden to apologize, but perhaps he should. If Mr. McCready didn't sack him on the spot.

His eyelids were starting to feel heavy, so he let them stay shut instead of trying to blink to keep himself awake. He let the darkness take him where it would, with blurred images of Dick's face, that last morning in the garden, and of Jack, cocking his head to stare at Oliver that first day in London. Staring at Oliver, ragged and haggard from walking seven days on almost no food but looking at him with an expression that, in retrospect, was calculating. As if Oliver were a bright new toy that Jack had just found; something for Fagin to use as he would. Though Oliver had no doubt that Jack had had no part of the deal between Monks and Fagin, Jack had, to be sure, gained from the introduction of the very young Oliver to the kindly old gentleman of his intimate acquaintance. Money, perhaps? Or extra recommendations as Jack moved up in the ranks? Oliver might never know.

And the worry stirred in him again as to how it might have been different had he taken Dick with him. Would that he had taken another turn that day or kept going or stopped sooner. Then he never would have met Jack. Though, in truth, it wasn't Jack's fault, or even Noah's that put Oliver where he was now. In serious disgrace, and at the risk of losing everything. But what price that, if he answered to his own heart?

The last thought, which draped itself about his mind as a well-worn velvet cloak, was what on earth Jack had been doing in Barnet, so far from his normal stomping grounds. Oliver had wondered that, on and off, through the years; it had never occurred to him that he might take the opportunity to ask.

CHAPTER 21

The Consequences Of Oliver's Passionate Nature

Oliver awoke to the stumblings and mutterings of Henry and Tate squabbling over the hot water that the girl had just brought up. He heard her steps going down and Mrs. Pierson's loud shouts for something or someone, and he knew he had to get up. Face the day. Face his workmates. Face Mr. McCready.

For their parts, Henry and Tate merely nodded at him as if yesterday had been an ordinary day. Which it had not been, though whether or not Tate and Henry had talked to each other about it, Oliver didn't know. But they were not unkind boys; it was not in them to torment, or in Tate's case, tease overly much. They both knew the grace of their stations; to become ill-mannered was to chance losing it. For as anyone could see, a McCready's Haberdashery boy was a cut above an unemployed ex-apprentice.

"Water's yours, Oliver," said Tate as he finished pouring his slops in the bowl. "Better get a move on for breakfast; you must be starving after yesterday."

"Yes," said Oliver. He made himself get straight out of bed and wash up. But he forgot and rolled up the sleeves of his nightshirt too far, exposing his forearm and the jagged half circle of ridged flesh. Both Henry and Tate stood there with open mouths and wide eyes. They might have heard of what had happened, perhaps, but now they had the evidence of it with their very own eyes, that Oliver came from a very bad background.

"Not looking's just as bad as staring," said Oliver, his heart racing, trying for some levity as he imagined that Jack might at a moment such as this. Though why he felt that being like Jack was ever a good thing was beyond him to comprehend. Jack might laugh when he told him, if he ever did.

He made himself finish washing up and put on his clothes as if this were any ordinary day. He went to his bed and put himself in order, straightening his suspenders, tying his boots, taking down his brown waistcoat from its peg. He felt the stiffness of the whipping from the day before. It began in the back of his neck, as if all of his muscles were fully joined together, locked in iron. He had to roll his shoulders before he could pull the waistcoat on.

He could go on this way, feeling guilty, or he could apologize; Mr. McCready said he might, if he was able. Mr. McCready always kept his word and let bygones be bygones once reprimands had been made.

Straightening his waistcoat and adjusting his shirt collar, he followed Henry and Tate down the stairs. They all clomped, of course they did, in spite of the many injunctions against it both by Mr. McCready and Mrs. Pierson. But with the good smells of a hot breakfast, even Oliver could not help but hurry.

In the kitchen, Mrs. Pierson was alone, with the table half-set and she with her hands dirty with coal.

"Can I assist you, Mrs. Pierson?" asked Henry, gallantly.

"You can load this coal and deal with this fire while I finish up this porridge."

"Has the new girl gone off already, Mrs. Pierson?" asked Tate. He took his seat with a little smile, as if he were on the verge of finding the whole disarray of the morning extremely funny.

"No, the master wanted extra hot water, and so I sent her up. Oliver." Mrs. Pierson looked directly at him as though yesterday's events had never happened. "Be a dear boy and go find that orphan. I've called and called, but there's been no answer."

Oliver nodded, glad to be of use and out of the kitchen while it was so unsettled. He scanned the kitchen, noting Henry's industry and helpful movement around the oblivious and already-seated Tate, and saw only the empty stool where the orphan sat during meals. He checked the scullery and the store room, only a little way off the kitchen, but still a viable pair of rooms where an orphan might hide and sulk. He even checked the door to the larder, but it was locked and only Mrs. Pierson had the keys. A quick check of the coal cellar revealed the same. The orphan was not in the most obvious places.

Feeling a moment of pure concern followed by an odd sensation of dizziness, Oliver climbed to the main floor and walked around the quiet shop, gloomy on account of the shutters still hanging on the other side of the windows. The room was clean and empty, with not even a scuff mark or a bit of dust to indicate anyone had been there since yesterday. The whole of the shop was entirely silent, with only the barest of noises from above and below to indicate anyone was nearby.

Oliver determined to go to the warehouse, though it would be cold this hour of the morning with no fire lit and the upper windows opened to let out the smoke from the day before. When he opened the door, he could still smell the smoke, though the air seemed clean and brisk, and the morning's church bells came through on the damp breeze. He stood at the landing with one foot on the top stair and scanned the warehouse, the narrow spaces between the shelves, noting that the small door inside the big door was firmly shut and locked from the inside.

Thinking to go and kneel next to the long table under the window to look for Martin there, he heard a small, stuttered sound, and when he turned to look for it, he saw the orphan. Martin was tucked against the wall on the floor, his knees pulled up to his narrow chest. His skin was white and he hadn't even the strength to shiver nor, it seemed, the sense to reach up and take down the warehouse coat to wrap it around him. That Mr. McCready had neglected to bring Martin in after his punishment of solitude was obvious, but the night had been cold enough to leave frost along the edges of the windows, enough so that Oliver saw his own breath cloud in the air.

Oliver rushed down the stairs and over to the orphan, and as he knelt on the cold stone floor, Martin gave several hitching gasps, and when he turned to look at Oliver, he could barely open his eyes. They were dim, clouded over, and his lips were blue. When Oliver touched the orphan's face, it was as cold as Uncle Brownlow's face when Oliver had kissed him good-bye. Colder, even, because inside the small frame was a beating heart; the contrast was too horrible to contemplate.

Oliver stood, pulling the small boy into his arms. Martin, still and cold, huffed a breath, a small, icy movement of air against Oliver's neck, and then went still. There was no respite from the panicked thud of Oliver's heart, though he hurried as fast as he was able with the bundle in his arms, up the wooden steps to the shop and then down the stairs to the kitchen, where Mrs. Pierson's coal fire waited.

"What in heaven's name—" Mrs. Pierson broke off as she watched Oliver kneel on the stone floor, unfolding Martin into the slow warmth that circled in waves around the cast-iron stove.

"Why, Oliver, has he been in the warehouse all night? And on such a cold night?"

Oliver looked over his shoulder, but only for an instant. Mrs. Pierson had her hands to her face, mouth open, a soundless heaving of her bosom. Likewise, Henry and Tate had stood up from their places at the table, frozen as though uncertain what was going on. Oliver turned his back on all of them and watched as his own hands reached out, feeling numb and mindless, as though he were watching himself do this from a long distance away. There was no feeling in his fingers as he stroked Martin's face, touched his temples, chafed his wrists.

And as he gathered Martin's hands in his own, the small fingers with permanent grime scoured into the knuckles, Martin's hand was still, so still, and the fingers did not clutch back.

They merely slid from Oliver's hands like small, boneless ribbons.

There was a silkiness to Martin's hair as Oliver pushed it away from Martin's forehead, which Oliver, to his horror, realized was damp from the frost melting in the warmth of the room. Martin's eyes, a milky blue, were open but did not flicker nor did the narrow chest rise and fall. Between the moment Oliver had lifted him from the warehouse floor and this, Martin had breathed his last.

"He's not breathing," said Oliver, barely able to speak the words. "He's—he's *dead.*"

"Nonsense," said Mrs. Pierson. She gave Martin a nudge with the tip of her black shoe poking from beneath her skirts. "Get up, you wretch, there's work to be done, so none of your lollygagging."

Oliver touched the skin beside Martin's eyes, but Martin did not even flinch. Oliver wanted to shove the cold body away from him, but he thought of Dick and gently cradled the back of Martin's head as he laid him down on the stones. The warmth of the fire was quite thick now, but though it dried the dampness from Martin's hair, his skin remained ice cold.

Oliver stood up. "Leave him be," he said to Mrs. Pierson, to the room. "He's dead, so leave him be."

Mrs. Pierson's hand flew to her bosom, face white as she took a step back.

"Why, Oliver," said Mr. McCready as he stepped into the kitchen from the stair. "How dare you speak to Mrs. Pierson so. Apologize at once and avoid further disgrace. You, boy, get up from the floor now, and go to work."

"The only place he'll be going is to a pauper's grave," said Oliver, feeling as though he were roaring as he spoke the words. "Don't you understand? He's *dead.*"

"There's no need to carry on so," said Mrs. Pierson.

"No, indeed," said Mr. McCready. He came fully into the kitchen now, moving past the boys and Mrs. Pierson to come right up to Oliver. "There was no reason for you to get attached to him. Besides, there are plenty of orphans at St. James's; we can easily get another."

"*Another?*" Oliver heard his own voice rise out of him, boiling up from his chest, a live thing with no master.

"Do you think there's an endless supply of small boys for you to dispose of at a whim? No!" Oliver reached out and only meant to shove Mr. McCready back, as far away as possible, from Martin's still form on the floor. Instead, he slammed Mr. McCready in the middle of his chest. "You left him in the warehouse and he froze to death, and you imagine that you can simply acquire another? And then another after *that?*"

Mr. McCready's eyebrows rose up, color rising in his cheeks as though affronted by Oliver's less than temperate remarks, as if it were horribly inconsiderate of Oliver to stand up for a dead orphan.

And of course, up to that moment, Oliver had been, to all intents and purposes, the obedient boy that everyone wanted him to be, expected him to be. Even, as queer as it might be, the sort of boy that Jack had mocked him for being. But something was moving thickly inside of him, like huge timber beams on a ship tossed at sea.

"He was never sturdy, Oliver," said Mr. McCready in the same tone he'd used with Mrs. Pierson the morning the stove had broken down. A tone meant to be soothing and pleasant but which only made Oliver's blood pound quicker still. "Some of the warehouse boys, why, a stiff breeze would knock them over; I'm quite sure the workhouse council and the beadle will understand that."

All of the breath in Oliver's body left him as though sucked out by the gasping, silent, gaping roar that seemed to fill the room. Oliver reached out his hand and grasped the handle of the cast-iron frying pan that was warming on the stove in preparation no doubt for thick slices of good bacon, and hefted it in the air. He had one split moment of thought, a whispered caution, one that almost stopped him, but momentum had built up in his body as he swung the pan in the air and slammed it against Mr. McCready's head. He jerked upright for a second, his whole body tightening, tight, and then he toppled to the floor, blood pouring in a red wave, forming a lake across the stones.

The iron pan vibrated against his palm. Oliver dropped it and stepped back from the blood that splashed up, and it hit the edge of his boot. Mrs. Pierson, her shrieks hitting Oliver's inner ear in dull echoes, ran to the door that led up to the street. He could hear her yelling, yelling for the constable, at someone passing by on the damp street above to go and fetch the constable.

And then, as Oliver looked at Henry and Tate and they at him, the moment became as frozen and still as a pauper's grave might be, as Dick had been placed in, as Martin shortly would be. The thought of it shuddered through Oliver, leaving him trying to breathe, gasping gulps past which no words could be eased. He could not explain that striking Mr. McCready was not what he meant to do, let alone—

"You murdered him," said Tate, hardly above a whisper. And of course it was Tate who would speak first; Henry remained silent, his expression tightening as though with some deep disdain for Oliver that he hardly had expressed until that moment.

"No," said Oliver, protesting against not only the accusation but also against the hot tumble in his belly that rose to his chest, threatening to choke him outright. "I only meant to—"

But Mrs. Pierson was stumbling back through the door, the air of the frosty morning leeching the warmth out of the room. She clutched her apron and skirts out of the way, and as she backed up, Oliver could see, through the narrow top of the window, a pair of booted feet clattering on the top step. Oliver moved, skirting the pool of blood turning to brown on the floor as it dried by the heat of the stove. He scrambled up the wooden steps to the first floor, mouth open, panting, arms aching with emptiness. He'd left Dick behind so callously. He'd failed Martin, leaving him to all the misery of abject neglect that he could manage. And now this.

His head felt as though it was sparking black dots in front of his eyes; he could barely see as he came to the narrow corridor on the ground floor, the door that led to the chilly warehouse. Without thinking, hands and limbs numb, Oliver grabbed the warehouse coat and threw it on, noting the dull flowers of red and brown on his shirt bosom, pulling the jacket over it. He could barely manage the lock on the small wooden door that led to the courtyard; it was stiff with cold. Oliver bent close and breathed on it, his fingers tugging all the while until it loosened and shot open under his hands. He could hear shouting from the kitchen; he had to hurry or they'd catch him, and he knew, his heart thudding painfully against his breastbone as he stepped through the opening and into the cobbled yard, that there was only one place he could go. Only one person he could turn to. So he started running.

CHAPTER 22

The Flight; Or
At The Three Cripples

As he flung himself into the cobblestone yard and out through the alley that led to Soho Square, he thought he could hear the clink of sturdy hobnail boots on the muddy cobbles of Wardour Street and the shrill, ear-piercing whistles of constables on the alert. But that sound was soon dampened by the ragged breaths in his own throat, the pounding of his heart as he ran through Soho Square, churning up chunks of black snow in his wake.

When he skidded into Oxford Street, he skulked at the corner, clutching his arms around himself. It was too wide and well-traveled a street to do otherwise, and he was already too visible, particularly in the grime-stained warehouse coat with the splatters of blood on his shirt. He looked as out of place now along the spine of Oxford Street as Jack had while standing in front of the haberdashery.

He crossed the street as quickly as he could, jumping between horse-drawn carriages and carriage wheels, keeping the jacket clutched around him. Then he ducked into an arched alleyway between two fine buildings, behind which lurked narrow lanes of mud-stained rookeries and leaning, half-timbered houses that were so old the bricks had crumbled through the whitewash, leaving red stains, as iron might, in weeping trails beneath the rudely shuttered windows.

With an edgy, bleak gasp, Oliver made himself head up the slight slope along the narrow lanes, ducking under timbers propped in the middle of the oozing, muddy streets, his sturdy boots splashing in half-frozen mud, getting it on his pant legs. Not caring. Not letting himself care. He just ran along the grime-painted back streets that, though parallel to Oxford Street, were as different from it as were the white flakes of snow absorbed by the muddy, moving boil of the Thames.

His feet slipped, mud and half-melted snow seeping between the cobblestones. Panting, he only partly realized where his feet seemed to be taking him, but at least the whistles of the constables seemed to have faded from being directly behind him to several streets over. From around the corner. Down the hill. Anywhere than from behind him, so that was something.

Spars of sunlight half-banked off brick walls, heating them, and melting the snow, bringing a fulsome smell that swirled up around him. He pushed passed it and kept moving. Surely he was not lost, surely the tavern was just beyond this narrow lane, thick with drapes of handkerchiefs and shabby goods for sale. Surely the Three Cripples was just ahead on the left. He couldn't be this confused about where he was going, not after having been the best delivery lad McCready's establishment had ever known. Mr. McCready had said so.

Oliver ran till he thought his heart would burst, till at last his feet found a familiar intersection, and his nose told him that the leatherworking shops near Saffron Hill were just along on his right. And that if he kept on going on Charles Street until it met up with Saffron Hill, he would get there.

But what would he do if Jack weren't at the tavern? Or if Noah Claypole *was* there and the only person known to Oliver? It was bad enough he'd sunk so low that the Three Cripples might be his only refuge. Or maybe, seeing as they were only thieves and housebreakers, they might not want a murderer in their midst. So what was he to do then?

His hands shook as he pulled open the door to the Three Cripples. He was not only unexpected but uninvited, and overwhelmed by his actions of that morning. The way his head ached and the welts from the whipping from the day before—how had he fallen so far that such a low place was the *best* that he could do?

The brown door streaked with street-splatter came open, sagging slightly, as it always did, letting in more than a smattering of weather, as it always did, so that the seats and tables by the door, swathed in damp, were reserved for those low enough not to demand better. He'd seen that in his few illicit visits; maybe those would be his seats now, if they even let him in at all.

He pulled. The door opened and he stepped into the steamy, hops-laced air of the Three Cripples. The crowd was very thin; it was early even for regulars. Oliver scanned the tables and then peered into the little alcove where a coal fire was often burning in the afternoon, and where he'd found Jack on previous visits. He told himself it was foolish to expect to find Jack just there as Oliver had last seen him. As if Jack had nothing to do but wait for Oliver, tipping back his chair and tapping his clay pipe against the scarred, dark surface of the table.

Jack wasn't there, but then neither was Noah, so there was a small blessing, at least. Conversing with Noah was as bad as trying to remain civil to Mr. Grimwig; hard words were the least of it.

As the door shut behind him, Oliver stood there, feeling the sift of cold leaking in from beneath the threshold. He felt almost naked without his hat and scarf. And as the barkeeper looked him up and down, Oliver became conscious of his bare hands, the filthy coat he wore. And, beneath that, the layer of bloody streaks that he knew was thawing in the warmth of the tavern, drying into an impenetrable brown; nothing would get those stains out.

He recognized no one. But if sanctuary was not to be found at the Three Cripples, then he had nowhere else to go. Maybe he should turn around now, walk out, find the nearest constabulary, and turn himself in.

"What you want?"

The barked question from the bar startled him and he jumped. When he opened his mouth, he hadn't the faintest idea what to say.

"We ain't open yet."

This was a lie, even Oliver knew that. Any fool could see the two men huddled over their pints along the window. Any fool could see the man with his long coat, which almost hid his filthy trousers, popping back a tot of gin as he stood near the bar. It might be early, but the Three Cripples never really closed.

"I'm looking for—" Oliver began, but then he stopped. It was as if to say it, to say Jack's name aloud, was to take the final step in admitting why he was here, even if only to himself.

"'E's Jack's," said a man, coming out from the back room wearing only a shirt and a greasy wool scarf around his neck. He grunted the words out. "Seen 'im 'ere, 'e's Jacks."

Oliver blinked; he'd only met Cromwell once, but perhaps it didn't matter, he recognized him now. Cromwell now had Oliver's ticket into some sort of safety, however temporary, if only he could open his mouth and clear his throat and inquire as to where he might find Jack.

"Jack!" Cromwell bellowed the name, raising his voice to the ceiling, and in the relative quiet of the tavern, the shout almost echoed.

After a moment of waiting, where Oliver looked at the bartender and was stared at in return, there was the sound of a door slamming. It came from overhead, from somewhere within the upstairs warren of the tavern. Footsteps came trundling down the hall and down the stairs, and then there was Jack. His shirt was untucked, his hair rumpled, and he was yawning from sleep and looking so familiar in the morning gloom of the tavern that Oliver almost started forward. But he stopped himself. It wasn't guaranteed that Jack would want to harbor a murderer.

"Jack, your mate's 'ere." Cromwell barked this, waving his hand at the bartender as if to indicate that this was no longer any of his concern.

Jack looked at Cromwell, who then jerked his thumb in Oliver's direction as if Oliver weren't the only out-of-place figure in the whole of the tavern.

Jack woke up slow and then fast, as Oliver remembered, and it happened now. He nodded at nobody, rubbing his fingers hard in the corner of his eye, and Oliver remembered the gesture from when they'd shared rough blankets in Fagin's den.

Oliver could see the expressions moving across Jack's face and imagined he could discern what each of them meant. And whether Jack would be serious or whether he would joke or whether he would dismiss the whole thing as beneath his notice. All of this flooded over Oliver, the memory of it coming as if spilling out of Jack in this one, unguarded gesture. But Jack was canny, and the expressions on his face smoothed away as Jack flashed what Oliver assumed was meant to be a careless smile. As soon as he focused on Oliver, Jack's eyebrows went up and he hurried down the stairs, barefooted even in the cold morning.

"Nolly? What you doin' here, then? Hell, it ain't even noon."

Oliver almost smiled in return but didn't. For thieves and housebreakers, the working day began much later than for a lad of Oliver's ilk. Though Oliver supposed that, being what he now was, his true working day would start when the sun went down.

As Cromwell walked over to the bartender, Jack walked right up to Oliver, seemingly unfazed by the rough coat and absence of the gentlemanly hat and scarf that marked Oliver as an apprentice at a very well-to-do haberdashery. Jack scanned him up and down, missing nothing, as he usually did, and then reached out to touch the edge of the lapel of Oliver's coat.

"You look at bit done in, Nolly," said Jack almost cheerfully, as if, indeed, Oliver's being down-and-out was a good thing. "Come upstairs, then," said Jack in a relatively normal voice, though it might really be too loud and too normal, especially for a chilly and mostly empty tavern.

But then Jack turned to him, and instant Jack really looked at Oliver, his eyes narrowed. That he could see all the evidence was easy to believe, even if he didn't yet understand any of it. But then, neither did Oliver himself. Jack caught Oliver's eyes with his own and held them there, looking, watching. And again, Oliver opened his mouth, panting, unable to speak, while the whole of yesterday, that very morning, started slamming into him.

Oliver opened his mouth, still struggling with the words he needed to say, must say. To explain it to Jack and to himself, the world, even. He'd never been of the opinion he was a person so evil as to take someone's life, but he *had*; his life had dragged him to this spot, and so there he stood. Mouth open, breath coming in short gasps, he was unable to say anything nor tear his eyes away from Jack's. Jack's brows lowered, his confusion making him look cross.

"Nolly?" he asked.

Just as Oliver took a breath to try again, the constable's whistle shrilled just beyond the door. It was too much to hope they were after a common pickpocket, not when they'd been hot on his heels all the way from McCready's Haberdashery. Not so early in the morning. Not in this slanting, freezing winter rain. Not if they didn't have to.

"Are those for you?" Cromwell asked, turning his head toward the door, eyes narrowing.

Oliver nodded.

"An' you brung 'em 'ere?" Cromwell asked this, forcing the words out through gritted teeth. "They're already lookin' at us, they're always lookin', an' you brung 'em 'ere?"

There was a pounding at the door, and before Oliver could even begin to stammer an explanation, let alone to understand it all himself, Jack whistled to the bartender and jerked his chin at Cromwell.

"I'm puttin' him away," snapped Jack. "You lot carry on."

Jack grabbed Oliver by the arm and hauled him up the dark narrow stairs he'd just come down. The smell of rot and damp barely pierced the panicked thudding of Oliver's heart as he scrambled up after Jack. Jack, who pulled on him hard and didn't let go.

At the top of the landing, the narrow corridor went to the left and Jack practically ran, yanking Oliver past narrow brown doors, through the fetid, still air that bespoke of windows shut tight against the cold night, to the end of the corridor. Jack stopped and pushed, not at the door at the very end of the corridor, but at the wooden panel along the wall. It opened upon a small space, about half the height of a man and not much wider than that. It gaped at Oliver like a dangerous, open mouth.

"In," said Jack, pulling on the scruff of Oliver's coat collar. "Get in an' stay down. An' keep your yap shut till I whistle, you get it? Otherwise, the peelers'll have us all if they're chasin' you an' find you here. Got it?"

Oliver nodded and Jack pushed him in the hole, not even waiting till Oliver was settled before he moved his hand along the wood panel to close it.

"Wait for my whistle."

The panel closed, leaving Oliver in the small space. He tried to settle himself, shaking, blinking as his eyes teared up, ice thumping in his veins. Bracing his back against the cold brick wall, he tucked his knees up. The room was so close around him he could barely get his arms around his knees. He could only tip his head low, chin against his chest, and close his eyes against the darkness.

Dimly, through the slatted wood beneath him, he could hear pounding and faraway voices, none of which he could recognize as Jack. He waited, teeth chattering, listening to feet walking across creaking boards, doors slamming, the feet coming closer as though they were mounting the stairs. Then the footsteps, several pairs, came down the corridor toward him, and he could now hear the distinction between different voices. Among them was Jack's, seemingly sleepy and, uncharacteristically, almost bored.

"Yeah, gents, here's the rooms," said Jack's voice, yawning. "But 'tis early yet for the likes of us.

"The likes of you?" asked a voice, stern and careful.

"We keeps a tavern," said Cromwell, and Oliver's whole body jerked with a start when he heard it. "Drinkin' ain't a sin yet, is it?"

"No," said the voice in a crisp way that made Oliver think he might be a constable who was only two feet away, and so very close; if Oliver so much as shifted, the constable might be able to hear the brush of cloth against cloth. "It's not a sin, although serving beverages before time is not legal."

"Them two rows a skiff on the river," said Cromwell. "T'other works the new ditch along Fleet. Surely it's nothin' to anyone to give them a bit of comfort against the cold."

"Ditchin's hard work," added Jack, making Oliver start all over again; Jack's voice sounded as though it was right on the other side of the wood panel.

Another pair of footsteps approached as Oliver heard several doors being opened and closed. Several low voices muttered in protest.

"Everything seems in order, sir," said the new voice, as though in response to an unasked question. "One of them below reported seeing someone of the description hurrying past the windows."

"And?"

"He seemed indifferent, sir, as though he couldn't be bothered."

"We'll keep up the search, then."

"What's he wanted for?" asked Cromwell.

"Not that it's anything to you," said the first constable. "But with the wanted posters going up this very day, everyone will know. He's an apprentice lad who's wanted for assaulting his master."

There was a silent moment as this notion sank in and then the footsteps started off.

"Take several men and go north of Holborn and search there," said the first constable. "I'll take the rest and head east along it, toward Smithfield. And get those posters up as quick as you might."

"Yes, sir," said the second constable, and Oliver's heart started to pound so hard that he couldn't hear anything else. Only his heart and the ratchet-like clicking of his teeth.

The darkness behind his eyes grew and he struggled not to move, to remain where he was, struggled not to shout out or leap to his feet and claw his way through the wooden panel.

He had murdered his master and everyone in the Three Cripples, Saffron Hill, even the whole of London, would know it inside the hour. The constables were after him; his would be a sentence of death if they caught him. He'd be hanged, just as he was born to, just as the man in the white waistcoat had predicted so many years ago. That was the day he'd turned nine; the day he'd met Mr. Bumble. The day he'd been separated from Dick and his life began moving from one misery to another.

He hugged himself hard and breathed deeply, telling himself he was too old to be afraid of the dark, although yes, he was not too old to be afraid to die. He couldn't be certain that Jack, in his irritation, might not simply throw Oliver into the street for the constable to take. And wasn't Noah an informer? If Noah found out, if Noah saw the wanted posters that told of Oliver's awful deed, surely he'd be first in line for the reward money. Whether or not Jack helped Oliver, Noah must never know, must never be told.

Oliver waited in the darkness for a long time; he didn't know how long. Just that his knees began to feel stiff and he longed to stand and stretch out, to take a deep breath. The cold of the wood beneath him, the bricks behind him, and some unseen draft soaked through the thick warehouse jacket and his good woolen pants. Even in his sturdy boots he felt it, creaking and freezing till he began to lose feeling in his toes.

Then a faraway door slammed and he heard footsteps racing up the stairs. He wanted to move, but Jack had said to wait for the whistle, so Oliver waited. Soon he heard it, piercing and low, not hesitant but quick. Then it came again, making Oliver think he must whistle in response to answer it. But before he could lick his dry lips, the panel slid back, letting in a stream of crisp, fresh air, and the outline of Jack. Of Jack's hand reaching for him, yanking him out of the small room. Jack hauled him toward the end of the hall to the farthest narrow door, the solitary door at the very end of a very narrow corridor.

"I've got him," said Jack over his shoulder, and Oliver had a brief glimpse of Cromwell and the barkeeper crowding the narrow corridor at the top of the stairs. "I'll take care of this."

"See that you do," said Cromwell, his voice slamming against the wall. "I don't want them constables sniffin' about more than they already do. And get 'im a different shirt," Cromwell said now. "That one's got blood on it. An' can you do nothing to rough up 'is edges? Take 'im, Jack, an' do something about that. We can figure out how to use 'im later."

"Got it," said Jack.

Oliver wanted to protest that he wasn't going to be used by anybody, least of all a criminal, but then, as Cromwell and the bartender disappeared down the stairs and Jack reached out to tug on his jacket, he remembered. He'd laid Mr. McCready low, left him bleeding on the flat stones of the kitchen floor. He was everything so many had thought him to be, had come to the very spot the gentleman in the white waistcoat had promised. If he wasn't guilty of more than a moment's murderous passion that so few might understand, then he had tipped himself into the verge by running from it. But how could he face anyone who wasn't also bad?

"Jack," said Oliver as he went where Jack was dragging him. "I want to go home."

"You can't," said Jack. "But don't worry, he won't want much, you'll be all right with us. Just do as he says, and you'll be safe."

But Oliver felt so far from safe, so very, very far.

Using a key, Jack unlocked the door and turned the small brass knob that glinted against the stained wood. The key and the lock seemed too feeble than to do more but keep out an errant passerby; if anyone wanted to get in, they could. But once Jack had pushed Oliver into the low gloom, he could understand why it wasn't important.

The room contained a low, old-fashioned clothespress, a low bed under the slanted ceiling, a square, wooden table, and a single chair. There might or might not be a candlestick on the shallow mantel, but since Jack did not move to light it, Oliver could not be sure.

Oliver landed against the far wall, sliding to the floor in the small space between the high, narrow window and clothespress in the corner, upon which was heaped a pile of garments, and slid to the floor. The pile of clothes was properly Jack's, or, more likely, stolen, waiting to be sorted and sold. But it didn't matter. Jack loomed over him, kicking the door shut with his heel, blocking Oliver's movement, leaving him no chance to stand up or escape or to do anything but look up at Jack.

"Care to share, then?" asked Jack, his voice tight, eyes sparking in the half dark. "Why'd you come here, bein' a murderer, knowin' it'd bring the peelers down on our heads, gettin' us all hanged on account of associatin' with the likes of you?"

Oliver struggled to push himself away from the wall, thinking he could think a great deal more clearly if he could but stand and talk to Jack man-to-man, not cowering in the corner. Because he'd not meant to, had never meant to—

Jack hauled Oliver to his feet, suddenly, and pushed Oliver against the wall. Oliver planted a bold hand in the middle of Jack's chest to hold him at bay.

"Goddamnit," he said. "Do you think I wanted to come here? Do you think I *wanted* to kill him?"

Rage pounded in his head and he swung his fist at Jack and clocked him right on the jaw. Jack staggered back, slapping a hand to his face. His eyebrows rose in surprise, just as Oliver realized he'd struck the solitary person who might not only have the ability to hide him, but who might also have cause. Jack himself could as easily turn him in as anything else, and Oliver knew he'd been foolish to let his temper get away from him, and that he'd been foolish to strike Jack.

"You must have done," said Jack, tightening his lips, snarling. "Otherwise, you wouldn't've."

"I didn't *want* to," said Oliver, almost shouting it. He pressed his back against the cold wall, knocking his head against the frame of the high, narrow window. "But he left the orphan, locked him in the warehouse all night. He froze to death, he—Martin's *dead*, don't you understand?"

Oliver stopped, eyes hot, fully expecting Jack to burst out with a derisive laugh and deliver some comment about how it was an orphan's lot to die in the freezing cold, and what of it? Orphans died every day.

But Jack was silent, brows furrowing again as he looked at Oliver. His green eyes scanned Oliver up and down. Oliver could almost see Jack's expression in the low gloom, standing as still as he was, calculating the risks and thinking about what needed to be done.

Oliver looked down at himself. The warehouse coat, with half of its buttons missing, had fallen open. There was a slash of blood across his shirt bosom and larger spots near his collar, and the placket was dirt-smudged where he'd clutched the orphan to him. The evidence of what he'd done was all over him; all Jack needed to do was to shove him out into the street and shout for the law.

Then Jack surprised him.

"Get them things off, quick now, afore the peelers determine to have another go at us."

Jack came at Oliver, hands divesting him of his coat and throwing it on the bed. He pulled Oliver's shirt out of his trousers without his permission, and before Oliver could stop him, he'd knelt and tossed the shirt on the low coals of the small grate. He poked at the cloth with a metal rod that served as a fire poker and breathed on the coals till the cloth caught. Warmth plumed into the room for a bare second and then faded away.

Then Jack stood, turning, walking toward Oliver. Oliver folded his arms across his chest, partly from the air, chill against his bare skin, and partly to hide the scar on his upper arm.

He shivered as Jack's hands landed on the bare skin of his waist, pulling on the buttons of his trousers. Jack half turned Oliver to better get at the buttons for the tabs, when he stopped, hands on Oliver's waist, still and warm on Oliver's icy skin.

"When'd you get these, eh?" Jack asked, using the tip of one finger to touch the welts that curved around Oliver's waist.

Oliver paused, not wanting to talk about it, let alone remember it. But it was hard to forget McCready's red face as he'd shouted, and Oliver's own temper, like a live thing, refusing to back down when all prudence, and Mrs. Pierson, had suggested he do just that.

"Yesterday evening," said Oliver, for what did it matter now? He was a murderer, so a thrashing from his master was hardly of importance by comparison. "Mr. McCready had hard words for me after I—well, I objected to his treatment of the orphan, and then he—" Oliver stopped, flinching as Jack's finger traced the curve of a welt. "Never mind it. It doesn't matter now."

After a moment during which something flickered across Jack's face, Jack was all business as he gave the waistline of Oliver's sturdy brown trousers a tug.

"Then take off them boots; get out of them trousers."

"Do you have a shirt? Let me put on a shirt first, please?" Oliver asked this, not even attempting to pretend he wasn't embarrassed, as Jack was as likely to mock him in any case. But he wasn't about to willingly stand completely in a state of nature in front of Jack.

Jack surprised him again by nodding. He reached around Oliver, bumping him out of the way, digging through the pile on top of the clothespress to pull out a shirt. He leaned back and tossed it in Oliver's face.

"It's one of mine. It's not exactly clean, but that don't matter. Be quick about it. An' if you're going to be stayin' with me, at any rate, you'll be givin' up them fancy manners of yours. Otherwise, you'll stick out, plain as a Chinaman."

Oliver pulled the shirt over his head, blinking against his confusion as to why Jack would help him. Or maybe, more, it was that he would be determined to shelter anyone for whom the constables were searching. *We look after our own,* Jack had once said. But did that mean Jack would now consider him to be one of his own?

The shirt was of thick linen, ragged along the cuffs and with a long burn mark along the collar. No doubt being so thick and fine, it was stolen. But it also hung halfway down to his knees, which meant he could keep most of his modesty as well as cover the scar as Jack knelt at his feet and began to unlace his boots.

Oliver tried to pull his foot from Jack's reach, but Jack grabbed an ankle and looked up at him.

"Quit your fussin'," said Jack. "These boots, your whole kit; a peeler an' everyone else for streets could spot you quick in a crowd as being out of place. Like I said. You stay here? My lodgings, my rules."

Oliver became still, heart thumping as Jack forcibly removed his boots and threw them against the door. They clattered and fell with a thud, and Jack stood, coming at Oliver again.

Oliver held up both hands to stop Jack. "I'll do it," he said. "I will, just let me alone."

Jack paused, eyes glinting, and he was at the ready, it seemed, to divest Oliver of every stitch if he didn't do exactly as Jack wanted. Oliver fumbled with the buttons, hastily, and pulled the trousers off, feeling the bite of cold air against his legs through the linen shirt. Then he threw the trousers at Jack, who caught them, fingering the sturdy cloth, heedless of the recent intimacy of Oliver's skin against the wool. His mouth pursed in a thoughtful line. Oliver could almost see the pennies stacking up in Jack's eyes.

"These'll bring a price," Jack said, bending to gather up the boots. "I'm goin' to get you a different coat an' hat as well as trousers, so you can be one of us, instead of one of them."

Never mind that the warehouse coat was shabby and worth nothing, and Oliver never wanted to see it again. He was struck by how the whole of the exchange reminded him of the last time he'd been taken up by Fagin's gang, how Jack and Charley had taken every valuable piece of clothing off of him, and how Fagin had given him worn, thin brown garments to wear.

And then how Fagin had locked Oliver up for days at a time till he thought he might go crazy. Had gone crazy, in a way, with nothing but books about killing and death to distract him from the shadows of the day and the darkness of each night. Would Jack, as well, keep him prisoner until Oliver proclaimed to be willing to join him in any of his lawbreaking acts? But then, Oliver was already a murder, so what did it matter?

Jack plopped down on the low bed, dumping his bundle beside him while he pulled on stockings and tied up his own boots. Standing up, he shoved Oliver a little out of the way to dig for his coat and hat then took up the bundle of Oliver's clothes and boots again.

"Get the door, and lock it fast. Stay here, quiet like, till I gets back."

"Will you whistle?" Oliver asked, shifting on his stockinged feet as the cold leached up through the floor.

"Lord, no," said Jack as though disgusted at Oliver's green-
ness. "But lock the door after, an' I'll call when it's me."

CHAPTER 23

A New Hat Represents
A New Life,
One That He Is
Hesitant To Accept

Jack swung the door wide as he stepped through it and slammed it shut behind him, leaving Oliver alone in the room, naked except for his stockings and a stolen shirt. Oliver flipped the latch, thinking again that the thin, faded brass was not very much to keep anyone at bay who might be determined to make their way in, and tried not to shake as the confines of the room pressed on him. His eyes darted around, taking in the half gloom, ears ringing with the racket of the street beyond the thin glass, the sounds of shouts, the raspy bark of a dog. He'd barely escaped being taken by the constables today, but would tomorrow promise the same?

To stave off the fear of his rampant thoughts, he stepped over to the small fireplace and knelt in front of it. Lifting the metal rod, he poked at the charred ribbons of his shirt, which lay smoking and dark against the coals. The warmth, brought to him by the stirring of the coals and his closeness to the fire, oozed slowly toward him, but was wicked away by the cold in the room before it had time to do much good. Besides lacking in much fuel, the grate needed a good cleaning, a stern blacking. The soot had built up around the mouth of the fireplace enough to absorb the heat and send smoke into the room. Not that Jack or anyone at the Three Cripples probably cared. Not since Jack probably used the room only to sleep in, and not much else—

He realized he was shaking, not so much from cold as from the panic that threatened to overtake him and send him running, half-naked, into the streets. Oliver scooted back from the useless warmth of the fireplace and sat on the low bed, which was shoved under the long, narrow window just beneath the eves. The dirt on the surface of everything was making Oliver's skin itch, but he stayed where he was, teeth chattering against each other, and each jagged, jumpy breath burning in his throat.

As his eyes became accustomed to the scattered light from the window, he could see the clothespress and the hump of items on top of it. The small brown table with the single chair. And then, along the near wall, the outlines of the fireplace and the scarred wooden mantel with a single candlestick and what looked like a clay bowl for Jack's pipe. Over the mantelpiece, on a series of nails hammered into the wall, hung a curved string, where Oliver supposed Jack might dry his stockings. Or, more than likely, hang any stolen handkerchiefs out in a row where they might more easily be sorted. Other than that, the room was bare; Jack probably carried anything he needed on his person, in his pocket, or in his hatband.

Oliver concentrated on this, the mundane reality of any lack of ornament rather than the panic rattling in his belly. Would he stay here? Could he? With Jack? But where else could he go? Jack was the only person he knew who would not instantly, at this very moment, turn him over to the law. He shuddered all over and buried his face in his hands. He bent to his knees by the bed, unable to pray, curling and uncurling his stockinged feet against the uneven floorboards, and told himself that it was too late to cry; this moment had been his destiny all along.

Then, startled by a creak of wood in the hall, he looked up and saw the scarf, the red scarf that Jack had stolen from him and which Oliver had not seen around Jack's neck recently. It was a tad unraveled at the edges, but it was still bright and soft where Jack had arranged it in loops across the slat of wood that served as the headboard of the bed. Oliver reached up, stroking the red wool, his fingers leaving a slight streak, just in the center. He drew his hand away. He didn't know what the scarf was doing there, laid out as though it was a favored piece of finery, but if he was to take it back, take it back from Jack, then Jack would have something to say. And Oliver was not up to a heated discussion about what belonged to him and what belonged to Jack.

It was a good hour, by the chiming of the church bells from nearly every steeple, before Oliver heard footsteps from beyond the door. His teeth had been chattering for some time, and he'd vaguely remembered pacing back and forth across the floor before he'd sunk next to the fire, wanting to climb into it, wanting to be anywhere else other than where he was. For what kind of life would this be, living with Jack, consorting with thieves and pickpockets?

He'd done it before, of course, but this time, he'd be doing it because he had to. Brownlow had taken him away from Fagin's gang and the low gutters where thieves lurked and given him the comfortable surroundings of the white townhouse in Pentonville. Then he'd taken Oliver to the sturdy stone cottage in the country with Aunt Rose and Uncle Harry. Gifted him with books he'd read beside a quiet fireplace, much better lit and cleaned than this one had been in many a year.

And again he thought of the portly man in the white waistcoat and his dire predictions of Oliver's future hanging. Then of Noah's taunts about how bad blood, Oliver's gift from his mother, would always come to a bad end. And finally, of Mr. Grimwig, who'd never trusted Oliver from the very first. Mr. Grimwig had been proven right, along with the rest of them, those forgotten workhouse wardens who'd muttered or scolded or tormented him. They'd all been proven right. Whereas, anyone who'd been the least bit gentle with him, even for the barest second, had been proven wrong.

So maybe he deserved it, this bitter point, this dark and dreary place. Maybe he'd truly been meant to be one of Fagin's boys from the very moment of his birth. Maybe he had. He had all the evidence to support it and nothing to support anything else. He nodded to himself, determined to manage that much, even if everything, every kindness and civility he'd ever known must be shoved to the most remote part of his memory.

He scratched the back of his neck, out of nervousness or, what was just as likely, the family of lice now making their way from the patched bedclothes and up his spine.

Then he heard Jack's footsteps, and then thought that was odd— how did he know the footsteps were Jack's?

"Nolly," said the voice that went with the footsteps. "Nolly, open the door."

Oliver leaped up from the hearth, sending dusted soot into the air, and opened the door. He stepped back as Jack barreled in with a bundle of clothes under one arm and a pair of scraped black boots slung over his shoulder, dangling by their laces. In his free hand, he held a small brown jug. He pushed past Oliver to lay everything on the table with a thump.

He turned to appraise Oliver. "Been rollin' in the soot, have you?"

"Just sitting by the fire," said Oliver as calmly as he could manage, but he knew that the quaver in his voice was giving him away.

"These are for you, then, an' somethin' to wash the blood off."

Oliver stood up and went over to the table; he used the small pitcher of water to get the blood off his neck and dried what he could with the edge of his sleeve. Jack seemed so matter-of-fact about it, as though Oliver's showing up looking as he did was something that Jack dealt with every day. Although, maybe he had seen and dealt with things like it when he'd been in Australia, and certainly when he'd been part of Fagin's gang. Oliver didn't know, didn't want to ask.

As he ran his hands over the bundle of clothes, he knew that if he put the articles on, he'd be yet that much further from everything he knew. And yet, if he didn't separate him-self from it, it would all catch up with him and would be over. In spite of these dark thoughts chasing around in his head, he unfolded a pair of pants from the bundle and put them on. They buttoned in the front, and the button holes were dark with grease.

"Thank you," Oliver said with a nod as he tucked his shirt in.

"Such manners you have, ever so," said Jack. He was laugh-ing, but it was an edgy laugh because Jack must be fully aware that if he couldn't hide Oliver well enough, he too would be brought down.

"All right, now, I'm gonna do somethin'. You won't like it by half," said Jack. "But it'll keep you safe, this, what I'm about to do. Got it? Now sit down."

Oliver could only look at him, his hands fisted on his thighs. He wanted to move, to run, but he couldn't even imag-ine to where or how. He had no money, and he couldn't go back to Aunt Rose, not like this. Not today. Not ever.

"I said sit down." Jack's exasperation was laced with some worry.

Oliver sat on the chair next to the table with his back to the dusty fireplace and waited.

From the small clothespress, dented with a rusted lock that looked centuries old, Jack pulled a short knife. It was probably the one he used to cut his supper with or to shave pieces off wood if he were the least bit inclined to light a fire. But he came at Oliver, holding the knife to one side, and pressed in close, his thighs brushing against Oliver's knee. Then he touched Oliver's head.

"What are you doing?" Oliver asked. He jerked his head back and looked up at Jack.

"Helping you," said Jack. "It'll grow back, never fear. You'll have the golden locks of an angel again within a week." Jack put his hand on Oliver's head, tipping it toward him, the heat of his fingers running through Oliver with a shock. Tugging, Jack pulled strands of hair away from Oliver's scalp and cut through them with the knife. There was a *scra-scra* sound, and tugging, and Oliver closed his eyes and pretended he didn't care. The cutting made his skin shiver, whispers of hair falling on his cheeks and down his collar, though it seemed Jack paused after every other cut to bend and toss the strands in the smoking fireplace. Finally, the cutting stopped, and Jack ran his hand over Oliver's head, the palm of it cupping a circle along the back of Oliver's skull, the touch feeling close and warm without the thickness of hair.

"Now there," said Jack. "You look a wee bit rougher, so that'll please Cromwell."

"I don't care to please him," said Oliver, feeling some stirring of anger in his breast.

"You'll care to remain hidden, so let me do this next bit, with no fussin', mind you."

Oliver opened his eyes and kept staring at his knees, seemingly the only safe place in this entire day, and sensed Jack moving to the fire. He put the knife on the narrow mantelpiece and bent to the grate. When he came back, he showed Oliver his hands, black and dusty, and before Oliver could open his mouth to even comment, Jack took his fingers and traced them along Oliver's jaw, past his ear. He ruffled the edge of Oliver's hairline, pushing his fingers against Oliver's scalp, running his fingers deeply along the top of Oliver's head. Oliver shuddered; no one had ever touched him like that. Not in his whole life.

Jack bent down and took both of Oliver's hands in his, looking for all the world like a courtier bending to kiss his lady's hand with the laying on of compliments. But he didn't kiss anything, only used his thumbs to smudge the back of Oliver's hands, pressing between the veins, moving the bones around, leaving smears that pretended to resemble work-worn grime.

"It'll only work if you keep your hands to yourself an' not wash 'em," said Jack, still holding Oliver's hands in his. Then he leaned forward even more and moved his face close to the hollow of Oliver's neck. If Jack had not been holding his hands, Oliver would have drawn back and way from this intimacy, so sudden and uninvited.

"You've got the hands of a gentleman, you have," said Jack, the breath of his low words whispering against Oliver's skin. "An' you smell like a spring mornin' compared to the lot down there. Soap an' water, I expect." Jack drew back, unexpectedly sudden, smiling down at Oliver. "Could be quite the draw for the ladies, if I ever determined to take up bathin'. So much maintenance though."

Oliver's skin felt jumpy, and alarmed, he brought his hand to his neck.

"That's the ticket," Jack said, and Oliver realized he'd just smeared more soot on his skin, which was to the better if he was to survive any of this.

"It won't matter," said Oliver, his lips numb, completely undone by all of this. "They'll find me. I was born to hang, that's what the man in the white waistcoat said. He said it several times."

"Who's that, then?" Jack stepped back as if surveying his handiwork.

"The man in the white—oh, never mind. He's long dead now." It was too hard to explain, with his hammering heart and the echoing of voices from below sounding like a faraway storm that was just about to reach him. The man in the white waistcoat had taken one look at him and pronounced him bad, oh, many years ago when he was just nine. No older than Martin had been, just yesterday. So very small—

"I think I'm going to be ill," said Oliver, standing.

"No," said Jack. "You're goin' to get drunk first, an' then you're goin' to be sick. Gettin' drunk first makes anything worth it."

Jack held up a jacket and helped Oliver into it, as gravely as any manservant. The jacket didn't quite fit as he was used to jackets fitting. It was dark blue and made of fine, thin wool, much finer than the warehouse jacket, with a high, old-fashioned collar and cuffed sleeves that were too long. The coat also had along the front a double row of shiny gold buttons, too tarnished to be real gold, of course, and a set of cut-off tails, resembling a gentleman's finery, trimmed back.

"It's too fancy, Jack, it's—" Oliver stopped himself, unable to continue in that way, in the way that a criminal might, because when he considered his outfit, he could see how it might look to the police. And why was that so easy?

"It is fancy, but it's the last thing a bloke on the run would wear, eh? It's a distraction, that's what it is. Here's a kerchief for your neck."

The kerchief was a rusty black, and as Oliver, with trembling fingers, tried to tie it into a turn of cloth that resembled a cravat, Jack shoved his hands away and tied it for him. With his head bent to his task, Jack was close now, so close that Oliver could see the faded freckles across his cheeks, the thin white scar next to one eye, feel the breath from Jack's mouth. See the way he held his tongue against the inside of his cheek as he folded and looped the cloth.

When he was done, Jack looked up at Oliver and handed him a hat. It was unlike his apprentice cap in every way that mattered; it was a low top hat, just like the one Jack wore, except that this one was brand new; the felt still shiny, falling in a smooth circle beneath his hands as he petted it. Being a fancy type of hat, so new and so bold, it would probably separate him from his old life better than the rest of the outfit put together.

As Oliver adjusted it on his head, he saw Jack smiling at him. It was then that he understood, at least part of it. Oliver was here, in Jack's lair, in Jack's world, and whether Oliver had come of free will or because he had nowhere else to go, to Jack, it was a good thing and worth smiling and drinking about. For the briefest of seconds, Oliver could feel that thought pushing away his own worries; to Jack, this was a good day, even if Jack didn't realize it.

Oliver looked down at himself. He looked, already, as if he was one of those sort of men that loitered on the street corners looking for day work, or lurked in the doorways of taverns hoping to find a score of some sort. He looked like he belonged to the lowest level of quality, but if that was the only way he was going to escape the hangman's noose, then, therefore, so be it.

Jack went to open the door, and the runaway galloping feeling came back into Oliver's chest, leaving numb spots where his heart was, roiling fear in his belly. It was obvious that Jack didn't expect him to just stay in the room all day, and it was likely that going downstairs constituted more of Jack's plan of distraction. That his being there, amidst the crowd of regulars that made up the Three Cripples, would be the best disguise possible.

With a jerk of his chin, Jack looked at Oliver.

"But only tie up your boots an' come down; Cromwell wants to see you."

"Why? What does he want?"

"He owns the Three Cripples, as you well know. I'm sure he'll want to make certain arrangements."

"But I'm here with *you.*" Oliver could feel it already, how the darkness of the world that Jack lived in crept in when he wasn't fully ready for it yet.

"Shouldn't worry," said Jack. "He just wants his pound of flesh, an' that ain't so much to pay when there's the alternative lurkin' about."

This was true; the alternative was so much worse. They hanged murderers, plain and simple, and Oliver had seen what that fate had done to Fagin, how it had broken him. Oliver knew he'd be broken like a snapped twig if they sent him to prison to await that fate.

"Yes," he said. "Just let me—" He needed a minute, just a few minutes, alone, before he could bear facing any part of Jack's world. He'd met Cromwell and had been greeted with grunts and assessing looks; he couldn't imagine what Cromwell would want, or how he, Oliver, could ever manage to provide it.

Jack nodded. "I'll go tell him." And then Jack was gone, through the door, leaving not so much as a trace of his being there behind. The warmth of the fire was flickering down, sucked out by the coldness of the room, and Oliver told himself his hands weren't shaking, that his teeth weren't gritted so tightly that he could feel the blood pounding through his jaw.

CHAPTER 24

As It Was
In The Old Days

When Oliver had finally calmed his fingers enough to lace up the new, scuffed boots he'd been given by Jack, he managed to make his way down the stairs, his heart hammering. A strange man, one of Cromwell's he assumed, showed him into a small room behind the bar where there was a little fire choking in its grate. The room held a table and chairs; the table was thick and heavy and almost too big for the room. He saw Jack out of the corner of his eye; Jack didn't come in, so Oliver was sat in one of the chairs on his own. It seemed that the man himself, Cromwell, was going to make Oliver wait. Someone brought him a pot of ale, but Oliver couldn't bring himself to touch it. Ale made him sleepy and he couldn't sleep, not yet.

Oliver's stomach was growling by the time Cromwell's frame filled the doorway of the room. His head was bare and his tie was still undone, though it was getting toward noon. Whatever he'd been doing, Cromwell looked relaxed and smudged, and to Oliver's surprise, he had a small smile to share.

"So, then, young Oliver," Cromwell said as he took a seat across from Oliver. He looked at Oliver and nodded, as if admiring Jack's handiwork. "In a spot of trouble, then, are you? Want to be stayin' on with us? That'll cost you, but first I want to know what you did."

Cromwell folded his arms, his sleeves rolled up to display the thick muscles of his forearms, on the table in front of him. The table was not so wide that he couldn't reach Oliver if he wanted to, and if the goal was to intimidate, then Oliver, if he'd been able, would have congratulated him on his success.

"An' if you lie," said Cromwell, pointing a finger at Oliver, "then I'll know it, an' believe you me, you don't want me catchin' you at that. So fess up, then."

Oliver opened his mouth but couldn't speak. Cromwell shoved the pot of ale at him. Oliver took a sip of ale and then licked his lips. "I murdered my master," he said, wanting to get it out. It was a horrible confession to make, and it still seemed unreal.

Cromwell's eyes crinkled up like he didn't believe Oliver and was going to laugh in his face at any moment. "An' 'ere I was thinkin' that they were lyin', that you'd stolen from the till an' gotten into it with one of your mates or somethin'." Then, without hardly changing his expression, Cromwell snapped out his questions. "So you killed him. Why? Speak up, you."

"He—he locked the workhouse boy in the warehouse, and he died, come this morning. And Mr. McCready didn't seem to care, so I—"

"You killed your master out of spite? *You?*" There was a flicker across Cromwell's face as though he were trying to assess how this could possibly be true. "You sit there lookin' like an angel, all sweet an' rosy an' well fed, an' you tell me this?"

"It's true!"

Cromwell laughed at him now, mouth open, teeth flashing, and something in Oliver's breast sprang up, hot and insistent. "I hit him in the head and he fell to the floor, bleeding."

"Hit 'im? With what?"

"A frying pan. An iron one."

Now Cromwell bent forward and howled while he pounded the table. Oliver got up, pushing back the chair, intending to leave, intending to march right out into the street. He'd thank Jack for his hospitality, he'd find other shelter, he'd find a way out of London, and then he'd be on his way.

But Cromwell sprang from his seat and blocked Oliver's exit. His shoulders loomed as he bared his teeth, the smell of the street thick in the air around him.

"You've got a temper on you, boy. Wouldn't know it to look at you, sweet as you are, but I'm tellin' you, you'll do as you're told around 'ere, temper or no."

Cromwell's body filled the doorway, bending toward over Oliver, his fist next to Oliver's face.

"You're not my master," Oliver said, barely managing it with Cromwell's face so close to his, so close that Oliver could smell the beer on his breath.

"Oh, yes I am. I very much am, an' you raise one 'and to me an' you'll find yourself floatin' down the Thames."

Oliver's heart pounded, but he made himself stay still, glaring as Cromwell brushed his clenched fist against Oliver's face and then gave him a shove into the corridor. Jack waited there with wide eyes, watching and careful, but Oliver could see he was somewhat undone by Cromwell's threats, even if they weren't directed at him.

Cromwell grabbed Oliver by the scruff of the neck and escorted him over to the alcove where he shoved Oliver onto the bench seat with his back to the main room.

"I want you should stay 'ere, all day, like nothin's wrong, you got it?"

Oliver rubbed the back of his head, nodding. He could sense that Jack was nearby but didn't let him turn his head to look. Jack had done nothing to stop Cromwell and had not spoken up on Oliver's behalf. But then Oliver dismissed the feeling of irritation, which was soon overridden by the chill, sharp bite of fear; Jack and the Three Cripples was his only escape.

Oliver spent his day, the brunt of it, sitting in Jack's alcove with his back to the door, in the seat closest to the doorway. After Cromwell had gone, Jack slid into the seat across from him.

"Unless someone comes right through an' looks you in the face, no one'll take any notice of you. Why, you look just like a regular customer." Jack added this last as if it were a good thing, seeming a little proud as he took Oliver's hat off and put it next to his own on the table. He smiled as though well pleased with the obvious success of his ruse, though Oliver didn't return his smile.

And it was a mad idea, all the way around, just sitting there like a coney, and it made Oliver edgy, doing this. But Jack insisted on it and brought him a bowl of stew that Oliver couldn't eat and some ale that Oliver wouldn't drink and made him stay there. It wasn't until later, when Oliver felt as though he'd been nailed in place, when more customers came in and the tavern filled with noise and movement and the smell of wet wool drying in the chancy heat, that it seemed that Jack relaxed his vigil.

The din of the Three Cripples crowd seemed distant and muted, the comings and goings, the stamping of feet, the click of a glass, the call for another round. Oliver watched out of the corner of his eye any time a figure passed in front of the light or stopped at the door to speak to Jack. Oliver found he couldn't bear to look any of them in the eye, lest they be the one to come and, as Jack might put it, put the finger on him for Mr. McCready's murder.

Uncle Brownlow would be horrified, and even old Fagin would have been astonished to find Oliver sitting there with the shadow of a man's blood on his hands. As for Bill Sikes— though he didn't know why he might think of him at a time such as this except that he had himself murdered someone. What would he think of Oliver now? Would he still pull out his revolver and hold it to Oliver's head, making sure that Oliver would do as he was told? Or would he, upon finding out, stand back, tipping the brim of his hat as a sign of respect? And since when had Oliver fallen so low that a housebreaker and murderer would be willing to pay him respect with anything as courtly as that?

Oliver looked at his hands. They were filthy but still were much cleaner than the tables and the floor. Cleaner than Jack's hands. And the neck and hands of the boy that brought another pot of beer that Oliver simply couldn't bear to drink.

Shaking, Oliver brought his hand up to his face, wishing he could get a basin of hot water and some soap and wash all of this off of him. Then he touched his hair and scrubbed through the stiffness of it, feeling the curve of his scalp, feeling exposed. He could hardly bring himself to stop doing it, raking his fingers through the bristle, till finally, Jack reached out across the table and touched Oliver's face.

"It'll grow, by-and-bye," he said. He brushed a stray lock from Oliver's forehead and patted his cheek gently, and Oliver made himself be soothed by this, although it lasted only a moment, that feeling of comfort, and then it was gone.

When the afternoon crowd pushed in and the main room was a throng of men in coats and boots, Noah arrived, dressed in his fancy suit that made him stand out from the Three Cripples crowd. But that was fine for him; he wasn't a criminal on the run. He came right through the open doorway to the alcove and stood at the end of the table with the firelight shining on the sheen of his cravat and on the spots of frozen rain on his hat as he held it in his hands. He was grinning, looking down at Oliver, mouth open, tipping back on his heels as if this, this sight, this room where Oliver waited to hide from the hangman's noose, were the best joke he'd ever heard.

"Oh, how the mighty are brought low," he said, crowing it, eyes shining as he looked at Jack as if wanting him to join in. Then he looked at Oliver again. "So proud, so proper, an' yet 'ere you are. An angel-faced murderer, all ready for the 'angman's noose." He slammed Oliver on the shoulder.

"We'll keep him from that," said Jack. "Never you mind him now, Nolly, we'll keep you from that."

Oliver knew that Jack would do his best to try, but if Noah was involved, and given what Noah did for a living, it wasn't a sure bet that he wouldn't take it upon himself to hand Oliver over to the law.

"I see you've 'ad your 'air cut as well, no longer lookin' such a swell, more like one of your everyday street weasels."

Oliver jerked, stopping himself from brushing his hand along his head, which he'd done several times that very hour, bringing a shade of soot to layer his trousers.

"And you did 'im in with a fryin' pan, I 'ear," said Noah. His mouth moved over the words, smirking. "How your old, dead mother would be proud, so very proud."

The invisible leash that had held Oliver in one spot broke with a snap and he lunged out of his chair, reaching for Noah, reaching for his throat. Noah, unprepared, stepped back, mouth open, hands flailing as he lost his balance as Oliver slammed into him and shoved him against the wall.

Oliver felt the roar of loss and the futility of it all, everything he'd done and tried to be, and clocked his fist back and hooked it, just under Noah's chin. Noah's jaw clicked, and Oliver punched him again, making his nose bleed. Then he slammed him in the neck, cutting off Noah's breath, making him tumble to the ground, clutching his throat while Oliver stood over him, legs spread, heart thumping.

"You'll not speak of my mother to me," said Oliver in a voice that was thick and stern and almost not his own. He glared down at Noah, who looked up at him, gasping. "I told you once, don't *make* me tell you again."

His breath was thick in his throat, but it felt good to best Noah, as he had that day so long ago. But this time, there were witnesses who would know the truth of it. Then he was grabbed from behind and pushed up against the door jamb, Cromwell's grime-drawn face close to Oliver's.

"He had it coming," said Oliver, defending himself, fury still gritting his teeth. Noah deserved to be beaten.

"Boys, boys," Cromwell said giving Oliver a shake, but it wasn't a hard one. "You'll be mindin' your manners and not makin' such a fuss in my tavern. Take it outside next time."

Cromwell let him go, and Oliver watched Noah struggle to his feet, unaided. No one helped him, but no one stopped him from going. Only Cromwell followed him into the main room, toward the front door, to make sure Noah left.

The irony of it was that, at the Three Cripples, fighting like that was a scolding offence; whereas at Mr. McCready's, there would have been discipline and shame. As for murder, here it got laughed at, and Oliver knew, as he should have known, that coming to the Three Cripples was a mistake. But at the moment, it was a mistake he couldn't undo.

"Come on, then, Nolly," said Jack.

Oliver looked up, waiting for the heat in his veins to simmer to something less fiery before he could focus.

"You've had a day, then, haven't you." Jack's voice was almost soft. He touched Oliver's face with his fingers, making Oliver jerk his head back. "Come here to me then, sit closer to the fire. You're all flushed, but your skin is cold."

Oliver didn't feel soothed, but Jack wanted him to be, so he got up and moved closer to the fire. Jack scooted along the bench and pulled Oliver down on it to sit next to him.

The heat of the fire hit his skin, his face, yet he was shivering as he sat down. The fire seemed unable to reach him, and his blood rattled against his bones. He couldn't understand why both Cromwell and Noah found his actions amusing, but it seemed to matter a little less as Jack pulled Oliver close to him. A serving girl brought in a plate of food and a tumbler of gin, placing them on the table with rude thunks. Oliver inhaled the smells rising from it, the tang and the heat of juniper.

"It'll be all right, Nolly, it will. You won't miss that life so very much, an' it won't take long, I promise."

Oliver looked at Jack, at the freckles across his blunt nose, at the smudges around his chin, on his collar. He could smell the sweet funk of unwashed skin, the grime under Jack's nails as he touched Oliver's wrist. He couldn't understand what Jack was doing, why he was sitting so close, and touching him like that. But it was a damned sight better than Noah standing over him, mocking. Or Cromwell, bristling and threatening.

"Yes," said Oliver, though he didn't really understand what he was agreeing to.

He reached for the plate of food; it held slices of beef, roasted, and bread, scraped with drippings, and boiled eggs; there was enough for a fighting cock, and Oliver's stomach rebelled. So he took a sip of sweet, warm gin and reached for the bread. The dripping on the bread was crisped with grease and salted, and that was fine, it went with the gin. He flicked his gaze up to Jack, who was watching him.

"There's enough for two," said Oliver, around a mouthful. He could barely stand to think of eating all of it, even though his stomach was growling and empty, and he was still shaking from the aftermath of his rage at Noah.

"Yes?" asked Jack. He reached for a slice of beef, and he ate it with his fingers as the skin around his eyes crinkled up with pleasure.

It took Oliver back to that time when food was spare and shared. He didn't know if Jack was remembering that time as Oliver now was, or whether it ever ghosted across his thoughts. But because he didn't know, he didn't feel bold enough to mention it. Especially not now, when Cromwell was no doubt just beyond the door, or had listening ears nearby.

Oliver pushed the plate with the remains of the dipping bread at Jack, using the edge of his hand that already held a slice.

"Here," he said. "You can have the rest."

"You're ever so sweet to be so generous," said Jack in a lilt that told Oliver he meant to tease Oliver about his manners, but that the sharing had undone him. Though, as Jack had probably enough to eat at the Three Cripples, Oliver could not figure out why it might be so that Jack would be so pleased that Oliver had shared his meal. But he was.

Jack ate with relish, and his shoulder brushed Oliver's and he also seemed to relax on the bench near the fire. Being there, as they'd sometimes done in the past. Not saying anything, just sharing a meal with the warmth of the low coals layering the air around them. And as Oliver polished off the gin and sugar and warm water, he realized he was too tired to pay more attention to any of it, that he needed to rest, and was it yet time to crawl under some blanket and block out the day?

He watched as Jack ate mouthfuls of the beef and boiled eggs, a flush of color coming into his cheeks. He didn't ask to share Oliver's gin, though he did call for a pot of ale, which he drank with several large gulps, wiping his mouth with the back of his hand afterward, looking at Oliver as though measuring him.

"You look ready for nighttime prayers, then, Nolly. Prayers an' bedtime stories an' all that." His eyes went unfocused for a moment, as if he were remembering something, then he looked at Oliver, blinking.

"I'm beyond prayers," said Oliver, feeling the shortness of the statement badly balanced by the enormity of the truth of it.

"You're floggin' yourself worse than any monk," said Jack with a sharpness that told Oliver he had little patience for that sort of behavior. "Besides, with that face, you'll never be beyond prayers." Then he snapped his mouth shut as if he couldn't believe he'd just said it.

It wasn't a comment that Oliver was unused to, and he shouldn't really be surprised that even in the glow of a fire inside the Three Cripples, Jack would look at him and think it. But his face, however beautiful and graced by angels, had never done anything to save him, and in fact, had gotten him into more trouble than it seemed to be worth.

"Anyway, when you wear your new hat, it ain't like your old cap," said Jack. "You'll look more like one of us, like Cromwell said."

Oliver wanted to protest because whatever Cromwell had in mind for him, a new hat wasn't going to make any difference at all. He'd be up to his neck in metaphorical blood and mud well before long if he let his imagination run away with him.

"Yes," he said to Jack anyway, feeling Jack's thigh pressed against his. His mind was humming and his body felt slack, and the day had gone on too long, simply too long. He'd only vaguely heard the bells for nine o'clock, and though he'd often worked a harder day at the haberdashery than this, he still felt it.

"Can I just—" He wasn't presuming on Jack's hospitality; Jack had already said he could stay. Cromwell had already said he could stay, even. But he wanted to leave the heaving throng, to turn his back on what, to Jack, must be only the young start of the evening. "I simply cannot—"

Jack shook his head. "Come along then. I'll come up with you, I'm supposed to—"

"Keep an eye on me," Oliver finished for him. He'd not considered that it was like this for Jack, that for all of Jack's posturing in the street, his roughness with Oliver, he was not, in fact, his own master. Even as he'd mocked Oliver for doing as he was bid at the haberdashery, Jack was doing as he was bid by Cromwell. But then, to Jack, belonging in a place that held so much of Fagin's history and Jack's own past was well worth the price.

"But have another drink first. It'll help you." Jack gestured to the girl, who brought more gin and a small pitcher of hot water and lumps of sugar in a bowl. "It'll help you sleep, keep that worry from your eyes. I'll have some too," Jack added as he put hot water in the gin.

Oliver looked at the two glasses, almost clean this time, sparkling in the light from the fire, closed his eyes, and took a breath. He sipped the gin, everything unfocused and soft, and there was Jack, sipping at his glass, looking at Oliver with ladened eyes that bespoke of a contentment Oliver could barely begin to understand.

The doorway through to Jack's life led down to low streets and mean places. The way was slanted and steep, and Oliver felt himself slipping as though the path were slicked with ice. One drink then, and now, and later, and the whole focus of the world would be edged in fog and nothing would matter very much anymore. At which point, he would be giving up his dream of that bookshop, but then, murderers didn't own bookshops. Then again, there was Jack's smile, soft, the sharpness of his features worn smooth by the warmth of the fire and the pots of beer he'd already drunk.

When they were done, Jack pulled the glasses to the edge of the table, not seeming to care if they dashed themselves to the floor or that someone else would pick them up, or anything. It was simply not Jack's job to worry about that nor Oliver's. Jack pulled Oliver to standing and Oliver followed him up the stairs that suddenly felt too steep and too long, and Oliver felt as though he'd been at the Three Cripples forever, that now the dirt was beginning to soak into him. Jack tugged on Oliver's jacket and wouldn't let him pause along the way.

"With me, then, Nolly," Jack said without turning his head to check on Oliver's progress.

A cold dampness filled his mouth and nose and the smell of sewage from an uncleaned cesspit leaked through the cracks in the boards. Oliver wanted to stop where he was and turn and run, but there was nowhere else for him to go. He was a wanted man; it was either this or the hangman's noose.

But Jack made him go where he was bid, back up to Jack's room. Oliver followed Jack, made himself do it. There was nothing else except to do what Jack said.

At the doorway, Jack left Oliver's side, and Oliver could hear him fumbling for something along the mantelpiece.

"You can sleep next to the wall," said Jack, his voice coming out of the darkness, his face appearing in the soft, silvery glow of the candle as he lit it. "That way, I can beat off the rats if they come for you."

Oliver felt himself start in surprise because, of course, Jack must be joking. Then again, maybe he wasn't.

"Is there no more water to wash with?" he asked, looking at the jug of water Jack had provided for him earlier.

"No," said Jack, seemingly unabashed as he took off his hat and jacket and tossed them on the clothespress. "But there's a public bath in Smithfield; you can scrub the bed lice off you there for a penny."

Now Jack was laughing at him straight out, and Oliver wanted to lay into him much as he had Mr. McCready, only he didn't have a frying pan, and the rage ebbed as soon as it flared. He was just tired.

"Come on, then," said Jack.

Oliver watched Jack unbutton his blue waistcoat and sit on the chair to take off his boots. Then, as Jack slid back the blankets from the bare, flocked mattress, Oliver knew there was nothing for it but to do the same. So he sat on the edge of the bed, which proved to be hard-edged and thin, and took off his boots, unlacing them with exaggerated care. He pulled off his jacket and had no idea where to put it; he could not remember if there were pegs in the walls. Instead, he stood up to lay it gingerly on top of Jack's clothes with his coat balanced on top.

Then he blew out the candle, and still mostly dressed, crawled over Jack and tried to arrange himself comfortably against the wall.

It was dark and the room was cold and Jack was the only warm spot anywhere.

"Back-to-back, then," said Jack, yawning.

This was how they'd slept when they were boys, back in the old den, back-to-back or tumbled beneath the blankets, knees banging against each other when Jack would turn into him with a cold nose and cold hands, burrowing into Oliver as if searching in his sleep for some long-lost comfort that he could not speak of when awake.

Oliver had forgotten that for so long, forgotten the feeling of another body pressed close, another beating heart nearby, another's warmth in the darkness. Now it came back to him with a slamming weight. There was so much loneliness in the dark, and none of this was Jack's fault, and besides, Jack was there, and no one else was. The nearness of Jack didn't remove his fear about being hanged, but it was muffling it to a low, dull roar. He turned toward the wall and pressed back till his shoulders met Jack's and their spines fused, hips low, pressed together. He made himself breathe and kept this eyes closed, willing sleep that never seemed to come.

The dark deepened, with church bells tolling, vibrating through the mist and the dank fog, slithering over the rooftops. Oliver found himself huddled down with his arms across his chest as though folded for some eternal rest. Which made his heart thud wildly, breath coming short, thinking of death after a short life where nothing pleasing ever lasted, and everything he'd ever come to care about had gone or pushed him away, and here he was, in this black place, on the edge of a pit that he was sure led straight to hell that burned with angry tongues of fire, and where he would forever and always be eternally alone.

The bed grew hard beneath him and the scratching of the rats grew loud and sharp in the ceiling. Oliver shifted away from the sound, turning, thinking that he might be half-asleep, praying that he was rather than sobering up from too much gin. Then he awoke, startled, as Jack turned also, curving his body into Oliver's, burrowing under his chin. He was warmer, suddenly, with Jack pressed up against him that way, heat soaking through his clothes and into Oliver's skin. Jack wasn't even properly awake, making only a sound, small and drowsy and low, as he reached up to tuck his hands against Oliver's chest. It was the first moment of ease that Oliver had felt since the orphan had come to the haberdashery, the first moment of warmth he'd felt all day.

More, this was the way it had sometimes been between him and Jack back in the den, when the frost was on the windows and Fagin hadn't gotten enough dross and goods to sell to buy firewood. In the dark chill of no firelight and barely even a rush of candlelight, Fagin's boys would burrow together amidst scraps of blanket and tags of wool, and always Oliver had stuck close to Jack and lain in the dark with him. And so, though it wasn't right or proper, Oliver opened his arms and pulled Jack to him. He would say nothing of it to Jack in the morning, but then he never had.

CHAPTER 25

Pies Eaten In The Street And A Night Spent In Newgate

Morning brought a light breaking through the window and a brisk wind that rattled the panes. Oliver's head thumped with a platoon of drums marching up and down inside his skull; he couldn't remember the last drink he'd had the night before. Only that Jack had been there, urging him on, ordering more and then still more, and all the while looking at Oliver with green eyes and a lazy smile that had tendered the message that everything would be all right if only Oliver would take one more drink, just one more.

"Gerrup," said Jack, pushing his hand against Oliver's shoulder. "Get me some coffee, you."

Oliver blinked across the bed and rubbed the back of his hand across his mouth, which tasted sour with remains of the night before. Jack, only inches away, was sleep-tumbled, almost gentled with it. Oliver pushed him back, nearly content before the events of the day before began to rattle down on him.

"As though I'd know where to go to get some." Which was true; he'd hardly know where to get coffee on his own. Not in this part of the City.

"Go to the kitchen. Light a fire, if someone hasn't already. Put water in a saucepan, add some coffee, an' heat it up."

This made Oliver remember where he was and why he was there. It sparked through him, a cold shaft that made him feel frozen even where Jack was touching him.

"I'm not doing that," said Oliver. His voice shook as he said it. "I'm not going down there. And I'm not waiting on you hand and foot."

Jack opened sleepy eyes and smirked, as though he'd meant it as a joke all along. Oliver turned away and scooted to the edge of the bed to reach for his boots and look for his jacket. He put the boots on and did up his laces and looked around the room for a washbasin that simply wasn't there.

Behind him, Jack was moving, getting up to go to the clothespress, pulling on his waistcoat and thumping down beside Oliver to push into his boots. His hair was mashed to one side; he merely flattened it with some spit from his hand. As he pulled on his jacket and stood up, his eyes glittered at Oliver.

"Something on the street then? Pies?"

In spite of his thick, addled head, Oliver's stomach rumbled at the thought of pies, hot and peppery, with dense crusts and unidentifiable fillings. It didn't matter what was put in there, one bite of those would be enough to almost make him forget Mrs. Pierson's cooking. Almost. And he hoped Jack had money, for he had none. He'd not gotten his pay the day before, and his four pounds, two shillings, and sixpence were far away, locked in his chest at the haberdashery.

"Grab your coat an' hat, an' we'll scoot out before anyone wakes up an' sees us," said Jack. He didn't mention Cromwell's name, but Oliver knew who he was worried about. He'd told Oliver that Cromwell would want a pound of flesh, but that pound had not yet been stated; even so, Oliver doubted that Cromwell would fancy Oliver wandering off without some sort of deal being struck.

Still, Oliver needed fresh air more than just about anything else, so he did what Jack said and followed him down the stairs. But when they got down to the main room, Noah was waiting for them, jingling change in his pockets, looking bruised about the eyes, his lower lip puffy even as he smiled at them.

"Come along boys, all that drinkin' and carousin' leaves an empty belly just waitin' to be filled."

When Oliver stopped to button his coat and place his low top hat properly on his head, he looked at Noah askance. Yesterday, he'd pummeled Noah as he'd always wanted to do, and yet there Noah was, standing and waiting, as if they were all the best of friends.

As Jack put on his own hat, he brushed past Oliver to go out the door to the street.

Noah followed, shrugging. "Cromwell bade me to make amends, an' so here I am."

He didn't seem sincere in voice or manner, and yet Oliver had already seen that the word of Cromwell was something that made men jump to attendance and scurry to do as they were told. He didn't doubt that Cromwell had had words with Noah; he'd had words with Oliver as well and wanted things the way he wanted them. The Three Cripples was his domain, and he considered all within to be his. So Oliver nodded, not saying *yes* or *thank you* or even wanting Noah along on this particular morning when so much was a-tumble in his own head. But Jack smiled and tugged on Oliver's coat sleeve, and so the three of them went into the morning, into the damp and the wind.

The street was not yet thick with people, but the passage narrowed as they walked along down the dip into Field Lane, turning just onto West Street toward the sounds and smells of Smithfield. Oliver had not had much cause to venture even this much near the place, not since Bill Sikes had dragged him through it one wintry spring morning so long ago.

He could still feel the clasp of Bill's hand, strong fingers, hard along the edges with calluses, smelling like dirt and oil. He'd never let go of Oliver's hand till they'd met up with a cart that had taken them the rest of the way. Toward the house with the silver plate, toward the fullness of Oliver's destiny, though neither Bill nor Oliver had known it then. To Bill it had been a good opportunity for plenty of goods to fence, though Oliver had wondered, from time to time, why it was that Bill had picked that house, so far away, when there were acres of houses between Smithfield and there just ripe for the taking. Maybe it had been part of Monks's plan all along, though it seemed a far stretch even for Monks.

When they came to the edge of Smithfield, Oliver's musings came to the point that they always did. He would never know the whole of Monks's plan; there was no one to ask, and most of his kin were happy to put the whole event behind them. His Aunt Rose, when he'd asked her once or twice, had gone into a swoon and had taken to her bed with salts and lavender water. Prayers had soon followed, making Oliver suspect she knew more than she'd ever told him. Knew more that she thought he ought not to know. Which was frustrating; it was his story, wasn't it?

"What're you doin' there, Nolly, starin' off like that?"

Oliver looked up. Jack had his hands on his hips, scowling.

"I'm lollygagging," said Oliver. He could never explain it to himself either, how and why his mind would go off into the past.

"I've got sixpence," said Jack, rolling his hand in his pocket.

"But I don't want no bath."

"Then don't get one," said Oliver, thinking that Jack could do with one. Only in Jack's world, as he could see, as he knew, washing up was less important than other things. "Let's get something to eat or buy a pot of coffee."

Jack's eyebrows flew up, and Oliver thought it was perhaps based on surprise that Oliver gave in so easily. Then, with a nod, Jack began ambling along the edges of the market with Noah close at his heels, the two of them stepping along as though pleased, as though the air wasn't snapping with cold and the wind wasn't carrying the dank smell of muck and fresh manure and the sweat of animals marched too far too fast.

They were headed for a row of temporary booths lined up along an old Roman wall, their thick canvas awnings bouncing in the damp wind. Oliver could see the hand-lettered signs announcing pies and hot drinks, so Oliver followed close behind on Jack's heels. He let Noah pick three pies and pay for them, getting his change and handing one of the pies over to Oliver. That Jack had let Noah pay for them was a marvel in and of itself, but perhaps this close to home, to the Three Cripples, where Jack was himself to be seen regularly, using those light fingers wasn't an option.

"Go ahead, Oliver, it's not made of cat or nothin'." Noah smirked, and to prove his words, Jack bit into the edge of the crust, holding the pie up to his mouth with both hands. His mouth smacked as he chewed and Oliver did the same, more gingerly, nibbling at the crust and tasting the presence of salt and grease more than any meat or potato. Still, while Jack smiled at him, it was a good enough moment for him to enjoy it in spite of the throng of people growing in the market and the smells cast about by the cold wind.

As Jack chewed, he wiped one hand on the side of his jacket, already darkened by grease, and Oliver tried doing likewise. But it was hard. He was used to cloth napkins and basins of water to wash in, both before and after. He wanted a table and cutlery and Mrs. Pierson in her wide, white apron, clucking over him if he ate too fast or not enough. But Mrs. Pierson probably hated him now, despised him, had actually raised her voice to call for the constable. There'd be no going back to that now, to her kitchen and the warm fire reflecting off the clean black grate.

"Hey?" asked Jack, interrupting his thoughts.

Oliver started. Jack had come up so very close without him realizing it. He blinked, clearing his mind. It might be harder to walk away from that life than he realized.

"You want coffee?" asked Jack, tipping his head close to Oliver's and reaching out to touch Noah's shoulder as though the three of them were sharing some type of secret rather than a perfectly ordinary conversation. "There's a cart over there;

maybe he's got tarts, an' if you can go without a bath for a bit, we'll have both, tarts an' coffee."

Jack's stomach was in charge of all until filled, that was obvious to see. Noah, for his part, didn't seem to mind that Jack was suddenly determining how Noah's money was to be spent. Indeed, Noah didn't even seem to mind that Oliver benefited, even if the scuffle the day before had left Noah with a bruised face.

"Yes, that's fine," said Oliver. He could manage for one more day and find a way to wash up later. And to figure out what he was going to do now that he was a murderer.

But between the three of them, they'd only enough for one tart and one large pot of coffee, which they shared between them after Oliver made sure that Jack put enough sugar in. The tart he mostly left for Jack to eat; after Mrs. Pierson's puddings, it tasted like plain paper. But it pleased Jack, who smacked his pastry-speckled mouth just before he wiped it with the back of his hand. Noah, Oliver noted, didn't partake but was watching them both.

"Ready for it then, Nolly?" asked Noah.

"Ready for what?" asked Oliver, not thinking to correct Noah that only Jack called him by that name.

"Why, for—"

A jumble of commotion started up behind Oliver—deep shouts coming from several men. When Oliver turned around, he saw three constables coming at him at a fast clip with batons raised. The crowed parted to let them through, and the shouts led the rough-jacketed men, the woman with the torn grey apron, the bottle washer, and the man who'd just sold them coffee—all of them—to turn and look at Oliver.

Jack moved, tugging on Oliver's jacket to make him follow, but it was too late. Hard hands gripped Oliver, and something hit him along the back of the head with a stiff clonk, and the sky, windblown and grey, dipped above him and sank below the roofline, over and over again.

Two of the constables had him fast with large, curled hands, and the other one, the one who'd hit him with the club, stood in front of him and was saying something about *charges* and *assault*, and Oliver's gaze flicked about as best it could, looking for Jack. Or Noah.

Jack was gone from sight, had dodged himself right into hiding. But Noah, smiling, with his hands in his pockets, remained standing by against the brick-crumbled Roman wall. With a sinking heart, Oliver realized that Noah must have planned this and turned Oliver in for the reward because the constables had come straight for him, right in the market where Noah had led them to.

And now they dragged Oliver off; there was even a waiting cart with a black box on it with two black horses and a black door with an iron grid. They opened the door and shoved Oliver in and shut it with a clank. He had barely enough time to settle himself before the cart lurched off, throwing him to the floor, making him scrabble on his hands and knees for balance. But he couldn't understand, what did they mean by merely mentioning *charges* and *assault*? He'd assaulted Mr. McCready, yes, but he'd *murdered* him, so why wouldn't they have mentioned that?

The horses trotted along at a brisk pace, rattling along the cobblestones, and Oliver could imagine that the dark cart made many—pedestrians and carriages alike—move quickly out of the way. He didn't have to guess what their destination was; it could only be Newgate, and even as the cart slowed down, he had only to close his eyes and imagine the dark, grey walls rising up from the street, bold as iron against the moving throng of the people, devoid of any ornament save the jagged edges of the gate.

When the cart stopped, the back door was flung open and he was hauled out, his feet banging against the iron steps. He had barely a moment to right himself and look across the crowd for Jack, though he knew better, he really did, before he was drawn inside through the smaller door inside the larger gate to a courtyard he only barely remembered. One of the constables held him, hard by, his baton jutted under Oliver's chin, while the other two talked in low voices to a man in a black coat. Oliver could hardly hear them above the roar of his heart as it thudded against his breastbone. He was going to hang by morning, just as Fagin had, and he wanted to faint upon the stones.

Then, one of the constables nodded and broke away from his conversation with the man in the black coat. He came over to Oliver, eyes narrowed. Without a word, he nodded at the constable that held Oliver, and the two of them began walking toward a narrow door along one side of the courtyard. They dragged him through the door and down a corridor lined with dripping grey stone that narrowed as the guards turned down a passage that led to a flight of steps going down into the darkness. These were not the cells where Fagin had been kept. They were going underground; there would be no windows.

Oliver started, pulling himself up. And as they passed beneath the stone lintel, Oliver struggled, trying to catch his breath to protest where he was going. He could not understand how he'd come to this. Many a soul had rebelled against a harsher master, many more a boy had taken to idleness in the street and not been cast so low.

"No," he said. "*No.*"

The constables, with hard hands and impassive faces, gave his arms a yank.

"Come along with you, then, you young snake," said one. "The magistrate said one night's keeping, and that is what you shall have."

Oliver choked on his own indrawn breath, stumbling down the first step, and they held him up. The walls became darker with damp, the stone steps were slippery, and the way was lit by rough candles in iron sconces. Staring at them, he burned his eyes till they grew hot, so he could hold the memory of their light through the long night. Otherwise, he was not going to make it.

They came to the first barred cell door, and one of the guards let him go long enough to turn the iron key in the lock. He was pushed inside. Not hard, really, but with enough force to let him know there was no backing out. No slipping by the guards to run up the stairs and into the light. The door was shut and locked behind him before he could even turn around. He could see the profiles of the two guards through the long bars in the door, only half-lit by the single candle on a sconce in the wall in the corridor.

"You'll be right enough come morning," one of them said. Oliver could barely see his mouth move. "If the damp rot don't get to you first."

They rattled their keys and marched back the way they came, leaving Oliver in the cell with only the distant flickering of a single candle to keep the darkness away.

The cell was big enough to stand up in, long enough to lie down in, but narrow. Oliver could have reached out each arm and touched the walls with his flat palms, should he have wanted to come in contact with the seeping stone. He could smell the tartness of mold, dimly see the greyish-white triangle of niter growing up in the corners. It was a solid, sealed tomb of blackened air, beyond which came noises that could have been metal on metal, or steps on stone, or the dark scatterings of rats' claws as they scurried through unseen tunnels.

He stood to the bars and grabbed them with his hands. The candle in the iron sconce along the corridor wall had perhaps three hours in it. Maybe less. His hands circled the iron; chips of rust came away on his skin. He would make it as long as the candle held. Beyond that, he could not promise himself anything.

Shaking, he made himself let go of the bars and paced, feeling bits of dirt under his boots as he walked, sensing the slime on the walls but not touching it. In the corner was a long narrow board hung on chains from the wall. It might be intended to serve as a bed, but there was no mattress on the wood nor even straw. The long ends of the cell were an almost comfortable six or seven paces, but the short ends were only three or four paces across. His shoulder began to hitch up every time he had to turn so sharply to miss the niter in the corner. Something slid down his neck as it dripped from the ceiling. Filth began to cling to his shirt. The air, already dank, began to clot in his throat. He willed the candle not to flicker.

But it did, not more than an hour later as he paced on and off. Someone else was being marched down the hall, past Oliver's peering face, and thrown into a cell some doors away.

The iron door was slammed and locked, keys were rattled, and Oliver was no longer alone. He stopped near the doorway to listen and watch, eyes wide.

The new company might have improved the condition of the dark, except for the keening sound that wavered with drunken tones almost right away. And the candle. As the guards went past it, the shadow of it dropped low and then grew larger. Oliver held his breath. The guards clanked up the stone steps. The light grew brighter. The keening waned for a bit. Oliver resumed his pacing, feeling his chest tighten, his breath shorten.

Beyond the stone, beyond the gate, somewhere in the open air, he could almost hear the bells tolling the hour. But the sound was too dim for him to be sure he'd caught all of the bells. Was it afternoon? Or was it later? Maybe one o'clock, he guessed. Could he last until morning? No. He would not last the night at this rate; he would be dead by morning from the pressure of his heart bursting out through his breastbone.

When he'd been young, much younger, though he felt so very old now and that time so far away, he'd hid from nights such as this with his hands over his face, crying in the corner. That cell's floor had been scattered with straw, and the stones paper dry to the touch, but it was much the same. He was much the same, the impulse was the same, but if he sat down to howl, he would be soaked through come morning and gaol fever would come upon him. He'd heard of it happening. The air in a jail cell was so thick and poisonous a man could die of it in a day. Or a night.

That would not be him. He'd stand all night if he had to, but if he did that, he would be awake to see the candle's last flicker, which would come long before midnight. If he was asleep with his eyes closed, he would not know it when the candle went out, would not know that the darkness was upon him with its smothering grip and silent scream. Yet he could not lie down.

His mind stuttered over this and he made himself continue pacing, continue thinking about how it had all gone wrong. He should have been more clever when he'd first run away and hit the streets to leave London. He could have gone to Aunt Rose and Uncle Harry to begin with, and why had he not thought of this? Killing your master was a sin, the worst kind, but perhaps Aunt Rose, especially, could have found it in her heart to forgive him. To hide him, at least for a time, till he could figure out where else to go.

But no. He'd gone to Jack, to the Three Cripples, and the honor of thieves be damned, Noah had turned him in, and he wondered whether Jack had known. At the thought of it, his heart ached as though it had been pummeled with a fist. They hadn't been the closest of comrades, but when Jack had taken him in, the next assumption was that Jack would have kept him safe.

The night darkened. The light of the candle seemed to have dropped low at an alarming rate. Oliver tried to listen for more bells but could not hear anything. The bottoms of his feet burned, but he could not bring himself to huddle in the corner or even to sit on the hard board of the bed. Perhaps if he sat in the middle of the floor. He lowered himself straight down, crossing his legs, wrapping his arms around his knees. The floor made him cold straight through, but his feet thanked him for it, just the same. He would stay in this position for a bit and then stand up. Then sit again. He might make it through the night. If the candle kept burning.

But then the candle went out. Without warning or even a flicker to indicate that something was amiss. Perhaps a stray breath of foul air had done it in, or it had guttered itself silently to smoke. He did not know. Only that he was shoved into pitch-darkness as swift as death, and his breath jammed in his throat.

Even the keening from the distant cell had stopped, its occupant passed out, perhaps, or sleeping. Could Oliver sleep, then, now that it was dark? He could barely breathe, let alone unclench his body enough to relax even that much. He felt as though spots were forming in front of his eyes, though he could not see them, and that at any second, now the heavy night had descended, the darkness would swallow him whole. The back of his neck felt like a thick band of wire was waiting for it, his thighs shook so hard it was all he could do to remain seated. But if he stood, his movement would be noticed by the dark, and something, *something* would grab him.

Now arrived the moment he'd been dreading as waves and waves of panic foamed up from within. He shot to his feet, feeling the high-pitched sounds his throat was making, feeling the bands tighten around his chest and his legs, the cold film of ice across his flesh. He ran to the bars and held them. Jammed his head against them, let the jagged crusts of rust flake against him, against his face. He could almost taste it on his tongue, the iron and the salt and the unwholesome funk of something leaching through the rocks above. He wanted to howl, wanted to bite, and shoved his fist in his mouth, which stopped the first urge and satisfied the second. He tasted his own blood, which pushed past his lips with an unsaintly speed.

The sudden fear that he would gnaw himself to the bone made him yank his fist away, but as he swallowed, he could taste his own salt, feel the jumpiness of his blood. His heart. And now he was seeing things.

Something flickered along the wall; he heard footsteps. The man in the other cell gave a hard keen, and then Oliver heard the sounds of him turning over, quite clearly. And then snoring.

The lights came closer, and the footsteps. There were voices, talking low, and the rattle of keys. For a second, he thought it would be the guards and the hangman, or the ghost of Fagin. In an instant, Fagin would be there with his large mouth and crooked teeth, and those dark eyes glittering in the candlelight. Making threats, demanding that Oliver accompany him to hell. Oliver uncurled his palms from the bars and stepped back from the door. Not that he could hide or run, but at the very least, Fagin would not be able to see Oliver's expression in the shadows.

Two figures stopped in front of his door; the light from a lantern shone through the bars. The first figure was a guard with a circle of keys. And with him, to Oliver's dazed surprise, was not Fagin's ghost that stepped out of the shadows, but Jack. It was *Jack*.

"Nolly," said Jack, looking unfamiliar in this place, though he was dressed the same as always, and in fact, looked as he did that very morning. The guard held the lantern and Jack motioned for him to hold it higher. "You in there? Or have you gone missin'?"

By these words, Oliver knew that Jack wanted to cheer him up, but Oliver did not want to be cheered. He hid his bloody fist behind his back and made himself take a step forward.

"What are you doing here?" he heard himself ask. His voice shook and he flushed, thinking of Fagin in the cell the night before his hanging and how he'd gone mad.

"Ask you the same thing, I would, 'cept I was there. You've been a bold one, gettin' yourself collared on the street."

Oliver scowled. Jack was getting pleasure out of this, in an almost perverse way, watching people squirm, being trapped while he ran free.

"You've already gotten your reward from this no doubt," said Oliver, his voice low. It came out more pathetic than he could stand, and he began to turn away when Jack stepped up to the bars.

"Nolly," he said in a voice meant only for Oliver. "T'warn't me, I never turned you in."

"I didn't see you once they grabbed me."

"That's why they call me the Artful," Jack said. In the lantern's light, his eyes sparkled, somehow making Oliver feel a bit better. "But I came to you soon as I could."

"I know it was Noah," said Oliver quickly, having always known this, even when speaking to the contrary.

Jack nodded, his face darkening. Honor among thieves meant something to Jack, that was for certain, even if it meant nothing to Noah.

"Five minutes," said the guard.

Jack turned and handed the guard something.

"Did you just give him money?" Oliver asked, shocked. He had not considered this, though now that he thought of it, Uncle Brownlow must have paid the guard to let him in to visit with Fagin. Prayers had not calmed the Jew nor had pleas freed him. The guards standing by had been impervious to both, though the whole of it had left Oliver in tears and feeling weak at heart for days after. The guards had only cared about the money. So of course, that's how Jack had gotten in, though Oliver very much doubted that Jack would be getting down on his knees and asking Oliver to join him in a quiet word with the Lord anytime soon. It almost made him smile, but then he thought better of it.

"How much?" he asked.

"Every penny I had," said Jack. "That's the last of it, just now."

Jack did not seem the sort of lad who hoarded his gold in the first place, so as to how he'd come by enough for the guard, Oliver could not fathom. Perhaps he'd taken a collection at the Three Cripples, though that image seemed as far-fetched as the idea that Jack took his earnings to the Bank of England to deposit them.

"I'll repay you as soon as I am able," said Oliver, finding it somewhat comforting to be concentrating on these mundane facts rather than the darkness behind his back and the hangman's noose waiting for him in the morning.

Jack did not remark upon this, though his eyes, in the uncertain light, seemed to speak for him, that it was nothing, that he did not expect anything back. Leaving Oliver, once more, confused as to the type of boy Jack was. He'd never really known, back in those days in Fagin's den. He realized he knew even less now. And then Jack nodded to indicate that he would go along with whatever Oliver wanted to do.

"And hello?" Jack was looking at Oliver, wanting his attention. So Oliver came closer, enough so that he could see the shadow of Jack's lashes against his cheek. "You're not a murderer, after all."

"What?"

"He's alive, your old master. You clonked him pretty good, but he's alive. He's pressin' charges against you, of course, for assault an' runnin' away, an' you're in it deep, but you're not a murderer. You'll not hang."

Oliver tipped his head forward; his heart pounded. He could not imagine that Jack would lie about something such as that, whatever else he was, whatever else he might do.

Oliver felt something on his face, some damp, perhaps, falling from the ceiling, but as his fingers touched his cheek, he realized he was crying. Maybe the darkness hid this, maybe it did not. But the circle of the cell's darkness around him made him feel that perhaps it did not matter for this one night, and that Jack would not mock him. He certainly did not say anything as he watched Oliver and did not look away.

Then Jack surprised him, reaching through the bars as though the guard simply was not there, and cupped the side of Oliver's face in his hand. The warm skin of Jack's hand was rough against his cheek, but Oliver stayed motionless. And as for Jack, surely he could feel the dampness of Oliver's tears but did not pull away.

"Nolly," said Jack, slowly. "The morning will come."

Without regard to the guard standing there, Oliver turned his face to cup it more firmly inside of Jack's palm, feeling the skin of it against his mouth. He was surprised that Jack did not take his hand away, not for a long, still time. His thumb moved across the edge of Oliver's jaw with careful strokes. His eyes were dark and Oliver made himself look into them.

"Time," said the guard.

That was it. Jack was out of money and the guard had better things to do. Jack drew his hand away and then jerked his chin upward as if telling Oliver to rally himself, the morning would be there soon, and without the hangman's noose. The guards motioned with the lantern and then took it and Jack away. When the darkness was full on and the footsteps had faded, Oliver sat in the middle of the floor, folding his arms around his knees, waiting for his tears to slow. The floor was cold and soon he would have to stand, but Oliver's heart was warm and there was a candle in it.

CHAPTER 26

Wherein Oliver Appears Before The Magistrate

When Oliver had finally deigned to lie down upon the bed, his teeth had been chattering too hard for prayers, and his ears too sharply tuned to the sound of scurrying claws beyond the walls and the constant drip of water upon the stones. He'd fallen asleep in spite of that but only realized it when he was woken up by the clanking of a key in the door to his cell. Two guards came in, pounding and stomping, pausing only long enough to put metal cuffs around Oliver's wrists before dragging him out of the cell and down the long black passageway.

It was morning, and he could tell this by the bare grey light that eked its gloom along the stone-lined corridor as the guards dragged Oliver up the stairs, down another hallway, and threw him into a holding cell.

While Oliver waited, with his hat in his hands that one of the guards had given him, sitting on the narrow bench against the wall, his hands in shackles, the movement around him had

421

come to a halt. He'd been arrested, yes, but for a moment, as he awaited the magistrate, it was as if nothing had happened. He was in another room, locked in, to be sure, but just waiting there. Waiting. Nothing had happened to him, and maybe he could pretend that nothing was going to. What could they do? He'd struck Mr. McCready, yes, but Mr. McCready was, according to Jack, still alive.

There was a snap of cold air. The door opened and two guards stood there to take him into court. It hadn't been a long wait, though long enough for Oliver to lie to himself, for his body to get used to the wooden bench along the wall. For the weak grey sunlight to come in through the barred window in a place that reminded him, a little bit, of the cell that Fagin had spent his last night in. But this was not that place; it was a different jail altogether.

"You, up," said one of the guards, and Oliver stood, cold dust filling his mouth, sharpening behind his eyes with bitter teeth. He walked toward them, and they grabbed him up under his arms as if he'd already made a motion to run. He wasn't running. There was nowhere to go.

The corridor leading to the courtroom was short, and as Oliver stepped into the room, the metal around his wrists clanking as he shook, he was struck at how this room resembled the last courtroom he'd been in when he was nine years old. That room had been as cold and still as a meat pantry, grimed with soot along the ceiling and littered with scraps of paper and ash along the floor. This room was exactly like that one except that there were two high windows along the far wall instead of one. This situation, as well, was almost exactly like then except that while he was still an orphan, he was taller and could speak for himself if given the chance.

The courtroom was packed with people who had nothing better to do than to come to see the excitement and to entertain themselves on other people's miseries. He imagined that their eyes reflected only their rapt attention at the dissolution of the life of someone who they felt to be beneath them. The thought of it was making him shake again, so he made himself think of something else, let his eyes sweep the room, seeing Mr. McCready in the front row, a white bandage under his hat covering a swath of forehead. He looked pale and ill and furious, his eyes sparking dark. As his eyes swept Oliver up and down and took in Oliver's shorn hair and disreputable coat, Mr. McCready's eyebrows went up, as they had often done when something had been amiss in the shop, and Mr. McCready had been obliged to step in and set things to rights. Only this time, he couldn't, not even if he wanted to.

Next to him, unexpectedly, sat Mr. Grimwig, his cane between his knees, his hands resting on it. He smiled at Oliver, that slanted ugly smile he used when he felt someone was watching. Why he'd come, Oliver had no idea, but it could not be to support Oliver.

Oliver turned away from the crowd and climbed up into the dock when told to. He held on to the railings and thought about being nine, and hungry and thirsty in front of a magistrate who did nothing but drink, and who assumed Oliver was a criminal before he'd even opened his mouth. This magistrate did not drink, though he seemed of a piece with the glasses and beard, eyes stern as he reviewed the page before him. Or that's what Oliver assumed he was doing. He certainly was ignoring Oliver, and the movement of the entire courtroom, the chill of the air as it whooshed through the room from some unchinked window or crack in the paneling.

Then the magistrate looked up and pounded on this desk with his wooden block. He rattled off his office, that the court was in session, and he wanted a verbal description of the offender in the dock before him. Oliver's mouth fell open and the full weight of the moment slammed into him as though it were a runaway cart. He was under arrest. He was well and truly under arrest, and the shock of it was that he was *guilty*. For running away, for assaulting his master. All of it. Uncle Brownlow would have been so disappointed; Fagin would have been pleased. And what's more, Mr. Grimwig had not been wrong, which would make him quite proud of himself, so at the very least, Oliver had not let *him* down.

The prosecutor stood up and read the charges. "Before us stands Oliver Twist, who is charged with assault and running away; he attacked his master without provocation. The court recommends deportation."

"And under what auspices of the law do you recommend deportation and for how long?" The magistrate looked up at the prosecutor; he never looked at Oliver. He seemed serene.

"We recommend permanent deportation on the basis of the remarks which are to follow. In that Oliver Twist has not merely broken one law but two, and at the same time, demonstrated a wild disregard for person and property and proven himself to be a danger to his community."

"Continue."

"Two days ago, Oliver Twist ran away from McCready's Haberdashery, where he was occupied as an apprentice shop boy. That he ran away is a crime unto itself, for he signed an agreement with Mr. McCready to provide services until he was twenty-one. Oliver Twist has, in effect, stolen himself, and the charge is theft."

The magistrate nodded, and Oliver felt his skin shiver under his shirt.

"On the same day, Oliver Twist got into an altercation with his master with regards to some trifle, and we attest that Oliver Twist willingly struck his master to the floor, opening his skull and leaving him to die in a pool of his own blood. All witnesses state that Mr. McCready treated his boys humanely and with compassion, so there was no reason for Oliver Twist to strike out."

"It's a lie!" Oliver's mouth opened and the words came out before he could stop them.

The magistrate looked at him. "You will be silent until given leave to speak, young Twist."

Something ripped through him and Oliver looked down at his hands, linked by metal, gripping the railings, feeling the heat behind his eyes. Yes, he'd struck Mr. McCready, but it hadn't been because of a stray moment of ill temper.

"But he *murdered* an orphan." Oliver's voice broke on the last word, sounding shrill and young in the echoing space of the courtroom. He heard titters and the gabble of talk, and he flushed. "He left the orphan in the warehouse and he froze to death, and when I found him, Mr. McCready said that he—"

"Enough." The magistrate banged his block of wood. "There will be silence in this court. And if I hear one more word out of you, Oliver Twist, one more word that is not directed by me, I shall end these proceedings and have you deported directly. Is that understood?"

Oliver felt his cheeks grow hot; he should have known better. The world had never cared about small boys such as Martin, and it never would. There were too many of them; they were disposable and forgettable. There was no way to rescue any of them, let alone a single small boy. What's more, the full weight of the law was behind Mr. McCready, and would stay there forever.

"Yes, sir," he said, his voice low, thick in his throat.

"Pray continue, Mr. Prosecutor."

"As I was saying, Mr. McCready was struck down with violence and intent to kill, and left on the floor, bleeding from his wounds. A pursuit was activated, but Oliver Twist disappeared in the streets within moments. Mr. McCready, luckily, was tended to by his housekeeper and has recovered. To continue, the second charge is assault with attempted manslaughter. Either of which deserve deportation, which is what the prosecution recommends."

The magistrate wrote in his book and considered his notes for a moment. Then he cleaned his glasses with a soft cloth; he tapped the edge of his pen on the desk. "I have a question. How are these charges brought, and by whom?"

The prosecutor nodded, checking his handful of notes. "Mr. McCready, the victim in this case for both charges, placed notices with the police, and in due course, the defendant was arrested by virtue of an informant, coming forth with information for a reward."

Oliver gripped the bars between his hands and made himself not talk, made himself stay silent, even as wanted to shout to the entire courtroom what kind of man the informant was, and that whatever Noah Claypole had to say was either a lie or the truth for his own benefit.

"May we hear from the informant, please, Mr. Prosecutor?" There was a pause. The magistrate looked at the prosecutor, and Oliver followed him. The prosecutor was not just checking his notes, he was reading them. He looked up, his mouth a stiff line. "The informant declines to testify; his written statement is asked to stand in his stead."

"What?" barked the magistrate. "But he received a fee, did he not?"

"Yes, he did, but he declines to testify. But he's a known informant, so the information is good."

The magistrate appeared to think this over. "Very well. Proceed."

"The testimony is given, and statements from witnesses have been presented to the court. The crime itself is not in question, but Mr. McCready is here to testify, regardless."

The magistrate nodded, and Oliver turned his head to the courtroom behind him while the whole room shuffled to look at Mr. McCready.

Mr. McCready was in the front row, sitting at the end as though he'd been prepared for this moment. He nodded at the prosecutor, white-faced, his hands in his lap, and then he caught Oliver's eye. Oliver could see the disappointment and the fury there, and he looked away. Maybe deportation would be for the best; he deserved no better, at any rate.

Mr. McCready got up and walked to the front of the courtroom and was sworn in. He mounted the dock adjacent to Oliver's. He stood straight and folded his hands; his head bandage shown, a white flag against his skin, as he took off his hat. He was a model citizen in his black suit, white collar, and cravat. His boots were Sunday polished, hair slicked down. His eyes were like darts as he looked at the magistrate only.

"Mr. McCready, I understand that you would like to give a statement against the boy."

"Yes, sir, that is correct."

"You understand that anything you say will be captured in the records of the court."

"Yes, sir, I do."

"Then proceed." The magistrate waved his hand in Mr. McCready's direction.

Mr. McCready cleared his throat and began. Oliver made himself listen. "My name is Evan McCready. I own a haberdashery at Number 116 Wardour Street. For the last fifteen years, I have devoted my life not merely to making a good living but to providing worthy boys the training in running a shop so that in the future they might be gainfully and reasonably employed."

"Do all of your boys gain good employment?" the magistrate asked.

"All of the boys I have trained, without exception, are now employed in London in respectable places. My most recent is now working for Harrods."

"You take them at fourteen, I understand, and let them go at twenty-one, is this correct?"

"Yes, sir, that is correct."

"And yet, Oliver Twist, by my records, came in at seventeen years, is this correct?"

"Yes, sir, that is correct."

"Can you explain this discrepancy?"

There was a pause as Mr. McCready dipped his head to look at his hands. There was a flicker of memory across his face, and Oliver had to look away. He knew what had happened that day, how kind Mr. McCready had been at Uncle Brownlow's funeral reception, and the intercession that Parson Greaves and Mr. Beauchamp had organized.

"Oliver Twist," began Mr. McCready, his voice a little rough. He cleared his throat and continued. "Oliver Twist is the adopted charge of a friend of an acquaintance of mine. When the friend, Mr. Brownlow, passed early this winter, I learned of Oliver Twist's situation. He had no place to go. However, he was educated and a good candidate for this sort of training, for all he was almost too old to begin."

"And what did you do then?"

"I attended Mr. Brownlow's funeral, I was introduced to Mr. Grimwig by mutual friends, and made my proposition to take in the boy."

"And who is Mr. Grimwig?" The magistrate looked at the prosecutor. "Do you know of this man?"

The prosecutor stepped up, waving his notes over the courtroom to point at Mr. Grimwig, who preened and straightened up at the attention. "Mr. Grimwig was a friend of Mr. Brownlow's and took on temporary responsibility for the boy at Mr. Brownlow's demise."

"He was concerned that Oliver should be able to make his way in the world," added Mr. McCready.

Oliver scoffed under his breath at that, catching Mr. Grimwig's eyes with his own. Mr. Grimwig smirked at Oliver and looked away. Mr. Grimwig was only concerned with Mr. Grimwig, and any needs of Oliver were an inconvenience at best. But he didn't say anything. Couldn't, not when the energy of the court was focused on seeing Oliver get his due, or at least as the prosecutor saw it.

"And so you took the boy, Oliver Twist, into your shop?"

"I did. We discussed the matter, and we both came to the agreement that this would be in his best interest. He was desirous of owning a bookshop one day, I believe."

"And when he is twenty-one, he comes into some money, as I understand it?"

"Yes, when he is twenty-one, he comes into three-thousand pounds, which is now in an account with the Bank of England."

"Do you have any interest in this money?"

"No, sir, I do not." Mr. McCready seemed insulted by the very idea of the question. "My only concern is training the boys under my care. My shop garners me sufficient profit to make a good living and pay decent wages."

"And to what might you ascribe Oliver's turn of attitude, from the day you interviewed him and found him worthy, to the point at where he attacked you. With what was it?"

"A frying pan," said the prosecutor. The crowd made sounds of amusement and jostled and moved in their seats.

"A frying pan," said the magistrate. He frowned at one and all, making the object serious once more.

"At first, he seemed to settle in." Mr. McCready looked up at Oliver, his eyes bleak, mouth in a straight line. Oliver was surprised by the sudden thickness in his chest. He *had* settled in; he'd liked working at Mr. McCready's. "He was quite— happy, as all my boys seem to be. They are well fed, trained, have time at liberty."

"Then what's the problem, do you suppose, Mr. McCready? Can you provide any demonstration of how it wasn't working?"

"Oliver Twist was a good worker; however, he seemed somewhat daunted by the amount of physical labor involved, though he went at it with a good heart and seemed to want to do his best."

"And the problem?"

"There was a young man," said Mr. McCready. His jaw worked as he thought over his words, his eyes unfocused as he stared at the floor. Then he looked up, putting his shoulders back. "There was a young man of Oliver's acknowledged acquaintance, who by his apparel and his voice, was from a low place, and whose identity I've never been able to ascertain. He kept coming to the shop. I warned Oliver to send him off, warned him of the consequences of the association, but it did not stop. They were even seen together in the street, when Oliver was on an errand, making deliveries. I had to whip him for it, and still it did not stop. I believe Oliver was influenced by this boy, to an unhealthy degree, and for reasons that I cannot fathom. Someone encouraged Oliver in his violence and sheltered Oliver when he ran away; I can only imagine that it was this same individual."

Oliver's heart felt cold in his chest. He'd not realized that Mr. McCready had been so impassioned to save him from what he saw as an acquaintanceship with someone of the streets. To have wanted so very badly to save Oliver from Jack, and not for any personal gain, but for Oliver's own sake—it was true kindness. Well, it was too late for that, nor could Mr. McCready have ever saved Oliver from himself. As for Jack, well, everything that had happened since Jack's return to London, from that day to this, seemed a foregone conclusion.

Oliver made himself remain calm as he looked over the courtroom, keeping his gaze low. He looked at Mr. McCready in the dock and at Mr. Grimwig in his seat, cane steady between his knees. He even caught sight of Mrs. Acton, up in the side rows where other elegant ladies sat to watch the commotion and the human drama. But he didn't see Jack, and was glad, so very glad, that he did not. Oliver could not be saved, but that did not mean that he had to drag Jack down with him.

The magistrate sat up in his chair, and raised his eyebrows. He settled his glasses once or twice on his nose as he contemplated Mr. McCready's words. "You seem somewhat impassioned by Oliver's association with this unknown individual."

"I admit to my own vanity in this, but I have never had in my charge a boy go astray to the degree where he could not be saved. And I—I would ask that the court would be lenient with Oliver Twist if I could ascertain the nature as to how this—this street ruffian—managed to work his way into Oliver's association. So easily. So *disastrously*." Mr. McCready's voice shook as he said this, color dashing across his face.

"How do you know he's a ruffian? How do you know the person who sheltered Oliver is the same one as was seen with Oliver in the street, who visited Oliver at your shop? Do you have a description?"

"I have no knowledge, your worship, but a glimpse of the back of his head. His hair is dark, and the two young men are of a height, and that is all I know." Mr. McCready paused, florid with restraint. "But Oliver could not have disappeared so easily, had he not known someone and had somewhere to go."

"But is it the same young man?"

"I believe so, your worship." Mr. McCready twisted his hat in his hands, rolling the brim around and around, then he stopped himself. "I believe so."

The magistrate turned to Oliver, holding up his hand to stay any comments from the prosecutor. "Oliver Twist," he began. "This companion of yours seems to have caused you some trouble. But is it the same individual who sheltered you and took you in when you were wanted by the constabulary?"

Oliver's whole frame went absolutely still, a freezing-cold hand clutching at his heart.

"That a young man of good prospects is unduly influenced by someone from the lower orders is not a crime, Oliver. But if this same companion sheltered him, after an assault such as you wielded against your master, then that *is* a crime. Do you understand?"

He could not speak. During Mr. McCready's recitations, he'd been lulled almost into a stupor, his body working up a heat to keep him warm in this cold room, his brain spinning as though it was a wooden cog, grinding itself into dust. They wanted Jack. Wanted his name, wanted him cornered and brought to heel. Oliver knew his name, knew it fully, knew all of Jack's names and faces, and all the rest besides. Jack Dawkins. The Artful Dodger. The Dodger. *Jack.*

And still Oliver could not speak.

"Oliver Twist, at Mr. McCready's urgings, and out of his passion to do right by you, as a good Christian man, I might be inclined to do as he asks and decrease these charges to three month's hard labor. That is, if this young man can be proven to be the reason behind your decline into the gutter of society. Can you give me his name?"

The courtroom fell into a hush. There wasn't so much as the creak of a wooden seat or the rustle of a petticoat to be heard, though Oliver felt the wind in his ears.

"Oliver Twist, will you speak?"

Oliver kept himself from shaking his head; he needed to think. While Jack might not be the most respectable of citizens, the truth of it was he had taken Oliver in, not once, but twice. And while the first encounter could not exactly be described as auspicious, Jack had done the best he could. He'd done his best the second time as well; he'd taken Oliver in even with his own head on the line, for surely he'd known that if Oliver was ever arrested that his association with Oliver, in return, would be questioned. And *still* he'd done it.

Uncle Brownlow would have said, had he been there, that a man never turned on a friend, never. Fagin, who no doubt had seen the inside of many a court, would have said much the same thing, only differently, *Fagin's boys don't peach.* And while Fagin was a reprobate of the worst order, and it would have come out differently, through rotting teeth and stringy fingers, a declaration of such paucity and paranoia so as to seem almost insane, the sentiment was the same. But while they would agree on his course of action, neither one of them was here to advise him. Perhaps that did not matter, for in the current moment, he was neither completely Uncle Brownlow's boy nor Fagin's boy. He was his own boy, and besides, he could never give them Jack.

"Oliver Twist, will you give this court the name of your companion and allow the law to lessen your sentence?"

Oliver took a breath as the courtroom fell to utter silence. He heard a board snap, as though under the weight of someone shifting where they stood. "I will not."

There was a roar in his ears, and then he realized it was the complexity of raised voices, the half shouts and exclamations that the magistrate's wooden gavel could not quite yet contain. The collection of sounds whirled up the ceiling and bounced off the walls. And still the magistrate pounded.

Through the din, Oliver could hear a single voice, rough-edged and slightly familiar, saying, "Sir, if I may speak before the court, if I may speak—"

The magistrate pounded his block, sending his pens to rattling until the crowd subsided, leaving Oliver feeling as though he'd been swamped with their reaction. Of course, they'd never understand, no one of any decency would. He might have a hard time, himself, explaining it to Jack, would that they ever met again.

"The court will come to order," said the magistrate in the first silence available to him. "And I have no other recourse but to—"

"Sir, if I may speak."

It was the same voice from before, and Oliver scanned the courtroom, trying to figure out where it had come from. He saw a man rise and come forward, without permission but with his black low top hat in hand. He was washed and shaven, looking clean and awkward, but the expression around his eyes gave Oliver pause. There was someone with him, a younger man, also newly cleaned, pious in a narrow white collar and black cravat; he had nothing on his person except for his cap in his hand. He had dark hair, and his head was bent down as they both walked forward. Then he lifted his head, and his green eyes glinted at Oliver.

Oliver's mouth fell open. *Jack.* Then he recognized the man: it was Cromwell, scrubbed and shaved and cleaned up to look respectable and concerned. With his hands clasped around his hat and the meek line of his shoulders, the dip of his head in the direction of the magistrate and prosecutor, all made him appear that his only desire was to be of use.

"Who is this man?" asked the magistrate. He waved his block at the prosecutor. "Tell me who this man is, or I'll have him removed from my courtroom."

"I do not know, sir," said the prosecutor. He adjusted the wig on his head. "But he appears to want to speak on behalf of—"

"On behalf of the young man, your worship," said Cromwell. "I am William Howard, come from the Holborn Society's Aid for Boys. We aim to assist young men out of a life of crime by giving them a good home, and—"

"So you appear to appeal for the boy? His sentence is about to be passed, you realize."

"Yes, your worship, but I come to the court every so often, to listen and learn from the great wash of humanity." Here Cromwell stopped to throw a generous wave over the crowd, which had gone very silent, listening to the dramatic rise and fall of his voice. "And in this young man's case, I truly believe that his problem is more temper than temperament."

"So you believe he was pressed into the assault?"

"By his own passions, your worship," said Cromwell. Then he patted Jack on the shoulder, sending a small cloud of dust up from the velveteen shoulder of his jacket. "This here's Isaac White, late of the streets and current resident of my honest establishment. I cleaned him up, taught him some manners, and he's not a pickpocket anymore. Are you, Isaac?"

The crowd was silent, enthralled. Even Oliver found himself leaning forward to hear Jack's reply. Of course, Jack and Cromwell believed none of what they were saying; it was all a joke to them. But it was so very well told, a lie to echo Mr. McCready's own tale, complete with the sweet-faced Jack, who managed to look shy and bold at the same time, flashing his smile, looking up from under his lashes at the magistrate.

"Yes, sir," said Jack, almost softly. "I would have died on the streets had it not been for the Society. Was about to go on a lark of stealin' an' that, when they found me."

"And how long have you been with them?"

"Only six weeks, your worship," said Jack. "But long enough to learn the difference between right an' wrong."

As the crowd broke into an excited rumble of talk, the magistrate considered the pair, and Oliver held his breath. Of course, a man as clever and learned as to become a magistrate would not be taken in by two men so obviously of the street, masquerading as both the saver and the saved. A quick run across London, as well, would easily prove that there was no such thing as the Holborn Society's Aid for Boys. But no one moved to do this.

"Can we beseech you, your worship," said Cromwell, raising his voice above the thrust of the din, "to consider the fate of this good English lad, led astray by his own passions, if he be sent into a country so far away from his native soil? To be surrounded by true convicts and dark natives with no sense of their own God? Wouldn't he be better off here, among his own? To be saved and set on the good road where he can be of use to society? I can't save everyone in the world, but I can do my best in my own little corner of it. And this poor lad, just look at him, at that face, surely he deserves saving?"

The crowd turned, of a body, to look at Oliver, standing in the dock with the shackles hanging heavy around his wrists and the backside of his breeches stained with gaol mud. His hair was scraggled and black with soot, his face was grimy with sweat and ash, and he knew that he was no doubt jumping with lice, and still they stared as if at something they wanted for themselves. He felt himself flushing and there was a murmur from the seats, a small cry from a despairing woman; Oliver ducked his head. Stared at his hands. Let the pull of emotion from the courtroom wash over him; he had no control at this point, only the magistrate did.

"Mr. McCready," said the magistrate. He had no need to bang his gavel; the crowd was absolutely silent, pitched forward in their seats, waiting on his next words.

"Yes, sir."

"An alternative to deportation has been brought before the court, and I for one am loathe to be overly punitive. Discipline and training on English soil is always preferable in cases such as these. Yet, as the victim of this crime and, indeed, his master, would you countenance this? Or yet take him home yourself and deal with the matter in your own way?"

Before Oliver had a chance to consider whether or how he might handle going with the man who he thought he'd killed, Mr. McCready shook his head and sliced through the air with his hand. "I'd as soon nurse a snake to my bosom," he said. "But I have no objections to the Holborn Society's Aid for Boys, if they take him, and good luck to them, I say."

"Then I hereby remand Oliver Twist into the care of the Holborn Society's Aid for Boys." The magistrate banged his gavel and sorted the papers on his desk. "Mr. McCready, William Howard, if you can come forward and sign for the boy, then I can close this matter and get on with my work."

Having not been otherwise bid, Oliver remained in the dock, waiting, while one of the constables standing by fingered his keys and jingled them a bit. There was talk in the crowd and Oliver could hardly believe the court system of London had fallen for a bit of velvet coat and grand speaking by a man who so obviously thought the lot of them to be fools. And Oliver was a fool as well if he went with them, but where else was he to go? Mr. McCready didn't want him, and Oliver didn't want to be deported. There was no other way.

The two men went up to the judge's bench and took pen and ink, bending over the prosecutor's table to sign a document that looked far too short to be recording all of the events of the morning. Or maybe it was only in Oliver's head that the time in the courtroom seemed overwhelming, never ending. The crowed rustled and stirred as if to voice their common displeasure that the next event wasn't already underway. The constable came up and unlocked Oliver's handcuffs, neither harshly nor gently; he was just doing his job.

"Off you go, young'n," said the constable. He seemed sensible, and the look in his eyes told Oliver that he might be among the few to see the truth behind Cromwell's lies. But it wasn't his job to say anything about it. Or maybe he knew that Oliver wasn't truly evil. Or maybe Oliver was dizzy from the final judgment and reeling with being saved from deportation.

From months at sea, trapped in a little boat, to live the rest of his days on rocky soil far from home.

CHAPTER 27

Old Bridges Are Burned And New Ones Unwillingly Built

The constable guided him to the doorway to wait with him while Oliver rubbed his wrists and longed, suddenly, almost painfully, for Jack to be there.

And all while Mr. Grimwig hobbled through the crowd. He was clacking his cane on the floorboards as he rudely made his way to Oliver, who couldn't imagine what they might have to say to each other should they pause to exchange greetings. And yet, there Mr. Grimwig was, resplendent for his non-speaking appearance in court, hair oiled back, a black armband around the sleeve of his dark green coat, his silk black waistcoat, and the shiny gold of his timepiece pinned to a scarlet ribbon. He was as he had always been, and Oliver felt startled to see him up close, as if it had been years since they'd seen each other instead of only weeks.

"Oliver Twist," said Mr. Grimwig, not bowing his head in greeting. Instead, he tilted his head back, looking at Oliver down his nose, showing everyone, anyone who was watching, exactly what he thought of his friend's ward.

"Mr. Grimwig, not a pleasure," said Oliver, not aiming to be pleasant as he might have done in the past. And this in spite of who was watching; he didn't think much of his guardian's friend and was well past the point of giving a damn what anyone thought about it.

"I see you have again swayed the entire English judicial system with your fine airs and cherubic looks, which, in spite of your shorn hair, which makes you look like a dock worker, manage to give lie to the impudence within." Mr. Grimwig nodded at the throng of the courtroom as people moved into the newly emptied seats or moved past the two of them on their way outside for fresh, damp air.

"I didn't—" Oliver began, meaning to explain that it hadn't been his words that had released him from his fate; it had been Mr. McCready's. Who was coming toward them, slowly, almost reluctantly, carrying something in his hands that Oliver couldn't quite see. "It was Mr. McCready—"

But Mr. Grimwig interrupted him, poking a sharp finger in the middle of Oliver's chest to get him to pay attention. Mr. Grimwig's brows lowered fiercely, and he was scowling, white-faced, angry.

"You ruin the life of everyone you come in contact with," said Grimwig through clenched teeth. "They are pulled in by your pretty face, your fine manners, and you plunge your dagger in their hearts, and afterward, they are never the same. You killed my best friend with your duplicity. You broke his heart, and you are well on your way to breaking the heart of Mr. McCready, though he is wise if he sticks to his word and never allows you darken his door again."

Oliver backed up, surprised. While he'd always suspected Mr. Grimwig felt thus, he'd never before spoken these particular thoughts out loud.

"And because of this, everyone you have ever known will turn from you." Mr. Grimwig stopped, panting, short of breath, as though his passion had taken it from him. His eyes were wet and his face flushed; he pulled out a handkerchief from his waistcoat and patted his face with it.

Oliver felt as though he'd been slapped, in public, in front of dozens of people, and his whole body jerked, stung. But before he could make a reply, Mr. Grimwig turned away, stuffing his handkerchief back in its pocket, thumping his cane on the floorboards to make way for himself. Then he slipped into the crowd and was gone.

The constable took Oliver's arm and hustled him to the doorway, where Mr. McCready met him. And indeed, marched passed them.

"With me, Twist," he said, and Oliver scrambled behind him, through the narrow stone corridor, out into the rainy morning. He sensed Cromwell and Jack close behind him, though they didn't say anything. Perhaps they meant to jump Mr. McCready when no one was looking; something that Oliver already knew he had to be on the lookout for.

Mr. McCready was talking to a constable, standing there with a box in both hands. It was Oliver's box from the haberdashery, the one that contained his clothing and books and his money. He turned to Oliver and held it out. "Didn't know where you'd be bound, but I thought I'd bring your belongings."

The look on his face was grave; Oliver felt that fist in his throat, a familiar hard ghost of regret. He'd done badly by this good man; in spite of his treatment of the orphan, Mr. McCready had only been doing what he thought to be right.

"About the orphan," Oliver began, meaning to explain, though he was never going to apologize.

Mr. McCready's expression darkened. "They're a penny a dozen, Oliver Twist, as you should well know, being one of them."

It felt as though Mr. McCready had slapped him. He shoved the box at Oliver, roughly, and as Oliver reached for it, it slipped from both of their grasps and dashed itself to the curb. A quick-stepping carriage hustled past; one of the wheels caught the largest edge of the box and dragged it, snapping and cracking, splashing it with gutters of rain water. Smashing it to pieces. Oliver's books, his mother's small portrait, the letters from his Aunt Rose, the small box containing his money, all of it, became unrecognizable and floated away on the narrow tide.

With a scowl, Mr. McCready tipped his hat at Oliver and plunged into the traffic on the wet street, slipping between a milk float and a band of street workers. And then he was gone.

Cromwell, close on his heels, brought Jack with him.

"Eh, then, Oliver," said Cromwell. He came up behind Oliver and clapped him on the shoulder. "You're one of us, then, my good lad."

Oliver was about to say something to refute this; he'd already made up his mind about that. But Jack came up on the other side, touching the back of Oliver's hand with his own as they watched the refuse of his belongings float away in pieces in the gutter.

"I knew you was never goin' to turn me in," said Jack. The brightness of his tone seemed to hide something else beneath the layers and the lies.

Oliver turned to look at him and opened his mouth to explain why he had not. But there was too much about the orphan and Mr. McCready and Mr. Grimwig that he couldn't explain, not in the street this way, not in front of Cromwell. And there was too much brightness in Jack's eyes. Oliver let the thoughts fall where they would.

Jack took the brown cap he'd been carrying in his hands and put it on his head, managing to look much younger in it than Oliver ever could, and Oliver felt a bit of softness that he'd believed to have died.

"No, Jack," said Oliver. "Never you." He watched as one last piece, the corner of the box, perhaps, or the edge of a book, floated down the gutter. "Never you."

The walk to the Three Cripples was brisk, uphill all the way, it felt. As the walkway narrowed, begrimed beneath their feet in spite of the rain, Oliver felt himself being sucked into the darkness. The number of folk increased, and the pavement became crowded, rotting wood rising around him, the dank smells thick beneath the rain. He was soaked through and shaking by the time they came to the door of the tavern.

"Get him cleaned up, you," said Cromwell. His voice had dropped to its normal tones; gruff and certain. "We don't want 'im to stand out, but 'e shouldn't suffer neither, not with that pretty face." He reached out as if to pat Oliver on the cheek, but Oliver jerked away, not saying anything, but jerking away, just the same. Out of reach. He was used to people, to Jack, saying he had a pretty face, but not in the way that Cromwell did it.

Jack, as if sensing it, pulled Oliver out of reach also, opened the door to the Three Cripples, and dragged him inside. It was cold near the door, but Oliver could feel the heat of at least one coal fire, smell the familiar dust and the damp, as if he'd been away for ages and not merely a day or two.

"You hungry, Nolly?" asked Jack.

Oliver shook his head. He didn't think he could manage food; he had no idea how he would manage any of this.

Cromwell came in behind them. "Get 'im cleaned up, I said."

Jack scurried, pulling Oliver with him along the bar, through the room, into the alcove that was Jack's. There was no fire, and Oliver hesitated, but Jack tugged, and Cromwell was muttering to someone in the main room, Oliver went and sat down in the seat next to where the fire was supposed to be and buried his face in his hands.

"Nolly?"

"Give me a moment," he said. "I shall be all right, in a moment." But he wasn't going to be. Not in any way that he could think of. He'd committed a crime and had had his day in court. His penance was this place and what it represented; he'd thought he'd left it behind, oh, so long ago. There had been years of goodness and cleanness between that day and this, so how was it that he'd ended up right back here?

"Nolly?"

Oliver sighed with his whole body. He took his face from his hands and looked up at Jack. Oliver, at that moment, noted that while Jack had a white collar over his green velvet lapels, there was no sign of Oliver's red scarf. But Jack didn't move as Oliver's eyes searched him. He only stood there, blinking, a little pale, that brown cap still on, the mud from his boots tracked right across the floor. As well, in the cold, stillness of the room, Oliver could smell himself. His own boots looked beyond repair, and he'd smeared mud right up to his shirt.

"It's goin' to work out, Nolly, you'll see. You're with me, now, ain't you?"

That this was a plus, Oliver could readily admit. But that it was going to work out was another thing. Jack was content, so Oliver should be too; to try and convince Jack otherwise would be wasted air.

"Yes," said Oliver. He made himself sit back a little bit; the seat was hard and cold beneath him, reminding him unduly of the night before spent in the prison cell. "But I still need a wash, and maybe after that, something to eat."

Jack nodded. "That's the spirit. Come on, up you get." He reached down to haul Oliver to his feet.

As they went into the main room, Oliver heard the noises, a door slamming and footsteps. From down the corridor near the stairs that went to the labyrinth below the tavern, Oliver heard a low cry. He followed Jack to see that Cromwell had Noah by the collar. Noah's nose was swollen and bleeding, and he looked sore about the mouth, as though Cromwell had just smacked him.

"Teach you to turn evidence in my place," Cromwell said, harsh. "Teach *you!*" Then he hit Noah again.

Noah cried out so piteously that Oliver started forward, only to be held by Jack's hand on his elbow. Though why he would want to help Noah in any case, he didn't know, except that he couldn't just stand by and watch.

"'E collected the rent on you," said Cromwell, seeing Oliver there. "Collected the reward an' all, as 'e does, the slimy toad."

"The reward," said Oliver. He'd suspected it had been Noah, but for some odd reason, it didn't make him feel any better to be proven right.

"'E went straight down to Newgate, when 'e found out about you, an' reported you, an' 'e collected the reward of five pounds. Pocketed the whole lot."

Which might be the problem. If Noah had split the reward with Cromwell, then he might not be hanging from Cromwell's fist looking like a drowned rat.

"Might 'ave cost me the use of you, besides, 'ad you been deported."

This stopped Oliver cold. "Use?"

"Of that pretty face," said Cromwell. He shook Noah to keep him still. "'Cause I own you now, owned you the second you walked through that door. But now, with the signature of the court to back me up? I own you for good and all."

Cromwell let Noah go to stumble against the yellow-stained plaster wall, nursing his nose with a snowy-white handkerchief that soon turned brick red. "An' one step out of line? Out you go on a ship to sea."

"No," said Oliver. "You don't own me, the paper merely said—"

Cromwell surged toward him, backing Oliver up, pushing right past Jack to back Oliver against the wall, pushing chairs aside and slamming the wall beside Oliver's head. Then he shoved Oliver's shoulders, hard, and moved close, pressing his body close, one thigh between Oliver's, his face only inches away.

"You're mine," he said. "I own you, body an' soul, an' besides, you're too pretty, far too pretty to be out on your own." Cromwell raised a hand to stroke the side of Oliver's face. "I'd take you myself if you weren't so valuable in other ways."

Cromwell was so close, his breath skittering across Oliver's cheek, that Oliver pulled back as far as he could, though Cromwell shook him, making Oliver's head clonk against the wall. "So valuable in other ways. An' you're mine, don't forget that."

Cromwell let Oliver go, shoving back off of him, the ghost of the heat of his body shivering on Oliver's skin. He stomped out of the room, leaving Oliver gasping. Jack's eyes were wide in his face, though he crossed to Oliver's side, touching his fingers to the edges of Oliver's jacket. And Noah, still bleeding, stared at Oliver as though this was his fault, and nothing but his bloody nose was amiss.

Suddenly, Jack marched over to Noah, holding out his hand. "Hand over a third, you," he said. "I know Cromwell's taken his bit, and I want mine."

To Oliver's surprise, Noah dropped the handkerchief long enough to count out some coins, and whether the change was right or not, Jack pocketed it and turned to Oliver with a small smile. "Noah an' me'll treat you right, Nolly. Though I don't think Noah's up to a wash this mornin'."

Or any morning. Oliver would sooner go with a shrieking devil than to walk the streets with Noah Claypole. Though as he watched Noah snuffling into his handkerchief, seeing the low line of his shoulders, the blood spotted on his shirt, it was apparent that being Noah was its own punishment.

CHAPTER 28

Jack Tempts Oliver With Food And With Drink

Jack took Oliver into the kitchen, which was a clattering mess of unwashed pots and pans and a hot stove that was sending smoke into the room; every level surface was covered with grease, and mouse-droppings littered the windowsill, the corners of the room, along the wall. A woman struggled at the dry sink to scrape dried remains off platters, while another was cutting slices of bread with a too-dull knife. In the middle of the room, a man hacked away at a side of beef that was green round the edges and looked to be more fat than meat. His cleaver whacked into the wooden table with each slice, sending rolls of flesh onto a sheet of newspaper.

Ignoring this, Jack dragged Oliver between the table and the stove, from the thick, sour air of the kitchen, out into the crisp, wet air, along a narrow path between the frozen mud, to the pump at the end of the alley. He kept a lookout as Oliver sluiced his face and neck in the icy-cold water. When he was finished and there was nothing for him to dry his hands on,

Jack pulled out his shirttails and offered Oliver that. Oliver kept his complaints to himself that he was now cold *and* wet and still not very clean, kept his mouth shut and followed Jack up the alley, through the foul kitchen, and back to the tavern.

Compared to the weather, the Three Cripples was a haven from the snow-flecked rain. Someone had lit a fire so the alcove was relatively warm, although the constant dusty damp clogged Oliver's nose as he sat by the fire, watching the bustle of customers, the door swinging open and closed every five minutes, bringing with it more air and cold, the push of damp bodies. But for all that activity that he watched for a good hour, he could see no pattern. During that hour, Jack went upstairs to change into his regular clothes, and when he came back down, Oliver refused the offer of a beer. It wasn't just that it was so early in the day, more, it was because Jack obviously wanted the beer for himself—for all Oliver watched, he realized that the order and passage of the day was nothing that resembled the haberdashery. Well and truly nothing like it.

The floor never got swept, the counters and tables went unwiped, dirty glasses and beer pots collected like litters of unwanted children at the end of the bar, and men spat on the floor wherever they would. And the girl, Doreen or Polly or whatever her name was, behind the counter, slopped beer over her hands and licked them, and pushed back her stringy hair and put her fingers in glasses, and on and on until Oliver felt as disturbed as a foreman inspecting a gang of drunk bricklayers in the street. It was easy to see that nothing was done with any eye to improving custom or making the place anything other than what it was: a local and disreputable but handy tavern, where the beer flowed and nobody cared about much of anything else.

"You all right, Nolly?" asked Jack. He stood up, finishing off the beer, tipping his head back to catch the last drops. Then he brushed his shoulder against Oliver's. "You're free now, remember? No more errands, no more gettin' yelled at for nothing, no more stupid job."

And that, right there, in Jack's unassuming statement about the world as Jack saw it, was the problem. Oliver could try to explain it, how the status of being an apprentice gave him a place in the world, put him several steps closer to his dream of owning a bookshop, but Jack would only look at him and frown and urge another drink on him. Because for Jack, the dream was today, only this minute, this small circle of space where they stood. For Jack, tomorrow was an uncertain mess and not worth bothering about, and certainly not worth planning for or working toward. For Jack, all of his tomorrows were a chance proposition at best anyway, so why not enjoy it while you had it? To explain it otherwise would be a waste of Oliver's breath.

Besides, as he looked at Jack, at the smudge on his cheek, which apparently had been there before the trial and lingered after, on account of Jack never had much affection for soap or hot water, there was something to it. Oliver remembered this feeling from the old days, of feeling lost, standing in Fagin's den with his cap in his hands, not knowing how or when or where the day would take him. And of Fagin, letting Oliver pick initials out of stolen handkerchiefs and praising him all the while. He'd not known where his tomorrows would find him then either. And strangely, he was right back there now as he had been then, next to Jack, who tilted a smile at him. At least Jack was something familiar and solid in a world that kept shifting around him. Jack was the only thing—

"It's just that—" Oliver began, thinking at least, in part, to try to explain it. "I don't quite know what to do with myself."

"It's true," said Jack, nodding. "You're usually deep in it by this time, elbows and arseholes, workin' your heart out, sweatin' it that your master will be displeased by somethin'. But here?" Jack waved a hand, dirt under his nails, over the company at the bar, the men at the table. "Here, there's nothin' you need to be doin' until we get sent on a job."

That was the problem. Not only was there nothing that needed doing, Jack obviously expected, now that Oliver had a prison record and no means of employment, that he would, naturally, operate in the world, as Jack did.

Oliver wanted to put Jack off, to say some comment that would enforce the notion that whatever else Oliver would be doing, stealing wouldn't be one of them. Which to Jack would seem laughable because, of course, whatever else was there to do? Besides sleeping in and drinking beer for breakfast and thinking, as you looked at a black-shouldered group of men doing the same thing, that you were having a grand time. That this was the life.

Well, it wasn't. And besides, Oliver's stomach began to growl, a low, persistent feeling deep in his gut. He was already missing Mrs. Pierson's good cooking, the stately platters of food and buttered bread, not to mention the cleanliness of her kitchen.

"Nolly." The way Jack said it came out half annoyance, half warning. It was as if Jack wanted to point out that this was Oliver's life now, and he'd better get used to it, and it suited Jack, so why didn't it suit Oliver?

It was somewhat disconcerting that he could feel all of this in the single utterance of a pet name.

"I need a purpose," said Oliver, shifting his shoulders, not thinking that Jack would understand.

"Cromwell'll give you a purpose, right enough," said Jack, as though this were a good thing. He even nodded as he said it with a little jerk of his head.

"Not that kind," said Oliver. He should start explaining right at that moment that he wasn't going to work for Cromwell, not ever. And why he should just button up his jacket and go out that door this very minute and march his way to Aunt Rose's. Leave all of this behind him. But he felt frozen somehow, and whether it was indecisiveness or just plain exhaustion, he didn't know. He could leave. But he couldn't bring himself to do it.

"I merely need something to do," he said. "I cannot put it any plainer than that."

"Come have a beer with me, then, if you're so set on doin' somethin'. The day's better, when you've had beer."

Jack picked up the pot from the table and dragged Oliver's jacket sleeve with his fingers to make Oliver follow him as he made his way to the bar. Jack shouldered his way up to the front and snapped his fingers at Doreen, who snapped her fingers back and pretended for a whole minute that she didn't see him there.

Determining that a beer would fill his stomach for the moment, Oliver followed Jack and stood close behind him, ignoring the startled looks he got, which Oliver wanted to believe was on account of his chopped hair and outdated jacket, but which he suspected was something else, as it always was.

Jack reached back through the throng and pulled Oliver up to the bar to stand next to him, pushing men aside, and why shouldn't he? He worked for Cromwell, who owned the tavern, and so Jack could do as he pleased. Not that any of the men at the bar could have been aware of that fact. Still, Jack nodded at the girl and ordered two pots of beer and ignored the dark looks he was getting.

Doreen took his pennies and pushed over the beers, which slopped on the damp wooden surface, slipping in the grease and liquor. Oliver made himself take one, fingers circling around the dingy metal edge, and then he drank from it. The beer wasn't bad; it smelled and tasted fresh at any rate, perhaps the freshest thing in the tavern, so Oliver concentrated on that, breathing in the hops and tasting the bite behind each swallow. He preferred gin—gin was sweeter when laced with sugar, but this early in the morning, midday, not even noon yet, beer would give his stomach something to do and dull his mind a little.

After about five swallows, he still had half his beer left, but his brain started slipping apart as the beer tumbled into his empty stomach.

"Jack." Oliver raised his eyes to Jack, who was standing there, finishing off his second beer of the day, wiping his hand on the back of his jacket sleeve, and looking at Oliver as though all of this was normal, all of this was good.

"I need something to eat." He felt desperate, having not gone this long without food since he'd been back at Hardingstone Workhouse. Even when he was with Fagin, he'd never been this hungry, his stomach a hollowed-out shell. He thought back and realized he'd not eaten since the pies on the day he'd gotten arrested. Two days ago. There might have been something offered to him in the jail cell, but he couldn't remember. His body was reminding him now though.

"Beer's what's to eat," said Jack, smacking his lips.

"No," said Oliver, feeling it hitting him, a swamp of hunger, his stomach grinding itself from the inside out, and waves and waves of dizziness.

Jack looked at him, brows drawn down in a dark line; Oliver felt the sweat popping up on his upper lip.

"You're a pretty miss an' twice as fussy," said Jack, critical, frowning. "But then, you always was."

Oliver shook his head, turning away, thinking that he might go and sit down amidst the filth and trampings of boots and the soot from the clogged fireplace, and lay his head in his arms and not get up again until his head stopped spinning. But Jack was there, pulling on his sleeve, cupping his hand around Oliver's wrist, startling Oliver at the gentle touch amidst the throng of men and the disaster that his life had become.

"Got a few pennies, how about we get you some pie?"

"No," said Oliver. "Just some bread. Some bread and butter." To his surprise, tears sprang into his eyes, feeling as though they were hot diamonds about to burst, so he swallowed and tried to straighten his shoulders. "And coffee. From a stand. You know?"

Jack looked at him, and Oliver thought he could see the recognition there, flickering in Jack's eyes, and the memory of that day when Jack had roughed him up and Oliver had sent him away with two pennies, and had often and thereafter thought of Jack eating bread and drinking coffee. Or had they gone together, sometime after? He couldn't remember. It was all muddled now, and gone, that life. His old life, the one he'd wanted.

Jack went and grabbed his low top hat and Oliver's hat from the table and ushered them out the front door, into the rainy street. The pavement ran with water, and the refuse and strings of straw gathered in clumps along the edges of the gutter. It wasn't raining hard, but it was constant, and though light, had built up, sparkling around the edges of the buildings, women's bonnets, the scarred backs of horses, on the hooves and beshatted hides of horned cows being driven to Smithfield along Saffron Hill.

Putting his hat on, Oliver ducked his head down, his chin touching the kerchief around his neck, the buttons cold beneath his fingers as he did them up.

"There's a cart down along here, I think," said Jack. He jingled his change in his pocket, Oliver's change purse having been traded or lost some time ago, it seemed, and Oliver followed close behind and tried not to stare at the cripple on the corner covered with a burlap sack and asleep under it, or maybe dead. Or the woman with the goat who was trying to sell milk under an awning that simply was too full of holes to keep out the rain. He couldn't look at any of them because if he did, the reality of it would come to him too hard and much faster than he was ready for. This place, this street, these people, this was his home now, as if he'd been destined for it so many years ago. And while the man in the white waistcoat back had Hardingstone Workhouse had been in error, he hadn't been very far off the mark.

"Can we—" Oliver hurried to catch up and walk beside Jack, hogging the pavement, bumping into people, getting dirty looks. "Is there enough for extra sugar in that?" he asked. They stopped at the cart. Its awning was solid cloth, at least, and they stood under the lip of it and warmed their hands over the brazier, breathing in the steam rising from the pot.

"Anything for you, my petal," said Jack, smirking. Oliver bumped his shoulder against Jack to get him to stop, but the coffee man, smiling, looked at Oliver, up and down the way people did, just the same.

"Two coffees," said Jack. "Sugar in his."

"Cheaper if you buy one big one, besides, I only gots one cup at the moment."

Jack nodded and handed over three pennies, and then one penny more, and pointed at the sliced bread, slightly soggy around the edges, stacked in the narrow metal bucket next to the fire. The man handed over a slice and prepared the coffee, putting in it, as Oliver could see, several large lumps of sugar. Jack gave the bread to Oliver, and with motions of his hands, let him eat the whole thing. Oliver sighed as he chewed, his throat a little tight as the bread was old and there was no butter, but he ate it anyway, swallowing as fast as he could and watching Jack take the first sip of coffee.

"You like it with sugar," Jack noted, handing over the cup.

Oliver held it between his two hands, bending down to suck the crumbs from his thumb, glancing up to see Jack staring at him. The coffee man was looking at him as well, with round, eyes, curiously watching as if he'd never seen anyone lick crumbs from their skin. Oliver looked away and drank his coffee, gulping two hot swallows that sent the warmth fusing through him, racing to his stomach, warming him from the inside.

"Better than beer?" Jack asked, still watching him.

Oliver cast his eyes over the passersby, the stream of people along the muddy streets that simply never stopped moving. "Yes," he said. "It's better than beer."

"Not better than gin," Jack said. Now he smirked. "Gin with sugar. Or, with you, anything with sugar, eh?"

Jack poked him in the stomach with his elbow, seeming to find this fact funny, though Oliver couldn't understand why. The whole day roared ahead of him, a great, big, vast empty wasteland of filth and damp, and Jack was as happy as a spring thrush.

"Yes," he said. "Anything with sugar." Or anything served on a platter, on a clean white tablecloth, preceded by the niceties of hot water and soap, and followed by a dry place to sit and read afterward, with no one stomping about, shouting.

"Nolly?"

Oliver looked at him and handed over the rest of the coffee. "I miss my books," he said. And although he'd only owned barely a dozen, in that box, now broken and dropped in the rain, it was the idea of them. That and the bookshop, which he was even further away from owning. Could he explain that to Jack, and would Jack ever understand? "Especially the one I'd only just bought, *The Arabian Nights*; I hadn't even had a chance to really read it before Mr. McCready threw it in the gutter."

Jack nodded, though his expression told Oliver that he didn't understand, not really. Jack's possessions amounted to, had always amounted to, what he had on him. Anything he needed he could trade for, or, yes, steal, and so the whole world was his closet, his clothespress. His shelf of books.

"Let's go down to the river," said Jack. "That'll take your mind off it, then."

Jack started walking and Oliver hurried to catch up, thinking how he'd walked with his thoughts and his grief the day of Uncle Brownlow's funeral, and how he'd met Jack in the snow. Now it was raining, and he was still with Jack.

The traffic, horses, carts, and people, thinned out a bit as they slipped and splashed down Field Lane, which was too narrow for many, and too dirty for most. Then along Farringdon, which spread out such as a fat woman's skirts, the throng picked up, out and about in the rain. These folk were made of women in cloaks and clean aprons carrying bundles, or men with shovels and warm scarves. Though they were not of the higher quality sort as would be found on Wardour Street, they were somewhat nicer than skulked around the Three Cripples.

After a brisk walk downhill, they arrived at the mouth of the pale grey-stone Blackfriars Bridge, the humped stone arches reaching into the rushing brown water. The wooden pikes and clouds of sail rocked on the water, damp and draped in the rain, the tide pushing in against the muddy shoreline, and low birds flew over and ducked into the water, picking at trash and bits of refuse, wheeling and crying over their heads, and all of it surrounded by the smell of the water and the mud, and the steam of a pipe emptying thick red fluid into the brown water.

Jack raced up to the low stone wall that separated a portion of the street from the river and half flung himself over it, as a child might. His face was bright with excitement as he looked at the rushing water, the movement of the boats, the ferries being rowed back and forth, the tumble and clack of carts over the bridge, racing in the rain as though to get out of it. A gust of wind picked up, wet and drizzly, and smacked Oliver in the face.

"I missed this, when I was away," said Jack. Unexpectedly, it seemed, for he'd not yet talked about his time being deported except for a few wild stories and attempts to show Oliver his tattoos. "It was such a dry place there, I felt like I was a dried sultana half the time."

While Jack had been away, a convict, Oliver had been in the country, warm and drowsy in the summer, cozy and fire-lit in the winter. Studying at the table before it was cleared for meals, or in the little front parlor, where nobody ever went, and nobody minded if Oliver was in there, for he was considered a good boy and mindful of where he was. Well, he was no longer a good boy, but he could be mindful, and was as he looked at Jack, who didn't, and never could, understand that this was no life. Not for a young man who wanted to make something of himself. But for Jack? The river and the view was enough. This moment was enough.

Jack, leaning on his elbows on the stone wall, looked at Oliver. "Tell you what. I'll pick some pockets an' get you somethin' to eat, a proper meal, would you like that?"

"What?" Oliver felt as though he'd been smacked. This whole morning, the issue had been that Jack wouldn't understand Oliver's life, but might, if Oliver would be able to explain it clearly enough. Yet the real problem was that even if Jack did understand it, it wouldn't matter to him. Because here he was, talking of picking pockets as if it were a grand option, and fair game on a rainy morning.

"No," said Oliver. "I'd rather go hungry."

But Jack just tipped back his head and laughed, rain on his face, on his teeth, bare hands cold in the air by the river, red with it, and he stood up and reached up to pat Oliver's face. Gently. Cold fingers against cold skin.

"I could do it," Jack said. "Get you a meal, as easy as anythin'."

Oliver wanted to jerk his head back out of Jack's reach, but he didn't. The single touch was enough to still him there on the bankside, with the rain coming down in sheets of mist. And Jack was willing to do it, and Oliver wanted to tell him, *yes, go and get a fat wallet and buy me a slice of roast and steamed pudding*, but he held himself rigid until Jack took his hand away and shook his head.

"Or you could do it," said Jack, laughing with an openmouthed smile. "You still owe me from the time I got you ham an' cheese at the market in Barnet."

"I'm not picking any pockets, not even for you." Oliver felt fierce as he said it, but Jack moved his fingers across Oliver's face, sweeping away drops of rain.

"You'll get the hang of it, Nolly," said Jack. "By-and-bye."

The way he said it told Oliver that Jack didn't think it was a question of *if* Oliver would fit in at the Three Cripples. It was a question of *when*.

CHAPTER 29

A Strange Afternoon, Which Is A Sequel To The Last Chapter

The afternoon wore on just as a slow beast past its prime, struggling in a muddy field. When they came back to the Three Cripples, the crowd had ebbed and the fire was built in the alcove, and Jack planted Oliver there along the bench, nearest the warmth. He made him take off his jacket and chafed his arms and hands and generally fussed over him while Oliver let him and tried not to think.

Which was hard, because there was nothing else to do except stare out the doorway into the main room and watch the customers come and go, and listen to Polly and Doreen snapping and barking, and feel the wafts of cold air whenever someone opened the door. Eventually, he let his head fall on the scarred, dark table and rested his eyes, letting the coffee fade, letting the moment on the river fade, and letting everything become what it was now. This moment, and Oliver nowhere to go, no one to be.

He dozed—he thought he had when he opened his eyes, for the fire seemed brighter and there were two candles on the mantelpiece, and Jack was standing over him, shaking him.

"Here," said Jack, pushing something at him.

The something was a pot of beer, crisp and golden, about the only thing the Three Cripples managed to keep clean and do well. Oliver took it and brought his lips to the edge, savoring the moment when the beer touched his mouth, and he swallowed, almost smacking his lips, looking up into Jack's eyes and seeing the little nod he gave.

"You're far too glum," said Jack, sitting next to Oliver with his own pot of beer, pushing Oliver in so that Jack could fit. "Far too glum for a man who isn't a murderer, an' in fact, was let off just this very day."

"Jack—" began Oliver, meaning to put him off; he didn't want to be cheered, in spite of Jack being near.

"We're goin' to play cards; I'll teach you my special hand where you can foist an ace or two up your sleeve, an' we're going to eat, an' I've ordered a chicken roasted, an' you, my good man, are goin' to learn to smoke."

"No," said Oliver. He put his beer down gently, not thumping it. "I don't want to smoke."

Jack smiled, his eyebrows going up. "Then everythin' else?" He waved his hand and snapped his fingers, not waiting for Oliver to agree or not. "Wench, wench, more ale!" he shouted, though neither Polly nor Doreen was hardly likely to answer to that, and Oliver didn't even know if the Three Cripples actually served ale, though it was likely that they did.

At Jack's bidding, Oliver continued to drink, and the beer began soaking into him. But as Oliver watched Jack go out to get his pipe and cards, he realized that he needed to think about what he was going to do.

There was a danger in staying where he was, with the memory of Fagin's stories about how glamorous and charming a life of crime could be. Though it wasn't just that Oliver remembered laughing at those very stories and being drawn in. More, it was what Cromwell wanted from him, which was the very thing that Fagin had wanted from him, though if Fagin were here, he'd be able to inform Cromwell fairly quickly what a terribly useless criminal Oliver had been.

And he thought that, perhaps, the problem wasn't that he wouldn't be a good criminal; the problem was that he *would* be. Or so it seemed because instead of turning up the collar of his coat and taking to the road this very instant for Aunt Rose and Uncle Harry's home in Chertsey, he was *still* here. Chertsey was where he belonged; they would take him in, in spite of his brush with the law. Wouldn't they?

But Oliver was distracted by Jack coming back to the table and sliding into the bench across from him, shuffling the cards between his fingers, the begrimed edge of his shirt cuff falling back from his wrist.

"We're goin' to play whiskey poker," said Jack, splitting the deck and pushing it together.

"What about patience?" asked Oliver, his head swimming a little—beer on an empty stomach—thinking that he already knew the rules to that one, though he'd never gotten to practice.

"'Tis for one person only," said Jack. "You're with me now, right, so we play this. An' when you're ready, we'll move on to whist."

While Jack explained the game, Oliver paid attention, noting the pairs and triplets and colors, and how the backs of the cards were badly printed, the edges worn and stained. Oliver threw himself into the game, for, after all, what else was there for him to do?

As Jack won the first three hands, Oliver realized that the backs of the cards were more important than the fronts, and that Jack was cheating. But instead of saying anything about it, Oliver started keeping track of the backs of the cards too, and so his score went up. He smiled as Jack puffed on his clay pipe, clenching it with agitation between his teeth, waiting for the moment that Jack looked up at him and understood that his cheating ways would not be the best of Oliver Twist because Oliver Twist knew how to cheat *right back*. And when Jack did, indignation rolling over his face, Oliver threw back his head and laughed, right out loud.

It was a kind, almost harmless way to spend the afternoon as it turned into evening, drinking and playing cards, with no one telling Oliver to mind the shop or scrape the steps or carry in more coal because the orphan was dead now—

"Hey there, Nolly, you hungry?" Jack asked this quickly, as if he'd been paying attention all along. He touched the back of Oliver's hand.

"I have done the world a great wrong," said Oliver, wishing suddenly for some gin; it was much stronger than beer and it was what was wanted right now. But the smoky room was crowded, and he didn't want to go up to the bar to get some nor did he imagine he could ask Jack to do it for him. Instead, he swallowed the remains of beer in the metal tumbler and placed it on the tabletop. Waves and waves of a deep searing that tasted as dark as regret rolled through him. "I let that boy die, just as I let Dick die, and I'm a horrible person, you know that, Jack, don't you?"

"No," said Jack. His voice was low, and he seemed in earnest even when he didn't ask Oliver to explain about Dick, though it was clear to Oliver that Jack didn't remember. "You're not a horrible person, don't you get that? Because if you were...on that day, you remember that day?"

Oliver shook his head; he had no idea what day Jack was talking about. There were so many of those days, and Oliver had gone over them so many times in his head, in his heart, that he didn't want to do it now. But perhaps Jack had a different day in mind, a new one. Something better.

"Let me tell you the story. When we went out to Clerkenwell Green, you an' me an' Charley, to get some wipes, an' we took them off that old man, an' you went runnin' an' got arrested and in court—they threw it all out an' you on the pavement. Do you remember that?"

Oliver remembered the courtroom of days long ago: it had been much like the one that very morning, with the magistrate and his drink. Uncle Brownlow had been there, somewhat tousled from the roughness in the street, and the bookseller, Mr. Beauchamp, as Oliver knew him now, coming in at the last minute—but he had fainted just as that had happened, and had woken up, days later, in Uncle Brownlow's townhouse.

"You were tossed on the street, poor wee mite that you were, an' who should come an' rescue you? Why, the old man, your Mr. Brownlow. He took you into that carriage as tenderly as if you were his own. He wouldn't have taken you in, not a man like that, if you were truly horrible."

Looking down at the tabletop, Oliver curled his hands around the tumbler of beer, now empty, and thought about the days that had followed, the kindness and then the cruelty and then the happy ending.

Then he looked up at Jack. Not asking how Jack knew this story or whether it was true; Fagin probably had spies posted, and the word had gotten back to Jack, so that was how he knew. "I ended up back here anyway," Oliver said.

Jack nodded and smiled, and yes, for Jack, this was a good thing.

"Somethin' to eat; the chicken should be here soon." Jack scanned the main room and nodded. "Here it comes."

But instead of being what Oliver had thought it might be, a piece of thigh or perhaps even a slice of breast, it truly was the whole thing, an entire chicken, seared on the skin, done in a roasting jack with grease dripping down its sides. It came steaming, with roasted potatoes cut up with roasted carrots, carried on a tin platter by a slatternly miss and slammed on the table. There were two little bowls, salt and pepper each, and slices of buttered bread done up in paper, and as Jack paid the girl from his fund of money, Oliver's mouth was watering.

He didn't want to demand an explanation as he might have done only days before, he wanted to eat and not ask questions and not worry, for at least a score of minutes, about what his future might bring.

"Go on, then," said Jack. And then to the girl, "Go on, Doreen, an' get us some gin an' water, an' don't forget the sugar, mind." He handed her some more money and then reached for the backbone of the chicken and tore the meat and skin from it with his bare hands. Huffing against the heat, he laid the meat and skin on a tin plate and pushed it across the table at Oliver while it cooled.

Of course, at Mrs. Pierson's, there would be clean white china plates and snowy clean napkins and a knife and a fork, so they could eat as civilized folk did. But not here; and for the moment, Oliver simply did not care. He took a piece of roasted carrot, all charred on one side, and bit into it, tasting the juices and the butter and thinking it fine.

Doreen brought the gin in two small metal tumblers, a pitcher of water, and a bowl of chunks of sugar. Oliver did up his own drink as the girl went away, using his fingers to put the sugar in, pouring in the hot water, and not caring that he slopped it over when he took the first large swallow. It made his stomach warm in a way that the beer never did and took the bitterness out of the loss.

They ate the meal, he and Jack, in silence, beneath the crackle of the fire, the hiss of water on the coals as snow melted from the chimney top, the rumble of feet and talk in the main room. When Oliver saw that Jack favored the potatoes, quarters and halves baked in grease, he stuck to the carrots; he noticed that Jack let him have first take at the curve of breast meat. Between them, they ate the roast chicken down to the bone, and everything else on the plate, finishing up with slices of bread and butter.

While Oliver licked his fingers, feeling the risk and the shimmy-slide into complete disreputableness, Jack signaled for more gin and water and stood up, stretching.

"I'm going to get more for my pipe," he said. "And you, girl, clear this away."

The girl cleared away, and Oliver accepted the gin and water and sugar as the room swam, warm and easy around him. He made up a drink for Jack and drank half of his, his stomach warm and full, the glow of the fire soaking through him completely now, the din of the room falling away into a pleasant mumble and jumble of voices and sounds. He felt safe in his corner by the fire, with Jack returning, puffing on his clay pipe, holding it between his teeth, grinning.

"Scoot, then, you," said Jack as he sat next to Oliver, taking the place by the fire and making Oliver move over nearer to the wall whether he wanted to or not. But it didn't matter; Oliver moved and let Jack sit where he would, which, on the bench, was right near Oliver, Jack's shoulder brushing his. The edge of Jack's elbow would jostle Oliver when Jack would lift his pipe for a pull on it, setting it down in a shallow dish on the table while he pulled the deck of cards from his jacket pocket and shuffled them between his hands.

"Another game?" asked Jack. "You know, we could move on to whist, or there's this new one, angels an' hearts, but then we'd need more players."

Oliver watched Jack's hands while he shuffled and cut the deck; it was the same deck from before, with badly stained and marked backs and the colors running as though the deck had been used in the rain.

"No," said Oliver, his voice sounding low, as though his head were sending some sort of message to him. He didn't want anyone else at their table, to intrude, to draw their attention away. He touched the back of Jack's hand and spread the cards out in a fan in front of them on the table. "You play patience, and I'll watch."

"It's not very amusin' if you're only watchin'," said Jack in return, soft and careful. Barely teasing. But he did as Oliver asked him and took up the cards to shuffle them once more, clicking them down on the tabletop, one-two-three, waiting for the aces to come up, and when they did, laying them in a row as though they were a band of black and red soldiers.

Every now and then, Jack would lift his pipe and draw from it, letting the smoke slide out through his mouth or his nose, as he pleased, and would then take a swig of the gin and sugar and water, and return to the cards, flipping them down as quick as he would, and then take the pile up again to lay the cards down, one-two-three.

Oliver drank the rest of his gin and water and slumped on his elbows on the table, drawn into the rhythm of the cards, the rhythm of Jack's hands that moved as though no one, not even Oliver, were watching.

"Those cards are marked," said Oliver, leaning his cheek against Jack's arm to remind him that he was there.

"Of course they are," said Jack smartly, as if they'd been discussing this all along. "But I'm ignorin' them; I aim to win without cheatin'."

"You'll never do that," said Oliver, making a scoffing sound in his throat. "Best to get a new deck, or, you being you," he said with a small laugh, "best to *steal* a new deck and play like a man, without the temptation to cheat."

Jack paused, curving a card against the table, pressing it down with his fingers. "Always so righteous, Nolly, you are," he said. "What's wrong with cheatin' if you win?"

He looked over at Oliver, his eyes somewhat hazed with drink, but direct, for all that.

"Because it's too easy, it's not a challenge. There's nothing honorable about cheating against yourself," said Oliver, looking right back, feeling that his voice was slurring a bit, and that maybe he wasn't making himself quite clear.

"You see—" he began but stopped, in earnest to explain what he meant. How a man might make his way in the world, but that it had to be done right, with honor and a goodness of heart, and how was he to make Jack understand any of it when the deck he was using was stolen and marked? "It's not right if it doesn't test your skill," he said, finishing up, locking the rest of his thoughts away.

Jack stopped and laid all the cards down on the table, his begrimed fingers splayed out, his head tipped toward Oliver, saying something, so low that Oliver had to move in close to hear him.

"What, Jack?" he asked.

Jack took a breath. "I'm glad you came," he said. "All those years ago."

"What?" asked Oliver again. He knew he was muddled from drink, but he had no idea what Jack was talking about. "What do you mean, all those years ago?"

"In Barnet, when I met you, on the road from that place you ran away from. Sowerman, or something. The funeral place. When you ran away, an' I met you there, in Barnet."

The memory of that day pushed up, right to the fore, and Oliver saw it as clearly as he ever could from any of the memories of days gone by. Of himself, on that cold and dusty step, his feet bleeding, his stomach collapsed with hunger, exhaustion weaving through him, in and out, and no one in that village of a dozen taverns paying him much mind at all. Except for that boy, that strange boy, who crossed to and fro in front of Oliver before speaking and asking, *Hello, my covey, what's the row?*

And then, at that moment, had come from Jack a tumble of words, half of which Oliver had not the wits or energy to understand, except that Jack had stolen for him a half loaf of bread and some ham. Then, in a tavern, he'd rightly purchased a pot of beer and had fed Oliver with the ease of one long accustomed to doing so, and more significantly, in a way that no one ever had. Then Jack had taken him to the Three Cripples and Fagin's den, whereupon Oliver's life and destiny had ceased to be his own. But the fact remained that Jack had fed him, there in Barnet, and Jack had paid for all with money from his own pocket. As he had done so now, this very evening.

"Jack," said Oliver, letting the image of that time fade somewhat. "Whatever were you doing in Barnet, so far from home?" It was a good long walk from Barnet to the Three Cripples, as Oliver now recalled, and he'd wondered this very thing, on and off, through the years. "So far from home," he said again, looking up at Jack.

He saw Jack hesitate a moment, then put the clay pipe to his mouth as though about to draw from it. Then he said, with the very smallest of smiles, as though Oliver was dragging something out of him in the most painful of ways and he loathe to show it, "Waiting for you, of course."

The day slipped from afternoon into night, and finally, after one too many beers, Oliver's head sank to the table. He intended to let himself fall asleep there, it being the most sensible thing to do, until Jack drew Oliver to his feet. They left the litter of pots and plates on the table, weaving their way among the crowd at the bar, stumbling as they went up the narrow stairs and corridor to Jack's room.

There, when the door was shut, Jack used the coals of his pipe to light the single candle on the mantelpiece, and Oliver saw again the red scarf, bright against the dark wood, making soft angles as if Jack had recently arranged it with much care.

Oliver stared at it as Jack jerked his own jacket off, then Oliver's, making Oliver stumble on his feet, though he tried to remain upright.

"Get your head on that pillow before you fall down," said Jack, mumbling. Rather drunk, it seemed, as was Oliver himself.

He let Jack push him to the mattress, not even pulling away as Jack landed next to him, thumping his head on the single pillow next to Oliver's face.

"I kept it, you see," said Jack.

"So I see," said Oliver. Not sure that he'd said it quite clearly, he reached out over his head, stroking the red scarf with his fingers. After which, his arm collapsed across Jack's neck as the room swam around him.

"Let me get that candle," said Jack, grunting. "Or it'll gutter."

"Yes," said Oliver. He closed his eyes, not caring that Jack never moved nor, indeed, that behind his closed lids he could sense the candle flame dip and flicker, choking on its own wax, till at last, with a gasping click, it went out altogether, putting the room into darkness.

CHAPTER 30

An Expedition
To Whitechapel

The morning wind spat against the window, rattling the glass in the leading as though a gale howled through the streets of London. The hard rain startled Oliver, rattling against the panes, dampening the air around his face. He awoke in one moment and then was still.

The night before had been filled with drinks, which had been the proper way to celebrate Oliver's release from prison. The Three Cripples had been a tossed bowl of smoke and with warm bodies and coins clinking on the counter and golden beer flowing, it had been exactly the kind of night that Jack enjoyed. Bodies close along the bench, faces closer, stories spilled as the beer was swallowed.

Jack lay beside him in the bed now, curled in a bow, round as a sleeping dove against him, and Oliver guessed that Jack was still asleep. Jack tended to sleep when he slept, and be wakeful when he was awake. It was not Jack's way to be confused about what he should do nor would he question whether or not he should do them. Only he, Oliver, was awake now, in the raining dark, the room a damp tomb around him.

His head pounded a little as he got up sat up. The room was cast in a grey-brown light that came through the smear coating the window. The smell he'd thought he'd gotten used to from the night before was more pervasive in the chill of the morning, with damp plaster, grime from the tavern below, and clotted bits of mold, all weaving together into an almost unpalatable soup. On the floor were clumps of mud from Jack's boots, the hump of their jackets, Jack's trousers, spread across the end of the bed, jagged as a snake. And the red scarf that trailed across the single pillow, a river of scarlet.

Oliver could see the hoarfrost on the nails along the roofline. Spring was coming, but it was butting heads with winter, and the frost indicated that snow, or at the very least, icy rain, was coming, rather like an insistent, spoiled child. He clenched and unclenched his hands; every part of him was tipped with cold now that he was out from under the blanket.

He gave Jack a poke to awaken him, for perhaps that might do the trick. Then he drew away, thinking that maybe the cold hollow now forming next to Jack would wake him up. Oliver reckoned that Jack's head would feel much like a box weighted with stones and thrown into the Thames in either case.

"Eh?" said Jack. "What you want?"

He did not know what to say for a moment. Nor did Jack, who sat up on the edge of the bed, blinking against the cold with the blanket trailing off him. The blanket that he'd drawn away from Oliver, who sat shivering in the cold.

"What you want is somethin' to eat. Don't you?" Jack looked over his shoulder to ask this. "I've got fourpence; you can have it, get you somethin' to eat an' all."

If it was a bribe to start thinking about the current state of his life rather than the unformed future of it, it was a good one.

Oliver made a motion to the door, which was brown and looming in the gloom of the morning. "You're as hungry as I am, so we'll split it."

"Pies, then," said Jack. He rubbed his eyes and scanned the room, and Oliver got the sense that this was how it was, and how it was going to be. Each morning would begin with late rising, any old time would do, and a scrabbling for funds for food. Instead of the way it had been at the haberdashery, or at home with Uncle Brownlow, with food and supplies laid in and a regular rising time and a hot breakfast on a clean table, served by a maid with a clean white apron. Still, being here with Jack was a far sight better than waking in the cold Newgate cell or at the shipyard, waiting to set sail into the cold, wintry wind, or even already at sea, far away from everything he knew, everything he had been—

"Dreamin' off again, are you?" Jack smacked Oliver's arm with the back of his hand, lightly, more to make contact than any reprimand, it seemed.

"Just thinking about—" Oliver stopped.

"Tell me," said Jack. He shifted backward to curl his hips around Oliver's hips as he sat in the middle of the bed, forming a warm circle, the contact of skin beneath cloth that closed upon Oliver like a sea tide. Oliver let himself lean into it, but only a little.

"I'd forgotten what it's like, being like this. At Uncle Brownlow's, the morning bell came at eight, breakfast was at nine, and on it went. But here?"

"We hang about an' loiter." Jack's mouth opened, laughing, his teeth flashing against his red mouth, shockingly bright so early in the morning. "An' then we steal!"

Horrified, Oliver moved off the bed, feeling Jack's palm in the middle of his back, pushing him, snorting the whole while.

"You can do whatever you like, Nolly," said Jack, and Oliver searched for his jacket, standing barefooted in the middle of the room, his shirt hanging to his thighs. "Long as Cromwell ain't got somethin' else in mind for you, which he does, as he says."

"Where are my boots," said Oliver, ignoring Jack. He wasn't going to work for Cromwell, and if that was the case, what was he going to do to earn his supper? "Jack, you put them—"

He turned as two thumps landed beside his feet. Jack was along the edge of the bed now, gesturing under it, still sleep-tousled, and looking at Oliver in that way he had, as though Oliver was his best mate in the world. Which in a way he was, unless Noah was in the room, and then Jack beamed at Noah, his treasure, his history man, knowing almost as much about Fagin and his gang as Jack did. But still. Oliver could not forget Jack's words as he reached through the bars of the jail. *Morning will come*, he'd said, in a way that told Oliver that he believed every word of what he was saying. *Morning will come.*

Well, morning had come and now, here he was.

Oliver espied his boots in a clump along the floor near the table. He could hardly believe that he'd drunk enough to forgo the common niceties of putting one's clothes away, of washing one's face and hands before bedtime. Of prayers, those were long gone, of course, along with his inheritance, but that didn't mean that everything else had to be tossed aside, did it? No, it did not.

Oliver reached for his boots and dusted them, concentrating on that and not on the coldness of the room, or of Jack, who scurried out of bed and shoved his legs into his stockings as unconsciously as a child, quick and stumbling, hopping about, bumping into Oliver as if this whole thing were a lark. Which, to Jack, it was.

"Pies?" said Jack as he tucked in his shirt and laced up his boots. "I told you I've got fourpence, though I'll wager there's more coin left from last night." This said as if coin to spend magically appeared, and there would always be enough for more pies, more beer.

"Pies," said Oliver. He tucked his chin down as he did up the buttons on his shirt. It wouldn't make any difference to point out the benefits of economy or budgets, or how secure it would be to get a regular job with regular pay. Jack would scoff and laugh and chuff the back of Oliver's head, which, in fact, he did now as he tossed Oliver his hat and coat.

Still fumbling with their clothes, they trotted down the stairs and out the mostly empty tavern. Jack poked Oliver with his elbow as they went out the door.

"You wake up sour," Jack said, and it was evident by his expression that he didn't like it and wanted to fix it.

Oliver looked up and down the slanted street, at the plops of icy water that fell from the sagging eves, then at the sky that threatened more miserable, freezing rain. He adjusted his hat and pulled his coat collar up. "I lost the life I wanted," he said finally, not knowing how to explain it any better than that.

"Lost my life, once," said Jack. He tugged on Oliver's coat to get him to walk down the lane toward the nearest pie shop, and his unspoken message was clear: it was easier to keep warm if you kept moving.

"How?" Oliver could not imagine what Jack meant, or that he'd had any life worth the losing.

"You must know," said Jack. "When I got arrested an' transported, an' everything I knew was gone when I got back."

It was on Oliver's lips to retort that their respective situations were not the same at all when he realized that for Jack, it was.

"But you know, I just kept my head down an' counted the days," said Jack, biting his bottom lip as he remembered the length of time between his deportation and his return. "Knew I'd come home to London, one day."

"But I don't *want* to keep my head down," said Oliver. "I have a plan for my life, and I want to live it as I should."

"As a gentleman, you mean," said Jack, the corners of his mouth sneering.

"As a gentleman who owns a bookshop," said Oliver. His frustration was getting the better of him, making his voice sharp. "I can't spend the rest of my days drinking in a tavern and watching you play cards. I aim to leave London, and maybe you could come with me."

That he knew he needed to leave London was a given; the last had sprung, unexpected, to his lips before he could stop it. But before Oliver could make his point by adding the benefits of this plan, Jack actually yawned in his face.

"Well, you can wish for that till you're blue, but you won't get what you want just by wantin' it. Besides, London is my home, an' I aim never to leave it again."

Jack didn't mean to be mean, he just wanted Oliver to stay with him, and such talk of Oliver wanting more than what a life at the Three Cripples had to offer made him cross, that was easy to see. So Oliver touched his shoulder, and Jack shrugged, and the two of them walked down the slant of Saffron Hill to the corner of Field Lane to the pie shop.

It was busy as they approached it, the squat square windows slightly dirty and making Oliver doubt all over again the quality that they would find there. And he was shy about it, having been arrested when buying and eating pies only days ago. But no one in the street was looking at him, making him feel as though, to his benefit, he wasn't standing out at all. Then once within smelling distance, his stomach woke up and tore at him, reminding him that he needed to eat. He missed Mrs. Pierson's cooking; he'd not had his breakfast, and the warm smell of salt grease and hot pastry pulled at him.

Jack walked in ahead of him, pushing his way in with self-assured shoulders, and Oliver followed close behind. They did not have to wait very long; the shop was the cash-and-carry kind with no tables and only one counter, behind which stood two portly lads with white caps on their heads, serving pies as fast as they could. Their aprons were covered with flour and dark stains, stains which would have had both Mrs. Bedwin and Mrs. Pierson shaking their heads and steering them right back out into the street again.

But Jack was holding up his hands.

"Four, then, you," he said to one of the lads.

"Four?" asked Oliver to Jack's back.

"They're only a penny, an' I seen you put away one already the other day; I know you can manage two."

Oliver sighed, watching Jack hand over the pennies. He was hungry and the money would be well spent even if part of him, a large part, wanted to be saving against a day that saw them even hungrier than this.

"Four," said Jack, handing him two pies wrapped in paper. "One for now, one for later at the tavern, with a pint of cider in front of the fire."

He made it sound cozy, saying it in that way, his mouth wrapping around the words as if they were already wrapping around the pie. Oliver nodded, thinking that Jack took overly well to being in charge, or thinking that he was, but knew at the same time, that he, himself, would rather not have to think. Nor to remind Jack that if they wanted a fire at the Three Cripples, they would more than likely have to build it themselves, after having cleaned out last night's ashes and blacked the grate. He did not imagine that Jack would want to hear any of that.

He unwrapped the first pie and tested the corner with his fingertips. It was hot but not overly so, and he bit into the crust, tasted the meat and the gravy in one gorgeous mouthful, and let the crumbs flutter down his chin.

Jack was tucking in as well, making short work of the hand-sized pie, and then licking his fingers of pastry crust and wiping his chin with the heel of his hand. Oliver blinked at this and then remembered that in the old days, Jack could out-eat any of them, and was always first to toast and eat slices of cheese, or be the first at the frying pan full of sausages. Fagin had remarked at least once or twice that Jack was a growing boy, and had usually followed this up by a cuff across the back of Jack's head. Not that that had stopped Jack.

"C'mon, then," said Jack, jerking his head in the direction of the door. He slid the paper-wrapped pie in his pocket to keep it warm, and Oliver followed suit, trying not to think of the slide-stain of grease they were leaving on their coats.

As they hurried up the hill, the wind blowing over their heads was getting colder, and Jack sniffed the air.

"Hope we don't get another blast," he said, and Oliver agreed. If they did, they would be stuck indoors, and there was nothing to do but stare at the fire and smoke and play cards. Which might hold some charm for a day, but not for longer than that, no matter what Jack thought of it.

But as they got closer to the Three Cripples, Jack slowed, even with the wind at his heels, and he looked at Oliver with his eyes big and something lingering there that Oliver couldn't quite understand.

"Let's not go back; I fancy some more walkin', will you come?" asked Jack.

Jack so seldom asked for anything. He would joke or boss or laugh, but never ask. So Oliver, patient with the connection of the night before still between them, licked his fingers and nodded. He wiped the palms along the side of his coat, thinking that gesture would get a nod of approval from Jack, which it did. He could see that Jack liked it when Oliver attempted to fit in to Jack's world, and since Oliver wanted to be able to think of himself as a likeable boy, there was nothing more for him to do.

Jack started walking back the way they had come, past the pie shop and down the lane, past Smithfield Market, where the smell of manure and old blood was strong in the icy air. The sounds of animals and of men shouting bounced off the brick walls as the lane narrowed before widening into the open area of the market. The smell was dank and foul, and Oliver averted his eyes as they passed along the sheds where the necks of geese were being placed on worn stumps before having their necks chopped off. He was grateful that Jack didn't stop to linger but hurried on, past the narrow rivers of blood beneath their feet and the stink of animals, distraught and suffering, and the unimpassioned expressions of the men who slaughtered them.

Jack led Oliver through Smithfield, and then over to Cheapside to follow the narrow lanes there, old buildings tumbling over each other. And the mud, the constant mud, which was a slippery carpet beneath their feet. They went down Aldgate and Cornhill to lanes Oliver felt he vaguely recognized, only he didn't know how or why. They went along a brick-blacked lane that was even more a-tumble than any around Holborn with the refuse of humans, clumps of foul snow, chunks of bone and hoof.

He stuck close to Jack, breathing through his mouth; Jack took Oliver's arm in a squeeze of his fingers, and Oliver didn't pull away.

"Is it much longer, Jack?" asked Oliver, hoping it wasn't but feeling indulgent, somehow, in this morning of spattering rain and wind.

"A little ways, Nolly," said Jack, turning away to lead Oliver up the street and down another small lane till they passed the Church of St. Mark's, and into another long, narrow lane, where the smell jumped up at him. He knew this smell somehow; his head pounded and his stomach wanted to rebel, though he knew better than to empty its contents in the street when those contents were so hard to come by.

Jack stopped as the rain began to splat down, on his face, on the bricks, circles of rain smashing into the clumps of old snow, as big as the palm of his hand. Jack pulled Oliver back against a wall, opposite the building he was starting at, a small alcove with a slate overhang that dripped into the street in long, sad grey plops.

The sun fought from behind the clouds for a moment, and sparks of stray light limned the bricks and wood of the building that now sagged like a craggy, dying thing. Sad beams of wood leaned against each other, and as Oliver watched, not understanding what he was watching, a brick slipped from the ledge of an upper story window, crashing through a faltering lath to shatter on the damp paving stones, scattering bits of red stone into the street.

"What is it?" asked Oliver. "Why have we stopped; shall we go back?"

"This here was one of Fagin's old dens," said Jack, his voice rusty. He pointed at the wreck of a building with his fist.

Now it made sense to Oliver, at least more of it, that Jack would bring him here and look, as though he was searching for the sound of Fagin's voice. And while Oliver might find satisfaction in visiting memories in his mind, Jack preferred to attempt to go back by visiting the actual location. How mournful and lonesome it must be to come back expecting to find some physical reminder of the past, only to find almost everything so changed as to not be recognizable.

"An' the last place I saw you, five years ago," said Jack now, unexpectedly. His head hung low, almost brushing against Oliver's breastbone. And when he looked up, his face was white, the skin tight around his eyes, making Oliver want to listen for Fagin's voice as well, in sympathy.

Somewhat shocked at this bald statement, Oliver shook his head. Jack was so easily dragging him back into the past, into the realm of once-upon-an-orphan that he needed to get away from. Especially the persistent thought of what Mr. Grimwig would say were he to learn of where Oliver was, and even though he never would, his voice was threatening to be a strong cudgel in Oliver's brain.

"Jack?" asked Oliver, dipping his head low to be a physical echo to Jack's frame, brushing his fingers on Jack's damp sleeve. "What do you mean, the last time?"

Surprising him, Jack jerked backward, moving away from Oliver to look up at the craggy remains of the building.

"I'd thought, you know," said Jack, somber, "that as I burned beneath that sun there, in Australia, carryin' water an' muckin' out stables or lookin' for stray cattle in the bush, that when I came back, everythin' would be as it was. As it always had been. Fagin in his fire pit, makin' sausages for one or two to feed ten, bringin' in bottles of gin, or screamin' at us to go out an' make more money. An' countin' those coins of his, late, late into the night."

Jack's memories of that time so resembled Oliver's own, and he was about to say so when Jack shook his head. He looked up at Oliver as though he wanted to cry, only he couldn't remember how. Oliver moved forward, somewhat alarmed by this show of deeper emotion of Jack's rising to the surface, and the memory of Jack's confession, similar in sentiment: *You're the only person I know in London.* But before Oliver could express how the revelation was causing something tender to shift within him, Jack moved away. He didn't want to be touched and he opened his mouth, struggling, it seemed, with the consternation that it was anywhere near as difficult as it was for him to say what he needed to say.

"We kept you here, days, weeks, even," said Jack, low, as if speaking to himself. "Feedin' you them books an' our stories about thieves—"

Suddenly Oliver remembered. "In seclusion, like at the dark room at the workhouse." As the memories sometimes did, this one came back to him in a rush, the dark single room where Oliver had passed so many hours alone that even the company of thieves and pickpockets and fences and their stories about the grandness of crime seemed preferable, even if only slightly.

"I laughed at those stories, Jack," he said. "Right along with you." Though why he was comforting Jack for having applied this cruelty to Oliver was almost beyond him. Indeed, he felt the heat of anger rising inside him with nowhere, really, to go.

"I just wanted it to stay that way forever, an'—an' you an' me to be there forever. I kissed you good-bye, an' Nancy took you, an' the next thing you was left in a ditch with a bullet in you, left by Bill—" Jack choked off, sending Oliver rushing forward with his hands outstretched.

"But I was found, Jack," he said. He didn't remember Jack's kiss from that night, but he did remember being dragged into the street and going all those miles with Bill Sikes in the cold, damp air. He stood now, close to Jack in the street, and the devil be damned if anyone cared. If even anyone in that street cared to slow down enough to see. Him touching Jack, his fingers as red and raw with cold as any common street thug.

"Found by my own people, you know. That story ended well, at any rate."

Jack eyed him, looking young and wounded, bringing to the surface the memory of his tenderness and comfort when Oliver was in Newgate. Oliver wanted to comfort Jack in return, thinking that he might attempt to explain to Jack that none of this was his fault, at least not wholly.

"Shot with a bullet an' I warn't there to protect you," said Jack, mumbling.

"You *weren't* there, so how could you protect—and why weren't you there?" Oliver asked, trying to dissuade himself from being moved by Jack's declaration. Besides, it didn't make any sense.

"Got arrested, you know that," said Jack, glumly. "For takin' a twopenny-halfpenny snuffbox."

"But didn't you once tell me—" Oliver stopped, realizing just then how astounding this fact was. "Yes, it was back in Barnet when we'd just met that you told me you were Fagin's particular *pet* and *protégé.* With all those skills—you? Arrested?"

"I—well." Jack stopped to tip back his hat and scratch the back of his head then replaced his hat with a jerk. "Fine, I'll tell you. I knew you wasn't dead, but then Nancy had a fit one night, an' Fagin tells me that in spite of it that you'd never broken to his teachin', that they was goin' to bring you back, that he had a plan. I knew it weren't right."

"Then why didn't you stop it?" Oliver asked this, though he knew that Jack, being only slightly older than Oliver at the time, wouldn't have been able to do anything.

"It was because—I was so, well. My mind was thick with the thought of it, an' I didn't want you back, but I *did.* Well, with one thing an' another, the very next day I was arrested an' sent to Australia soon after. Had a trial an' everythin'."

Oliver thought of that time, so confusing with its kaleidoscope images that shifted all around him. One thing was startlingly clear, that Jack had let himself be so distracted by Oliver's fate that he'd gotten himself snatched off the streets and deported. Oliver ought to be amused by Jack's fallibility, but he wasn't. He didn't laugh, not at Jack, because while everything else in his life had flung itself around like a mad bull and trampled every dream, every certainty he'd ever known, Jack was the only unchanging thing.

"You were well out of it," said Jack. "An' when I came back, I knew I had to look for you—I knew that you would never come lookin' for me."

Jack's eyes flicked as though seeking a place between the then times and the now. With Oliver standing absolutely still in front of him, he seemed to gain strength, and finally, Jack's hand tightened around Oliver's, making Oliver Jack's anchor in a storm. This feeling was new to him, and after having clung to Jack all those years ago and during the past few days, it made him feel strong, oddly, and perhaps for the first time in his life.

"I do have a scar from the bullet," he said, wanting Jack to look at him without that sad expression in his eyes. "From where they took it out; and I healed after that, and well, so you've no need to—"

"That's like a tattoo, ain't it?" said Jack, taking this idea up, brightening. "Like the one I got; a woman at the docks did it for me, afore I left—"

Knowing from the newspaper that criminals convicted for transport were kept locked up before they sailed, Oliver doubted this version of the tale more than he had any other. But he didn't chide Jack; it would ruin the story, and besides, he might be ready to see Jack's tattoo now. Especially now, in this moment, when he realized his bullet wound and the ragged shallow scar it left behind was, as Jack said, a tattoo, of a sort, in its own way. One of life's marks and something Oliver could trade with Jack to get a glimpse of the alleged tattoo, at which point Oliver would no doubt become more acquainted with the many, many stories behind it.

"Jack," said Oliver, gently, because he wanted to go back to the Three Cripples with its modicum of warmth and dry. Only he didn't want Jack to feel badly for having dragged him here to this place, with its dark and fear-stained memories.

"I missed you," said Jack, simply, looking at Oliver's hand curling around his own. "An' I was so—well, you was the only one prosperin' after I came back. I left an' I came back an' there was no one left but you. No one to tell my story."

"I know your story," said Oliver, soothing, as he pulled Jack away from the ruined building. "And besides, Noah knows your stories as well."

"Yes," said Jack, straightening up. "He tells 'em good, he does, all vibrant like. Except—"

"Except?" He let Jack pause in the middle of the lane as it slanted uphill toward the main thoroughfare, thinking that if Noah were to have told some story improperly or had made Jack any less than the most important player, Oliver would have more words with him and use his own fists for punctuation.

"Except he warn't one of Fagin's boys, not truly. Not like you an' me."

Giving Jack a shove, trying not to smile at Jack's easy dismissal of Noah's charms, Oliver began walking up the lane, toward the street that would take them back to the Three Cripples.

"Why is that?" asked Oliver, turning his head away as they passed a dead hog in the street.

"Because he peached on you, collected his winnings after. Something you never did, even when you could."

As they walked, side by side through the muck of Whitechapel, Oliver didn't point out that if Noah wasn't one of Fagin's boys, Oliver was even less of one. It wouldn't help to point that out, even though Oliver's lack of peaching had much less to do with Uncle Brownlow's teachings or even Fagin's precepts than it had to do with Jack himself. The memory of Jack's hands through the bars of a Newgate jail cell, telling Oliver that morning would come. A shared blanket on cold nights, a pat to the head, somehow gentle even amidst all of Jack's street hardness. And all these gestures and words from Jack when Oliver had needed them most. So Oliver said nothing of it, and together they walked back, eating their second serving of pies as they went.

Along Aldgate Street, thick with shops that looked busy and prosperous and a step above Field Lane, they passed a bookshop beneath a swinging, rain-dripping sign that said Grey Dove Books. The shop wasn't much like the one that Oliver hoped to one day own; the canvas awning kept off the rain but only barely, and the door frame and the window casing was badly in need of paint. But, for all that, the window had a shelf pushed right up against it, with the spines, dusted clean, turned out toward the street for easy viewing. Oliver stopped in spite of himself, causing Jack to tumble over his heels as Oliver pressed his face up against the smudged glass. The gold- and silver-gilt titles tumbled together in a row, and he read them, silently, thinking of the times with Uncle Brownlow when he had only to express a desire for a certain title, and the book was his.

"What's this then, Nolly? You want to go in?" Jack spat in his hand and was pushing back his forelock of hair in preparation, ready it seemed, to indulge Oliver in this passing fancy.

"No," said Oliver. He dragged his eyes away from the books to look at Jack. "There's no point in it, is there?"

"There is if you want one," said Jack. It was easy to see that he didn't quite grasp the siren's song that books had, especially ones that Oliver had not read before, but he was attempting, in his way, to be kind. "We could just—"

"No," said Oliver. He shook his head, knowing exactly where Jack's thoughts were running. Jack was imagining that they could sashay into the bookshop, tuck a book or two into their jackets, and be off as if nothing had happened. For one thing, their jackets weren't big enough to hide any book, and for another, well, it was inconceivable that Oliver would allow himself to stoop so low as to steal a book, of all things.

Jack nodded, seemingly interpreting everything that Oliver's rebuttal entailed, even if he might not quite understand the why of it. His eyes scanned the street, flicking over the row of books that glimmered from beyond the mud-spotted window, then he gave Oliver's sleeve a tug.

"Look there," he said, pointing at the window.

"At what?" Oliver didn't relish the idea of longing for books he shouldn't want nor for all that they represented.

But Jack was insistent. "No, not them. Look. Us." He pointed at the glass, and after a moment's confusion, Oliver could see what Jack was pointing at. For in the window, in a streaked reflection made gloomy by the rain, were two young men. One young man Oliver recognized directly as being Jack, the reflection of Jack, with his shabby top hat and his bright blue waistcoat and those coattails that banged against the backs of his knees. His spit-shaped hair reflected like black ink; his grin was a crooked, white slash; his eyes were two bright spots. That was Jack, a part of the streets he constantly roamed, a child of them once, a stamp of grit and sly ease that never seemed to leave him, and appeared clear, even in his reflection.

The other reflection was of himself—it could be of no other. The reflection of the top hat in the glass matched Jack's in height, and the silver-buttoned jacket seemed at once like a bright bird's wing, hanging from the shoulders of an entirely different person than himself. The trousers he wore hung badly, crumpled with mud and damp along the hems; the sleeves of his jacket were too long and uneven, and the whole of it reflected the filth that he'd been living in. He could not bear to look more closely at the reflection of his face; he did not want to see what it would tell him. He was so changed he wouldn't be able to recognize himself.

"C'mon, then," said Jack, his voice low, as if disappointed that Oliver was not pleased at how much his reflection matched Jack's. He tugged on Oliver's sleeve, and so, bookless, and feeling disjointed, Oliver followed where he was led up

Aldgate and Cheapside and past Smithfield Market, up Field Lane to the door of the Three Cripples, where custom had picked up and the Three Cripples was as popular as a town square on market day.

CHAPTER 31

Contains The Particulars Of Jack's Story, And Additionally, The One About Noah and Nancy

As Oliver opened the door and stepped into the Three Cripples, he saw that at a table in the middle of the room, Noah was sitting, with a pot of beer in his hands, with men gathered around. It appeared he was telling a story, waving his mug in the air. Then Jack, right behind, saw him as well, and went straight over to the table where Noah was sitting.

Oliver followed him, trying to hold his breath as he passed through the press of men, and some women, whose woolen coats and tattered, dragging shawls were stained with grease, and with the rain, smelled like old fish or untanned hides or whatever else it was they worked with. He thought he heard someone say, *Bet his backside is as sweet as his face.* Making

Oliver flush and again doubt his decision to come to the Three Cripples, and Cromwell be damned.

When he got to the table, Jack was already sitting next to Noah and had a mug of beer in his hands and his short pipe between his teeth that he was just lighting. The circle of smoke from the pipe smelled as though it had come from an unseen fire in some deep wood, and Oliver made a gesture to catch Jack's attention. Jack looked up, and the circle of men around the table parted to let Oliver through.

"So then I says," said Noah, continuing on, all but ignoring Oliver as he took a swig from his pot of beer. "Then I says, 'Whatcha carryin' around so many 'andkerchiefs for, Mr. Leaming?' Turns out, 'e was a fence, and not one of you lot, and all the while 'im a shop owner, carryin' on sellin' 'ardware for 'arnesses in the front and havin' illicit dealings in the back!"

"You are a card, an' a canny one," one of the men said, laughing. "Did you get the reward, then?"

"Indeed," said Noah, patting his breast pocket. He took a slug of beer in his mouth, cheeks puffing out, beer sliding from between his lips and down the side of his mouth. "This'll keep me till spring, I wager."

"Till you lose it on the ponies again!" The man barked this out, his laugh spreading beer on the air in a fine mist. "You never could stay away."

Noah dismissed this with a jerk of his chin. He leaned back in his chair. "There you are, Nolly." He held out his mug. "Be a lad an' bring me some more beer, eh?"

There was a single moment of silence as the men around the table drifted away, and as Oliver looked at Noah, and Noah looked steadily back. The bruises on his face that Cromwell had left had barely begun to fade, but Noah seemed oblivious of them, only daring Oliver to disobey him. Jack gave a shrug and pushed some coins over to Oliver and Oliver took them, thinking to buy himself and Jack a beer as well. Telling himself that it would have been rude to respond to such a simple request, but before he turned away, Jack unsettled himself from his seat to cuff Noah upside the head.

"I told you once, only I calls him Nolly," Jack said, his voice even. "Don't make me tell you again."

Then he sat back as if nothing had been said, and the sounds from the tavern filled in the space around them. And all the while Noah sat there, his mouth open as if astonished that Jack had dared to lay hands upon his person. But Jack merely shook his head and put his pipe back between his teeth. He looked up at Oliver, who nodded, turning to get the beer, feeling glad that Jack, finally, did not seem to be pleased by Noah as much as he had. Oliver shouldn't be gladdened by that, but he was.

He went up to the bar and shouldered his way through, pushing over the coins and asking for three pots of beer. Then he returned to the table, carrying the pots, wondering how his life had resulted in the fact that he was waiting on a table for Noah and Jack, and then thought better of his anger. Still, he wouldn't do this again, at least not for Noah.

Jack was appreciative upon getting his beer, swallowing half of it at one go before Oliver had even sat down next to him. Noah was staring into his beer, frowning, as if drawn into the dapple of foam along the surface. Oliver wondered why they weren't in Jack's alcove instead of halfway to the middle of the floor, with the draft from the door at their necks and too far away from the single fire for it to do any good.

As the door opened again and sent a squall of damp air to settle around them, Jack shuddered and drew up his shoulders. "It's ages till spring comes," he said companionably, to no one in particular.

"Till then, winter has full sway," said Oliver in return.

"I wish I was a lizard," said Jack. He smirked as he said this, for now he had Noah's attention. "Like one of them lizards, down below, an' I could spread myself on a stone till my blood boiled. Then I'd be warm. But a lizard can hardly be a thief, can he? No fingers an' thumbs." Jack laughed, open-mouthed, at his own cleverness.

"You don't need fingers an' thumbs if you've got a gang of boys, workin' for you. Did you ever think, while you was away, of startin' your own gang, then, Jack?" Noah asked this directly to Jack as if Oliver wasn't even there.

With another swallow of his beer, Jack nodded. "Certainly I could do it, certainly. Start off with a small boy, one or two, make myself known to the fences, set myself up. Be known as dependable to my acquaintances of a particular circle."

"Except," said Noah, with that small curved smile he used, that Oliver remembered from when Noah would badger Oliver at Mr. Sowerberry's beyond Oliver's ability to resist the temptation to kill him. "Except, sad to say, you would no doubt run across your very own little Oliver, who, as you recollect, upset a very decently balanced apple cart."

When Oliver started in his chair, Noah turned to him, *tut tutting*. "Oh, don't make a face, the one you always do, that pious little face, all your worryin' and prayin', an' never you mind. It's Fagin who told me who messed up that job, that pickpocketing job—"

The words struck him like a blow. Oliver rose in his seat, intending to smack Noah directly across his pasty, smug face, but Jack stopped him with a hand on his arm and made him sit back down.

"If you'd have stuck by my side, Nolly," said Jack, leaning forward earnestly, attempting, it seemed, to make a circle of conversation between the three of them, "all would have been well. You could have been a workin' member of the gang an' brought in loads with that face of yours."

Oliver couldn't understand why Jack was talking to him like this. Then he heard Noah chuckle under his breath and realized why. It was the stories; Jack loved stories, and Noah had been telling this one, so to be of a kind, Jack told his in return. That was all there was to it.

"You know I'm no pickpocket."

Jack saluted Oliver with the pot of beer, sloshing some over the rim. "That you are not, my friend, that you are not. Your face gives you away, dirty or clean."

"Well," said Oliver slowly, considering, wanting to steer the conversation away from crime and pickpocketing. "I do want a bath, it is true, after our jaunt to Whitechapel this morning." He looked at Jack to remind him of what he'd said during that walk, how he'd said it.

"What?" asked Noah, sitting up as if suddenly interested that Oliver was actually at the same table with him. "Whitechapel, whatever did you go down there for?"

"Oh," said Jack. "It's a long story, a sad tale; you've no interest in it, I'm sure."

"Just a stroll in the fresh air," said Oliver, finally drinking from his beer at last. It was cool in his mouth but slightly bitter, as though it were the dregs from the bottom of the barrel.

"In this weather?" Noah shook his head. "C'mon, tell us. What were you about, then? C'mon, Jack."

Jack sat up in his chair, pulling the pot of beer to him with the curve of his hand, ready to give Noah what he wanted. But it was a private thing, what Jack was about to display, what they'd shared in that dank street, confessions given and taken, the memory of something between the two of them that Oliver wanted to keep for his own. The memory belonged to him and Jack. Was Jack really going to share it with Noah?

Just as Jack opened his mouth to speak, Oliver caught his eye, a frantic pounding in his heart. There was no way, really, that Oliver could impart his meaning without actually saying the words aloud, but he did not want Noah to know anything about them. The whole world could know; Oliver didn't care about that. But Noah? He could not bear it if that were true.

"Well, then, since you insist," said Jack in that way, cavalier, tipping his head back to assay his audience and determine what type of story they truly wanted. "It was old times for me an' Nolly, takin' a walk, you see, into the wintry wind." He took a drink of beer and smacked his lips. "We walked to one of Fagin's old dens—"

"Is it one I'd know?" asked Noah. His eyes were wide and searching as if desperate to find out whether he'd missed something good.

"Don't know," said Jack, shaking his head. "At any rate, this was an old den, we kept Nolly there, weeks an' weeks it was—"

Noah snorted out a laugh, shrugging because, of course, he couldn't help himself, not at the idea of Oliver being held captive against his will. The sound of his jagged breath made Oliver want to smack him all over again.

"We worked weeks to try an' make a good hand out of him, something Fagin could use. But he's so—I mean, look at him." Jack took his pipe and waved it at Oliver, then took a good strong draw from it, letting the smoke flay out in tides from his nostrils. "Too pretty for words, an' while that might be useful, it goes *through*, gentlemen. It goes *through*, all the way to the bone."

"What does?" asked Noah, and Oliver, frankly, wanted to know as well, in spite of his irritation at Jack's cavalier reference to that dark time. Because while his face was often a cause for discussion, his features didn't go down to the bone, not in the normal sense.

"Piety," said Jack, pounding the table with the pot of beer. "Piety, goodness, cleanliness, all of it. This is a boy who, when he says his prayers, he means 'em! There was no turnin' him, and Fagin nearly tore his hair out havin' made such a bad judge of things."

Noah considered this, his face falling as though he were crestfallen that the story wasn't a better one. And Oliver realized that Jack had done it on purpose. That, in fact, he wasn't going to tell Noah anything that mattered, anything about what had happened that morning. Noah had gone and cut himself out of Jack's confidence when he'd peached on Oliver for the reward; Oliver wondered if he'd be getting drunk enough this evening to tell Noah exactly what Jack thought of him, and whether he'd laugh in Noah's face while he did it.

"That's not the truth of it though," said Noah. He grabbed the skirts of a passing barmaid and gave her backside a pat. "Three more, my lovely, an' haste with it!"

"Truth of what?" Jack asked. He tapped his pipe and laid it sideways on the table.

"Of what Fagin wanted."

"He wanted Nolly to steal, that's what he wanted." Jack nodded at his own truth, and for him, there was nothing more than that. "But Nolly's a terrible pickpocket, ain't you, Nolly?"

Oliver nodded, but he sensed that Noah was intent upon telling a different kind of story. It was in the way he sat, leaning forward, tapping his finger to his nose. His eyes were narrow, and when they looked at Oliver, they flickered with hate. Noah had something for Jack; the thought of Oliver and Jack in the streets looking at one of Fagin's old dens had brought it out.

"I know why Fagin was 'anged," Noah said.

Jack swallowed. "Because someone peached," he said, trying not to look at Oliver and failing.

Of course, the identity of the person who had peached was what Jack wanted to know, what he always wanted to know; he felt that somewhere there was a tattered ribbon of a memory of exactly what had happened, of a story that no one he knew could tell. What Oliver had delivered up to him, when threatened, had been scatterings, and nothing to satisfy.

The knowledge of that time, when anyone would talk of it at home, usually had Oliver sent out of the room when his elders had discussed it, when Uncle Brownlow had the parson over to their parlor for tea and everyone bowed their heads to pray. It was after the prayers and the tea that Oliver was sent out, for a walk, to fetch a book, or for a slice of cake in the kitchen. Anything. He'd lingered when he could to get the rest of it, but the story had always come in snatches, and he could never know the whole of it.

"Ah," said Noah with the exact type of smile he'd had back at the undertaker's shop, gloating and rude and triumphant. There was beer foam on his mouth drying to a crust, and he took another swig and belched. Oliver pretended he hadn't; bad manners were rife at the Three Cripples and there was nothing much anybody could do about it. "But I knows how an' I knows by who."

"How could you possibly?" asked Oliver. It was a demand more than a question, but it seemed if Noah got his way, he'd string this story on until it was thin and weak, and Jack, poor Jack, would get no sustenance from it. That or Jack would be drawn in so hard there would be no separating him from Noah from that point onward in spite of the fact that he'd peached on Oliver for money.

"Because I was there, Work'us. I was *there.*"

The name stung, but Oliver made himself not react to it, though everything—his limbs, his hands, his heart—made him want to launch himself across the table and make Noah shut up. But at the same time, Jack was enthralled, and so the story must be told.

"How?" asked Oliver. He knew he sounded disdainful, and he was. His experience of Noah was that he tended to say a great many things, and all to a bounded and specific effect, whether true or not. "How? Tell us that, then. Otherwise, it's just a story, and I think Jack has better things to do. And I do as well." Though what, Oliver couldn't imagine. There was bad weather outside and bad company within, and no real retreat from any of it.

"Be still, then," said Noah, "an' listen. The day after I gets to London, I 'ooks up with Fagin 'imself. 'E sends me to the courts to watch Jack get sent abroad for that snuffbox—"

"I know this part," said Jack. He had a small, secret smile, but he was looking down at the tabletop rather than at Noah or Oliver, and Oliver knew why. It was because this part was in the court rolls, and a part of written history forevermore. That was the meat of it; there was no denying that Jack felt it the pinnacle of his career.

"—with Jack demanding his privileges an' talking back to the magistrate, insisting 'e'd an appointment with a gentleman in the City—"

"An' don't forget," said Jack, "that my attorney was breakfastin' with the Vice President of the House of Commons."

"There isn't a Vice President of anything in the 'Ouse of Commons," said Oliver, blinking, being left behind in their joy and ridicule of the whole situation.

"Yes, yes," said Noah. "But that's not it. When I saw Fagin, I told him this, an' 'e told me that 'e'd lost his very best 'and."

"Who's that, then?" asked Jack, though Oliver suspected he already knew.

"You, Dodger," said Noah, looking fairly pleased with himself. "'E says to me, 'e says, *Is there one of you that could touch 'im or come near 'im on any scent?* And then, the other fellow says, *Not one, not one.*"

"Who said *that?*" Jack's mouth hung open. "Was it Fagin?"

"Fagin said the first bit, an' the other, well, I don't know 'is name, properly, but 'e 'ad 'is 'ands in his pockets an' laughed a great deal of the time."

"Charley," said Jack; his voice was low, almost a whisper, something reverential and private. Oliver knew Charley, a brash young man, finding humor everywhere and laughing even when there wasn't any, as though this were a nervous reaction and not anything real. Jack had adored him, in his way; it was Charley who had taken the hand-off of the handkerchief on that day so long ago. "They said that, Fagin an' Charley said that?"

"As I live an' breathe." Noah took a large swallow of his beer, finishing it down to the dregs. When he came up for air, he looked at Jack, his mouth wet, and he wiped it with the back of his sleeve. "There's more though."

"More?" asked Jack in a way so expectant, so hopeful, that it gave Oliver a twinge, remembering wanting more, and how painful it might be if Jack were not to receive it. "How ever so?"

"When you was taken," said Noah, "you were 'is best 'and, an' not one to take up the job of dodging a certain female by the name of Nancy."

This stopped Jack, but he only considered it for a moment before he asked, "He had you follow *Nancy*? Why?"

Oliver had heard something about this; he knew where the story was going, knew that Nancy had met with Uncle Brownlow and Aunt Rose late one night, but he'd never gotten the full of it, what was said or why they'd let her go back to her old life. Aunt Rose tended to cry into her handkerchief whenever Oliver had asked her about it, so he'd stopped asking long ago.

"Because Fagin suspected she was up to somethin', an' she was, oh, definitely. Tryin' to get word to that Brownlow fel-

low about where Oliver was and 'ow to get to 'im. Somethin'
about that whole conversation set Fagin off, an' 'e told Bill, an'
then Bill—"

"But how do you know of this?" Oliver found himself asking the question, knowing that Noah was leaving something
out. He half feared to hear it, but perhaps, at last, it was time.

"Because, you daft, pious, workhouse boy, I told you. Fagin
sent me to follow 'er, which I did. I stood there on the steps of
London Bridge an' 'eard everything they said. When I went
back to tell Fagin, 'e 'ad me tell it again to Bill. Which I did. I
know all of this because I was *there*." Noah turned to look at
Jack now, only at Jack, because of course, it was for Jack that
he was telling anything at all.

"I 'eard 'er tell of 'aving drugged Bill Sikes so she could get
out an' meet with 'em. She met with your old Aunt Rose,
Oliver, not once but twice, gave 'em Fagin's name, an' Monks,
an' told of that arrangement whereby Fagin would get Oliver
to be a thief an' Monks would pay 'im. It 'ad to do with your
inheritance, Work'us."

"The inheritance I won't be getting," said Oliver, feeling
the severity of his own tone through clenched teeth. On the
heels of that was the shock at finding out that Aunt Rose, delicate, fragile Aunt Rose, had actually walked London's streets
in the middle of the night to meet with a whore in the shadows of London Bridge. He could hardly allow himself to believe it, yet the location of that meeting, one of the elements of
that time that no one had been willing to tell him, could
hardly be denied. Noah's details were too specific, and in the
end, it made sense. Aunt Rose, or anyone, would have been
more willing to tell him the facts of that meeting had they not
been so squalid.

"Fagin wanted to make a good profit off Oliver, you see," said Noah to Jack, ignoring Oliver's gloomy statement. "For Monks's sake, but it was Nancy who did you all in, don't you get that?"

"How's that?" Jack's face tightened. "What do you mean, *Nancy* did us all in?"

"She gave a description of the dens where Fagin could be found, a description of Monks, an' she cried after she did it, but she did it anyway. She told 'em about Bill, the man she wouldn't leave, Bill, who she 'ad drugged, mind you, to peach on all of Fagin's lot, includin' him. Bill was in a terrible way when 'e found out, gnashing his teeth and spoutin' off about poundin' people's 'eads into the ground. Which—"

Noah paused as he arched his head and pulled on his lapels because, of course, this was the moment, his moment, his and Jack's. Oliver wanted to get up and walk away from the table. He'd not heard the whole story before, had only gotten brief sketches of borrowed conversations he was never supposed to have overheard, and now, when he could hear the whole of it, he didn't want to. Besides, he knew the end of it.

"Which he did, Nancy's 'ead, that is." Noah smacked his lips around the juiciness of this revelation. "Killed 'er in their rooms according to the records an' the newspapers. He beat her with 'is pistol an' left her to bleed on the floor. Then 'e ran from the coppers, an' anyway, the game was up for Fagin an' all, what with Nancy 'aving told Brownlow, who, it seems, went straight to the law for it."

The thought of Nancy with her blood soaking into the floorboards made Oliver feel cold inside. Nancy had been a stout, friendly girl, untidy about her person and confused enough by life to consider staying with Bill Sikes her best option. And in her way, she had been kind to him. She didn't deserve to die, not that way, not *any* way, and surely, she would not have—

Just as he thought it, Jack reached up across the table to grab Noah by the lapels, one in each fist, and never mind the pot of beer upset to spill musty suds across the table to spatter into Oliver's lap.

"She *never* would," said Jack, baring his teeth, almost growling at Noah. "She never would give up Bill, an' you don't know anything about it!"

"She did," said Noah, baring his teeth right back. "I was *there*, I tell you, an' I 'eard what she said, she told about Fagin an' the dens, an' about Bill—"

"She didn't!"

"She *did!*"

Jack was shifting his weight, standing up, resettling his hands on Noah's jacket, coming around the table as if ready to slam Noah to the ground and give him a sound thrashing, something that Oliver knew Noah deserved for telling the story in this way. Making Nancy out to be the culprit for the loss of Fagin's gang and ruining Jack's last memory of her.

"Jack," said Oliver, standing up, putting his body right next to Jack's. "Come away, then. The story is old; Noah's brain is addled by drink. You have the right of it, I'm sure, for Nancy would never—"

He had to stop because he didn't know what Nancy had said or whether she loved Bill enough to avoid talking about him. That she'd said something about Fagin and his gang to Uncle Brownlow and Aunt Rose that dark, far-ago night was true enough, but there was more than one pair of ears be-

tween Noah talking and Bill hearing. If Noah's message, either
twisted or true would be of use to him, Fagin would see it
within his rights to wreak revenge, and for the execution of
his plan, Bill was the best weapon that he'd had.

Jack shook off Oliver's hands, twitching away, straightening his neckerchief as Noah backed away from the table.

"She never would, now, would she, Nolly!" Jack shouted,
and he didn't seem to care how many heads in the Three
Cripples turned to stare. "And you, Mr. Bolter, should know
better than to say such things!" Jack actually shook his fist at
Noah, his own breast heaving, watching Noah with narrowed
eyes as Noah adjusted his lapels and took up his hat as if he'd
meant to leave all along. Leaving Oliver standing there, with
Jack next to him, shaking, so angry at what he considered to
be lies, though Oliver imagined that Noah had saved this particular story for when he wanted to draw Jack in the most.
Except it had, evidently, the exact opposite effect, much to
Oliver's secret pleasure.

And—yes, there was something else. On the night before
Fagin was hanged, he'd muttered about someone named
Bolter, and how it was he, and not Nancy, who should have
his throat cut, sawed off, in fact, because, as Fagin had said,
Bolter was *somehow the cause of all this*. Bolter, who was actually Noah Claypole, and how on earth was Oliver going to be
able to explain that to Jack without Jack coming at him? To
admit to Jack now that Fagin had gone quite mad before his
execution wasn't something Oliver ever intended to do, but he
had been quite clear as to who was to blame for the demise of
Fagin and his gang. But if Jack found out, he'd be right after
Noah and end up with blood on his hands, and be clapped in

irons on his way to Newgate before the day was over. No. Oliver couldn't do it. Not to Jack. Not now.

The group of men next to their table had gone silent, but as Noah walked off, the talk started up again, the beer set to flowing. Oliver never wanted to be as far away as possible from the Three Cripples as he did at that moment, but it seemed inevitable that he was where he was.

CHAPTER 32

After Whitechapel

They moved from the table in the middle of the room to the small alcove. Oliver stood by, holding his hat and Jack's as Jack shoved and threatened for the current occupants to leave, which they did, muttering and stomping off. But Oliver didn't care how rude it was, what Jack had done, he couldn't stand being in the middle of the room with all eyes upon them, watching and listening. Especially after Jack's display of temper. So the alcove was much better.

Much better, that is, than being at a table in the center of the main room, but that did not mean it was better than his old life, not by half. Since he could ever remember, things had gone from bad to worse, and even when they'd gotten better, as during those dear, gentle years in the country with Aunt Rose and Uncle Harry, they'd gotten bad again, in the end. His own attempts at setting his life to rights had led him back here, to this very spot, at the Three Cripples. With Jack.

Jack, who, even if he'd come from quality people, or if he'd been a lord, someone of a higher station, would always be like he was, a child of the streets. Nothing would ever change him, so even if Oliver's world whirled around him like a sand-storm—

Raising his hand to order them something to eat and drink, Jack took his cards out of his pocket, shuffling them between the fingers of one hand. He took his hat from Oliver and laid it on the table, pushing his dark hair back from his face, distract-edly staring at nothing.

When Doreen brought them some food, Oliver eyed the tin plate of slices of beef that looked none too fresh, and the boiled eggs, which had a tinge of green around the yellow yolks. He stuck to the beer, drinking huge swallows, and thinking it fairly fresh beer, drank the rest of the pot.

Oliver looked at Jack, seeing the spark of candlelight re-flecting off the silver buttons of Jack's blue waistcoat, seeing the flash in his green eyes. With the arrival of the food, Jack became his usual self, relaxed, scanning the crowd, keeping an eye out, taking a drink from the pot of beer when it was brought to him. But there was something edgy in the way he sat, the tightness of his shoulders, the lack of even the slightest smirk. Perhaps he was expecting that Oliver would ask Jack to teach him a new card game in spite of Oliver's rather emphatic declaration that he did not want to spend his life this way. So why was he continuing to do that very thing?

Now that the afternoon was still, becoming evening, what Jack had said to Oliver earlier kept coming back to him. Jack, who so rarely spoke about how he felt about anything, and never about himself. It was as if Jack had given Oliver some-thing that was only Jack's to give. Even Jack couldn't steal someone else's heart; he could only give his own. Then Jack looked at him, flipping three cards face up in front of Oliver as if inviting him to play a game. And in that moment, in the quietness beneath the wildness of Jack's eyes, Oliver saw a place there that was for him and him alone.

No one had ever said anything like what Jack had said to him. No one had ever looked at Oliver that way, as though he meant something, that he mattered—but Jack's expression now, the furrow between his brows when all he was about was a drink and some cards and his pipe, as usual—so why—

Perhaps it was that Jack feared he'd said too much.

You was the only one I knew in London...I knew I had to look for you—I knew that you would never come lookin' for me.

In spite of these heartfelt comments, Jack was now the very figure of equanimity. As if ignoring the fact that Oliver was staring at him, Jack drew from the pipe and laid it aside.

"What you frownin' at, then, Nolly?" Jack asked, tapping the edges of the cards against the table.

"Nothing," said Oliver, ignoring the galloping of his heart. "The beer—it always goes to my head."

"You always could suffer the gin better," said Jack. "Shall I get you one?"

"No, I just want to—I need to put my head down." And this not merely because the room was becoming dim and booming around him but also because he couldn't gather his thoughts, was unable to collect them into a tidy bundle that would indicate to him what he should do. That first he should do this, and then, second, that, and then after that—Oliver cast a glance about to take in what Jack was seeing, though nobody was looking at them at all.

"I just need to lie down."

"C'mon then, you," said Jack. He stood up, taking up the cards and the clay pipe, still smoking, in the cup of his hand.

He shoved Oliver before him on the bench, pulling Oliver to a stand as though he were some enfeebled elder or some young child who needed a gentle hand to the back to guide him through a narrow, dark place. And Oliver let him, feeling the heat of Jack's hand through layers of wool jacket and muslin shirt that seemed, now, quite thin.

And though some far away part of him, brisk and annoyed, heeded caution, Oliver followed Jack through the crowded tavern, close behind, up the stairs, and down the narrow brown hallway, amidst the gloom of the dimming afternoon light that was leaking in from somewhere. Their footsteps echoed on the worn floorboards and Oliver waited, leaning against the doorjamb as Jack took out his key and undid the useless lock, the metal jaws of the key scraping loudly against the rusty tumblers, in a severe and focused way that let Oliver know that if he didn't lie down, and quickly, he would be falling down, right there in the passageway.

Jack walked into the dark room, with Oliver close on his heels. Jack went over to the mantelpiece, a dim, narrow shadow along the wall above the dark maw of the cold, empty fireplace. He didn't light the candle but stood there a moment, drawing the last mouthfuls of smoke in preparation for dampening the ashes in the pipe to put it in the bowl on the mantelpiece. Oliver closed the door, leaning back against it.

"There should be a fire in that grate," he said.

"I'll go get one," said Jack, though he made no move to go past Oliver or to open the door or anything.

Oliver had an impulse, then, that came from someplace deep within him, a place so still and untrammeled by grief or sorrow or doubt. A strong, deep place in his heart that still believed in blue skies and that all would be well. A place that had enough strength to weather any storm. If Jack didn't want it—if he hadn't meant it—then he could simply push Oliver away and continue smoking his pipe. The risk would be all his.

There was a tiny pause as Jack held his breath, and before he could do anything else, Oliver walked over to him, and standing close, kissed the smoke from Jack's mouth. Pausing with his lips over Jack's, sensitive and shivering, he drew the smoke in, tasting it on Jack's breath, and the beer, and that faraway day when they'd met, when everything had changed, and nothing that had happened since had been able to stand in the way of this moment.

"Oh," said Jack, holding his pipe to one side, not pulling away, his mouth moving and then bestilled. "If that's what you're about then—"

And it didn't matter, Oliver was warm through, his hands on Jack, warm, tugging on Jack's coat and touching the skin of his throat. The room was dim except for the glitter of the street coming through the dirty window. Oliver could barely see; the only light was the spark of charred ash from Jack's pipe.

"Here," he said, holding the pipe to Jack's mouth. Jack took it and drew in a breath, holding the smoke till Oliver kissed him again and tasted the smoke. Then he took the pipe, and in the darkness, put it in the bowl on the mantelpiece. The wooden ledge was narrow, but the pipe would be safe there till morning or later in the evening or whenever Jack might look for it again. But now there was Jack, in the dark room, coming close, pulling off his coat, which Oliver heard land with a thump on the floorboards.

But he didn't remark on this, Jack's slovenly habits, because it didn't matter. His own jacket fell to the floor also, and the night would hide the scatter of boots and stockings and the loose collar of Oliver's shirt that Jack unbuttoned with slow and careful hands. Then Jack drew his hands on Oliver's neck, pushing the collar away and down, untying the kerchief around Oliver's neck, putting his mouth on the curve of Oliver's jaw, sending a shiver through him. Many a hero in the books he'd read had kissed his princess, but the descriptions had never indicated that such a kiss would send his whole body shivering. Nor was his reaction described in the Bible, even in the passages with the women letting down their hair and singing the song of love, no written word had ever described it quite like this.

But whether it was love, as written of in the books he'd read, or something brought on by the drink, his body pushed into Jack's hands, which stroked his hair and pulled at his trouser buttons and seemed to be everywhere all at once. And Jack did not say words of love nor even really speak, though if he was speaking, Oliver was sure he could not hear him over the thudding of his own heart, the effect of the beer seemingly burned away by the heat of his skin and the sear left behind in the trail of Jack's fingers.

"Will you, then, Jack?" Oliver asked, not quite clear on what he was asking or why. Jack answered him, just the same, undoing his own trousers and then Olivier's, and pushing Oliver on the bed, tipping him back, suddenly, to land against the hard, flocked mattress.

It was an uncomfortable bed at best, but when Jack was on him, his thighs straddling Oliver's thighs, his hands stroking the bareness of Oliver's ribs where his shirt rode high, he for-

got about the bed, for Jack was hard and soft against him all at
once, the dust and the salt from his skin so close as Jack
shucked the shirt he wore, trailing the long tails of it as he
pushed it aside.

Jack would be cold that way, all on his own, so Oliver
struggled to put his hands on the folds of his shirt, to pull it
free from his trousers, arching his back. Jack helped him for a
moment and interrupted the motion as Jack pressed Oliver's
hand to his crotch where the hardness of his sex was outlined
as an iron brand. He moved Oliver's hand on him, over the
trousers, then pulled Oliver's hand inside, where the skin was
soft and shockingly hot.

"Come along, then, Nolly," said Jack, when Oliver's hand
jerked to pull away. "Just a little bit; it won't hurt you none,
and then I'll show you. Right?"

How Jack had his wits about him enough to speak, Oliver
didn't know; he couldn't imagine being sane or clear enough
to articulate a sequence of events, the end to which Oliver
didn't know, had never known. But Jack did, and he leaned
low and kissed Oliver on his temples, brushing softly as he
kissed Oliver's eyelids and his nose and then his mouth, a little
rough and tasting sour from the worn-away beer, but sending
shocks through Oliver's body that felt like small, sharp flickers
of lightning.

And when Jack pressed even lower, their chests touching,
Jack's bare one to his shirted one, Oliver's arm was trapped
between him, and only his hand could move. So he did, curling his fingers around Jack's hard sex, dampened by Jack's
pleasure, the hair of Jack's private body scratching against
Oliver's wrist. When he moved his fingers and did it again,

Jack made low sounds in his throat that Oliver had never heard anyone make before, seeming to be from desire but expressed in anxious pleas and some unspoken pain. And desire, as Jack thrust into his hand, pushing faster than Oliver could keep up with, and finally, his hips against Oliver's, shoving one time so hard, that it almost hurt, pulsing in Oliver's hand, leaving hot dampness behind.

Then he flung himself backward on the mattress, sideways, almost knocking Oliver off, and before Oliver could get up from the bed, shocked, eyes wide with it, Jack reached for him, pulling, saying, "Come here, come here."

And laying hands upon him, he pushed down Oliver's open trousers. Taking Oliver now, hard as a brand against his belly, the sin of it clanging inside of his head as the pleasure of it, of Jack's hand, moving up and down, overrode that like a thundering horse until sin was only a vague notion. And Oliver squirmed against Jack, feeling the wildness of his body, out of control, as Jack stroked him up and down, and chastity vanished as his whole body clenched and sweat and heat raced up his spine, and he spent himself into Jack's hand, curling forward with a violent spell of heat that left him panting into Jack's shoulder, sweat freezing along his almost-bare hips, the small of his back.

"There, then, my petal," said Jack, whispering into the crown of his hair, kissing him there. "You belong to me now, as ever you was."

Oliver could only nod, struggling to breathe, thinking to pull up his trousers and tug his shirt more into place as Jack reached behind him to drag the thin woolen blanket, pulling it up over them. Letting the scratchy edge be tucked under his chin as Jack refused to let him go, wrapping his arms around

Oliver's shoulders and pulling him close till they were both on the bed, squarely, the pillow beneath Jack's head, and Jack himself for Oliver's pillow.

"Sleep now," said Jack, his voice mumbling off in the darkness.

And Oliver would, part of his brain thinking of Jack's shirt and how he would be cold without it, but he could barely manage to move his arm enough to make it comfortable, discovering that his arm was across Jack's belly, rising slow and deep, in sleep, where Jack already was. Oliver's eyelids flickered to that blue sky, now husking low into in a slow, darkening night. Where there was peace and stillness and a river inside of him that overflowed and seeped gently across thirsty green banks. Oliver closed his eyes and let himself follow Jack.

CHAPTER 33

Treats Of A Bathhouse In Smithfield, Wherein Oliver Considers His Future

W hen Oliver woke up, he stared at the brown-splotched ceiling, thinking for a moment of the places on his body that Jack had touched, his mouth that Jack had kissed, the stroke of a hand, gently, along his neck, and with more urgency, the flesh between his legs. His skin, all over, seemed to hum, a silvery-toned hum that bespoke of the results of it, the spill of his seed along the bare surface of the flocked mattress, the scent of him mixing with Jack's, like salt from the sea. An ancient holy sea which he'd been taught should never be troubled with being spent in pleasure; it was a sin to do so, a waste of a man's capacity, and a crime—what he and Jack had done was—

He sat up, jerking the blanket back, realizing he was naked from head to toe and feeling the hot wave climbing up his chest, his face. He was almost vibrating with it, the shock of realizing it, the memory of Jack's hands, and the length of Jack's body next to him, the warmth and the closeness, the intimacy—he didn't know whether he was hot with shame—and he should be, he really should be—or whether it was something else. Because even with the heat of discomfort, the sense of quiet deep within him was good as well, and it settled him, as a long walk down a summer's country lane might have done. Had done, in the past, when he was young and the world a green and blue and innocent place.

His skin ached for clean water to wash with. But was he going to wash away the sin of it, wash away what had been between him and Jack? How could he? He couldn't, even as confusing as it was. Not with the memory of Jack's hands upon him and Jack's mouth upon his. Jack had touched him as no one ever had before and kissed him and said, in a low, husked voice, *You belong to me now, as ever you was.* There was still the unsettled future, choices to be made where roads diverged. But with the streets of London before him, now that he had Jack at his side, the world seemed wide open.

Not that Jack was anything lawful or even good, and perhaps not even steady. Jack was a sprite, a child of the streets, pulling Oliver to him as the sky pulls toward the blue, and that was enough for Oliver. He did not know what Jack would think of the night before, and while Oliver knew his own mind about it, it was too new an emotion to share.

Jack sat up on his elbow, eyes puffy, hair mashed on one side, eyes sparking. He looked up at Oliver as though trying not to smirk. "Been wallowin' in the grief of sin, have you?" he asked.

Oliver felt uneasy for a moment because what they'd done was a sin, not only in the eyes of the church but in the eyes of the law. But then he looked down at him, at Jack, bare beneath the woolen blanket, his collarbones pushing beneath his skin, the dirt around his neck. And the smudgy marks of kisses around his mouth that Oliver had left there. If Mr. McCready could walk the street a free man after the willful neglect that had killed Martin—well, passion between two people, regardless of their status or gender, could hardly help but be the lesser evil. Oliver felt he might struggle with this, but not that morning, not with Jack looking at him that way.

"I don't think I'm as shocked as you think I ought to be," said Oliver, letting his mind have its way with his mouth even though he was shocked, down to his bones. But not enough to forget it.

He watched as Jack's eyebrows flew up and he pushed his thumb in the corner of his eye, perhaps to disguise his delight at this news or perhaps just to wake up faster.

"I'm going to go have a bath," said Oliver.

This made Jack frown as he struggled with the blanket as if attempting to get up and delay Oliver from his departure.

"Will you come back?" Jack asked.

"Yes," said Oliver. "I'll come back."

The bath house in Smithfield was a low, two-story building, cobbled together from a collection of houses around a lopsided court. Oliver could see steam coming from stained upper windows and the growth of mold on the frames of the doors, the slimy, dark moss on the cobblestones, the slick of mud and damp that covered every surface.

As he went in the main door, his head felt muzzy in spite of the chill of the pennies in his pocket that Jack had given him. As well, the bath house wasn't a good place, but he was here and he needed a bath, so there was nothing for it but to carry on.

Once inside, there was a lady in a bottle-green skirt. Her apron was more grey than white; she seemed to be covered with a layer of damp as well. Her smile missed teeth but she was pleasant enough and took Oliver's pennies with an open fist.

"Tuppance for first water, and hot, thank you, sir. For another penny we can brush and set your clothes to rights."

Naturally, the woman wouldn't concern herself with *why* his clothes looked as they did, in particular, Oliver's, with the stains of Newgate prison still on him. With Jack's scent pushed through the cloth, along with the sea-tang of what they'd shared.

"Yes," said Oliver, swallowing as his sense of nervousness ate at him. "Thank you, miss."

"We'll send a lad by, once you're in," she replied, taking the additional coin from Oliver.

If he kept going as he was, spending money as soon as he'd acquired it, he'd be more like Jack, who had no sense of thrift or savings and would spend it all as soon as it came in like the criminal he was, living day to day.

A lad, dressed in a thin shirt and trousers in deference to the steamy heat, led Oliver down the hall and gestured to an alcove that had a narrow tin bath full of water, a bowl of soap, and a thin towel. Some unseen breeze chased through a gap in the windowpanes.

"Is this the best you have?" asked Oliver.

"No refunds, mister," said the lad. He trailed his fingers a bit in the water, which steamed up around them.

Oliver's skin began to itch, and he started pulling at the buttons at his neck.

"Fine," he said.

Then the lad pulled back the curtain on the little, fogged window. This seemed to let in light and air, and made him feel a little better.

He got undressed, laid his clothes on the chair, and climbed in the tub, trying not to look at the bruises on his legs or the state of himself. His body had been through enough; it didn't need to be examined for faults and flaws. But there were marks there. Marks from Mr. McCready's switch, from the handling of the constables, the bricks of the jail cell, from Cromwell's hands. And finally, from the lumps of Jack's mattress and Jack's calloused hands, gentle in the night. The bullet scar from where Giles had shot him that Jack had yet to see. It was all over him, everywhere that he'd been. The question was where was he going?

Settling back in the water, he sighed. It wasn't hot enough, and the metal of the tub was cold where it touched his skin. As he reached for the soap, he could hear, through the thin walls, other people splashing around, probably without any real idea as to why bathing was not only the next thing to godliness, it was also civilized, and therefore desirable.

He rubbed soap on every part of him, standing up for a moment to get it all over his skin, and then he sank back in the water to soak. When he returned to the Three Cripples, he wanted to tell Jack about soap and hot water and how good it felt, but he doubted that Jack would believe him, preferring, it seemed, to live with the lice on his skin, the nits in his linen. Oliver refused to admit how easy it was to think of going back directly to the Three Cripples with the intention of talking Jack into taking a bath. Especially when the Three Cripples and all that it entailed should be the very last destination in his time on the earth.

A lad came in and took Oliver's clothes from the chair, sparing Oliver only the briefest of glances. As he left, the cotton curtain swayed damply in the breeze, giving Oliver a quick view of the narrow brown corridor, letting in the smells and the damp and other people's perfume, or lack of it, and Oliver closed his eyes.

He would bathe and get dressed in his disreputable clothes, and he would go back to Jack at the Three Cripples. After that, he didn't know what he'd do. Cromwell seemed to think that Oliver belonged to him now and felt he had the papers to prove it. Oliver knew he could leave London and go to Aunt Rose, but now he was a person of low quality with his criminal record that included not one but two visits to the dock to stand in front of a magistrate, with Oliver's guilt presumed to already be a foregone conclusion. She didn't deserve to have to shelter him in that state. Except she would, she very most likely would. Still, she didn't deserve that trouble, no one did.

And really, he couldn't leave Jack, who, in spite of his rough ways, was a tender anchor against a world that constantly shifted beneath his feet. He could still feel Jack's hand on his face, reaching through the bars to comfort him, tender in spite of the grit of the rusting bars, gentle in spite of who Jack was, where he had come from. Still feel Jack's kisses and his hands, hot on Oliver's skin, but silk-soft in contrast to the rough wool of the blanket.

Oliver's face grew hot again; he felt as though he might be boiling inside of his skin in spite of the cold water. Jack had been there then, and Jack was here now, and there didn't seem to be any way of getting away from that. Unless Oliver determined that what had happened between them the night before was never to happen again. Which he should do, if he had any sense.

"You done, mister?" asked the lad from beyond the curtain.

Oliver sighed.

"In a moment," he said. "Just give me another moment."

He heard other people splashing and muttering, making the whole affair as intimate as if he were bathing in the same room with them. Oliver sank low into the water. He pretended the back of his neck was comfortable against the rim of the tub, and that the water was much hotter, the soap softer, less gritty against his skin.

He scrubbed the length of his forearm and closed his eyes against the drops of water on his skin, on the rim of the tub. Unless he could convince himself not to go back to the Three Cripples, he was well and truly lost.

After getting out of the tub, drying on the thin towel, and getting dressed, he headed back to the Three Cripples, for he could not come up with any other direction to take. He followed West Street, where the wind whisked across his hair, still damp against his neck, making him feel cold. Water ran in the center of the street, ripples of the runoff of grey and melting snow, making Oliver feel as though he should have taken one of the back alleys, as malodorous as those were. But instead he'd chosen this way, splattering his trouser legs with damp and mud, with feckless drops from the overhanging rooflines making their way down his neck. Then, to make matters worse, as he turned the corner into Field Lane, he ran, literally, into Noah Claypole, who had, it seemed, been making his way up Field Lane toward the Three Cripples.

"'Ang about, Work'us, where's your manners?" demanded Noah, his shoulders pushing forward beneath the narrow cloth of his jacket.

"As to that, where are yours?" Oliver demanded in return.

Noah raised his fists as if he were about to give Oliver a good walloping, and why not? Even though they were out and about in the streets, they were *sans* Jack, and more importantly, without that particular audience, Noah could do whatever he pleased, as he always had. But then, so could Oliver.

Then Noah stopped, fists unfolding as his fingers spread out. He leaned forward to sniff along Oliver's neck. "What you been about, then, Work'us?"

"I *am* allowed to be out-of-doors, Noah," said Oliver with some tartness. "I'm not a prisoner, however much you'd rather I was. I've just had a bath, if you must know."

There was a look in Noah's eyes, a narrow, calculating gleam that struck Oliver as it had in the old days. He was looking at Oliver as if he knew exactly what Oliver was thinking and feeling.

"Thought you smelled like a posey," said Noah. "But what I can't imagine is why for?"

"That's none of your affair," said Oliver. He started to attempt to sidle by Noah when out of the corner of his eyes, at the top of the street, just where it began to slope down from

Saffron Hill, he saw Jack. He had his low top hat on and his jacket buttoned over his waistcoat, and he'd not yet seen Oliver. But there he was, resplendent and confident, hands in pockets, even whistling, and Oliver knew, right then, that there had never been any getting away from what was between them, if ever there had been.

"Eh?" said Noah, and Oliver whirled back to face him.

"Quit following me," he said, turning on his heel to march up the lane to meet Jack halfway at least. Naturally, Noah was quick to follow him, annoyingly close, as if with the intent of being as intrusive as possible.

Just then, Jack reached them, coming up breathless, his hat far back on his head. He looked at Oliver, his pleasure that Oliver had, indeed, returned, warring with some hesitation that Oliver knew to be caution. What he and Jack had shared the night before, whether or not it might ever occur again, was never meant to be for common consumption.

And yet, there they were, with Noah as their first audience, witness to the furtive glance that Jack gave him, to the flush that colored Oliver's cheeks because he didn't know whether to reach out and touch Jack on the sleeve, at least, to reassure him. But the tense line of Jack's jaw, the stiffness of his shoulders stopped Oliver even as he wanted to explain his own confusion while at the same time resolving Jack's. That is, if Jack *was* confused, perhaps he wasn't. The flash of his green eyes in the crisp air of the street brought back the warmth of the night before, so perhaps, regardless of what Jack was feeling about that, his current irritation might not be about Oliver at all—

Feeling warm from Noah's gaze, Oliver turned to look at him, dragging his attention away from Jack with some reluctance. Noah was looking at Oliver and then at Jack, his gaze flicking between them as though they were the newest curiosity since the lions had been brought to the Tower. Oliver froze as Noah's eyebrows shot so far up into his hairline that they disappeared, and his mouth had fallen open.

"'Ave you an' Jack—" Noah stopped, and Oliver attempted to tighten his face so that Noah could not see the memories of the night before there.

But with that and Jack's slight cough, it seemed too late to hide anything. And evidently, Noah did not need Oliver's face to find out hidden secrets. He pulled at the buttons on Oliver's collar, which popped open and bounced in the street. Noah's eyes were on his neck, and Oliver knew what he was seeing.

"Bloody sodomite," said Noah, giving Oliver a shove, anger sparking in his eyes, and Oliver knew that Noah was furious not only because of the crime, and indeed, in *spite* of it, but the fact that—well, no matter how many clever stories Noah had told Jack, this was the one story that only Oliver could tell.

"I can smell it on you, Work'us, as 'ard as you tried to wash it off, an' I can see it on your face." Noah almost snarled this. "You're better off leavin' an' goin' back to the workhouse; you're not one of Fagin's lads, an' you never were!"

"I'm more of one than you ever were," said Oliver, feeling the heat of it in his breast and forgetting that he'd ever denied it heretofore that moment. "For I never peached on one of my own."

It was almost in slow motion that Noah clenched his fists to demonstrate to Oliver exactly what he thought of it all, but Oliver, faster by seconds, punched him in the nose and smiled while he did it. Noah staggered back, clutching his face, blood streaking down his chin.

"What's goin' on, then?" Jack asked, jumping forward to clap a hand on each of their shoulders as if they were all the best of friends. "Why ain't you two gettin' along?"

"You know why," said Noah. "Besides, 'e 'it me!" he said, his astonishment muffled beneath his hands.

"What? Nolly?" Jack shook his head as if he'd not just seen Oliver do that very thing, though it was plain to anyone that Noah was the only one bleeding. "Why, he's as delicate as a petal an' wouldn't hurt a child."

Oliver could not help but smirk at this, the evil gladness racing through him; it was one thing to best Noah, he'd done it before and would do it again. But to have Jack take his side was worth giving up all the hot baths in London. Worth the stiff confusion that sprang up between them as they looked at each other.

"You'll regret this, Jack," said Noah, licking his lips and wiping his nose with the back of his hand. "You just see if you will."

But before Jack could say anything, perhaps placate Noah, as he might have done, Noah stormed off back down Field Lane to where it led out to Holborn, banging through puddles as if he might melt them with his fury.

"Eh?" asked Jack, turning to Oliver, reaching out briefly to touch a mud-splattered lapel. "He knows, then?"

"For all he's a fool, well—" Oliver tried not to jerk back from Jack's hand, his eyes flicking to Jack's, feeling a quail of nerves and foolishness and the terrible intimacy of it, to look at someone and have the memory of the curves of their body, the taste of their mouth, their scent up close—he saw the worry in Jack's eyes then and stopped the train of thought with a twitch that seemed to run through his whole body. "He's a fool, but he's very astute, and I'm not very good at lying to him fast enough to avoid him finding out the truth."

"Never you mind, Nolly," said Jack as his touch turned into a full stroke of Jack's hand on Oliver's neck. "It'll work itself out, by-and-bye." Then Jack leaned in, his cold nose beneath Oliver's ear, where his hair was still damp.

"Besides, you smell lovely, an' how can I be angry when you smell like that?"

"Soap and hot water, Jack, is all it is," said Oliver, shivering with the faint touch of Jack's skin on his but not moving away.

"You were comin' back," said Jack finally, pulling himself upright so, as seemed likely, he might rescue him and Oliver from being a spectacle on the street, though it was far too late for that.

"I told you I would," said Oliver.

Jack shook his head. "Not with that look on your face, the one you had this mornin'. It was like a storm come over them blue eyes of yours."

The thoughts from the bathhouse came back to Oliver then, as did his resignation. "I do need to leave London, Jack, as I told you," he said. "I don't know as to where, but—"

"You know I can't come with you," said Jack interrupting him. "And besides, you don't need to leave ever so quickly, do you? Stay with me awhile, won't you, an' I'll help you get a kit together, and some brass, so you won't be starvin' on the streets like the poor, wee mite that you are."

Jack's causal answer belied the fact that he believed he would, in time, be able to convince Oliver to stay. Besides,

Oliver had never been able to resist how he felt inside when someone offered to feed him, and he did not resist it now. Not when Jack was looking at him as he was, with a flash in his green eyes, sharp as a mirror.

To Jack, any of this, anything anyone thought, and whether or not it regarded the rules written by man or God, mattered very little to Jack. He wanted Oliver to stay, and that was all there was to it. The thought of leaving in the face of that desire was not impossible, for it was quite true that many had looked upon Oliver as an object to be gained or even, simply, as though he were something good to eat. Oliver was used to leaving it behind, ignoring it, pretending it wasn't there. But not when it came with that smirk that half bespoke confidence and half whispered of something else, something that Jack had only let Oliver reach. If Oliver would leave, it might not be directly; he had no plan to speak of, no direction to head. There was London, and there was Jack, the rain and the wind whistling down the lane where they stood, within eyeshot of the Three Cripples.

Jack smiled. "No long faces," he said, stroking his thumb along Oliver's jaw.

Oliver resigned himself to having his heart broken by a street thief.

CHAPTER 34

Which Contains The Substance Of A Pleasant Interlude

In that moment, silent and somewhat sweet, between them, Oliver cast his eyes down the mud-drenched lane, where Noah had so recently gone. Jack did likewise, then back at the Three Cripples, at the throng along by the door as if he couldn't bear to charge his way through it, but had to, just the same. Then he tipped his head back, hand on the crown of his low top hat.

"Say, Nolly," said Jack, interrupting the thread of Oliver's thoughts. "I've gots an errand to run—will you wait here, or come along?"

It wasn't quite as sudden as a smack to the face, but this was a moment Oliver feared would come. Jack was going out to pick pockets; Jack was a thief, and not all of the angels in heaven could change him from that. It might suit Oliver better if they could, but what other employment could Jack gain? Oliver could not imagine him clerking in an office or even chasing bullocks in a field. But he didn't ask what Jack was doing nor implore him not to go. It wouldn't change anything anyway.

"I'll go back—I'll wait for you here," Oliver said, taking a side step up the lane. "But not forever, so hurry back."

Jack's whole face cinched up in a smile, one that reached his eyes. He touched Oliver's face with his fingers.

"That's somethin' old Fagin might have said." He was laughing at Oliver outright, and Oliver tried not to return the smile but failed.

"Well, then," Oliver said, clearing his throat. He knew the words, remembered Fagin saying them, but couldn't dig up the charming oiliness of Fagin's voice to say any more. "Hurry on, then," he said, just the same.

With a wave and a smile, Jack turned to go, swallowed up by the crowd on this rainy day, leaving Oliver on the slanted, damp paving stones, to be looked at by rough men who shouldered past him, bumping into him because they could. Or because they wanted to get close. And they stared; people did, but without Jack as his shield, or even Noah's annoying presence, Oliver felt naked and bare to the soul.

Gritting his teeth, he shouldered his way in amongst the men; there were women too, with slatternly hair and singed aprons, and they made way for him with saucy smiles and too much toilet water applied about their person.

Oliver pushed up the street till he was through the door of the Three Cripples, looking through the smoky haze of the coal fire at the crowd drinking their dinner, thinking again of what Mr. Grimwig would say. Of how he would pound his cane and state, for anyone to hear, that this was Oliver's lot. To live amongst the unwashed, to shelter in such a place, to consort with thieves.

Oliver hurried up the stairs, and when he got to the door, he opened it; the lock gave way at the slightest push. It was true, what Mr. Grimwig might think, either in part or in whole, depending on the moment. The room that he and Jack now shared was littered with clumps of mud, the bed was unmade, the mattress grimy and stained, cobwebs in the window and soot streaking across the old brickwork that surrounded the unlit fireplace. So Mr. Grimwig was right, Oliver lived as he deserved to live, with thieves, in fetid, small quarters. But at least he had Jack, he had that, though for how long, Oliver didn't know. He needed to leave London, only he didn't want to leave without Jack. Which meant staying. Which also meant, as he waited for Jack, that he needed something to do. Or at least until Jack talked him into joining him on the streets, or Cromwell made good his threats to make use of Oliver. Until then, Oliver was on his own.

He took off his jacket and laid it on the back of the chair and doffed his top hat and put it on the table. Then he began to make use of his idle hands. He pulled the blankets from the bed and hung them on the string over the narrow mantelpiece to air. He leaned the mattress up against the wall and somehow found a scrap of cloth to dust the slats and turned the mattress to the other side. Not that it made much difference; the stains on both sides made it look as though someone had died there. When he tried to open the window, it was jammed shut, and looking at it, Oliver knew he'd need a lever of some sort to open the window, not to mention hot water and soap, and then he realized that he needed an army of maids to make any real difference in that room.

Oliver took the jug from where it sat on the floor, and went back down the narrow corridor and down the stairs. Skirting the crowd as best he could, he went past the bar and through the side door that led to the kitchen.

It wasn't as busy as the last time he'd been through it, though there was the same slovenly woman stirring something on the stove while completely ignoring that there was ash from the flames getting into the pot. The same man from before, with his red-and-brown stained apron, was using his cleaver to cut the last bits of scraggly meat from bone and putting it with bare and unwashed fingers into a large wooden bowl. There were dried leavings on the long, thick table, a pile of bread that had been scorched, some lump of something that had flies all over it and smelled, and, wrapped in torn blue paper, an old, well-scraped cone of sugar.

The fireplace needed cleaning worse than the one upstairs did. The grime on the walls was thick, and there was something splashed darkly on the windows, tar, perhaps, or old wax, he wasn't sure. He couldn't imagine that he'd actually eaten food prepared in this room. But he wasn't going to do anything about the kitchen; he only needed to keep his hands busy until Jack returned.

He put the jug on the table, but neither the man nor the woman turned around to ask him what he was doing or what he wanted. After looking around one more time, Oliver left the jug there and decided against attempting to find soap in a kitchen like that, along with the water he knew he could get from the pump if he went outside into the alley. Instead he found a stiff wire brush and a small pail and went over to the fireplace and took up sticks and scraps of wood from the wood box. When he slunk through the main room, he kept his head low and used rusty tongs to grab bits of live coal from the fireplace in the alcove.

Back up in the room, he tried scouring at the coal dust on the grate with the stiff brush, but while his efforts cleaned the fireplace a little, his efforts mostly resulted in coal dust flying up all around. In spite of this, at least he could place the coal and the woodchips in the grate and feel the warmth of the low flames and how the chill of the room eased up, and at least most of the smoke went up the flue.

He straightened the bed, put the blanket and pillow in order, and dusted the windowsill and the mantel with the scrap of cloth he'd used on the bed slats. Then, on his hands and knees, he went over the whole of the floor, pushing clumps of mud and layers of dust between the seams of the floorboards, where no doubt they would fall unnoticed onto the shoulders of the customers in the main room below.

He knew he wasn't cut out for a life of this type of grimy work, but there was something to order and structure that filled him up as much as a good meal did. In spite of this, once the fire was lit and the room done up, there was nothing much for him to do. He sat cross-legged in front of the fire and held his hands out to the glowing coals. His palms were dirty, and the knees of his trousers were black with coal and street grime. No doubt his face and the back of his neck reflected the same state in spite of his recent bath. And he wondered when Jack would return. And wondered, after that, what they would do, he and Jack, together. Or apart. He did not know.

⁓❦⁓

When the bells of St. Andrew's Church were striking the hour of two o'clock with long, slow tolls, Oliver realized that he'd fallen to dozing in front of the fire, and that the coals were down to a level where they needed building up and the ash shoveled away, or the fire would die out altogether. As he stood up, rubbing the back of his neck, he wondered where Jack had gone to, and whether maybe he should have gone with Jack instead of staying behind. But what if Jack, while pinching another twopenny snuffbox, got himself arrested again? And how was Oliver really going to manage being with a common thief?

He shook this off—made himself shake it off as he straightened his clothes and went down to the main room. It was still thronged with people, the air thick with damp because the door to the tavern was closed against the rainy weather. He saw that one of the fires had been built up, small flames flickering and jumping as the rain came down the flue, the wind whistling through the grate.

There was Jack, coming through the front door with a sack in his hand and bottle under his arm. He was almost soaked through, and Oliver went to him, trying his best to ignore the looks he got with his jacket off, the buttons broken from his collar, and his kerchief loose, his throat bare.

"Jack," said Oliver, and then, on an impulse which found his body quite unable to resist, he cupped his hand around the crook of Jack's elbow. "Come, then. We should eat, and I built a fire in the room, although the chimney is no doubt still choked with soot, and the fire smokes—"

"You built a fire?" asked Jack, letting himself be turned away from looking at the men who now piled in the alcove that Jack considered his.

"Yes," said Oliver. He nodded and tugged on Jack's arm. "I built it for the both of us, and I'm sure it's died down by now, but I can build it up again."

"Maybe," said Jack in a way that seemed to indicate he was wondering which fire, exactly, that Oliver was talking about. Either way, he shook off Oliver's hand and settled himself in his damp jacket. He held out the sack, which was mud-stained and ragged along the edges. "I got you somethin'; was going to share it with Noah, but—never mind him anyway. Here."

He lifted up the sack and handed it to Oliver, finally looking him in the eye; though his brow was furrowed low, at least he was attempting to forget about Noah.

"What is it?" asked Oliver, hefting it in his hands, his voice coming out high as a young child's on its birthday. The burlap sack bulged with corners and points and was heavy as a small anvil.

"Upstairs," said Jack. "I honestly thought you weren't goin' to be here when I got back."

Oliver ignored the statement, which seemed to beg for re-assurance from Oliver that he would *always* be there when Jack got back, because he could not, in truth, respond to it. Instead, he let himself be led up the narrow stairs and down the brown hallway to Jack's room, where, indeed, the fireplace was smoking as the fire had died out, and there wasn't enough heat to take the smoke up the flue. Jack made Oliver sit on the bed and arranged the sack on Oliver's lap.

"Only for you, mind," said Jack, seeming to get some of his spirit back. There was a small, low light in his eyes, as if, once in the room, alone with Oliver, he could let it show. He handed the bottle to Oliver as well, though Oliver's hands were already occupied with the sack.

"Very well," said Oliver, trying for some sternness to keep his voice even. It didn't quite work, so he concentrated on Jack's gift to him instead. He balanced the bundle on his lap with one hand, and with the other, he shook the contents of the bottle and looked at the cork, which was sealed with brown wax.

"It's brandy," said Jack.

Oliver had never had brandy before and wondered at the cost of it before belatedly realizing that, of course, Jack would not have enough on him to actually have *purchased* the bottle at a shop. "Thank you."

"An' there's more," said Jack. He reached into the sack, shifting the weight of it on Oliver's lap, and pulled out a still-warm pie, large enough for a family of four, that had a lovely baked crust and smelled like onions.

"Rabbit pie," said Jack. He put the pie on the bed near the pillow and sat down next to Oliver, taking off his hat and laying it aside. "Go on, then."

When Oliver pulled three books out of the sack, he was astounded. They were used books, with the edges a little battered, but still fine, the faded gilt on the covers promising that the pages had been well-thumbed because the stories were good. One title, *The Castle of Otranto*, he thought he'd seen in the townhouse; the other title, *The Last of the Mohicans*, was entirely new to him. The last book was a worn copy of *The Arabian Nights*, exactly resembling the copy that used to belong to Oliver, back in the day when his life, while troubled, lacked the confused stumblings the memory of Jack's kissing him now brought.

As he held the books in his lap, he moved his fingers along the edges. He should feel worse about it that these were stolen, though he was thinking more about how he'd missed out on the pleasure of browsing among the titles with Jack at his side. Indeed, his chest ached with the pleasure of it—that Jack had thought to acquire these for him. Then he looked at Jack.

"You didn't *steal* them," he said. It was more of a statement than a question because while it might be defendable, in certain circumstances, to steal a bottle of brandy and a rabbit pie, it was an entirely different action to steal books from a bookshop.

"Of course I did," said Jack stoutly. "However else would I get them for you?"

Oliver knew that he should push the books aside and admonish Jack that although stealing to survive was one thing, for pleasure? Most assuredly not. But there was Jack's expression to contend with, much improved from his encounter with Noah. And then there were the books themselves, inviting him with covers and edges and titles. "I've never read this one, *The Last of the Mohicans*, it says. Have you?"

"Do you take me for foolish?" asked Jack, drawing back. "I have more important things to do."

"And this other one, I think I saw it on Uncle Brownlow's shelf, but I was never allowed to read it. It would addle my head, Mrs. Bedwin thought."

"Which one's that, then?" Jack moved closer, tipping his chin down until it rested on Oliver's shoulder, as if wanting to share in the moment where Oliver stroked the book with reverent fingers.

Oliver traced the title, his skin prickling a bit with delight at the warm feel of Jack's breath on his neck. "*The Castle of Otranto,*" he said, reading aloud. His fingers itched to shove everything from the bed so he could begin reading *The Arabian Nights* without any moment of delay. "Really, Jack, wherever did you get them?"

"Nolly," said Jack, taking off his jacket and tossing it on the floor near the bed. "You don't want to know, trust me. But I'll get more wood for the fire, or coal, or whatever's to hand, an' when I come back, we can eat, an' then—"

Jack paused. He stood up, looking down at Oliver, and brushed the dust and grit from his trousers and reached for the bottle to uncork it. Taking a swig straight from the bottle, he swallowed some brandy and closed his eyes for a minute.

"Do you want me to read to you, Jack?" asked Oliver. He felt a shiver that was akin to comfort. The boys at the haberdashery had never allowed that reading was good or pleasurable; any time spent in the room with them as they lolled on the beds when he tried to read, their idle chatter had been a constant interruption.

Jack's eyes flew open, and there, yes, was the glitter of desire. For after Noah, Jack needed a new story as much as Oliver needed the book to tell it from.

"Here," said Oliver. He scooted back on the bed till his back was against the low headboard. He crossed his legs; that his boots were still on didn't matter, the blanket was filthy already, and besides, a book awaited him. But Jack took a moment to undo the laces for him and to pull off Oliver's boots and throw them aside. Oliver didn't let himself make a comment about this since that was how Jack was with his own clothes. And, besides, Jack was now undoing Oliver's neckerchief and pushing his collar open, taking a small moment to place a feathery kiss on Oliver's temple. The hairs on Oliver's neck stood up, making him want to tip his neck aside for more of the same, but he took a deep breath and didn't move and waited till Jack sat back, smiling at him.

Then Jack took off his own boots and kerchief, and his blue waistcoat besides, while Oliver thumbed through the pages, noting the slightly worn edges, the thumb stains from a cup of tea, perhaps, or a splash of something else. The book had been well read and well loved, but it was Oliver's now. He didn't let himself think about how the original owner might miss it, and he wasn't about to ask Jack how he had stolen it.

"C'mon," said Jack. He lay on the bed next to Oliver and arranged himself, using the whole of the pillow. He pulled the pie onto his stomach, wedging the bottle of brandy between them. "Don't be stingy; if you are goin' to read, then read."

There was enough light to see by, streaming in through the grit-dappled windows. Oliver opened *The Arabian Nights* and turned to the first chapter, and tracing his finger down the page to settle it, began to read about Scheherazade and her stories about the jinn and magic lamps and mystical, faraway places. At first his voice felt shaky and rough. But then, between bites of pie that Jack handed to him and mouthfuls of brandy, supplied to Oliver's mouth by Jack with care so as not to splash on the pages, it smoothed out to the tones that Aunt Rose would praise when he would stand in the parlor on a Sunday and read out loud from stories of the Bible.

As Oliver read, the words about places he'd never been to were enchanting, with images of desert hills dappled with glowing stones and deep caves of secrets and adventure, and turbaned Moors sitting on fine wool rugs with the frankincense-scented smoke from gold-bound lamps settling on their shoulders. From there, the tale continued, and all the while, Jack finished off most of the pie and half the brandy, continuing to feed Oliver and giving him swallows of brandy, as he remembered to do it. And then, with a satisfied sigh, Jack sank even lower, and curled on his side, his head resting on Oliver's thigh, an idle hand draped across Oliver's leg.

Eventually, Jack began to breathe through his open mouth and fell asleep. The sight of him, the relaxed slope of his shoulders, the contented curl of him on the bed, made Oliver's eyes droop and want to close. And that, added to the brandy and the last of the rabbit pie, made him want to put the book down and curl up next to Jack. So he did. He put the bottle on the floor, as there was still some brandy left, and put the pie on the floor next to the bottle. He did not let himself think that it was the middle of the day and that most of the world was at work, being useful, being industrious. And yet, he was here with Jack, on a rainy afternoon, lazy and adrift with thoughts of a faraway land contained within the worn binding of a stolen book as he put his head down on the mattress and pulled the blanket over them both.

CHAPTER 35

An Unpropitious Interruption By Cromwell And The Results Thereof

When Oliver awoke again, Jack was already sitting up, shirt half-jumbled around his waist. He was taking a long swallow of the brandy, and when he offered the bottle to Oliver, Oliver shook his head. It was bad enough to sleep away the day, but to drink it away as well? But then, they'd already done that, what of it? So he held out his hand and took the bottle, and indeed, finished it off. Jack took it from him and then put it on the floor with a clunk.

There was shouting at the door, and the wooden panels shuddered under the banging. Jack got up, pulling his shirt straight, buttoning his trousers as he went to get the door. As the door opened, Oliver thought the better of them admitting they were within, but it was too late. Cromwell stood there, broad shoulders filling the doorway, looking rough and dressed for the weather.

"I'm 'ere, as you see," he said, smiling with his teeth. "An' now you're goin' to work for me."

"I told you," said Oliver. The blanket scratched across his arms, bringing back sleep-dappled memories of Jack, half-awake, petting Oliver's hair as he might a cat. There had been softness and pleasure from Jack's hands, made even more welcome by the brandy in his head. But now the brandy chased itself unpleasantly in his stomach. "I'm no thief."

"An' he ain't," said Jack. He was about to find his boots on the floor and put them on as if to regard some semblance of modesty, though Oliver suspected it was merely because it was chilly. "He can do other things, scholarly things. Or—"

"I'll 'ave him stealin'," said Cromwell. He didn't come any closer in the room, but then, he didn't have to. "Or I'll have 'im, I'll 'ave you *both*, up on charges of sodomy. That's still a 'anging offense, ain't it?"

In spite of his attitude, that of carelessly buttoning up his waistcoat, arranging his clothes as if Cromwell was of no account, Jack's face went chalk white.

"Or maybe it's castration an' deportation, I can never remember which." Cromwell bent to pick up Jack's jacket and handed it to him. Jack took it with a snap, his hands shaking.

"Make up your mind, then, Cromwell," said Oliver evenly, with a calmness he didn't feel. Either of those punishments would suit the crime they had committed between them, but whether that was worse than the fact that Noah had probably run straight to Cromwell with the news of what was between Oliver and Jack, he didn't know. What he couldn't bear was to see the way Jack, normally a bright spark no matter how gloomy the weather, was standing. Cringing, really, his shoulders drawn, as Cromwell watched him finish dressing.

"And you mind your mouth, orphan," said Cromwell with a snap. He made a fist of his hand and pointed his thumb at Oliver, shaking it at him as if it was meant to be a threat. "I'll come up with somethin' you're good at, you see if I will. A lad as pretty as you, there's all kinds of ways you can be useful to me. An' if you don't, why—"

"Cromwell," said Jack. "I'll talk to him, like I said I would. I will, if only—"

"See that you do." With a snap of his head, Cromwell left the room, leaving a trail of his smoky sweat behind and slamming the door after him.

In the silence of the room, Jack picked his hat up from the floor and ran his fingers along the brim. He wouldn't look at Oliver, not even for a minute.

"What did you mean, like you said you would?" Oliver tugged on his shirt, his fingers becoming tangled with the red scarf, which had fallen down upon the mattress.

"Get dressed, Nolly," said Jack. "Just get dressed. I only said that I'd talk to you, not that I'd make you."

"Make me what? Steal?"

"Well, yes," said Jack, looking at Oliver now, though hesitating to hold Oliver's gaze for long. He came over to the bed and sat on the blanket, making it harder for Oliver to move away since Jack was sitting on one of Oliver's sleeves now as well. "What else could you do, but what I do?"

"I've told you," said Oliver, muffled as he tugged hard enough to be able to pull the sleeve away from Jack. He did up the buttons on his collar, his fingers noting the missing ones, and sighed. It was happening already; Jack's world was taking him in, and there seemed nothing that Oliver could do about it. But it wasn't Jack's fault, for all his expression said that he was aware that Oliver would be resistant. To Jack, this was the world, and if Oliver was with him, then why wouldn't he want to be a part of it?

Jack pulled Oliver's trousers from beneath the bed along with one of his stockings. Oliver put his feet over the edge of the bed to pull them on then put his bare feet on the floor, rolling and unrolling the stocking between his hands.

"I'm not meant to be a thief," Oliver said finally, to the stocking, his hands, the floor. Anywhere than at Jack, who would be very disappointed to find out that this was so.

"It'll just be a few times," said Jack. "To satisfy Cromwell, then you'll have some brass an' you can be off."

"I can be off anyway," said Oliver. "I walked seventy miles from Hardingstone to London with only a penny in my pocket, as you'll recall. I imagine I can do the like again." His voice felt cold and there was a chill in his throat. He and Jack had come, once again, to this particular crossroads, and for no man but Jack would Oliver even deign to discuss it. "But I can't stay in London, there's nothing here for me now."

Jack moved as if to get away, scrabbling around on the floor to find Oliver's other stocking.

"Besides," said Oliver, taking the stocking. "Stealing's a crime and a sin."

"Other things're a crime an' a sin but that don't seem to bother you none." Jack came up to Oliver and tossed his hat on the bed. He stood close to Oliver's knees until Oliver looked up at him. "A crime an' a sin," said Jack again, his green eyes hard.

"But we're not hurting anyone then," said Oliver, somewhat shocked that Jack, like Cromwell, would think to use that to convince him. "Not taking anything from them."

"But rich people deserve to be taken," said Jack, earnest, as though glad with the change of subject, gesturing to the window as if to include the wide world beyond it. "They deserve it!"

"Just because someone is rich doesn't meant they deserve to be stolen from." Oliver didn't bring up Uncle Brownlow because this wouldn't convince Jack in the slightest.

"Well, some, yes, like your old gentleman," said Jack, surprising Oliver with this insight. "But what I mean is those rotters who walk around with their noses in the air an' won't trouble themselves to toss a penny to a beggar, them's who I mean."

Oliver couldn't speak, for he was one of those. Not rich as a king, no, but not willing to give a beggar a penny, not willing to pay the street sweepers, not willing to hand out even a crust of bread.

"Ain't there a one?" asked Jack now, insistent. "One among them rich folk, so rich an' mean that they might deserve to have something lifted? Cromwell never goes to the same place twice, but it would teach 'em. Surely you could come up with someone to give him."

Unwillingly, as he got up from the bed to grab his boots from where they were by the door, Oliver thought of Mrs. Acton. Of her fine gowns and grasping arms. Of the tea set, all over silver. And of her cruelty to him. She could have taken his rejection with much more grace, seeing as how there were plenty of young men in London who would only dream of being in her good graces, lolling in her bed among her perfumed sheets.

"Well, then?" Jack hurried to urge Oliver to sit back on the bed, while he put Oliver's boots on him and did up the laces, looking up into Oliver's face with bright, hopeful eyes.

"You see? You've thought of someone, haven't you?"

Oliver shook his head, but it wasn't to disagree with Jack. More, it was his surprise Jack had seen, so easily, the wicked thoughts in Oliver's head. Mrs. Acton didn't deserve to be stolen from any more than Uncle Brownlow had, or even, any more than Mr. McCready, because while Mrs. Acton had been cruel, cruelty wasn't the same as being dishonest.

Putting his booted feet firmly on the floor, Oliver reached out to touch Jack's face but withdrew the tender gesture at the last moment.

"He won't want to stop at one victim," said Oliver. "I had the whole of London to deliver to; I know a good many places with silver plate and more besides."

"That you do," said Jack as he stood up, trying not to smile and failing. It was in the flash of his eyes, the snap of his smile, how pleased he was by this turn of events. Oliver didn't have the heart to bring it up once again, that he was leaving London as soon as he was able. Because in Jack's mind, his will for Oliver to stay would be more than enough to make it happen.

Jack pulled on his coat as he reached for his hat. With a quick grace, he took up Oliver's coat and hat as well.

"I'm ready," he said.

Of course Jack was ready; Jack was ready to steal day and night, and Oliver knew that, had always known it. Jack would never stop, and for Oliver to expect him to was madness. That way led to madness.

When they went down to the main room with the intention of having a pint or two of beer in their alcove, Cromwell appeared, as he always seemed to do, and gestured for them to follow him back to his room beneath the arched ceiling.

"Don't you forget, pretty one," said Cromwell with a snap when Oliver merely looked at him, "that castration is just a-waitin' for you, the second you think to cross me."

Oliver felt it, that rush of fear slithering through him at the thought of it. He looked at Jack as Jack looked at him, wary and uncertain. Of course, Jack knew that Oliver would never peach, but he seemed uncertain whether Oliver would protect him from the surgeon's knife or another trip across the ocean, or indeed, whether Oliver would cut and run, right then and there, leaving Jack to his own devices.

Knowing he could make a decision for this moment only, Oliver nodded and walked down the passageway beneath a ceiling that lowered, the white plaster becoming dark with soot, Cromwell close on his heels. Once in the small room, Cromwell gestured that Oliver should sit across from him; for Jack, there was no chair. Cromwell pushed a scrap of paper and a stub of lead across the table.

"You only need give me one name, from all of your deliveries that Jack said you was on," said Cromwell. "Just write down an address for us to go to. Of course, you'll come with us, but we just need a lookout, is all."

If Oliver had known Cromwell better, he'd say that his tone was coy. And besides, with a man like that, like Cromwell, and like Jack, there was always a lie behind a deceptive truth. Oliver pushed his hair out of his eyes and tried to think of a way to say no with a gentleman's grace, although he wasn't sure why he was trying to be polite to a thief

"You're going to give me that address," said Cromwell, as level and assured as if he'd been speaking to a willing accomplice. "And then you me an' Jack, we're goin' on an inside job, a little bit of breakin' and takin', if you see what I mean. You could be the lookout for 'im, a guardian angel, like."

From where he stood by the wall, Jack looked at Oliver. The expression around his eyes was guarded, dark hair falling over his forehead as he looked away, willing, it seemed, to keep silent rather than object to what Cromwell was saying. Oliver felt an ache in his heart at the sweetness there that only he could see. This was no way to live, but Jack didn't know any better. Didn't want to know any better.

"C'mon, Nolly," said Jack in the silence, as if it was up to him to make this happen. He pulled himself upright against the wall, shoulders back as he put his hat on and tipped his head back to settle the hat more solidly on his head. "Safe as houses," he said, looking at Oliver directly. "All you have to do is stand watch, an' if the peelers come, you whistle. So say yes; you'll be bored witless else." Jack reached down to hand Oliver his coat and hat. "Say you will. Then, when we come back, you can read to me some."

Out of the corner of his eye, Oliver could see Cromwell's eyebrows go up, but Jack was only looking at Oliver, so Oliver shut his mouth into a firm line. Then he nodded. Being the lookout for a crime wasn't actually a crime. Was it?

"I'm only giving you one name," said Oliver, feeling stern as he looked at Cromwell, knowing that it was his pride that lied to him that he might have been able to give some other answer. "And it will be someone who might deserve it because I can't stand by and watch you take from someone who's good." Oliver took the paper and stub of lead and bent his head and wrote Mrs. Acton's address down in a slow, careful script. He ignored the fact that if anyone were to acquire this particular piece of paper, the crime would lead directly to Oliver, and there would be no stopping the hanging that had long been foretold for him.

But as Oliver pushed the piece of paper across the table, trepidation becoming thick in his heart, Cromwell just laughed and ordered some beer and food for them.

"It's on me, fellows, so eat 'earty."

Then Cromwell waved to someone in the passageway, and a man came and whispered in Cromwell's ear, taking the paper and going back down the hall without another word or even a glance in Oliver's direction.

Doreen came with a platter ladened with pots of beer and a plate of cuts of cold meat and slices of bread and cheese.

"Come then, Jack, that's a dour face you've got on," said Cromwell, with a gesture at the table. "'Ave some beer to take it away."

There was no place for Jack to sit, making him a tense accomplice to the meeting that had mainly been between Oliver and Cromwell. But he took up a pot of beer and drank it as if this were any other evening and their intended activity merely the normal course of things.

"My friend there has gone to scout out the 'ouse," said Cromwell, "because I like to know where I'm goin', as you may as well know. Besides, I ain't the type to sit on a job, unlike some. I like to get in, grab, an' then get out. It's fast, an' that's safe, an' just you remember that." He was pointing at Oliver with his beer pot in his hand, sloshing the suds over his knuckles. "So drink up."

Oliver drank some of his beer and took a piece of bread to calm his stomach, knowing that the beer on an empty stomach would make him dizzy and short-tempered. The afternoon's sleep he and Jack had shared, though, had left him wide awake even with the light along the corridor from the main room dimming in angles and shadows along the floor.

They waited more than an hour, till the beer was drunk, and Jack, propped up along the wall, looked as though he were about to fall asleep. Oliver's legs had gone numb from sitting so still for so long, and Cromwell dozed while looking into the dregs of his beer. Then, there was a motion along the passageway, and Cromwell stood up.

"Drink, drink!" he said to Oliver and clapped him on the back and made a gesture with his hand that Jack and Oliver should follow him. Which they did, clattering down the narrow corridor and through the busy tavern into the damp, chilly night. There was a mist coming down, laced with bitter fog, but it wasn't snow, wasn't anywhere near as cold as it had been. If spring was coming, which it was, then whatever Oliver earned on this job, he'd take with him when he left the City. This would be his only job and he would tell no one. He'd make sure Jack wouldn't tell anyone either. Cromwell wouldn't tell anyone, so that was that.

They trekked through the streets, which were growing dark as night came, skirting any lamps, staying to the shadows, keeping to the walls of the Old City, ducking beneath curved and crumbling archways while the water dripped down on them. At first, while his heart hammered, Oliver considered that they might be headed the wrong way, toward the river. But as they went uphill and he recognized Grey's Inn Gardens, he realized they were heading north. When they crossed Little James Street, he knew they were headed in the right direction, though, truly, it was the wrong direction, and when they got to Doughty Street and slipped into the back alley, he knew it was wrong, deep down inside.

"We can't rob this house." Whether it was Mrs. Acton's house or another, the fine, graceful building in a nice neighborhood of terraced dwellings was not meant to be stolen from.

But his second thoughts, however delayed they had been, were smashed through when Cromwell grabbed his jacket and pulled him back, pushing him against the damp wall. "You chose this bitch for a reason, slammed down the address like a tinker's plug. You know the inside, you know your way around—"

"I'm not going in," said Oliver, hissing. "I'm not."

"You will," said Cromwell. His face was only inches from Oliver's face, glittering with rain as the twilight came down. "You *will* come in with us. You'll show us the right stairs that'll take us directly to the silver. Unless you want to stand 'ere in the street an' wait for the peelers to find you."

Cromwell's additional threat, that of turning them both over to the courts for sodomy, went unspoken. Oliver's mouth fell open; he tasted the rain on his lips as he looked over at

Jack. Jack merely shrugged because, of course, none of this was his fault.

"So you will come in," said Cromwell. He grabbed Oliver by the lapels and pulled him even closer. "You will, as it will be better for Jack if you do. Safer for 'im if 'e knows what to contend with when 'e goes in there, if you're with 'im."

Oliver felt the heat in his face. It was as if Cromwell knew what was in his head, his heart. That was the key, then, the hook to get him to do what was wanted. Fagin had never used Jack against him, but then, it might not have worked back then anyway. Oliver struggled in Cromwell's grasp, but it was a flutter of movement only, a protest, a mere shrug, meant to make a point that Cromwell would never get.

"We have to go in through the kitchen area," said Oliver, finally. "The stairs to the ground floor are to the left. She has three, no, four servants. And the things, they're on the sideboard on the ground floor." These things, silver and polished and valuable, were always out to show how stylish Mrs. Acton was, though any acknowledgement from the upper classes would be of no use to her once they were gone.

"Showy," said Cromwell. He let Oliver go, and pulled out a thin, narrow, leather-bound case from an inside pocket of his coat.

When they went skulking down the stairs to the kitchen area, Cromwell bent down and took out some spiked tools from the case and then went to work on the lock on the narrow door. The door opened with a click, and Cromwell and Jack slipped inside, leaving Oliver in the dank area, alone for a moment, with the rain coming down and the full darkness like a cloak overhead. He couldn't imagine that a constable would come around the block, checking on the mere chance of a single break-in along the middle of a grand city.

Then again, Oliver didn't know; he had never paid attention before. But in that second, he could see it. If you watched the constables on their beat, you could figure out where they weren't likely to go and then go there, to that dark place beneath a constable's vision. And that was the way Jack saw things. But he, Oliver, didn't want to see it that way nor live a life full of thoughts of evasion and trickery and skulking about when nice people, regular citizens, walked in the light of broad thoroughfares and took hansom cabs or the omnibus and paid their fares and purchased goods at a store, and were regular. Ordinary.

Except his heart was beating. Beating like drums against his breastbone as he waited in the dark, his eyes widening to every sound, feeling the hum and clatter of the traffic from a nearby street, feeling it in his stomach. He was helping while Jack robbed someone, and giving in to Cromwell's threats, and all to punish a woman who had done badly by Oliver. While it was a crooked justice, it was justice. Not to mention that it was a far cry from the time he'd watched Jack and Charley rob Uncle Brownlow of a very fine silk handkerchief; this time, he knew what they were doing, and he was *helping* them do it.

Just then, Cromwell reached through the open door and grabbed Oliver by his rain-spattered lapels and yanked him in so hard that his teeth clicked together. The wickedness of it tasted like copper on his tongue, but his whole body was tight, the blood humming in his veins as he trod softly up the wooden stairs behind Cromwell. Jack was already at the landing, a burlap sack unrolled in his hand, standing there, quite calmly, it seemed, in the darkness, as if he were on an every-day errand. And that, rather than robbing someone of their goods and silver.

At the sight of this thief, *his Jack*, functioning in the world that he knew best, that of darkness and theft and law-breaking sin, calmly unrolling a sack in his element, Oliver's whole body started at the shock of it. At Jack, looking up as Oliver came up the stairs, showing a flash of white smile, ready to steal. And though no words came forth, and Oliver's heart was bursting in his chest, it wasn't right to see Jack like this; there should always be a curtain, however shadowed, between Oliver and Jack's world. But that was gone, permanently gone, and when Cromwell gave Oliver a shove, Oliver went, leading the way to the main parlor where the silver was.

It didn't take them long in the gas lights from the street to jam the silver in the bag, lining the objects between times with wads of linen handkerchiefs and some points of lace to keep the plates and the enormous tea pot from clanging together. Oliver's mouth went dry as he took the silver creamer, now washed and clean, between his fingers and put it in the sack.

Now there was no backing out of it, that particular fact, because he, himself, had assisted in the theft. He could have stood by, complaining and praying as he would think himself wont to do, had done in the past, but no. He was standing be-side Cromwell, looking at Jack, who opened the drawer to find the silver tea spoons and flat little butter knives, also sil-ver. And the little gilt butter plate with its cunning curved lid and dozens of other tableware, all in pure silver. Oliver had never seen Jack like this before, so calm, self-possessed, fingers nimble, so steady and so sure. And he wasn't sure that he should feel a sense of pride, as he did, when the object of that, with what Jack was doing, was so wrong.

But Jack was concentrating, seemed oblivious, and all of the silver things went in the sack, and a few in Cromwell's pockets besides, and when Cromwell flicked Oliver on the back of the neck, Oliver was jolted out of the spell of it, like a blind man coming to sight, gasping, the chill of it on his face.

"Time to go, dreamer," said Cromwell with a whispery hiss. "I knew you'd never be as bad at this as Jack always claimed."

Whether or not Oliver should be insulted, he didn't know. Nor did he have time to contemplate, as there was a rustle of feet from upstairs, and Jack hauled him by his collar to race down the stairs to the kitchen, across the flagstone floor, and out the door. Cromwell took a moment to lock the door behind him, which, as Oliver could see, would give the mistress of the house, and the peelers, if they were called, some confusion as to what had happened in the night. Nothing had been knocked over or broken or damaged. It was only by the light of the morning, or by a dozen candles, if someone was awake enough to light them, that the Acton household would discover all that was missing.

Oliver's heart hammered, racing as if with pleasure from one of Jack's kisses. His mouth open, he tasted the rain and ran to follow Cromwell and Jack. Cromwell suddenly stopped, making both Jack and Oliver jostle on their heels as they neared the corner of the block. Oliver could hear footsteps, the steady tread of a constable on his beat.

As Oliver rubbed the back of his mouth with his hand, Cromwell stopped and handed him the sack, inside of which the bits of silver dully clattered.

"'Ere, you, look sharp." Then Cromwell's hands were on him, turning him back the way they'd come. When Oliver looked over his shoulder, Jack was already walking in the other direction, away from Oliver, as calm as could be.

"No, don't look. Just walk it, walk it through. If someone stops you, say you're on an errand for your gran or whatnot. With that face, well, they won't even think of stoppin' you."

But Oliver's hands were shaking so badly at the sudden realization of what they were doing, what they'd done. And the blurred darkness that was swallowing Jack, whose footsteps were fading away in the dark. He dropped the sack at Cromwell's feet, making the silver jump and clang, accompanied by the high sound of crystal breaking.

"I can't carry it," said Oliver, dancing back as Cromwell reached out to throttle him. "I can't—" And he couldn't explain it, not even if he tried, not with his very breath leaving him, his heart clenching at the thought of it, the truth of it. That if Jack had remained at his side, he would have been able to do it, but that without him, it was impossible.

Without a word, Cromwell picked up the sack and gave Oliver a shove toward the lights in the street, in the other direction from Jack. Oliver was already walking, doing it without thinking, down the alley and to the street, his heart pounding. He'd assisted in stealing goods from Mrs. Acton's house, and while he might have objected when the going had gotten beyond his ability to deny the truth of it, he'd still done it. Cromwell was taking the bag of silver in another direction, and Oliver was the last person anyone would suspect, so he was going to get away with it. The thudding against his breastbone was so hard he thought his chest would break open, rend him into bits right there on the street. And still he kept walking.

His thoughts of Jack, walking along the darker streets of London somewhere, wove in and out of his head as he walked down the street, past Little James Street until he got to the paving stones of King's Road. He was about to head downhill until he got to the Three Cripples, but just as he was about to turn left, he felt someone touch his shoulder from behind.

When he turned, it was a constable. He was dressed in impeccable blue wool, and a shiny black half top hat. He was sturdy and tall and looked down at Oliver, holding his bull's-eye lamp high to spread the light better.

"Why are you going down that way, young fellow? It gets dark down that way, not a very nice place, you see."

Oliver was having the same feeling as he had when Jack and Charley had stolen the handkerchief that day, so long ago. Oliver had been trembling and shaking when Uncle Brownlow had turned and shouted *stop, thief,* and Oliver had been the only boy in sight. But then, there was Jack, in Oliver's mind's eye, heading down another street, hands empty, innocent as a rose.

So now, Oliver tried to calm himself by chewing on his lip. Then he said, "I'm on my way to see my grandmother," he said, his voice coming out a bit higher than he thought it should as he told the lie that Cromwell had suggested. "To pay her a visit, with her being so ill and all. The cholera, Mother says. Her house is right there." Oliver pointed to a row of houses, several of which had a light in the window. The constable might know whether or not an elderly woman lived in any of them better than Oliver would, but it was something. "Just going there," he said. "Not much farther. Grandmother expects me, and then Mother wants me back directly, you see."

It wasn't just the lie that had his pulse racing, it was the easy way that the lie was taken as truth, and this in spite of the fact that he'd beaten Noah any time that one had called his dead mother's reputation into question. Oliver hoped that she would forgive him. And Fagin had always told him that Oliver's face would be his fortune, and now, yes, he was right. After years of hearing it in his head, here, now, was proof. Beneath his skin, something lurched, something dark and slippery, coming up to the surface, tasting bitter, but oh, how easily it was sliding through his veins.

"I must be going, sir," he said. "Grandmother is waiting for me."

"I see," said the constable. He waved his lamp at the paving stones. "Well, mind how you go, it gets a bit uneven along here. Going downhill."

There was something to the way he said it, so that Oliver watched him as the constable walked off, and he realized that he was right. That Oliver was going downhill, in more ways than one. That his first step onto the London road, back, oh, so many years ago, when he'd run away from Sowerberry's shop full of black coffins, had been downhill. It occurred to him that he might have been better off taking Gamfield's offer of being a sweep. At least then he would have found honest work. His face would have been permanently stained with coal dust; no one would have thought he was pretty, and he could have slunk into his life without being pulled this way and that. Gamfield would have beaten him, to be sure, but that would have been it. There, at least, in that life, there would not have been this horrible crossroads, situated permanently beneath his feet as if to constantly demand which way he would choose to go.

But now, he'd ended up this way, doing *this*. That he'd gotten away with it this time was obvious, the reasons for it clear. That he could again, also, yes, he could do it. And could keep doing it.

He kept walking, thinking these dark and unpalatable thoughts, his feet taking him directly to the Three Cripples where the lights shone through the dirty windows and the door opened to present Jack to him. In his shirt and unbuttoned blue waistcoat, the sleeves rolled up on his arms. Smiling, pipe between his teeth, smoke swirling away in the cold air. Oliver's conundrum was still there, but Jack was also there, real and alive, and bursting with joy that sparked out of his eyes like warm lights on a cold river.

At the Three Cripples, Jack nodded and pulled on his arm, so that meant that it was okay and Oliver could let go of the tenseness in his body. He felt as though he'd been shaken, hard, all over, and was only now coming to a calm spot that would, soon, it seemed, turn to movement again, and he'd be sucked up into the world where Jack resided, and behind him, Cromwell. A world that was only waiting, had always been waiting, for Oliver to become a part of it.

"Shall we eat somethin'?" asked Jack, slowing down to walk at Oliver's side, pulling him along at the same time. With a flourish, Jack made men move from their spot in the alcove where the fire gleamed and vibrated with heat, and Oliver let himself be placed in a seat on the bench by the wall. Jack was there next to him, a warm barrier between Oliver and the rest of the room.

Oliver had committed a crime. He'd committed a very serious crime, and no one was chasing him. He was going to get away with it. He was a criminal. Again. Yet. *Still.*

"We'll wait, an' Cromwell will bring us our share," said Jack. He waved to one of the girls to bring some beer, and though Oliver felt he couldn't manage a single swallow, when the dented pot was handed to him, he drank half of it down with one gulp. With a shaking hand, he wiped his mouth with the back of his coat sleeve and looked at Jack, who smiled back at Oliver, green eyes glinting, mouth moist with beer, as though he'd not a care in the world.

"You did well, Nolly," said Jack. "I knew you'd be a good once you got goin'. Told Cromwell it was the better idea than tryin' to make you do the streets."

"You spoke to him about me, about this." Oliver wished that he were more surprised about it, that Jack would have ideas about whom and what Oliver should be. After all, Oliver had come to him, to Jack.

"Told you I did, but only in passin'," said Jack. He pulled out his pipe and lit it from the fireplace, pulling on the ashes through drawn lips. The smoke oozed out along the clay stem of the pipe, draping Jack with it, ashes lighting on the rim. "Told him you was too fancy for rough work but that you were an educated man, and we can always use one of them."

"I don't want to do this, Jack." Oliver looked around the room at the rough crowd, boots stomping on the floor, the drink spilling, the smell from the cesspits rising through the movement of bodies. It was appalling to think of the rest of his life being made up of what he saw before him. "I don't want to live like this."

"Yes, you do," said Jack as he reached out to touch Oliver's cheek where it was flushed with the heat from the room. Then Jack puffed on his pipe for a moment, spilling out smoke that traced its way across his skin. "Think of it this way. Mrs. Acton can afford more of what was taken, no one was hurt, so why are you bothered about it?"

"It's still wrong." Oliver's heart was beating hard now; he wanted Jack to understand just how wrong it was, but Jack never would. To Jack, that was how the world went, and Oliver had just better go along to get along because this was his world now. Which was what was tearing at him, this world, his world. It was not the one he wanted, with the clean streets and a tidy bookshop in a tree-dappled court. His vision was of a good place, with decent people and books to read. On that long-ago day, in front of the bookshop where Uncle Brownlow browsed, and just before the chasing had started, and the rest of it, there had been a moment. A deep, still moment where Oliver had seen into the windows of the bookshop, and had realized how it could be. How he wanted it to be.

He opened his mouth to protest all of it, Jack's ideas of how it should be and Oliver's place in it, when Jack pulled the pipe away from his mouth. He dipped his head and put his hand on Oliver's arm and in a very low voice, said, "I know it's not the dream that you've had in that pretty head of yours, Nolly."

Jack's face was close now, the breath of smoke a bitter taste on Oliver's tongue. "We'll steal books, you see. I'll teach you how. An' we'll collect a whole great many, an' then find some old, empty place, an' we'll take it over. We'll paint a sign over the door, *Nolly's Books*, an' you'll have your place. An' when I'm not workin' the streets, I'll come payin' a call, an' tease you from your work. It'll be fine, Nolly, you'll see."

The breath in Oliver's throat choked him, tightening up with the utter loss of it. He would never be able to explain to Jack that a good bookshop, the right kind of bookshop, wasn't full of stolen books, wasn't situated in some old disused and empty place that no one wanted. It must be new and well cared for and freshly painted and full of books that Oliver had picked out with particular care. It should be a place that people wanted to come to, not some dark, back-alley room that smelled, where the roof leaked, and all those mean conditions that Jack considered normal in his world were present.

But Oliver's impulse to bury his face in his hands was stayed by the look in Jack's eyes, the open, almost soft expression on his face. To Jack, the picture that he painted was the very idea of coming up in the world.

"It'll happen, by-and-bye," said Jack.

Jack lifted his hand to trace a line on Oliver's forehead, quite gently, then pulled out his deck of cards and began flicking them through his fingers, as if everything were settled between them.

"I need to leave London, Jack," said Oliver. He said it only to Jack, to that place inside of Jack where he imagined someone good and decent still existed. "Come with me."

"No," said Jack. He sat back, breaking through the hope in Oliver's heart. "You're far too somber for someone who's just had a great success. Doreen!" Jack half stood and waved to a girl, one who was not Doreen, but who nodded at Jack and stomped away to get them more beer.

"Gin and water," said Oliver, thinking that Jack wouldn't hear him. But Jack shouted, "Gin and water!" across the room, making several heads turn to look at them till Oliver tugged on his jacket and made him sit down again. They weren't going to discuss it. Oliver needed to leave London, to get the City in his hindsight, but Jack wouldn't go.

It would kill Oliver if he stayed, but it would break his heart to leave. So, in light of this, he lingered at the crossroads deep within him.

Oliver was on his second gin and water, with enough sugar to make it as sweet as tea and enough gin to make the room seem warm and pleasant. Cromwell came into the alcove, his shoulders filling the doorway and blocking some of the movement and din behind him.

"A fine evenin', gentlemen," he said, grunting at them as he sat down across from them without being asked. He took Jack's beer and tossed the remainder of the contents of the dented pot down his throat, swallowing it all without losing a breath. "And though I ought to give your friend 'ere the back of my 'and for droppin' the bag in the street like that an' leavin' me to carry it, I've got your take, less my cut, of course."

"Of course," said Jack, nodding, with not even a twitch across his forehead to indicate that he was the least bit interested in why Cromwell had carried the sack of silver rather than Oliver. Instead, he concentrated on the table before him,

572 ～ Christina E. Pilz

clenching his pipe between his teeth as he swept the cards off the table, piling them into a stack. The edges of the four and two of clubs stuck out from the edges of the other cards, as they always did, slightly larger than the rest.

"There's a fiver between the two of you," said Cromwell. He pushed a folded paper bill across the table at them, covering the bill with his grimy fingers until Jack took it up beneath his palm as if it were a code passing between them. "An' there's more of that, if your friend 'ere can come through." Cromwell jerked his head in Oliver's direction. "If 'e can stand to make a list of the other places 'e delivered, what sort of makeup they 'ad."

Oliver's whole body stiffened, fighting against the laxness created by the gin, and he looked at Jack. Jack gave a shake of his head and took a draw on his pipe.

"He won't say yes," said Jack. "But then, he won't say no, either. Will you, Nolly?"

After a shocked moment, Oliver realized that he was thinking of it. That it was in him to give Cromwell Mr. McCready's address directly. To tell him where the money from the till was kept until the end of the week, when Mr. McCready would take it to the bank. Where Mrs. Pierson kept the money she got from selling grease. Even to the chests in the attic where the boys slept and where they kept their pay packets. The silver knives and forks in the drawer. The old Bible, which might be worth something to someone.

"Perhaps," said Oliver, even though he knew he could never do anything like that, to give out addresses and the location of valuable goods, especially when most people didn't deserve it. Mrs. Acton had been one thing, but he couldn't do that again; he didn't want to become that kind of man, regardless of how satisfying it had been.

Cromwell seemed unaware of Oliver's duplicity and was mollified by Oliver's reply. He nodded as he got up and winked at Oliver before he turned and walked back out into the main room. His broad form was swallowed up by the press of bodies, the churn of brown coats and boots, the splash of beer, dull sounds from far away.

"I won't do it," said Oliver. He spoke to the table, addressing it, trying not to raise his voice. Jack couldn't help who he was, but Oliver *could* help the direction his own life would take.

"I know," said Jack. The back of his hand knocked against Oliver's, pushing the five-pound note into Oliver's hand. "Take the money, keep it safe. We'll use it to buy books, so you won't fret so about the sin of stealin' 'em. I don't want you lookin' at me like that; you'll get your pretty face frozen lookin' like that."

Oliver took the bill and tucked it in his trouser pocket, tilting his head as Jack touched Oliver's cheek with the back of his hand.

"Now," said Jack, taking the last swallow of his beer. "Drink up your gin, and we can rejoin to upstairs."

Of course Jack meant *adjourn* or *repair* or something like it, but Oliver didn't have the spirit to correct him. But he got up, just the same, slugging back the last mouthful of gin and sugar before following where Jack led. His heart raced but in a lazy way, pleasant more than painful as they went through the main room and up the stairs to the upper floor, down the narrow corridor to their room. It was gloomy and dark with no fire in the grate, but Oliver didn't need to see as Jack briskly tipped Oliver on the bed and pushed back his shirt collar, undid the buttons.

The weight of Jack's body was on top of him, between his thighs, pressing him into the flocked mattress, with Jack's hands busy pulling his shirt out of his trousers and petting Oliver's ribs. It felt good, as gentle as soft fur, leaving shivers running through him, and he tipped his head back to let the warmth of Jack's hands, Jack's breath on his neck, soak into him. Nothing else mattered but that touch upon his skin.

"So," said Jack. He shifted up to nip at Oliver's ear, and Oliver opened his mouth, waiting to feel Jack's mouth, waiting for the kiss. "If you had a list, like what Cromwell wants—"

With a snap, Oliver sat up, his head clonking on Jack's chin, shoving Jack in the chest with both hands, sending Jack tumbling from him. He heard Jack land on the floor, the scrabble of his boots as he picked himself up then stood next to the bed, a grey shadow in the darkness.

"What was *that* for?"

"You know I won't do it, Jack. I'm not like that." Oliver's chest heaved, and his body ached with the absence of Jack. But he couldn't help that; he needed to make Jack understand how it was to be. "You say that Noah was never one of Fagin's boys, well, neither was I."

"But you—you helped out with the house tonight, that delivery place of yours, an' you did a fine job."

Jack's knees bent, his body creating a dipped weight on the bed, and Oliver could see the grey outline of him now that his eyes had adjusted to the darkness of the room. He felt Jack plant a hand on either side of him, crawling up along his body to plant a kiss wherever it might land.

"You hurt me to the quick, you do, sayin' you weren't one of Fagin's lads." The tone of the words was joking because Jack liked to joke, but beneath it, there was a frail shake. Oliver reached up to take Jack's face in his hands. He kissed Jack somewhere near his mouth, and when he found his cheek, he moved his lips across skin, tasting salt and dust and the smoke from Jack's pipe. Then he pulled Jack full on top of him, enjoying the weight, the safety of Jack's body on his in the dark, Jack's legs tangled with his, the red scarf somewhere in the blankets, tickling his neck.

"Well," Oliver said, more gently now with the pleasure of having Jack so near, of it just being the two of them in the dark. "Cromwell is such a common thief, you see."

"Common?" Jack asked in the voice that said without saying it that he wanted more of the story. He peeled off his coat, arching above Oliver to toss it to one side. Oliver could hear him and feel him pulling his shirt out of his own trousers to float loosely about them. He pushed Oliver's shirt over his head so he could press his mouth to Oliver's chest. Oliver let him.

"Common, I said. A housebreaker is so terribly common nowadays, you know."

Jack grunted his confusion, rising up to kiss Oliver, nipping at his mouth.

"What I mean to say," said Oliver against Jack's lips. "That is, if we are going to be thieves, we should be highwaymen. Like Jack Sheppard."

"Who?" Jack stopped, the cloth of his shirt pressing against Oliver's bare ribs.

"I'm sure there's a book of stories about him; I'm sure you'll find one or two to steal." Oliver knew he was saying all of this to placate Jack. But it was working, so he continued with it. "Jack Sheppard, the notorious highwayman. He robbed from the rich and gave to the poor, as they say, and ended up in Newgate. From which he *escaped.*" Oliver put the emphasis on the last to make the tale a better one. "And when he was recaptured, they hanged him, and before he went, he tipped his hat to the ladies and blew kisses at the babies." The last part wasn't true; when they hanged you at Newgate, your hat was already gone. But he added, just then, "We'll wear masks that disguise our identities when we go out, and I'll ride a grey mare, and you a steel-black stallion, will that suit?"

This seemed to satisfy Jack. "Trust you," he said, squirming now so he could reach down for the buttons on Oliver's trousers. "Trust you to come up with somethin' high class like that. You an' me, highwaymen. I don't know how to ride; mayhap we could kidnap a ridin' master an' have him teach us."

Back in Chertsey, when Oliver had been living with Aunt Rose and Uncle Harry, Oliver had ridden the pony that pulled the trap. It hadn't liked it at first, having been trained to pull rather than carry. But Oliver had softened the pony's temper with lumps of sugar and sweet carrot tops, and the two of them had spent many a sunny afternoon galloping along the fields of golden rye and under the shade of the edge of the forest, Oliver's elbows ungainly, and him falling off half the time. So he already knew how to ride, after a fashion, but Jack seemed to like the kidnapping part of the story; Oliver only kissed him and sighed as Jack stroked his hardening sex.

"That bullet wound," said Jack, sounding a little breathless. "You were goin' to show me."

"Only when you tell me the truth about how you got your tattoo, which I have yet to see." Oliver caught his breath as Jack's hand swept up along the inside of his thigh.

"It's right here," said Jack, not able to point to anything in the near dark. "I did it myself with a bit of flint when I landed in Australia."

Oliver laughed, a scoffing sound in the back of his throat. The story might often be told but the truth of it never known, it seemed, and yet, what did it matter? Jack probably had never had a tattoo to begin with.

At the sound of Oliver's doubting him, Jack jumped up again and went straight to the mantelpiece, where he lit the candle with a single flick of a match. The smell of sulfur in the cold, still air was strong as it floated over to Oliver while Jack came and pulled Oliver to a sitting position and came to stand directly between Oliver's knees, looking down at him.

In the yellow light and the shadows that loomed across the floor, Oliver took Jack's hand and pulled it to his upper arm, the left one, and stroked Jack's fingers along the slightly off-shaped and ridged scar. There Jack's fingers rested while he looked at Oliver. Jack couldn't possibly know that the bullet wound was not something Oliver, readily or otherwise, ever showed to anyone. Or maybe he did, as he drew his thumb with some reverence across it.

"So," said Jack in a voice he might have used in church, were he ever to attend a service. "This is what you got that night. When Bill left you to die."

"He did carry me," said Oliver, remembering the light from the house that dimmed and shook as Bill's rough coat rubbed against his cold-numbed cheek. "As far as he could, and then he left me."

"What?" Jack had not heard this part of the story, not that Oliver had had any occasion to tell it, and his fingers tightened around Oliver's elbow. "Left you? Bleedin' and dyin' like you was?"

"He carried me as far as he could." Oliver repeated this with some insistence, thinking of Bill's voice, hoarse with panic and probably fear as Crackit ran on ahead, and with the dogs behind, Bill had shouted *Damnation, how the boy bleeds!* Then, just after growling, *Wolves take your throats* at the party perusing him, Bill had left Oliver in a ditch. But even in the midst of saving his own neck, Bill had not been without some consideration of faithfulness to a fellow thief, even if that thief had been an unwilling one, to leave him in the direct path of the local law and angry citizenry. No, Bill had carried Oliver, had wrapped something around his arm, painfully tight to slow the bleeding and carried him till his own sense of preservation had caused him to place Oliver in a low, damp ditch. That Oliver couldn't remember anything after that, not even crawling through the wet grass to the nearest door, didn't matter. He'd been saved then, and if part of that could be based on Bill's charity to him, even the smallest bit, then he was grateful for it.

But he couldn't tell Jack this, not now, not when his heart was hammering and he felt warm down the back of his neck, and his arms felt cold except for the one spot where Jack was touching him, which was as hot as an iron brand from a blacksmith's forge.

"Never mind," he said his voice uneven. He stood up, close to Jack. "Now you can see it. It's healed now, as is, I imagine, the tattoo you've spoken of so often."

With a small pet, Jack let go of him and pulled his shirt over his head, letting it land with a thump on the floor. His chest was pale in the candlelight, with the slightest tuft of hair along the center. He didn't seem shy as he looked at Oliver, but hesitant, looking down at himself, along his arms, his belly, his chest, where there was simply no tattoo nor any sign that there had ever been one.

The whole of it had been a lie, a merry chase of facts to suit the conversation, to entertain or distract, whatever was called for. In light of the smear of dark color across Jack's face and the fact that he never once had felt neither chastened by any remorse nor bent to any man's scruples other than his own except for this lie, this bold, colorful lie—well, Oliver couldn't find fault in him. Instead, he stroked Jack's pale, bare, unadorned arm and smiled in that way, that way that Mr. Grimwig used to accuse him of using on purpose, though he never had, not until this moment. With Jack, here in this room, and this one, single truth between them.

"Never mind that now," said Oliver. "There's no fire in the grate, and I'm going to come down with the fever if I stand here in practically a state of nature."

"I'll warm you," said Jack in as reverential a tone as might be expected from a street thief who has been caught in the web of his own making, threaded through with relief, it seemed, that Oliver wasn't cross with him.

He walked forward, making Oliver walk backward until his knees bent against the bed, and he was forced to sit down. Yet

Jack kept moving, inexorably moving, his knees between Oliver's, kneeling over Oliver till Oliver was flat on the bed, the pillow askew, the blanket rucked to reveal the rough ticking of the flocked mattress.

Jack pressed the weight of his body down, holding Oliver in place, kissing his mouth, sliding down to kiss his neck as he reached with his hand between Oliver's legs. He stroked Oliver roughly, the wool of Oliver's trousers between Jack's hand and Oliver's hard sex, the threads dragging as Jack's hand moved, pulling his hardness out to the chill air, making the thrum of energy building hotly along Oliver's spine sear right up into his brain. And all at once, Jack surged up and put his mouth on it, sucking on it, and licking the edges with his tongue. Oliver felt his whole body release, tightening up before he spilled his seed into Jack's hand.

Oliver dreamed about five-pound notes, and flickering through that was the memory of what had happened. That Uncle Brownlow had bet Mr. Grimwig that Oliver, with a new suit of clothes, a pile of books, and a five-pound note, would not return from his errand.

It is a standing and very favorite joke for Mr. Brownlow to rally him on his old prophecy concerning Oliver, and to remind him of the night on which they sat, with the watch between them, waiting his return; but which Mr. Grimwig contends that he was right in the main; and, in proof thereof, remarks that Oliver did not come back, after all: which always calls forth a laugh on his side and increases his good humor.

CHAPTER 36

A Debt Of
Five Pounds Is Paid

The bells were tolling early, and they were loud enough
to wake Oliver up with a start, the dream still skim-
ming in his head. He sat up in the bed, his head ringing with
the gin from the night before. He could taste Jack in his
mouth, the salt and the smoke, and took a deep breath. He
needed to do this today, before Jack woke up and stopped him.
He needed to do this and acknowledge the place he'd come to.
He needed to do this before he could move forward and before
he lost his nerve.

As quietly as could be managed, he slid out of the bed and
pulled his trousers on, tucking in his shirt, looking for his
stockings as he pulled on his jacket. He needed to be gone before Jack found out what he was going to do; Jack would be
furious in any case.

When he found his stockings, he sat on the floor and
pulled them on and laced up his boots. Then, unable to find
his own jacket, he borrowed Jack's, and Jack's low top hat besides, and slipped out of the room.

Once down the stairs and out of the front door of the Three Cripples, the fresh air was like a slap in the face; it was not quite dawn, and the air was damp with rain. But there was no smell of snow, only the quiet glimmer of rain on the pavement, early candles from inside of windows, reflecting on the glass. Oliver hurried past the windows, taking care to breathe in shallow movements, not running even when he came down the slope to the Strand.

From there, he hurried, before the gin wore off, before it became too late to say what he needed to say, he hurried, following the curve of the Thames along wide streets and skirting through neighborhoods where the lanes were narrow and quiet. Still, the sun was up and stirring behind a veil of clouds, and church bells were again ringing by the time he reached King's Road and turned onto Old Church Street. As bold as any delivery boy, he banged the knocker of the front door of the townhouse now owned by Mr. Grimwig and waited. When he heard no one stirring, he banged again, and then again after that; surely someone would have heard him.

And indeed, the parlor maid, not quite as spruce as she might be, but given the hour and that it was only Oliver, no one would remark upon it.

"Can I help you—why, Master Oliver, whatever are you doing here?"

"I've come to see Mr. Grimwig, can you roust him?" It was more of a demand than a question, leaving Oliver to wonder whether his haste had been in vain, that the gin had all worn off and he wouldn't be able to say what he'd come to say.

The maid hesitated, looking over her shoulder, and perhaps hearing something from within, opened the door a little wider. "You'd best come off the street, young master, and I'll fetch him."

That she hadn't turned him away was a miracle in and of itself. That she'd called him *young master*, well, it had been ages since anyone had called him that or treated him with some deference, opening the door for him as if he'd not the hands and arms to do it himself. It wasn't entirely comfortable, even as it was all too familiar.

Once in the front hall, the maid stepped away, leaving Oliver's eyes to track the familiar cleanliness of the hallway, the low shine of the black-and-white entryway, the spotless wooden floor, the fine, thick white tablecloth on the table in the parlor, the neat assembly of newspapers, perhaps only a day or so old, for Mr. Grimwig to read when he so desired it.

Before Oliver had a chance to step into the small front library, Mr. Grimwig appeared from his bedroom on the main floor. He'd been too aged to climb stairs for some time now, and so that back bedroom had been his. He'd not changed locations, it seemed, nor his habit of wearing a floor-length flannel dressing gown for most of the morning, and a nightcap of sheer white until it suited him to take it off. As was his custom, he carried his cane, and marched on Oliver with the boldness of a much younger, more able man. When he was within one foot, he stopped.

"You will tell me your business, and being quick about it, be upon your way, and never mind that you've disturbed an entire household with your shenanigans." Mr. Grimwig's face was mottled and red, his eyes blazing. "Come on, out with it. Or has an actual life of crime abused your brain to the point where you can no longer speak?"

"I've come to give you this," said Oliver. He pulled the five-pound note from his pocket and held it out. "Here's your five pounds." He wanted to spit a curse and shove the fine, crinkled paper down Mr. Grimwig's throat, but he only held it out, his hand shaking.

Mr. Grimwig reached for the five pounds, his amply cuffed dressing gown falling back from his wrist. But then he stopped. "What five pounds?"

Oliver stared at him, feeling the backs of his eyes grow hot. "This five pounds, old man. The five pounds I was to take to the booksellers, only I was grabbed on the street and the money and the books were taken from me. *This* five pounds."

Oliver held out the bill and flicked it in the air. "The five pounds you *never ceased reminding me of*, day in and day out, for *years*." Oliver's voice rose to a pitch that snapped against the ceiling. "I might now be a thief, as you said I always was, but I'll be damned if I'm charged with taking money from a beloved guardian. So here, take it and mark it in your ledger, and never mention it to me again."

"What do you mean, you're a thief?" Mr. Grimwig took a step back, and Oliver could see the parlor maid and the first footman lingering in the hallway near the back steps.

"I've taken to thieving. I've thrown my lot in with a den of thieves, and my future income is subject to ill-gotten gains such as this money." Oliver felt his jaw tighten as the effects of the gin began wearing away. But he'd come this far, he might as well finish it. "You were right all along, and I just thought you'd like to know it. I've lost my inheritance, thanks to you; you've probably already spent it, so what does it matter?" The room began to tip slowly up and down, the light reflected from the highly polished floor, and the candle the maid had lit was striking the backs of his eyes.

Mr. Grimwig took a breath, his eyes gone narrow, and as he straightened his back, pulling himself upright, he brought a change to the room as though a wind had swept through it.

"I've done no such thing," he said, sneering, haughty. "There have been no charges pressed against you, and so your inheritance remains intact. The money is in my care until you are twenty-one, but I, unlike you, am an honest man, and it will still be there until that day, as it ever has been."

As angry as Oliver had ever seen him, Mr. Grimwig now had righteous indignation on his own behalf. Everything he'd ever thought of Oliver had been proven true, from the first moment they'd met till this moment, in Mr. Grimwig's front hallway, and yet he was stating that the money that Oliver intended for his future bookshop was still intact, still available. Oliver felt his knees give way and he reached out to the nearest table, knocking over the candle, which snuffed itself out on the polished tile.

"What do you mean?" Oliver's voice came out in a gasp, and everything was tilting and grey before his eyes.

"It is just as I have said. I've explained it to you, did you not hear?" Mr. Grimwig waved his cane in Oliver's direction. "Now, you're drunk, and you need to leave before I call the constable."

"Call him, then," said Oliver, snarling. "I'll be gone before he gets here."

There was a sound from the back hallway, and in Mr. Grimwig's eyes, the first light of fear from the unaccustomed sight of Oliver's anger, full out and plain on his face.

"I'm leaving," Oliver said, reaching for the doorknob. His fingers failed it, and he was forced to clutch at the doorjamb. The five-pound note fluttered to the floor.

"And take that with you." Mr. Grimwig pointed to the note with the tip of his cane. "I will—"

Oliver grabbed the foot of the cane and swung it back, intending to strike with it, but Mr. Grimwig actually cringed backward, throwing up his hands. In all of Oliver's imaginings about what he might say to Mr. Grimwig were the chance offered him, he'd never thought this, that Mr. Grimwig would be afraid of him, to hold his arms across his body as if the thin, polished wood could break him. If Oliver so much as twitched, Mr. Grimwig would drop to the floor before the cane even hit him, and this, above all things, stopped him.

He thought to put the cane on the table, to lay it between them like a fallen sword, but Mr. Grimwig snatched it back from him, and grasping the long end of it, smacked Oliver with it, hard, across his shoulders. Mr. Grimwig was able enough to express his fright, and although the blow stung, it was far lighter than it ought to have been, and certainly lighter than many a blow from Mr. Grimwig had been in the past.

Oliver stepped back and picked up the five-pound note. He folded it back into thirds and put it in his pocket, all the while aware of Mr. Grimwig's gaze and the wide-eyed stares of the servants, several more of whom had crept up from the kitchen.

"You will not darken my door ever again," said Mr. Grimwig, his jaw tight, voice shaking. "Until you are twenty-one, and even then, send someone in your stead, for I do not wish to see your face *ever* again."

Oliver turned to go and caught his reflection in the gold-gilt mirror that hung in the front hall. It had been one he seldom used, and the odd feeling of looking into it now must have been what made the image there so unfamiliar. It was of a young man in a worn, low top hat and a gentleman's coat and tails, cut back to fit a smaller frame. The shirt, it was obvious to see, was of old, worn muslin, and was much stained with dribbles of beer and circles of grease, as might be seen on some careless person who didn't know the use of a knife and fork, let alone a napkin. And the face, it was streaked with soot and long marks of unwashed sweat. The only way he recognized it as being himself was because he was the only person standing in front of the mirror, and the eyes, still his own, were as blue as ever they were.

Oliver's whole body felt tight; not only did he more resemble Jack Dawkins than himself, the encounter he imagined, with the feeling of justice and right, hadn't happened. Mr. Grimwig was not impressed by Oliver's return of the five pounds and was even more morally indignant at Oliver's presence than he'd ever been when they'd lived under the same roof. Shoulders sinking, Oliver opened the door, the cool feel of the brass knob familiar beneath his hand, and slipped out into the silvery morning's rain.

CHAPTER 37

And Last:
Jack And Oliver

He struggled as far as the corner, where winter-bare trees clustered in a triangle of muddy earth, then sank to his knees to vomit in the gutter. The smell of gin, the sour taste of it in his mouth, made him feel faint, and he had to push away from the mess on the stones before he fell in it. The most he was able to manage was to sit on the edge of the pavement with his feet in the gutter, head resting on his knees and his arms wrapped around. Jack's low top hat fell at his feet and got knocked by a passing cart, and Oliver made himself grab it up before it floated away or someone took it.

He twirled Jack's hat in his hands, running his fingers along the begrimed brim, tracing the satin lining, worn raw to the felt in many places, and the corner of a torn-off ace of hearts jammed into the satin. It was of Jack's card tricks, aimed at cheating, or at denouncing a cheater, whatever was called for. And all the while, a light rain fell, until Oliver was soaked through to the skin. He couldn't get any wetter or have sunk any lower.

Sighing, he made himself put the hat on and got to his feet, staggering a bit until he could catch his breath and determine the direction he needed to go. What he needed, more than a precipitous arrival at the Three Cripples, that is, before Jack awoke, was to make sense of what Mr. Grimwig had said. The inheritance from his father was intact, as long as he didn't become a criminal. And thanks to Mr. McCready's sense of duty, Oliver was not that. Well, he was, but not charged; there was nothing on his record to implicate him; he was a free man. And when he turned twenty-one, he would be a rather well-off man, with enough funds to start that bookshop. Someday.

In the meantime, he needed to get out of London before Cromwell's influence, and Jack's, the worse of the two, headed him in a direction from which there would be no return.

The thought of his inheritance stayed with him all the way back to the Three Cripples, while the wind whisked light rain into his face and bits of paper across the tips of his boots. Oliver pulled up the collar of Jack's jacket; the wool lapels and silk lining smelling like Jack, and it made his heart jump. But he settled Jack's low top hat firmly on his head, paused on the edge to wait for a hackney cab to go by, and then stepped onto the cobblestones.

His shoulder throbbed as he hurried up the Strand, away from the river, away from the brisk morning activity of good, honest shopkeepers, and up Holborn Hill. Into streets where the buildings hung close and the air pushed even closer. The sky was filled with rain now, as if the clouds had lowered and become a river's current upon the stones, flowing with as much force as if to wash everything to sea. Rain glittered on the windows and on roofs and on chimneys unlit by coal or comfort.

By the time he got back to the Three Cripples, he was soaked through. The main room was full, taking with the morning crowd, it seemed, early risers intent on taking their breakfast in beer and spirits. Maybe someone had actually gone to the kitchen and cleaned it up in an effort to serve something hot to the customers, though Oliver knew this was his own imagining. The Three Cripples was, as it ever had been, a place for the drained and ragged souls of the City to come and drink and deal and swindle with no questions asked. The whole of the area, filthy and muddy and dank, was always going to be that way, and none of Oliver's observations or protestations, albeit unspoken, for the most part, would make any difference whatsoever.

He was just at the bottom of the stairs when Jack came down them, thumping on the narrow treads. Noah was at his side as if nothing were amiss. Jack had on Oliver's jacket, swirling Oliver's fairly new hat in his hands, and when he saw Oliver there, he frowned, obviously annoyed, for Oliver's coat hung on Jack like an ill-used sack.

"Where have you been, eh?" Jack's voice was hard, but he kept it low as he reached the bottom of the stairs. "An' give me that money; we're goin' to buy breakfast, us an' Noah."

"Cromwell wants to see you," said Noah, his lips curling as if he were well satisfied with this announcement. "Sent me to bring you."

"But we can have breakfast first," said Jack. He held out his hand, and Oliver gave him the five-pound note, the movement making his shoulder ache.

"That money was for—" he began, but then looked at Jack, shaking his head. Jack's promise about the money being set aside to buy books for the bookshop didn't matter now anyway. Any money between them was stolen money, and that was no way to start a new life, so it was best spent.

"Never mind. I would like coffee."

"Then coffee it is. Noah, you've a mind for coffee?"

They moved through the men at the bar and stepped out into the street where the air was damp and fresh, and Oliver took his first deep breath of the morning. The gin was well wearing off now, and he'd gotten his answer from Mr. Grimwig: Oliver was a ne'er-do-well of the first water and would always be considered so, especially after today. Yet, Mr. Grimwig had not hit him as hard as he might, and had let him keep the five pounds and told him—

Come back when you're twenty-one.

It struck him anew how few years away that was. And the freedom that the money would one day bring him.

Noah pulled ahead in the rainy street, skipping like a fool to avoid the puddles, which was an impossible goal, and Jack lingered back, his hand on Oliver's arm.

"Nolly?" asked Jack. His eyes were sweet, with damp specks across his cheeks, his oily hair hanging low over one eyebrow.

"You look ridiculous in my hat," said Oliver, feeling cheerful in spite of Noah's announcement about Cromwell wanting to see him.

But Jack seemed to know there was something going on, that something had happened to Oliver in the short time he'd been away. He hung close to Oliver all the way to the coffee shop, and when Noah stepped inside to grandly ask that a table be cleared for the three of them, Jack hung back, his hand on Oliver's arm, and regarded Oliver, his eyes wide, looking earnest and young.

"Nolly," he said, using his most convincing tone. "When you left this mornin', without me, I might add, you looked like your nearest an' dearest had expired. An' now, well, you look like you've got angels singin' in your head."

"I went to see Mr. Grimwig," said Oliver, ducking his head close to Jack's. "And my inheritance, three thousand pounds, it's still mine. That is, when I turn twenty-one."

Before Jack could do anything more than make a noise of surprise, Noah came out to get them.

"Come on, you louts, there's a table waitin' for us," he said in that bossy way he had.

The Cheshire Cheese was an old pub of dark wood, creaking floors, and coal smoke that had soaked into everything within its walls. And it was crowded as well, making them walk single file to a side room, where they were seated at a high-back table nailed into the floor. The good part was that it was directly next to a brightly burning coal fire; the heat came at them in delicious waves as they sat down.

Noah and Jack put their hats rudely on the table, and Oliver followed suit, for what did it matter now? Noah ordered coffee and bread and ham and never counted the cost because, of course, he wouldn't be the one paying for it.

As the coffee was delivered to their table with their food, Noah picked up a bit of ham with the tip of his knife to bring it to his mouth, and he was watching as well. Oliver took a large swallow of coffee, milky and smooth, from the bowl, and licked his lips.

"You made your dear friend quite anxious, goin' off like that, Work'us," said Noah, between bites. "'E was in quite a state, sure you wasn't comin' back."

"It's all right now," said Jack, slurping hot coffee from his saucer. "He went to see Mr. Grimwig."

"Who's 'e?" asked Noah, paying more attention to the sliced beef on his plate than the details of the conversation.

"None of your damned business," said Oliver. He felt the words almost explode from his mouth before he could stop them.

"Mr. Grimwig's that friend of his guardian angel, the one who passed," said Jack, more gently than Oliver had ever heard him. "Why did you go to see him?"

"To return something, only he didn't want it." Oliver put the bowl of coffee down; the beef and bread were as unappetizing as dust from the road. He had more to live for now and wasn't interested in the kind of life that stolen pennies could buy.

"The fact of the matter is," Oliver said, not bothering to hide the surprise in his voice. "I plan to leave London as soon as I am able. After I get my things."

He couldn't bring himself to look at Jack because by things, he meant the books, all three of them, that Jack had given to him. Those were his, stolen or not. That Jack had already expressed a firm dislike of leaving London with Oliver was known; he couldn't look at that face and see Jack's mouth saying the words again, denying Oliver the gift of his presence, so he didn't ask it.

"He got his inheritance," said Jack, into the bleak bit of silence that had fallen on the table. "It's three thousand pounds, an' with that, he can do exactly as he likes."

"Three thousand pounds?" asked Noah with a squawk as half-chewed food fell out of his open mouth. "A workhouse orphan like you?"

Feeling a flare of annoyance that Jack would be so free with Oliver's information, he made himself think instead on his surprise that Noah didn't know the story. But then, even if he'd been in Fagin's employ, Fagin was hardly likely to let Noah in on the arrangement he'd had with Monks.

"I have family," he said, taking some small satisfaction from that, in telling Noah that after all these years. "The Flemings, along the coast, Brighton, or maybe Lyme, I think, or near there. And my father left me money; three thousand pounds, it's in the bank till I'm twenty-one, and I intend to—"

He stopped. It didn't matter what he intended to do. Noah wouldn't care, and Jack wasn't going with him. Oliver would leave London on his own and come back when the time came to get his inheritance. Until then, he would have to find work, honest work, maybe as a clerk in a shop, for which he had skills in spite of having no reference from Mr. McCready.

"Well, excuse me, Work'us, I 'ad no idea I was dinin' with royalty." Noah got up from the table, shoving it back, sending the pile of bread scattering across the tabletop. The competition was both won and lost, as it ever existed between him and Noah, and not likely to change.

When Noah was gone and the table settled, Oliver could feel Jack staring at him.

"You mean to go, ain't you," said Jack. "No matter what I says."

"I can't stay in London, Jack, you know that. It never goes well, in spite of my best intentions."

Jack looked at the table, his fingers along the edge, looking a little lost without his pipe and cards.

"Well," said Jack, a shaky warble in the word. "If you've a mind to go, then best get it over with, before—"

Before *what* would never be known because Jack stood up, scattering the plates and calling for the young miss to give them their tab so he could pay her. Oliver watched as change was counted out from the five-pound note that Jack gave her, and he thought about the money in the bank and how different it was from any money in Jack's pocket, which got spent as soon as it touched Jack's fingers.

Without saying anything more, they left the tavern and strode up the street beneath a sky that was peeling clouds away from the rain, and into the Three Cripples. Something clutched hard at Oliver's throat as he climbed the stairs, Jack at his heels. He pulled off Jack's jacket and low top hat and laid them on the bed, hoping Jack would do the same without him having to ask for it. Then he pulled the books Jack had stolen for him from the mantelpiece; they were dusty with ash as if they'd not been touched in a decade or more, and this alone told him that he was about to do the right thing. For no book should be treated so; they should have their spines dusted and sit on their edges rather than their flat sides, and they should have their pages kept warm and dry—

"Here's your jacket, then," said Jack.

Jack was holding it out, and when Oliver turned to look at him, Jack's eyes were as they had been that first day, the day they'd met after so many years. The day of Uncle Brownlow's funeral reception. They were flinty, difficult eyes, and contained an expression to match that seemed to indicate that he didn't think much of Oliver and wanted what he wanted and would soon be moving on. It seemed a long time since Jack had first come calling, looking for Fagin's gang and finding only Oliver had made the most of it.

"Thank you," said Oliver, taking the coat and hat. He tried to swallow against the thickness in his throat, but he couldn't even manage that.

"Don't waste any of your fine airs an' graces on me," said Jack. His mouth was white as he said it, and his whole body was stiff.

Oliver took the red scarf from the bed and wrapped them around the books that Jack had stolen for him, feeling defiant while Jack watched. Then he put on his own coat and hat, feeling the dampness from where the rain had soaked through, smelling Jack's scent, the smoke from his pipe, the oil from his hair. He felt as though he was choking, but there was nothing for it but to go out the door and down the stairs, with Jack clattering behind him.

The main room was full of men, drinking at the bar, their bodies close and damp, creating that smell that he knew he would not miss. Not that nor the clutter nor the brown paint nor any of it. But he would miss Jack, even as he turned to look at Jack, and knew, deep in his heart, that Jack did not want to hear any sentiments that Oliver might care to express.

Jack's expression told him that Jack wanted a quick good-bye, and that Jack would be moving on, if you please.

Oliver paused, just the same, at the door to the alcove, wanting to say something in spite of Jack. But then he saw Cromwell, with Noah at his side, coming in the front door. Noah must have told Cromwell something, for his face was dark with fury, his shoulders bunched together, and when Cromwell spotted Oliver, his hands became fists.

Oliver skirted down the passageway that led to the kitchen, thinking to go out that way. He went into the kitchen, sensing that Jack was still following him. The kitchen was empty of people but full of dishes crusted with food and unscrubbed pots and the smell of spoiled food, old grease. There was also the din of the main room, bouncing against the walls.

From behind him, he felt a movement, as though someone had bumped into him, but it was far too early in the morning for anyone to be drunk enough to be so careless. But as he turned to rebuke the rudeness with his elbow, he felt a pair of large hands on his neck just as his head was dashed into the doorjamb of the alcove. He lost hold of the bundle in his hands as he tried to push off the wall, but his head was spinning and his feet couldn't quite manage to move the way he wanted them.

"That's enough, you need to learn when you've been bested," said Cromwell's voice, somewhere in the back of his head, ringing low, in the way of a solemn bell. "An' Jack, pick that up. You're needed as well."

With black spots filling his sight, Oliver couldn't figure out who Cromwell was talking to; it couldn't be him because with Cromwell's hands on his shoulders, dragging him, Oliver didn't have an option of not doing as he was told. He struggled, and Cromwell hit him again and slammed him against the wall. Sharp arcs of pain lashed through his shoulder, and he could barely stay upright as Cromwell shoved him through a doorway and finally let him go.

No one would come even if Oliver shouted; he was at Cromwell's mercy. And of course, Noah was there, smirking from his place by the door that led to the courtyard and the alley behind the Three Cripples. That he'd come directly to Cromwell with Oliver's news about his inheritance was obvious; he probably thought he was going to get a cut of whatever Cromwell might manage to take, though he'd be wrong. Yet, perhaps, for Noah, the cut he was going to get was the satisfaction of seeing Oliver brought low.

"You won't be so pretty, Work'us, when Cromwell's done with you."

That was Noah, all about his revenge and his satisfaction that Oliver had been, once again, brought so low. That didn't matter; where was Jack?

Jack was at the door to the main room, closing it behind him, slowly and carefully, as though he'd just been scolded for being too loud for being indoors. He carried Oliver's books under one arm, with the red scarf trailing down his leg to the floor. His low top hat was askew, and when he looked at Oliver, his expression was blank, and Oliver couldn't tell whether Jack was in on this or merely surprised by it. Either way, he was blocking the only other exit, and Oliver didn't know which pained him worse, Cromwell's blows or Jack's potential betrayal.

"What do you want?" asked Oliver, trying for boldness even though he felt faint, as though he couldn't get enough air.

"You 'ave an inheritance, I 'ear, my dear boy." Cromwell came close, his broad shoulders rising tall, his boots making hard sounds on the stone floor. "An' I want it, so 'and it over."

Oliver backed up. He allowed himself this, even though he knew it was the wrong thing to do; it would just make Cromwell come at him with even more cruelty.

"I don't have it till I'm twenty-one."

"Then I keeps you locked up till then, eh?" Cromwell took off his jacket and rolled up his sleeves above his forearms, until the muscles threatened to break through the thin cotton. "A good return on my investment, I'd say. A few pounds a year on you an' a three thousand return? I don't 'ave to be good at numbers to know I'll come out ahead. So which is it to be, 'and it over now or later?"

"It's in the Bank of England," said Oliver. He gritted his teeth as he saw Cromwell's fists bunching up. "I can't acquire it, and you can't mean to imprison me till then, someone will—"

"Someone will miss you?" Cromwell's smile was full of teeth, and he snapped at Oliver. "No one will. You've been dismissed from your position, an' no one cares where you are. Or where you'll end up."

One of his fists smashed into Oliver's face, and Oliver staggered from the blow, tasting blood, barely able to keep his feet.

"You're only an orphan that nobody loves anyway, ain't you, Oliver?" With another grin, Cromwell grabbed Oliver by the collar of his jacket and hit him hard enough to send Oliver tumbling to the floor. But Cromwell's grasp was solid and he kept hitting Oliver, smashing blows against his face until he stopped, Oliver hanging from his fist, blood seeping between his teeth.

When Cromwell pulled back his fist again, Jack suddenly flung the bundle of books and scarf aside and launched himself at Cromwell, hitting and kicking, but Cromwell only swung back enough to bat Jack across the face, sending him flying, his head landing with a thunk against the wall.

"No," said Oliver, roaring it. Cromwell had hit Jack, who, while not as gentle as he might be nor as innocent as an angel, was Oliver's friend. And no one, not even a hulking criminal such as Cromwell, had the *right* to hurt him. The awful rage, so long kept chained inside of him like an animal, escaped.

Oliver shifted his weight as Cromwell stepped back. There was enough movement for Oliver to wriggle free, grabbing up the first heavy thing his hands could find. It should have been a cast-iron frying pan, but it wasn't. It was the cleaver, still stained with old blood and bits of dried flesh, and Oliver hesitated only a moment as he hefted it in his hands and swung the sharp edge at Cromwell's shoulder. He felt it sink in, felt sick and glad at the same time, and watched the bright slash of crimson stain through the cotton of Cromwell's shirt.

Watching the blood flow in a tide down Cromwell's arm, Oliver pulled out the sharp edge, hefted it and swung it again, and as Cromwell lifted his arm, sank the cleaver into his ribs, hard enough so that Oliver could feel it hitting bone, could hear bone breaking. Breathing hard, Cromwell staggered, and Oliver hit him again, this time in the leg, the blade going in heavily, sinking to the bone, and Cromwell's trousers gaped open as they became stained dark red, and without a sound, Cromwell crumpled to the floor.

Stepping back, Oliver flicked the cleaver in his hand, holding it high so that none of the blood would drip on him. There was a tiny spot on the cuff of his shirtsleeve, but that could be easily explained away and be quite unnoticeable if he were to press some soot into it. As for his hands and face, he could wash them and walk the streets of the City, and no one would have visible cause to stop him.

Feeling the energy spilling through him, he advanced on Noah, swinging the cleaver in front of him.

"You'll not say a word of this to anyone," said Oliver, in a clear, level voice that did not quite sound like his own.

"What?" Noah's voice was high and he pressed himself back against the door to the alley, his eyes wide as he took in the lake of blood that was spreading across the stone floor around Cromwell's fallen body.

"I said, you'll not say a word of this to anyone, or I'll give you a reason to regret it." His voice was low, as though coming from a deep place inside of him, and now that he'd stopped moving, he felt cold all over.

He laid the cleaver down, where it sat, bloody and precarious, on the top of a pile of dishes. When Noah moved back, Oliver kept one eye on him while he went over to Jack, whose eyes were open and blinking. When Oliver pulled him up, Jack sat up and then got to his feet, rubbing his jaw one moment and the back of his head the next.

"What did you do?" Jack asked this taking in the body on the floor, barely moving, though there were low, jagged sounds coming from it.

Oliver shook his head. His heart was pounding now, and all the strength he'd had when he'd hit Cromwell left him. He felt dizzy, and his breath felt sharp in his throat, as though he were going to faint. He wanted to say something that the heroes in books always did, about having just vanquished his foe, but he couldn't even begin to form the words. So he merely pointed at the cleaver and at Cromwell, who was ceasing to move, and opened his mouth. He was going to try to talk, he truly was. He was going to explain it to Jack, so that Jack didn't think he was a killer by nature.

"No matter what," said Oliver, his throat catching over the words. "I couldn't let him hurt you, couldn't let him—"

"Never mind," said Jack. He took Oliver's hand and rubbed some of the quickly drying blood on his own hands, making it look like old paint or rust from an iron gate, nothing that would alarm anyone. Then he tucked Oliver's arm under his own. The blow to the head had left him pale, but he bent to grab his hat, and Oliver's hat and the books and the red scarf, and took Oliver by the elbow.

"You," Jack said to Noah, in that tone he used when all was not as he thought it should be, such as when there were people in his alcove, or Oliver was in need of fresh air and it wasn't happening fast enough.

Noah moved to the side so they could use the door. His face was white paper and he was shaking all over, but somehow resolute, he said, "Whether 'e lives or dies, you'll be a wanted man, you know that, don't you, Work'us?"

"And you'll be there to collect the reward, won't you, Noah."

Oliver realized he was lifting his hand to reach for the cleaver so he could use it on Noah because he'd be *damned* if some charity boy was going to terrorize him into giving himself up. But Jack grabbed his arm and made him put it down and started walking, right up to Noah, who had no choice but to move away as Jack reached for the doorknob to open the door. The knob was old and rusty and Jack had to make a few tugs on it to get it to open. The doorjamb splintered apart, letting the rain in, and the freshet of wind, which, coming from the alley, smelled none too fresh.

Jack stepped out into the small, muddy courtyard and slammed the door behind him. Then he looked at Oliver as if to ask him the way.

"I need to cross the river," said Oliver, his mind still barely able to think clearly enough to consider it. "I need to leave London.

It was a strange conversation to be having as the rain spattered against the cobblestones and the dank smell of mud and of cesspits rose around them in the sheltered yard. But he let Jack lead him to the pump at the end of the alley, where Oliver took off his jacket and washed his face and hands under the thin, icy stream while Jack pumped the handle. When Oliver put his jacket back on, he was shivering all over, his teeth chattering, unable to stop, until Jack came up to him, close enough so that Oliver could feel his warm breath against his cheek.

"Let's get you out of here," Jack said, tugging on Oliver's sleeve to get Oliver to follow him, to continue down the alley, and going down backstreets that Oliver had never known existed before that moment. The way was tricky and narrow and dark, but Jack knew where he was headed, and he took Oliver with him, all the way keeping close, keeping Oliver close to him, till they came to the narrow grey stones of Whitefriars Stairs.

"This way." Jack pointed to the last bit of dripping, brick-lined alley, the thinnest point between buildings along the path that led to Blackfriars Bridge. Then Jack moved on, with Oliver following close behind, along the narrow passage between the warehouses along the wharf until they got to Blackfriars Bridge.

They stopped on the north side of the bridge. The river moved beneath the great grey-stone arches, swelling with the rain and the movement of ships and skiffs, tumbling against its own banks, threatening to spill over into the streets of the City. Oliver remembered that day, after his release from Newgate, which he would remember for a very long time, the moment when Jack, with his rain-kissed face, had smiled at Oliver and, for a moment, the world had seemed a good place.

The world was no longer a good place, but as water dripped down his neck and beneath his shirt, he looked at Jack. And for that moment, rather long in the silence next to the roar of the river, Jack looked at him. Those green eyes were serious and they wanted to know, without any words at all, whether or not Oliver was going to be all right. Perhaps Jack thought it wouldn't have done for him to have asked this aloud, but he asked it all the same. Oliver lifted his hand and touched Jack's neck. Just once, then let his hand fall away.

"You don't have to follow me, you know," said Oliver, frustration cracking in his voice; he hated having to explain his decision over and over again only to have Jack tell him no.

606 ～ Christina E. Pilz

"I'm leaving London," said Oliver. He had to make this clear; he couldn't stay.

"I'm goin' with you," said Jack. There was a bright flush on his face, which Oliver could interpret as trepidation or merely the cold air by the river.

"But I've asked and *asked*, and every time you said no to me." Oliver felt the heat of anger as he said this, almost blasting it out, not able to believe what Jack was saying. "You said you weren't coming with me because London was your home."

"Not if you're not in it," said Jack simply.

This caught Oliver's heart and all the air in his lungs until he could barely breathe. But as he opened his mouth to remark upon Jack's statement, or at the very least, confirm it, Jack tipped back his head, giving it a jerk to straighten his low top hat on his head. There was a small light in his eyes, some shy, uncertain thing, and Oliver knew he could say what he wanted, in his heart, to say, about how it would gladden his life if Jack were to come with him, all the way to find his mother's people. Yet at the same time, Jack was not one for soft, sweet words or poetry from books.

"Do you mean it?" asked Oliver.

"'Course I do," said Jack as if this were the most obvious thing, and Oliver was merely being dull and stupid not to have seen it long ago.

Feeling undone by this, Oliver looked at the river and scrubbed his eyes with the back of his hand, telling himself it was the sharpness of the wind that pricked at him and not the dangerous secret that he and Jack carried between them. Or the fact that, at least for a while, while on the road to a destiny he did not quite understand, he would not be alone.

"Is that all right with you, then, Nolly?" Jack asked this in a perfectly clear voice, as if nothing were amiss or strange about their plan to walk out of London and into the unknown without even so much as a backward glance.

Oliver made himself nod, swallowing as he did so, and then looked at Jack, who was looking at him with that jaunty hat atop his head and the cut-back gentleman's tails, that bright blue waistcoat, all parts of Jack that resonated in Oliver's head, and in his heart. And in Jack's eyes, green and sharp against the grey weather, Oliver, just for a flickering second, saw himself as Jack saw him, someone worth being with, someone worth caring for. Then Jack smiled, as he did, with bright teeth and sparking eyes, and so Oliver nodded. The smile was Jack's message to him.

"We'll go together, you and I," Oliver said, keeping his voice steady. "All the way to the sea."

"Have you ever seen it?" asked Jack, pulling on his lapels, tipping his head back. "I lived on it for months, you know, being hextricated an' come back again, an' then next to it for years an' years, so I could show you."

"I'd like that," said Oliver. He looked at Jack's mouth, at the bruise forming from Cromwell's smack, at Jack's hands, grimy from the streets, and thought of what books had said about the sea, and of drawings he'd seen of the houses ringed around a cove of blue water. They might not ever find his mother's people, but at least he'd be out of London, where nothing good had ever lasted, and Jack would be with him. "I'd like that very much."

He stepped onto the bridge, watching Jack out of the corner of his eyes, then Jack tugged on his coat sleeve to stop him. Frowning, Oliver watched as Jack put the books on the damp stone of the bridge, as books ought not to be treated that way, but perhaps Jack didn't know that. Oliver opened his mouth to tell him, but when Jack took up the scarf from the books and furled it on the air, a bright red sail in the grey, rain-dappled sky, he stopped.

Jack took the scarf and stepped close to hook it around Oliver's neck, tucking the soft wool deep into the space between the coat's collar and Oliver's neck. Then Jack looped it, in the jaunty way that he did, in the way that had no sense of fashion, but felt, indeed, incredibly warm.

"I reckon you can have it back, then," said Jack.

Oliver did not quite know what to say to this. The scarf was worn from wear and dirty from Jack's hands, and yet Oliver felt warm, not just against the chill air over the river, but against the lonely places inside of him.

"Thank you," he said, not quite trusting his voice to say anything more than that. To cover the flush on his face, he bent to pick up the books, to tuck them comfortably beneath his arm, and straightened up to look at Jack.

Jack nodded, jerking his hat aright on his head, and smoothed his lapels one more time, not saying anything. Then he turned to Oliver and tugged on his jacket and fell into pace beside him. Side by side, they crossed the strong stone bridge, with the traffic flowing past them and the river flowing under them, the rain coming down, a grey curtain, till they could see the City of London no more, and the damp, paved street stretched out in front of them.

❧ The End ❧

Made in the USA
San Bernardino, CA
29 January 2014